CONTENTION

STEPHEN J. IRWIN

Contention © Stephen J. Irwin 2018

ISBN: 978-1-925732-24-5 (paperback)

Cataloguing-in-Publication information for this title is listed with the National Library of Australia.

Published in Australia by Stephen J. Irwin and InHouse Publishing.
www.stephenjirwinauthor.com.au
www.inhousepublishing.com.au

Printed in Australia by InHouse Print & Design.

No hour of life is wasted that is spent in the saddle

Winston Churchill

CHAPTER 1

The policeman put the key in the cell door, which woke Logan Weston and made him lift his head. 'He's dropped the charges. You're free to go, Mr Weston,' said the sergeant. Logan was slightly dazed, as there was nothing better to do than lay back on the pathetic excuse for a bed. He slowly rose as the officer turned the key and swung open the cell door. The relief on Logan's face showed instantly, and the sergeant escorted him back to the booking counter.

The officer at the desk handed Logan back his belongings, which were confiscated when he was officially arrested and brought in early that morning. The officer said, 'I just saw your fight with Angus Masters on YouTube. Jesus, man, you landed the best uppercut I've ever seen. You definitely broke his nose.' He handed Logan a ballpoint pen and motioned to a register book for him to sign. 'Off the record, mate, don't feel bad. Everyone is on your side, judging by the comments they're leaving online.'

The officer kept on talking, but Logan didn't have a clue what he was on about. He signed for his property, which included the stopwatch and black book he used on the track to record the gallop times.

'His new nickname will be Angus "Grub" Masters! First your wife, and now he takes your horse. He *is* a grub.' The officer took his pen back and placed it inside his top pocket. 'You are free to go. You take care, Logan.'

Logan nodded his thanks and walked to the exit, not knowing that his life was about to change forever; all he had to do was open the door.

The viral video of Logan Weston landing a beautifully-timed uppercut on Angus Masters' nose had clicked over 456,000 views in the five hours since it had been uploaded. One of the racehorse trainers in the watch tower was filming a horse for his clients to view when he saw Logan make a beeline for Masters. He had heard the news just minutes before and knew there would be a confrontation, and that it would not go down well.

In the video, Masters puts his hand out in a gesture to say 'no hard feelings'. Logan reaches for the handshake, steps in close, and suddenly grabs the back of Masters' head instead, then drives home an uppercut like a professional boxer. Angus Masters goes down for the count. The trainer who recorded the whole incident started the viral video epidemic by uploading it to YouTube. The video was quickly shared to Facebook, and the rest is history.

Logan opened the thick oak door of the police station and, as soon as he saw daylight, he heard the cries: 'Logan! Logan! Logan!' The press ambushed him with a bombardment of questions: 'Is it true the charges have been dropped?' 'Is it true My Blue Boy has been sold and Angus Masters is his new trainer?' 'How do you feel about this, four days out from the four-million-dollar W.S. Cox Plate?' Twenty reporters crowded around him, shoving recording devices and cameras at him.

Logan was in shock, as he was not prepared for anything but a quiet walk home. One reporter jammed a recorder up to his face and said, 'Angus Masters has now taken your horse, My Blue Boy, and your ex-wife. Can you comment on that, Logan?' Logan stood like a deer caught in headlights. Then he heard a familiar whistle, one he had known since he was a kid, and he spotted his best mate Pete across the road signalling to him. Logan pushed straight through the reporters, not saying one word, and jumped in the front seat of Pete's F-truck.

'What the hell is happening?' Logan asked, looking stressed, as Pete drove them away from the police station. 'Why's the press chasing me? Because I smacked an asshole in the nose, like he fucking deserved?'

Pete was always a lot calmer than Logan. 'Just settle, man,' he said reassuringly. 'Relax for a second.' Logan put his head back on the headrest and took a few deep breaths—in, then out. There was a pause and Logan knew Pete's dry sense of humour was working on a comment, and sure enough he quickly delivered. He held his nose closed with two fingers pinching the end and looked at Logan, mimicking how he thought Masters would have reacted. 'Asshole! You broke my fucking nose!' They both burst into tearful laughter.

When they had caught their breath, Logan asked, 'Where're we going?'

'My place,' Pete replied. 'Since I'm *preeetty* sure your place will not be peaceful.'

Pete's wife Suzie loved Logan like a brother. Pete had clued her up and she had cooked up some steaks to have with buns and salad. The boys walked in to Pete's house and Suzie gave Logan a big hug. She looked him in the eyes and said, 'The asshole deserved it.'

Pete grabbed the Scotch decanter and poured two glasses. He gestured towards the back verandah, and they walked through the house to sit outside. There was silence for a minute before Pete couldn't hold out any longer. 'What happened, man?' Pete, like everyone else, had only just heard the rumours.

Logan took two big gulps that emptied his glass. He waited for the burning to stop before he spoke. 'I snapped. I lost my shit. Everything had been building and simmering for years anyway. Last night, Lex called and told me he'd just sold My Blue Boy for 4.5 million to James Smithfield.

Suzie walked out onto the verandah and handed both men their steak sandwiches. 'Thank you, Suzie,' Logan said.

As Suzie went back inside, Pete continued his interrogation. 'He sold him? And you didn't know until you got that call?'

'No bloody idea! Four days out from the Cox Plate,' said Logan.

Pete sat quietly, in utter shock. Logan had picked My Blue Boy out as a yearling and had won five starts with him. A Group 3, and his last start winning a Group 2. He was now equal third favourite for the Cox Plate.

'He can't do that to you, Logan,' said Pete, gobsmacked at the truth.

'Well, he did. He sold him,' Logan said sadly. 'And there is a big kicker in there as well for him if he wins the race. Lex told me last night. I simply had to cop it on the chin. Lex was good to his word when he bought the horse from me that if ever a sale went down that I was on five per cent of the sale price. It was in the signed contract. I was told James Smithfield was to call by 7 a.m. with who his new trainer was, as he had made it clear that the horse would be moving. In the end, there is nothing I can do.' Logan sounded like the wind had been knocked out of him.

'I said I would work him this morning, as it was his last bit of fast work for Saturday's race. All night I wondered who the new trainer would be. David Turner has twelve in work for Smithfield, so I guessed he was the number one pick. I was okay with that, as he'd be my pick if I had to give a horse to a rival trainer. But then I saw Smithfield and Masters walking over to the trainers' hut together. Masters was showing his stopwatch to Smithfield with a huge grin from ear to ear. They had watched Bluey's gallop from the grandstands; I guess to hide from me. It was a winning gallop and he flew, but the rider was swinging to hold him from going faster.

'So, when I saw Smithfield, Masters, and his foreman walking to the trainers' tower and Masters with a smart-arse grin, I exploded. I knew Bluey's gallop was superb. In fifteen years of training, Masters had been given so many great horses that his clients had purchased, and he's always broken the best ones down. After they win the big ones for him, he doesn't care about the horse's future.

'So, as Bluey was heading back to the tie-up stalls after his gallop, I started to follow and that's when I spotted them walking towards the hut. I realised then it was Masters who was behind the buy, as he had wanted to get in a lot bigger with Smithfield for years. When he saw me, he held his stopwatch up and tapped the glass, indicating a great gallop. He would have to be the most arrogant prick on this earth. I guess I snapped. He kept walking towards me and, as he got close, he put his hand out to shake my hand, as if it was all just business. I didn't even think about what I was going to do, and the next thing I knew his foreman and two others had me pinned on the ground. That big bastard Alfie must weigh 140 kg; I couldn't move. I heard, "You broke my fucking nose," and then Smithfield said, "You all saw it. Don't let him go. I've called the cops." I looked up and saw his nose was crooked and pissing blood.'

By now, Pete's jaw was wide open. He paused before he said, 'So, you've lost your first ever runner in an Australian major Group 1 … not forgetting that Masters also took The Dreamer after he won a Group 1 Toorak Handicap for your father ten years ago.' Pete paused cautiously, questioning whether he should say what he was about to say. Logan seem to know what was coming and he subconsciously prepared. The two guys had grown up together so there were no boundaries and no holding back on the truth. Logan had braced for it, but it still hurt. 'And … the asshole stole your wife as well.'

Two years ago, Angela, Logan's wife, had been caught having an affair with Masters. To rub salt into the wound, they now had a nine-month-old daughter, Matilda, together.

'Has he got some vendetta against you or something?'

Logan didn't get to respond as his mobile rang. He looked at it and turned his phone to Peter to show him the caller ID: it was the head Victoria Racing Club racing steward. 'Fuck, it's Preston,' he said. Logan took the call, which didn't last more than two minutes, and it was Preston who did the talking. Logan hung up and Peter instantly said, 'Well?'

'They are pissed off. The YouTube video of the fight, he said, is at 1.3 million views now, and all over Facebook, and apparently

"The integrity of racing is at risk." I have to go in now to front the four stewards.'

Pete got up and piled their dishes to carry in. 'Sure, mate. I'll drive. Let's go.'

They arrived at Victorian Racing and Logan spent the next two hours going through what had happened. Preston was on Masters' side, as both their fathers were chief stewards in the 1970s and still close friends. Preston was a pompous prick as well, and loved the power of being the chief steward.

Logan knew he was in deep trouble this time. He had clashed with Preston just three months ago when his four-year-old gelding Trouble Road had a huge form reversal and had gone from a run of 7th, 12th, 6th, and last start—a four-length last—to winning at 165/1. Logan, Neale, and Pete owned the horse and had planned the sting. They'd set bets up around the country and pulled over $400,000 out of the corporate bookies, who squealed like stuck pigs for being stung on a rare occasion. No charges were laid, but it did make the front page of the sports section and Preston didn't like it at all. He tried his best to find Logan guilty of form reversal, but Logan was smart, and the gelding did win his next two starts. It had eased the egg on the steward's face, but now he had Weston where he wanted him, and gave the maximum penalty he could.

Logan was charged under rule 65D, for bringing racing into disrepute, and given an eighteen-month suspension and told to hand over his trainer's licence and received a $25,000 fine. Logan plead guilty and, to Preston's disgust, he pulled out his chequebook, wrote the cheque for $25,000, and handed it over with his licence. In his pompous voice, Preston said, 'I gather you won't be appealing the charges, Logan.'

Logan wanted to reply and say something he would regret, but he held his tongue and started walking out, but then hesitated. He turned. 'That's the most satisfying 25 grand I've ever spent. Good day, kind sirs.'

CHAPTER 2

'Are you serious? Eighteen months! Can't you appeal?' Peter said, disgruntled.

'I'm not going to bother. I've only got four others in work,' Logan said. 'I'm out of here. Shutting up shop and taking off. I'm done. I always promised myself I would take off one day and travel, and now I have no reason to stay. I have no one or nothing to hold me here now that Bluey is gone. He was my one shot at greatness, and we both know those types of horses aren't easy to come by. Now he's gone. Dad's gone, Angela's gone…' Logan paused, his heart aching. 'I'm fucking over this industry, just over it.'

Pete stood and faced Logan. 'This is a fucking joke. You get some balls and fight these pricks. I'm ringing A Current Affair right now! I will even ring Pauline Hanson to get a "Please Explain."'

Logan put his hands up and motioned. 'Just settle a bit, mate.'

'Nah, fuck this shit. The guy's a cock and he deserved it. Darren Hinch—yep, he's our man to take up the fight—'

'Peter,' said Logan, interrupting Pete's rant. This got his attention as only when his mother would call him that would he stop in his tracks. 'Are you going to fork out the cash to fight this, as I'm sure I'm not going to.' Pete was a real tight ass.

'Well, it's been a while since you've had a holiday, I guess,' said Pete.

Finally, he was off his high horse, Logan felt. 'I'm done and dusted. Maybe one day that prick Angus Masters will be brought down, and I hope I'm there to witness it.' Logan said.

Logan went home and, to his relief, the press had left, as it was now 9 p.m. Even though it was late, Logan rang the owners of the four other horses and they all agreed for their horses to transfer to Stephen Mitchell at Caulfield tomorrow. Logan poured a glass of Scotch and sank down in the recliner, reflecting on the last twenty-four hours.

He had lost Bluey, just like that. It had really hurt because he had bought the colt himself. He had paid $35,000 for him at the Magic Millions yearling sale in 2012 at the Gold Coast and bought him on spec, hoping to place him in the first few months with a new owner. No one could see what Logan could see in him, and this meant he had to pay for the horse and then race him himself. He had bought two more colts from William Inglis and Son in Sydney and placed both with new owners, but Bluey was the colt no one wanted. Masters basically had an open chequebook when it came to buying yearlings, with some very big racing owners, and also his father, backing him. His arrogance also appealed to many of the high-flyers who wanted the recognition of being in his stable. Masters could train, there was no doubt about that, but the good ones lasted one, maybe two, preps at their best, then never came back in that form ever again. Masters would not have even looked at the colt Logan had bought, based on pedigree and appearance, but Logan saw something in him. He walked like a panther, had a great shoulder and girth, and was very straight through the knees. He had very good gaskins and forearms, and great length hip to tail, plain and underprepared for the sale. None of this mattered, as Logan just had to put his hand up.

After twelve months, the ugly duckling turned into a swan. My Blue Boy had won his first start at Caulfield by four lengths. Logan had paid just $35,000 and the first prize was $45,000.

Logan had learnt his trade from his father, Frank. Logan had golden hands when riding; many said they were a gift from God. He could get horses to do what others couldn't. Everything was transferred through his body when he rode, and while on top of a horse, his life's worries always seem to disappear. Logan's mother June had died from breast cancer when he was only four years old, so Frank had raised Logan alone, with help from his mum's sister, Aunty Joy. Frank was the closest friend Logan had ever had.

When Frank died, after suffering a fatal heart attack at track work at Scone in the Hunter Valley, it tore Logan's heart out. Frank had been semi-retired and had just five in work. He would float into the racecourse for gallops and manage with just one extra rider. He still rode slow work most days. They found Frank next to his truck, which he had loaded up to head back to his little farm on the outskirts of Scone just minutes earlier.

Soon after, Logan found out that his dad still owed $235,000 on his twenty-five-acre farm, and he simply couldn't sell Pepper Tree Park now that both his parents' ashes were spread there under the weeping cherry tree.

It was around that time that Lex had made himself known to Logan, offering $200,000 on the spot for the colt. It was a fantastic offer, as Logan was down to only four horses in work, so they shook hands on the proviso that he would stay with Logan to train, and if Lex ever sold the horse, he was entitled to a five per cent commission on full sale price. Many trainers now had similar contracts, as many lost good horses sold to Hong Kong for large amounts and never saw a single dime for the expertise in selection. Logan used the money to pay off old Frank's farm, and Aunty Joy moved in to help keep it looking beautiful.

Logan took another swig from the glass of Scotch and picked up his iPad. He opened Facebook and scrolled down a few flicks and there it was, now with over 2 million views, titled 'Heartbroken horse trainer KO's his rival'. He pushed play and recognised the voice straightaway. 'Hey, Tony, this will be interesting. Weston just lost My Blue Boy to Masters, just in time for Saturday's Cox Plate.' The recording followed Logan as he walked up to Masters. 'Oh, he's heading for Masters. Tony, watch this.' Then, after the moment of impact, the voice exclaimed, 'Holy shit! He just KO'd Masters!' After the quick struggle of the guys pinning Logan to the ground, the video ended.

Logan hit replay. He knew it was P. T. Smith who filmed it. They hated each other, and it was always awkward sharing the training tower with him. He wasn't surprised by the upload as he and Masters were best mates, and they must have already spoken before track work that morning. Smith was expecting the confrontation.

One positive thing, Logan grinned to himself about, was at least he knocked the bastard flat on his back. He had wanted to do that for a very long time. It had been two years since Angela had the affair, and seeing Angus at track work every day made his blood boil.

Angela had grown up out the back of West Wyalong and had endured a tough life on her parents' 45,000-acre farm. All her life she had to work so hard for everything. After a three-year drought, the bank locked the gates and repossessed the farm. Two years later, her parents died.

Logan was heartbroken when Angela left. As far as he knew, they were working well together and heading in the right direction for a successful life and a family one day. They had dated for five years and were married for only two. He knew the ten-year age gap was a small issue, but he was still only forty-two, and there was plenty of time for children. Many times, they would struggle with the racehorse numbers, but like all trainers it was about finally getting the right horses on board. Angela was a great track work rider, and this skill was crafted from her days riding campdrafts, as she could sit on any racehorse better than most. Also, Angela had attended night university class studying marketing, and her skills led to the stable getting better-class horses.

Things were on the rise, but the cracks appeared when things started to go bad for Logan after he copped a $35,000 fine for using a banned substance. What had happened was a disgruntled track work rider, who had previously worked in Masters' stable, got back at Logan for firing him. The rider had, on more than one occasion, let horses gallop faster than Logan had asked. He had said they just pulled too hard and he couldn't hold them slow enough. This happened one too many times, and subsequently horses trained by Masters won the chosen race. Logan had had enough, and sacked the rider. It was a heated argument, and the rider didn't hand back his key to the stable door. He snuck back in during the lunch hour and gave a racehorse an anti-inflammatory shot on the day before the race. Logan put up a good case with a lawyer but, without sufficient evidence of tampering, Logan was fined for the banned substance that was in the horse's system. He was advised to tighten the security for his stable complex, but at least the penalty didn't carry any suspension time. The ex-employee had a bad track record and the stewards took this into consideration. It also helped that the horse ran well down midfield that day, and there were also no betting changes. But this was enough damage for the stable to lose their main client, and losing twelve horses of high calibre was a nasty blow and hard to recover from for a small-time trainer. You could guess what stable ten out of the twelve horses were moved to, and it wasn't long before Masters also got the Group 1 filly he had always wanted—Angela.

Angela was stunning in a country girl way; tough, witty, and smart. She had grown up this way to survive. She may have only been thirty-two, but she was tired. She had struggled her whole life, and it was no different with Logan, since he wasn't the big mouth racehorse trainer who could land well-paying clients. Logan had enormous ability as a trainer, but he couldn't sell himself. He was a bit of an introvert and slowly built a small group of very loyal friends and clients who trusted him. Masters was totally his opposite. He talked a big game and acted like an arrogant prick, so he landed the high-flyers with his confidence and salesmanship. Not to mention that he also had family money backing him, so he trained with a very large stable of over 120 horses and thirty-five staff. He was assured of success with the royalty of the best-bred thoroughbreds that could be bought.

Logan could never spoil Angela with gifts because they had to put everything they earned into the stable and horses. Sometimes they struggled just to pay the weekly feed bill. Their yearly holiday was in January, when they went to the Gold Coast for the yearling sales, as that was all Logan could afford. The Masters family was one of the top twenty-five richest families in Australia, and Angus was not some battling small-time racehorse trainer. He averaged three to five Group 1 winners each year. Many of them were trained by others before he got his clients to buy the horses, promising the world to them.

Angela saw her parents die from a life of never-ending hard work, and Masters had played on that. Logan knew it took two to tango, but Masters promised a better life, children, an unlimited credit card, and a luxury penthouse apartment with city views. Angela seemed to adjust pretty quickly to her new life; from a Holden ute to a BMW 5 series AWD, and from old Levi's jeans to Louis Vuitton. Since she left Logan, she didn't get horse manure under her fingernails anymore, and she finally got a child; a daughter named Matilda, now nine months old.

Angela certainly had the lifestyle to be envied, but she was conscious that Masters had probably screwed around in the past. Rumour was his first love fell pregnant when he was twenty-two, and she had confided in Masters' mother. Amazingly, the girl just seemed to disappear; some say paid off to never return, as the family didn't want a stablehand to bear a Masters child. Masters didn't even seem fazed by her disappearance. Besides, he was a spoilt brat, travelling the world on daddy's money, hoping to become a champion racehorse trainer.

CHAPTER 3

Logan was lucky, as he had backed Bluey in his first four starts. He jumped up in grade very quickly, and also met some handy horses, so that helped to get good prices. Logan didn't fill the press with BS like Masters did; he was the opposite, and hardly spoke to the press.

Bluey was 22/1 in his first start, and Logan won $22,000. At his second start, he was 8/1, and Logan won $16,000. At his third start, he ran second, and Logan still had him each way and won $4,670. At his fourth start, Logan jumped him to a Group 3, which wasn't common, as most trainers let the horse progress through their grades. Logan realised how good Bluey was, and at 33/1 won $76,000.

With five per cent of 4.5 million from the sale, plus the winnings in the bank and the farm paid off, Logan was finally debt free and he could afford to take a few years off.

Logan packed his bags and stable up, left Melbourne, and went back up to the Hunter Valley with a ute-load of training gear for storage at the farm. He felt he still had his integrity in racing, as most trainers would have loved to do the same thing if someone stole their prize horse. It was forever happening— trainers pinching horses from other trainers—and will continue to happen.

Aunty Joy welcomed Logan with open arms. 'The farm looks great,' Logan said.

'We've had four inches in the last three weeks, and it's been a great spring so far.'

It was only a small farm. Aunty Joy fattened a few steers and lambs, and Logan had a few ex-racehorses he would never sell living their life out there. Aunty Joy didn't need much cash as she had worked hard all her life and had plenty in her retirement fund. She had also bet on Bluey when Logan told her. She had cash hidden all around the farmhouse. Logan suspected it was well over $100,000 from the winnings as she was fearless on the punt when told to get on.

Aunty Joy had brewed tea, and they sat on the verandah and talked.

'What are you going to do, Logan?'

'I have no real plans yet, but I think I might buy an open-ended ticket and just go away for a few months.'

'Will you train again?'

'I honestly don't know. This one really hurt. I think he could be a champion, Aunty Joy, I really do.'

There was silence for a minute as they sipped their tea, taking in the scenery. Logan missed the Hunter Valley lifestyle, but to make it big he had to move to the city.

'Well, you know you're welcome to stay here as long as you want,' Aunty Joy said.

'Thanks. I think I will stay for at least a few weeks.'

'Well, dear, if you can take care of the farm in that time, I might take off and visit some friends up north I haven't seen in a while.'

'Oh, Aunty Joy, I'm sorry. It's probably been a while since you've had a break.'

'It's okay, dear,' she said. 'But two weeks away would be a real treat. You don't mind, do you?'

'No, of course not. I'll take good care of the place while you're gone. Maybe I'll also figure out where I want to go and what I may want to do,' Logan said with a sigh.

Never one to lose a minute, Joy got up and said, 'Well then, I best make some phone calls and write a to-do list for you.'

Logan laughed. His aunty hadn't changed a bit; always flat out when her mind was made up.

Aunty Joy's friends in the north had been overjoyed that she had some time off to visit, and told her to drive up as soon as possible. She quickly filled a suitcase and packed her car for the trip. She had given Logan a big hug, a list of daily chores, and her friends' contact information before driving off at 1 p.m.

It was now 2 p.m., and Logan sat on the couch in front of the TV, flicking through the channels until he found the racing. It was in between races, and the barrier draw had just been held for the Cox Plate. Bluey had barrier five. Good barrier, Logan thought. Then the race day presenter mentioned in the final acceptance that My Blue Boy had been accepted wearing blinkers for the first time. Logan just shook his head in disgust. He knew what Masters was up to. If he won with blinkers, he was the genius, but if he lost, he would say the horse galloped too hard on Tuesday morning. Logan thought that he did fly in that gallop on Tuesday morning and he was at risk of leaving it on the training track. But Logan knew his horses. He would back his judgement of the gallop. The best of the world were over for this race, and there was no point Bluey going in underdone. Suddenly pissed off, he decided to do a quick run into town to get some food.

Not much had changed in town. As Logan walked past the travel agents, he stopped and decided to go in. He was taken aback to see there was now only one person working, but quickly gathered that everyone must book online these days. Logan was still a bit old school and liked getting personal help with booking a trip. He smiled as he was welcomed with, 'Hello, stranger.'

'Hey, Sam,' he said, surprised to see her, as he leant over to give her a quick hug. They had dated in high school for nine months and lost their virginity to each other. She was still very cute and there certainly was still a bit of chemistry. They had broken up when Logan had headed to England to work in a racing stable at Newmarket. They were young, but it wasn't a nasty parting, as they both understood and needed to see the world. Logan left for England, but sadly Sam didn't end up seeing the world. She started dating Reg Johnston, the fullback for the local rugby side, and married him two years later.

They caught up as they planned Logan's trip. Sam had two sons, who had now grown up and left home, and she'd divorced Reg. Logan told her he was staying at Pepper Tree Park for two weeks, and that Aunty Joy had headed north to visit friends. Sam helped Logan plot out his trip; first to Britain for two weeks, then on to Canada, then see what happens after that.

As Logan left, Sam said, 'We should catch up one night,' and flashed him a slightly flirtatious smile. Even for a forty-year-old mother of two, she was still a stunner. Logan had not flirted with anyone since Angela had left, let alone been on a date. He had been completely heartbroken by the affair.

Logan shocked himself when he said, 'Sure. I'd like that, Sam.' He gave a small smile and wave as he walked out the door.

Hank, Logan's little Jack Russell Terrier, woke up and flew out the doggy door, barking excitedly. Logan sat up, looking at his watch; it was 9.26 p.m. He'd gone to bed around 8 p.m. Hank continued to bark and Logan got up to go call him back in, thinking it was probably rabbits that Hank had heard outside. As he walked through the house in his boxers, he heard the sound of a car door shut, then a woman's voice said, 'Aren't you a cute little doggy! You are so cute.'

Logan opened the door to be greeted by Sam walking towards him, lifting a six-pack of beer up. 'Thought you might be thirsty.' She was dressed like Daisy Duke and had brought Logan's favourite beer, Corona. Logan could tell she'd had a few drinks herself by the twinkle in her eye.

'Did you drive here drunk?' Logan asked.

Sam answered in an innocent whisper, 'No, of course not. But I may have snuck the back way from Ashley's house, just in case. We had a few drinks for her birthday.' Sam put her finger to her lips and said in a husky tone, 'Was that bad of me?' Sam executed the look and tone perfectly. Logan couldn't resist how sexy she looked.

Logan laughed and invited her in. She put the beers down on the island bench, turned around and leant against it. She looked at Logan with puppy dog eyes, 'Did I wake you? I can go if you want.'

Logan could be shy and socially awkward, but when he was behind closed doors with a woman he could turn on the charm. Logan knew what she was here for, and he had to admit to himself that giving the lady what she wanted for old time's sake would not be an issue. He looked into her eyes, waiting for the sign of surrender. It didn't take long for her to blush and that was his signal; she had not laid down any boundary and she was ready for whatever Logan was about to dish up.

Logan was only in his boxers, as he had no idea he was getting company after he showered before bed. He still had plenty of fitness and tone in his body as he rode his young horses in their slow work each day. He was tall, had rugged good looks, and was the type of guy that would fight for your honour. Not like Masters. Masters was an ex-jockey, so he had a small build. He would step over you to better himself, and Logan suspected he suffered from small man syndrome.

As Logan walked over, he noticed Sam's eyes drop for a split second to check what she was about to receive. Logan was three-quarters hard. He was not the biggest downstairs, but, like champion racehorses, it was girth that made Logan a winner. He took her hand and slid it to the front of his boxers, whispering, 'This is why you're here, isn't it?'

Sam was now fixated and at the point of no return. Seeing her eagerness, Logan unbuttoned her shorts and, in one swift move, lifted her with one hand and slid her shorts off with the other.

'You seem to know how to get the panties off pretty quick now.' She smirked.

They didn't kiss; Logan laid her back on the breakfast island and dropped his boxers. He slowly moved his hands up to her breasts. 'Wow, you had a growth spurt after I left.' Sam was as flat chested as Logan when they lost their virginity. Now she was more than a handful.

He knew she would be wet and, now fully hard, he slowly entered her. 'Jesus, you too.' She wriggled her body down over the edge of the kitchen bench a bit more. The anticipation had started at the travel agency that afternoon, so the sex was wild and extremely intense.

'Fuck me harder!' Sam locked her gaze directly on Logan's eyes, as she wanted to cum so badly and he was riding her home hard. But he couldn't hold on any longer and gave three hard thrusts. The only sound was their heaving and panting.

Finally, Logan broke the silence. 'I'm glad I called in today,' he joked.

'Well, I'm glad the champagne I drank didn't let me orgasm.' Logan stared at her and they both couldn't hold their laughter.

They were still in the kitchen. Like the true gentleman his father raised him to be, Logan gathered Sam up in his arms and took her to his bed. He knew she shouldn't be driving, anyway. He lay beside her and felt at ease. To have company for the first time in so long felt right. He closed his eyes, enjoying the feeling of her falling asleep, nestled up to his bare chest.

Logan woke up, carefully untangling himself from Sam's arms and legs. He guessed it would be about 3.30 a.m., which had been the start of his workday for over fifteen years. He looked over at his watch and was surprised it was 3.34 a.m. He grinned to himself, blaming last night for his body clock being out by four minutes. It was only the third morning since he quit the training ranks, so he had not yet readjusted to his new lifestyle.

He stared at the ceiling, thinking of Bluey trotting around the track this morning before his biggest ever race. No amount of money, or even multiple orgasms, could take away the pain he felt. His life and business had all finished with that one punch. He considered seriously for a moment if he regretted any of it. So many times in his life, he had let things slide, even when he got fucked over. He'd been too lenient. Logan hadn't felt the same inside since he KO'd Masters and walked away. He had fronted straightaway, hadn't taken any take shit from the stewards, and happily turned over his licence with ease. He knew he was the one who decided to throw the punch. His situation was the result of his own actions. Many lesser men might whinge and try to find someone else to blame, but Logan's father Frank had taught him at an early age to own up to his mistakes. 'If you stuff up, it's your fault. You're only human. If you stuff up over and over again, you're an idiot.'

Logan was wide awake and looked out the window at the darkness. *New day, new me, new chapter.* He knew he wouldn't fall back asleep so he got up, put the kettle on, and poured a coffee. For the first time in his life he was completely free; not one thing to tie him down. He felt good, as if the burden he had been shouldering for the past few days was finally beginning to ease. He sat on the couch, gazing out into the slowly breaking day, letting his mind go wild with where he would go and what he would do.

He was startled when he heard the toilet flush and then heard Sam brushing her teeth. He smiled, knowing she was using his toothbrush. He turned, still smiling, and he caught sight of her standing in the doorway. She looked very cute standing there in his shirt.

'Good morning,' he said in a tone that meant 'Thank you for last night.'

'I'm hoping it will be,' replied Sam in a seductive tone.

'Coffee?' Logan gestured from the couch.

She held his gaze with a smouldering look, and Logan looked a bit puzzled. Then the penny dropped. Logan put his mug down on the coffee table as Sam made her way over to him. 'You still owe me that orgasm.' This time there was no rush, no anticipation, and no performance level either one had to live up to after all these years. Sam got the trifecta.

'I think I like this start to my morning better than watching a slow one gallop three furlongs,' Logan said.

CHAPTER 4

The Cox Plate was the biggest sporting event for the weekend in Australia, but the online drama possibly made it the most popular sporting story in Australian history. Almost 38 million hits on YouTube and over 45 million on Facebook, with many now adding their own spin. Ninety-eight per cent of viewers were on Logan's side. Masters had been getting smashed as the villain on social media, and Weston was quite amused at the insults being slung at the guy.

It was certainly a story for the press to lap up. The video was mentioned in the newspapers daily. The media happily stirred the shit, knowing it would help sell papers, so they made it bigger than it needed to be, with headlines like 'Masters Gets Last Laugh' and 'First His Wife, Now His Horse'. Logan seriously thought about getting a new mobile number as the requests for interviews were insane.

The long driveway to Pepper Tree Park seemed to protect his privacy. Besides, he'd only been to town once and, except for Sam, no one had recognised him. Even though he had vowed to be a new man, it hurt to see the past brought up. It rubbed salt in the wounds for Logan to see his ex-wife Angela and her new daughter all over the news.

What had made it worse were the rumours circulating that My Blue Boy hadn't been 100 per cent sold, like first thought. Lex was told by Masters that under his care he would win Group 1 races, and it was he who could broker a 20-million-dollar stud deal with the big farms if he won a Group 1. This added fuel to the fire. The 4.5-million-dollar figure was a guaranteed sale, win or no win, but the kicker was another twenty-five per cent to Lex on anything above 4.5 million if the horse was syndicated at the end of his racing days for stud duties. Logan had accepted and signed the deal, and already had his percentage in his bank account. There was a clause in the contract saying whatever happens after the settlement was not to be challenged; his settlement was final. Weston signed off on it because he just wanted the money and the painful hurt behind him, and not to be tied down with lawyers and bullshit for years to come.

Luckily, Sam was a very pleasant distraction from the week of turmoil.

Race day started at 11 a.m., and Logan and Hank the Jack Russell settled down on the couch. Logan switched to Channel 7 to catch them throwing to an ad break. The host of the race day said, 'Next up, the controversial story the whole world is talking about. The behind-the-scenes drama that unfolded on Tuesday morning, when one horse, My Blue Boy, brought the biggest feud in racing between Angus Masters and Logan Weston to a boiling point. This story is coming up next.'

'Fuck this shit, Hank,' Logan said, getting up. 'The race is at 4 p.m. and I can't watch all this bullshit till then.' He felt so uneasy in the stomach that a text startled him. It was Pete.

'This will be interesting. You watching the story about to come on 7?' he texted.

'No. Going for a ride on the Harley with the dog.'

Pete knew by the blunt reply to leave it alone. He texted back, 'Wear your helmet.'

He wanted to ride the Harley, but curiosity got the better of him. Channel 7's exclusive opened with the reason the owners decided to transfer Bluey. Lex very carefully opened with a well-planned statement. He had a large cardboard box business and didn't need to lose face over the publicised drama. 'I'm not sure anyone could have predicted that this decision would have escalated like this. With respect to Logan Weston, the decision was extremely hard to make, as he had done a wonderful job with My Blue Boy so far. We were lucky enough to purchase at a price that Logan asked, and we agreed we'd stay with him to train. We also agreed that if My Blue Boy sold, Logan would be paid a five per cent commission. For the record, Logan received that five per cent at the time of the sale.

'Angus Masters is one of the top three trainers in Australia and has made some great colts into very good stallion prospects. This is not a personal hobby, it is a business venture, and I invest millions each year. Angus Masters has twenty-seven Group 1 winners to his credit and has the ability to land the right race at the right time. Our buyer, James Smithfield, has eight in work with Masters, and he is one of their top three trainers. Part of the deal was that the horse moved immediately to Masters. The decision was simply a smart business deal for myself and my family. When Logan resumes training, I would be very happy for him to train for me again.'

The interviewer waited patiently, knowing it would be a very well-rehearsed statement, but he wanted to stir up some shit for the TV ratings. 'I'm sure you knew there would have to be some fireworks after Logan Weston's wife moved stables two years before.' The interviewer didn't have an issue implying Logan's ex-wife was just like a racehorse.

Lex, being a smart businessman and a man of integrity, countered, 'Angela wasn't transferred like a racehorse. She is a lovely lady and has been an integral part of Logan's and Angus's lives. Both trainers are paid to train my horses, and that's where my comments end.'

The interviewer seemed disappointed he didn't get a decent sound bite, as he had hoped. 'Well, My Blue Boy is now as famous as Phar Lap thanks to the attention on social media. Many punters are calling for your head, especially if the horse wins today. Do you care to comment?'

Lex shook the interviewer's hand and said, 'Let's hope we talk in a few hours.'

Channel 7 then showed the video of Logan's KO with the Rocky music in the background, followed by a shot of Masters in the saddling stalls area with two of the blackest eyes you could ever see and a partially swollen nose. To his credit, many thought he wouldn't show today with all the hatred and personal attacks on social media. However, Logan knew he was too arrogant to stay at home.

He probably wants the win even more now, that pompous son of a bitch, Logan thought to himself. It was now three hours to the race and Logan was full of nervous energy. He hopped on the 64-inch zero-turn Toro mower instead of the Harley, and gave the lawns a touch up. Frank had planted so many trees that Logan was endlessly mowing round and round each tree base.

After jumping in the shower to wash off the dust, clippings, and leaves, Logan was seated once more on the couch. Hank hopped on and took control of a third of the couch. Logan switched the TV back on, and right there in his face was the pre-race interview with Masters. Logan said to Hank, 'Can't win, buddy.'

The Channel 7 interviewer asked, 'Angus Masters, in light of everything that has been happening around the world on social media, how are you feeling today?'

'I'm feeling confident about the race,' Masters said, with a sneer.

Gee, he looks like shit, Logan thought. He may have even felt a bit of remorse about his punch to Masters' face at that moment.

'And My Blue Boy, how is he today?'

'We've re-shod him. As soon as he got to the stables, I discussed with my farrier that he had *way* too much toe and was off balance on the near fore. He has worked well, and we haven't been able to fill him up eating since he arrived.'

Logan shouted at the TV, 'You little fuck!' Hearing that, Hank quickly got up and went outside, thinking he was in trouble. *No trainer with any respect to another in his industry would ever say that, let alone on national TV*, Logan fumed to himself.

The interviewer asked, 'And why the blinkers?'

'Well, sure, he's good but the blinkers will sharpen him up.'

'How do you feel about your chances in the Cox Plate?'

'We have LJ Smith on board, and he's won two Plates before and knows the track like the back of his hand. Not to mention the changes we have made this week, which have improved the horse by three to four lengths. He hasn't stopped eating, so fingers crossed.' An arrogant smile spread over his bruised face, and he looked directly at the camera. 'I'm ready to win my first W. S. Cox Plate.'

'You slimy piece of shit!' Logan kicked the coffee table forward and didn't care it marked the polished timber floorboards. He stormed outside in disgust, his blood starting to boil. His phone vibrated and let out a chime indicating a new text message. Logan whipped it out and read the message from Pete: 'Just settle down.'

Logan felt his anger slacken. Only a great mate would sense the timing and reach out to help. Logan texted back, 'Asshole!'

Pete instantly replied, 'Me or Masters?'

A small smile crept over Logan's face as he texted, 'Both.' He took some deep breaths and walked back inside; ready to face the TV again.

Pete texted, 'I reckon he will win. Too good of a gallop on Tuesday. Your polish is still on him, thank God.'

Logan replied, 'He basically buried my career on live TV.'

Suddenly, Logan heard Hank's feet scampering up the front steps and he burst through the doggy door, dragging something in his mouth. He'd just found or killed a rabbit and jumped up on the couch to pull its head off. 'Oh, for God's sake, Hank!' Logan quickly grabbed the rabbit away from Hank, but, to his surprise, Hank launched himself from the couch and snatched the rabbit in mid-air by the hind leg. He had a strong bite and Logan couldn't help but laugh. This was Hank's Cox Plate and he wasn't giving up without a fight.

Logan opened the door and managed to persuade Hank to let go of the rabbit long enough for him to throw it as far as he could out onto the front lawn. Hank leapt off the verandah and bolted after it as it hit the ground near the tree lane. In one fluid motion, he grabbed it in his mouth, not even stopping in his stride, and ran back towards the door. 'Whoa!' Logan said as Hank tried to side-step him, only to be stopped by Logan's size-13 foot. He ushered Hank back far enough to get the door shut and the doggy door locked. That was one thing he didn't need to deal with right at that very moment.

His mobile rang. This time it was Neale. He had always been very dry and, before Logan could say anything, Neale said, 'I thought his coat didn't look that good.' They both just started laughing. 'Very low blow, mate. You might have a case against him and Channel 7 for defamation of character. Let's talk after the race,' and he hung up, without Logan getting a single word in.

Bluey certainly looked super working to the barriers, but it seemed the fight was a more popular subject than the race. Some guys on a buck's day had dressed as Weston and Masters, and had signs that read: 'We want a rematch!' and 'Round 2?'

Bluey had drawn barrier five, which was Logan's lucky number. Logan had never been so nervous in all his life. He felt like he was going to throw up as they loaded in the barriers. The whole field stood very quiet, and not one horse was misbehaving. The gates flew open and the field jumped. The race seemed to be going in slow motion for Logan, but his whole attention was on one runner. The jockey, LJ, flew the gates, then eased Bluey. They were running third on the fence. Logan couldn't have asked for more. Still, it was all going so slow. Logan's heart was pounding so hard, he thought his chest was going to burst.

They approached the 1,000-metre mark and Bluey was full-on running. At 800 metres, the English galloper McFarland took off, with Malcom Hobson his jockey urging him on; Black Mountain also went with him. It was on, and many Cox Plates had started the battle of the champions from 800 metres. The majority of horses seemed like they were off the bit. Some jockeys had already given their mounts a few slaps with the whip to urge them on. Every horse was now in full flight, flat out, bar just one horse—Bluey. He was travelling sweetly, but under no pressure. Logan saw the look in his former horse's eye, the same look on his very last gallop on Tuesday; the look of a champion.

The field approached the 400-metre mark and now the field had stretched eight wide. LJ had not moved and he had a handful of horse under him, but he was blocked for a run. Logan was sure he could see LJ praying for a run. Quarter Back was still doggedly in front and fending off all the challengers. Society Boy was done, he had run his race, and the American import was starting to fade. LJ, as cool as he looked, must have been sick in the stomach, along with Bluey's ex-trainer Logan, and Masters as well. A slow horse coming back on top can break your forward momentum.

Then the stars aligned, and it happened. Turnpike wobbled around the turn and drifted two off the fence. Seeing this, LJ instantly gave Bluey two back handers and pulled the left rein and shot through the inside run. He had sat on some great horses before, but never had a horse shown a quicker turn afoot. LJ hit the lead with 150 metres to go, then exploded even more to cross the finish by 2.2 lengths. My Blue Boy had won the Cox Plate.

Logan gave a victorious roar and jumped, punching the air like Tiger Woods draining a 50-foot putt. He stood in shock and combed his hands through his hair again and again, letting it sink in. Tears welled up and his throat tightened. He walked out onto the verandah for some fresh air. Hank was still ripping the dead rabbit to shreds by the front door. 'We did it, boy, we won the Plate.'

Logan didn't care that he wasn't the winning trainer. He was the one who had chosen the ugly duckling, broken him in, pretrained and educated him to gallop. He had turned him into a superstar, and now My Blue Boy had won the Cox Plate.

As Logan made his way back inside, the post-race interview had started. The interviewer walked up beside Masters as he headed down to the track. 'How does that win feel?'

Masters spoke calmly and proudly. 'After the huge challenges all week, having to balance his feet and fill his stomach, I'm satisfied that the changes we made have paid off.' Then he strode out onto the track to meet LJ and Bluey without saying another word. The camera panned around at the crowd and focused on a person holding up a sign that read 'We love Logan and Bluey!' It was a small consolation and made Logan smile. As the horse, jockey, and trainer came back to scale, instead of the jubilant applause Masters had hoped for, boos and jeers were called from the faithful punters and the drunks.

Channel 7 was going to milk this for what it was worth. The interviewer raced over to Masters' wife Angela as she triumphantly made her way to the winner's stall. 'You must have mixed emotions,' said the interviewer, shoving the microphone eagerly in her face for comment.

'Why would I?' she quipped, not breaking her stride. 'We just won the Cox Plate!'

'You just won with a racehorse that, until very recently, was trained by your ex-husband, who is now banned from racing for eighteen months.' The interviewer was almost jogging beside her. 'That doesn't impact your feelings about the win?'

Angela stopped short. This instantly hit a nerve; there had been so much pressure leading up to the race day, with press hounding Angela for comments daily. It had obviously become too much. Angela was tough because she had been brought up to be that way, but Logan knew that when she was backed into a corner, she came out swinging. He waited for her outburst but had no idea what she would say.

'It's pretty simple to understand, isn't it?' Angela snapped at the interviewer. 'The better trainer gets the winning horse, just like the better man gets the girl. End of story. No further comment.' And she stamped away angrily.

The interviewer's eyebrows raised instantly, and he was suddenly speechless. They threw back to the panel of racing experts in the box, and they had the same expression. 'That was savage,' someone mumbled quietly to break the silence.

Logan hit the power button and dropped the remote on the couch. He trudged over to the fridge and grabbed a Corona. Any remnants of joy he felt from the win had vanished. His phone had been buzzing, but he turned it off and left it on the kitchen bench. He walked outside and sat on the verandah steps, looking out at the front paddock. Hank took a break from ripping apart the rabbit to trot over to Logan and get a quick pat on the head before he grabbed the carcass and headed to the garden bed to bury it for later. Logan watched as Hank struggled to dig a hole; his full belly almost bursting at the seams.

Angela had known Logan better than anyone. She knew Logan's darkest secrets, and two years wasn't anywhere long enough for his heart to heal. It didn't help that both trainers were training and racing on the same circuit, so every day he was reminded of what he had lost. Very few knew that over the last two years he had been battling severe depression and anxiety. He had even contemplated suicide, and had considered how he would do it. He had thought it out so many times, over and over at night when he was alone in his bed, to the point of actually writing a letter to the person who would find his body. All racehorse trainers had access to many drugs to treat the horses, so he thought about mixing a drug cocktail and injecting himself. He planned to fill up a saline bag with it as well, and set up a drip before he injected himself just to make sure he didn't come back.

A call to Lifeline had saved his life. After he had spilled his guts, the woman on the other end of the phone got him talking about what he was passionate about. It turned out she actually had a share in a racehorse with a fellow trainer who was a friend of Logan's. She got him talking about what he loved about training horses, and he told her about each horse in his stable. At that time there was only four in work, and it was Logan's lowest run of outs. He hadn't had a winner for thirty-four weeks. But the woman on the end of the line got him to talk about what he was great at and what he'd accomplished in the past. Gradually, Logan slowly started to believe in his own ability again. She asked him to break down his training style, and suggested that he think about studying other trainers who were getting better results to see what they are doing that he wasn't. When they talked about Angela, the woman asked Logan to consider if he thought his true love, the person he was meant to be with, would have bailed on him when he was in a rut, at a time when he needed her most. He agreed that he believed true love meant sticking with someone through thick and thin. They spoke for almost four hours and, at the end, Logan felt like they had become friends. Considering she knew a friend of his, he wondered if one day he would meet the mystery woman on the other end of the line that had saved his life.

Seven months later, Logan was at a Sunday race meeting at Sandown after My Blue Boy had just won his first start. Logan was walking back to the stalls and a woman stepped away from a group of people nearby and said quietly, 'I believe in you, Logan.' He turned around and she winked at him, and he knew instantly who she was. Logan froze and just stared at her, not knowing what to say. He wanted to thank her for saving his life but didn't know where to begin. She smiled knowingly. 'I want that Group 1 win now.' It was a Rocky moment; similar to when Mickey said, 'What are we waiting for?'

Logan felt a nudge under his arm, which brought him back to the present. It was Hank, covered in dirt. He must have successfully buried the rabbit. A few tears started to swell in Logan's eyes, then the floodgates opened. His body had finally decided it was time for closure. Angela's comments drove the final nail into the coffin. He had always held her on a pedestal because, to him, she was the perfect woman and could never put a foot wrong. But he finally saw a side of her that he didn't like; a cruel side. *Maybe that's who she's been all along, and I never saw it before now.*

After letting it all go, he felt better. He rubbed away the tears and wiped his nose on the sleeve of his shirt. Hank was sitting back, not knowing what the hell was going on, but then he saw an opportunity and went through the small gap in Logan's arms, and sat on his lap.

'Jesus, Hank. Your rotten, rabbit farts, you can't beat 'em.'

CHAPTER 5

Logan decided to leave his phone off and went for a walk up to the shed. In the back there was a tarp over his dad's old motorbike. Frank loved the Harley Davidson and had ridden it to town most Sundays, even if it was just going to get the paper. 'Gonna fire up the bad boy,' he would always say. The bike hadn't been ridden since he passed away as, bar the funeral, Logan had only been home twice since that day. He pulled the tarp off and there she was, still in perfect nick. Logan had never bothered with a bike licence, but he loved to ride. His father told him, if you let a bike sit for a long time, make sure you drain the fuel. He found the fuel container with fresh fuel kept for the mower, grabbed a feed dipper and drained the fuel, and refilled with new fuel. He wiped the dust off the seat, turned the bike around in three moves and hit the start button. After a bit more choke was given, she fired right up. It sounded great, always had, and that is one sound his father loved even more. He put the stand down to let it keep idling over while he found his father's old helmet. After a few quick brushes with his left hand and a few hard shakes, he was confident enough that there were no spiders. He didn't want any surprises along the way.

He sat back and gave the fuel tank a pat. 'Let's go, Frank.' He slowly rode down the driveway, showing respect to the Harley and also to old Frank's rules: 'Always drive slow and with respect in and out of the driveway to your house, and also observe your farm in and out.' Logan hadn't been on a motorbike for at least eight years. *Just like riding a bike,* he said to himself. 1,000-cc between his legs did make him slightly nervous as he felt the power, and he had always loved the sound. For the first time in five days, he was focused on just one thing—freedom.

About two kilometres away was Donnybrook Road. It was a nice road to cruise; twenty-six kilometres long, with a dead end. Normally not much traffic either. He hit the left indicator and accelerated through the gears up to 60 km/h through the outskirts of town, hit a right, dropped it back to third, then gunned it as he passed the 100-km speed zone. The bike would do 120 km in a second if needed, but he put it in fourth and eased back to sit on 110 and enjoy the ride. The area had new houses as the Bruce's had sold a parcel of 1,500 acres to a developer who had cut the parcel up into ten lots to build houses; some with sheds and some with stables. Most had new houses built already. His idea had worked well, and he got a premium for each lot. There was nothing worse than getting a lovely block, only to have the neighbour litter it with dead car bodies and crap houses.

It was pushing twenty-seven degrees; just perfect. He knew he was soon coming to the four bends next to Flinders' dairy farm, and then he had close to a four kilometre straight down past Choplin's lucerne farm. He eased back to 60 and 70 through the S-bends and, as he straightened and saw the clear straight ahead and not one car in sight or hay tractors crossing, he gunned it and the 1,000-cc spat out any cobwebs it may have had inside. It possibly missed a beat to the experienced rider but Logan said, 'Let's go, Frank!' and grinned from ear to ear, as he had never ridden the Harley outside of the farm before.

The end of the straight grew close quicker than he had anticipated; disappointment instantly set in. He eased back down from the 180 km/h, back to 90 km/h around the left-hand bend heading past Dunstan's feed lot for lambs. He was surprised to see the paddock, which he remembered filled with thousands and thousands of fat lambs when he was young, had now been radically reduced to maybe 300 lambs. The escarpment grew closer and the valley narrowed, and he knew he had two kilometres left. He had so many memories of this place, like hunting the valleys and hills for the red deer that had fled when the Greenies had cut the fence at the deer farm over the range one night, letting 650 deer loose. No one was ever charged, and only around 35 deer were recaptured and returned. Logan slowed as he came to the end of the valley and decided to stop and take in the view for a minute. *So many memories*, he thought.

He heard the distinctive sound of a land cruiser ute approaching through a paddock and turned to see it heading towards the gate Logan hadn't noticed he was stopped in front of. He walked the bike forward, dropped the stand, and hopped off to open the gate. He had never lost his country boy manners, and he knew this would save the driver hopping in and out twice to open and shut the gate. Logan smiled as the car drove through and stopped. 'G'day, Mr Rose,' Logan said.

'C'mon boy,' the man said as he leaned out the driver's side window, 'how many times have I told you to call me Don.' They shook hands. Don was one of Frank's best mates, and they had served in Vietnam together. Don had given the eulogy at Frank's funeral. 'I just saw the Plate,' Don said.

'Yeah, my boy did well,' said Logan with some pride and some sadness in his voice.

'I knew a guy once,' Don started, 'who lost his farm in an investment deal trying a new fertiliser that was going to yield him an extra twenty-five per cent profit per annum. It fucked him,' Don said. 'Ate him alive with the guilt of what could have been. After three years, his wife left as the guy had rolled over on life. Led to believe he was a failure, his negativity had killed him years before and he never recovered.' Don always had an example ready for any circumstance that needed sound advice. 'Don't be foolish and chase revenge, boy. Trust me, you are better than them both. If you don't show integrity, and if you carry a chip on your shoulder forever, you will never make it again in anything.' He patted Logan's shoulder. 'It was a great punch though.' He winked and turned back to the wheel. His ute clunked into first gear and he headed off down the road.

Logan threw his leg back over the Harley, but his finger hovered on the start button as his thoughts churned. He still had so much anger inside towards Masters and Angela. They had both showed their true colours today without a doubt. He knew deep down he had as much talent as Masters, and he also knew he had to be truthful to himself. He had always been a person who envied the success of others, could be very stubborn at times, and had tunnel vision. But Logan had spent the last week doing some soul searching and questioning his path in life. For the first time, he didn't really know what he wanted in life. He kicked the stainless-steel stand and fired up Frank, as he had now re-christened the Harley.

CHAPTER 6

Logan had started to change down gears as he approached the outskirts of town and eased back to 80, then down to 60 km/h. As he made his way down the drive to the house he spotted a Channel 7 satellite van pulled up at the front of the house. 'Are you fucking serious,' he mumbled under his helmet. He hit the kill switch and kicked the stand out and laid the Harley to the left.

Three men were squished in the front seat of the van. Logan was puzzled. 'Can I help you fellas?' he asked.

'Yeah, can you get that Jack Russell on a lead for us? He bit Nigel on the leg when he knocked on the door.'

Logan looked around and couldn't see Hank. He whistled and the little dog came flying out from under the van, looking as if he was ready to attack the trespassers again. 'Give me a sec,' Logan said, and he took Hank up to the verandah and clipped him to a short chain secured to a support post. Logan rubbed Hank on the head and winked at him. 'Good boy, Hank.'

Seeing that it was now safe, the three men clambered out of the van. Two were still smirking at how Hank had taken to the guy's leg like he did. The most well-dressed man spoke up, thrusting his right hand out to help ease the situation and show they came in peace. 'David Newman,' and he also pointed, acknowledging the camera crew. 'Logan, we were hoping you would have five minutes for an interview ... I'm sure you know what it's about.'

Don's words rang loud in his ears, and Logan took a deep breath. He saw the shock on David's face when he accepted without a problem. David didn't waste one second, and got the mic set up immediately. They chose a spot near a post-and-rail fence beside a three-year-old colt in a small paddock.

Logan was actually calm. He hoped this would get it over and done with. 'Okay, Logan, we are just about ready.' David didn't give any indication of what the interview was about, and Logan hadn't asked either, so both men were a bit wary.

The newsman had strict instructions from his superiors to get some sort of controversial comment for a spot on the 6 p.m. news or stay the hell up in the bush and not come back if he didn't. He now had thirty-eight minutes to do the interview, edit it, and email it back to the newsroom.

David smiled into the camera, so Logan guessed they were starting now. 'Good evening, I'm David Newman. I'm here in the picturesque Hunter Valley with the most talked about racehorse trainer in the last twenty-five years, Logan Weston, to talk about the video that has become a global sensation. It has reached 56 million views online in a week and has quickly become one of the most famous sporting feuds in history. After one of Logan Weston's horses switched stables days from the prestigious Cox Plate, Logan assaulted Angus Masters on Tuesday morning and was banned for eighteen months. Today, that horse, My Blue Boy, won the Group 1 Cox Plate for his new trainer, Angus Masters.' David turned to Logan, who was casually leaning against the fence. 'Logan, how did it feel today seeing *your* superstar horse win the Plate for your arch rival?'

Logan gave an amused smile. 'Oh, Angus isn't my arch rival, David. He is actually one of Australia's leading trainers.' He thought for a moment and continued carefully, 'The horse was sold in a deal last Monday night, and I got a very nice percentage of his sale price for the work I'd done with him. I'm very proud, and I'm happy with his win.'

But David was on a mission and prodded him for a more emotional response. 'But surely it must have stung to see Masters taking all the credit.'

Logan shrugged casually. 'Every trainer would love to be the one to hoist the trophy over their head and stand by the winning horse. It's a great achievement, and I congratulate Angus on the win and wish him all the best.'

'That's very modest of you, Logan.' David was starting to sound disappointed in the direction the interview was headed. He tried one last dig. 'It must be particularly tough to see Masters celebrate that win with Angela, your ex-wife. She made some pretty harsh comments today. Do you have any response to those?'

'Well, David, emotions are high on such a momentous occasion. When an interviewer stuffs a microphone and a camera in your face, and you haven't prepared a statement, you just react. I understand that situation, so I happily give Angela the benefit of the doubt. I congratulate them both for My Blue Boy's win. And before you ask, no, I have not made any plans to return to training just yet. Thanks to the lucrative sale of Bluey, I am taking a twelve-month holiday.' Logan smiled over at David and said, 'I think we got it.' He unhooked his mic and ravelled up the cord, placing it in David's hand.

Before David could say another word, Logan started walking over to where Hank was tied up. 'What do you think, Hank?'

'Just wait. Just one more question, Logan!' David was starting to panic, stuck between not getting the interview his boss wanted, and being attacked by the tiny dog.

'I'll give you a thirty-second head start,' Logan said, holding the clip. They knew they had enough for the news story, even if it wasn't controversial, and none of them wanted a Jack Russell swinging from their balls, that was for sure.

Logan watched and gave a smart-ass wave goodbye as they drove out down his drive. He unclipped Hank and he disappeared to fetch his decapitated rabbit, which had resurfaced from the garden. 'Jesus, Hank,' Logan said, rolling his eyes and locking the doggy door as he went inside.

He had left his mobile on the counter and now he saw that he'd missed thirty-eight calls and forty-six text messages. His voicemail was filled with motivational messages saying things like, 'You'll be right mate!' The texts messages were similar, except one from Sam that read, 'I'm horny, Mr Weston. What time tonight?' with a naughty devil emoji.

They both knew it would not go any further than this week, though they really did enjoy each other's company. Sam made Logan laugh and, after two years out of the saddle, he finally felt that he had his mojo back. Logan texted back, '8.39 p.m.'

Sam texted back, 'Giddy up, cowboy,' with a kissy face emoji. *Sam would be a great distraction tonight. Today felt like it was moving in slow motion*, he thought. Deep down, it had hurt seeing Masters win, and Angela's words had cut to the bone. Mental scars are bad enough, but knowing your wife left you for the other guy had made Logan doubt himself as a man in so many ways. He hated Angela and at times called her everything under the sun to himself, and seeing the asshole Masters at track work every day just rubbed salt into the wounds.

At 6 p.m. Logan turned on the news, curious to see how they would portray the interview. After twenty minutes, his story aired, and they discussed the interview for almost five minutes, which is a lot for a spot in the sports segment. Channel 7 had done a back flip and gone from trying to stir the pot to putting a positive spin on the story. Logan was happy he was portrayed as taking it on the chin and holding his head high. Logan was relieved he had taken Don's advice and acted respectfully. He felt he had given a good interview, and he just hoped the attention would settle down now.

Hank rose up from his spot on the couch next to Logan's left foot. Hank had heard something and was at attention. Logan looked at his watch—8.38 p.m. Hank knew there was someone coming down the driveway even before you could see the head-lights. He gave Hank a rub on the head and winked with a grin. 'I'm having someone staying over tonight.'

Logan didn't rush to the door as he didn't want Sam to think he was watching the time. He heard a small tap on the door and Hank scurried over, barking in anticipation. Logan opened the door and Sam was standing there wearing a black overcoat and black high heels, and holding a toothbrush and a bottle of Moët. She posed and gave him a seductive stare, trying her best to look like a superstar model. She held the stare for about four seconds before she burst out laughing. 'What's so funny?' he said, chuckling at her and letting her inside.

She steadied herself, took a few breaths in and out, then shook her hand in front of her mouth hoping it would help her keep a straight face. Now composed, she said, 'Well, I thought I would go to the drive-through bottle shop to grab a bottle of bubbly. Normally if the attendant Dale is on, he comes out and I don't need to get out of the vehicle. When I pulled up I couldn't see him, and I knew I was dressed inappropriately to go into the bottle shop. But there were no other cars there so, what the hell, I walked in. They'd changed all the shelves around so I couldn't find the French champagne. I was nervous already, as this jacket is short enough,' and she did a quick turn around and bent over to show Logan what she meant. He nodded, grinning.

Sam continued, 'I finally found it and as I was bending down to get the chilled bottle, I heard, "Sam?" I instantly knew the voice and turned red as a beetroot and turned around to see my mum and dad. And you know my dad is a smart ass, and he didn't miss this occasion. He goes, "Bit warm for a trench coat tonight, isn't it, baby girl?"'

Logan was by now laughing hard. 'I didn't know what to say, but he just walked me towards the counter. The attendant appeared, and Dad just winked and said, "My shout. Enjoy your night."'

They were both laughing hard and Sam said, 'So, after all that, let's open this bloody bubbly.'

They talked and laughed about the day they'd both had. Finally, Logan poured the last few drops into their glasses, then rose and walked to the door. He opened the door up, calling for Hank. Hank jumped down from the couch and looked at Logan, who went, 'Pss,' which was always a sign to stir him up and meant to get alert that there could be a rabbit or rat around. Hank flew out the door, and Sam looked puzzled.

'He will be looking for a rabbit or rat for an hour at least,' Logan said, as he walked towards her. He took her hand and pulled her up. With the other hand he cupped it behind her head and looked her straight in the eye. With one swift pull, he pulled the jacket waistcoat belt undone and it opened.

'I see, Mr Weston,' she said. 'But will an hour be enough time?'

Touché, he thought.

Forty-five minutes was probably closer, but Logan didn't time himself. *There was something about sex in your forties*, he thought. *It seemed a lot more relaxed, as you're more comfortable with who you are.* Sam had an appetite that had been dormant for three years, and they both felt like they were teenagers again. Maybe not six times per day, but they were enjoying quality, without a doubt.

Afterwards, Logan walked to the kitchen while Sam went to the bathroom. Logan walked to the fridge and poured two glasses of mineral water. Suddenly, Hank dove through the door with something squirming in his mouth. Logan shook his head and yelled, 'Hank!' The dog dropped the monster rat he was wrestling with. It quickly scampered across the room and hid under the couch. 'For God's sake, Hank,' Logan yelled, half laughing and half mad, still in the afterglow of a magnificent orgasm.

Hank darted around the couch, growling as he couldn't quite get under the couch, so Logan lifted it, hoping Hank would dart in and grab the rat that was the size of a rabbit. Hank dove for it and Logan felt the rat run over his naked foot. He instantly dropped the couch and he realised, after hearing a yelp, he had trapped Hank underneath.

As Logan was lifting the couch up again, Sam appeared in the doorway. 'What's going on?' she asked, very confused.

Hank was still sniffing around under the couch for the rat. 'Get out, Hank!' Logan yelled. Finally seeing Hank was clear, he dropped the couch. He looked back at Sam and said, 'This bloody dog just brought a massive rat in, and it's running around.'

Sam instantly went pale and her eyes darted around. 'What! Where!'

'I don't know,' Logan said, also looking around as Hank sniffed along the ground. 'We'll just have to wait until Hank finds it again.'

Taking no chances, Sam jumped on the breakfast bar, pulling her knees up to her chest. 'You told him to go get one, so you need to sort it!' Logan looked at her sitting fully naked on the bench and laughed. He walked over to her and she shooed him away, squirming in disgust at the thought of a rat crawling on her.

Hank and Logan walked through the house and there was no sign of the rat. *What a way to ruin a moment*, he thought. A loud scream came from the kitchen and Hank instantly bolted to the source and beat Logan to the kitchen. 'It's behind the fridge!' Sam shrieked.

She isn't smiling now, he chuckled to himself. Hank couldn't get behind the fridge so Logan got a broom and shook it down one side to spook the rat out. It darted out the opposite side and Hank was waiting to ambush it. No messing about this time as Hank clamped down hard on its neck and gave a vigorous shake to make sure. This repulsed Sam and for a split second she felt sadness for the rat.

Hank dropped the lifeless rodent and Logan was ready with the dust pan. He scooped it up and walked onto the verandah. Hank was bouncing behind him, barking with excitement. Logan flung the dead rat as far as he could and Hank bounded away. Logan walked back inside to see that Sam was still sitting on the kitchen bench looking dismayed. Logan locked the doggy door, as both agreed that was enough excitement for the night.

CHAPTER 7

It was 7.15 a.m. Sam was still sound asleep. Logan had been up for a few hours, as he still hadn't readjusted his body clock completely. He grabbed his mobile and turned it on. He wasn't worried about leaving his phone off now, as he had no clients and his close friends knew the landline number if there was a real issue. There were no new messages or text messages, and he felt relieved. He decided to delete every text and phone message from yesterday and start fresh today.

He poured another cup of coffee, two sugars with a dash of milk, but strong. He sat outside on the verandah to watch another beautiful sunrise, just like yesterday. His mobile rang and he thought, *Here we go*. He considered turning it off but saw that it was an international number and he was intrigued. He cleared his throat, as he had been caught before. 'Hello,' he said.

There was a slight pause. 'Logan Weston?'

'Yes.'

'My name is Cynthia Baker, Logan, and I'm calling from Newmarket in the UK.'

He could hear her British accent and was taken aback for a split second. 'Oh, okay. Hi, Cynthia. What can I do for you?'

'Logan, I'll cut to the chase. I am calling to offer you a job.'

Logan's eyebrows raised. 'Oh?' Now he was listening intently.

'I have 105 acres here in Newmarket and I have just finished building two private training tracks and forty stables. Everything is state of the art.'

'Sounds very nice,' he said, considering how expensive a set-up that size would be in Newmarket.

'I have twenty-two-year-old twin boys who are both crazy about racing. James is a jockey, but Tom wants to be a trainer. Both boys have done two years with Henry Coffey here at Newmarket.' Logan knew how good Henry was, as he had the backing of Jefferson Farm and had trained nine Group 1 winners last year in four different countries.

'James has ridden sixty-seven winners, Logan,' she said proudly. 'Unfortunately he had a nasty fall and has since lost his confidence. He's currently riding work, building his strength back up and his mental confidence as well. Tom has just spent eighteen months with David Lucas in the US and it's time they get their own chance.'

Logan sensed the two boys were her pride and joy and, like any proud mother, she was doing everything she could do give them the best chance.

'It sounds great, Cynthia, but where do I fit in?'

'Logan, Tom has studied your statistics of runners to winners, and also the winners to purchase prices, and you seem to have a unique knack for finding nice horses and keeping them sound.'

'I see you've been doing some homework, Cynthia,' he said, chuckling nervously.

'I've just read the notes Tom put together,' she said, and Logan sensed her starting to relax.

'Well, Cynthia, I'm flattered but my trainer's licence is actually suspended for the next eighteen months.'

'Yes, I am aware of your unfortunate circumstances, Logan. You appear to be a man who knows how to handle himself,' she said with a light chuckle. 'And Logan, to be completely honest, when I saw the story I thought to myself, *that petty man with no morals deserved everything you dished out.*'

Logan thought, *I'm starting to like this lady.*

'I am offering you an open-ended first-class ticket to anywhere you want to go. All I ask is that you first visit me here in Newmarket for one day so we can discuss the position I have available.'

Logan thought for a moment. 'Cynthia, I really appreciate the offer, but I will need to think about this first.'

'Perfectly fine,' she said. 'My PA, Mary, will call you the same time tomorrow for your response.'

'Okay, that sounds great.'

'One last thing before you go, Logan … Have you ever been at a horse sale and thought how it would feel to have a backer who had pockets so deep that you never miss out on a horse ever again?'

Logan grinned, shaking his head as he had wished for that so many times at the sales. 'I sure have,' he replied.

'Very good, then I look forward to meeting you in person very soon,' and she hung up.

He sat there is shock. Everything had been going so terribly, and now this call out of the blue. He quickly googled 'Cynthia Baker' on his phone, and there she was. 'Widow Cynthia Baker

sells Turkey Empire to Hobson International for 346-million—'.
He didn't need to scroll down anymore; he gathered she was about
his age or slightly older and now had play money for a tax break.
Every trainer wanted a backer who had disposal income. He had
seen so many whales* come and go in the racing industry, and
always wished he had a chance with one.

He was startled as Sam touched him on the shoulder. He'd
been so engrossed in his thoughts, he hadn't even heard her walk
out. 'Morning,' he said.

'Good morning.' She looked so sexy in his shirt. They walked
inside and Logan hit the kettle button back on and grabbed two
coffee mugs. 'Are you okay? You seem jumpy,' Sam said.

'I just got off a very interesting call from England,' he said.

Sam looked confused. 'England?'

Logan handed over his phone and she started reading the
article. 'Holy shit, I didn't know turkeys were worth that much.
So, what was the call about? Turkeys?'

Logan leaned back on the bench, chuckling. 'No, she's setting
up a racing stable and needs a trainer.'

'And a toy boy,' Sam quipped with a roll of her eyes, and her
body language had already changed. She knew she would still be
in the same town for the next twenty years, while Logan now had
no ties in life.

'Seriously,' he said. 'She said I have until tomorrow to make a
decision, and she's going to pay for my flight over there first class,
open ended. All I have to do is go and see what she has to offer.
No promises.'

---

* A 'Whale' is a term used for someone 'making a splash' in the equine industry.

'Wow, now that's exciting,' Sam said, and managed a weak smile. 'Well, it already sounds like you've made up your mind. There's nothing holding you here,' she said as she put the milk back in the fridge. They'd spent three nights together and the rules were made at the start—it was just sex. Sam knew she would be a Scone girl the rest of her life. Logan just shook his head in disbelief; he was as excited as he could ever remember.

She looked up at him and hugged him softly. 'It sounds like a great opportunity, Logan. You should go for it.' She couldn't hide the disappointment in her voice.

The kettle came to a boil and he turned to pour two cups. Sam picked up his coffee mug and said, 'I'll get it. You go hop in the shower.'

'Thanks,' Logan said, and he walked to the bathroom. His head was spinning with the offer.

He shaved, brushed his teeth, and tried to have a relaxing shower to get his thoughts in order. He dried off and walked into the bedroom to see a steaming mug of coffee and a note beside his bed that read: 'Safe trip. Thanks for the fuck.' Sam was gone.

CHAPTER 8

Logan was waiting for the call, and at 7.20 a.m. his phone rang. He let it ring four times and took a deep breath before answering. 'Hello?'

'Logan Weston, this is Mary—'

He cut her off before she explained further. 'Mary, I would like to meet Cynthia and discuss the position further. When do I leave?'

After a quick chat, he was booked to leave in five days' time on a first-class flight. He rang Aunty Joy and told her the news. She was so excited and said she would be back before he left to take care of the farm and Hank.

'Come here, boy.' Logan gave Hank a big cuddle before he left the farm. The last few days were spent talking to close friends and getting a few things sorted. He'd ordered in a truckload of hay and feed, paid the local mowing guy twelve months in advance for the yard maintenance. Aunty Joy hated that he'd paid for it, but she knew her knees were buggered.

Logan had one last very enjoyable ride on Frank's Harley, then drained the fuel and covered it with the tarp again. Logan honestly didn't know when he would be back. Aunty Joy drove him to the airport and she gave him a long hug at the gate. He had to shut his eyes most of the way, as she still insisted on driving.

Waiting to board, he looked at his phone before he would have to turn it off. He hadn't heard a peep from Sam, not even a goodbye text. He wasn't going to press it. *Once I step on this plane, I will see where life takes me*, he thought. *I need to have an open mind, free from complicated attachments. It's time to get my head straight.*

He couldn't believe he was flying first class on the Emirates A380. 'Welcome aboard, Mr Weston,' said the first-class attendant as she escorted him to his private suite. He had walked through first class on a few different trips to New Zealand, but he'd never seen anything like this before. The seat could be reclined to make a bed; he could take a shower if he wanted; he had so much room to spread out, and a personal attendant. Everything was amazing. He settled in and, before he knew it, they were climbing to the safe travelling height.

He flicked through the movie channels and settled on the life story of a down-and-out boxer who made a comeback. Logan previously never had time for anything but work, but watching movies helped him relax. His brain switched off for two hours or so as he became engrossed in the movie. The headphones were top of the line and shut out everything else. No phone, no work, just a new life filled with new opportunities. He watched another movie and had the most beautiful lunch he could recall. He'd never eaten salmon cooked so well in his life. He decided to take a nap and couldn't believe the comfort of the bed. He managed to get three solid hours of sleep before he got up and washed his face and tidied up. It was now 5 p.m. Australian time. The attendant invited him to join the other guests at the bar and lounge area. Logan looked a bit confused. 'Upstairs, Mr Weston,' she said, and gestured to the spiral stairs.

He walked upstairs to be amazed at the bar and lounge area. He took a seat at the bar and was given the wine list—no prices. He settled for the barman's selection on a red wine. The red was superb, and it wasn't long before he had another in front of him. He didn't even need to ask. He certainly felt out of place surrounded by so many wealthy-looking people. Luckily, he had invested in some pricey suit jackets, sports coats, slacks, and jeans for the trip and the interview with Cynthia Baker.

He had never been a big drinker. When you get up at 3.30 a.m. six days a week, you can't afford to be hungover. The two reds had gone down so smoothly that he opted for the third and felt the relaxation sink in. The barman said, 'Excuse me, sir,' and Logan looked up to see him gesture to the left.

Logan swivelled in the seat to see a man in his mid-sixties sitting with his wife and a slightly younger female. The gentleman smiled warmly and spoke quietly, 'Would y'all care to join us, son?'

Logan had never really been the social type, but the red was working and he knew he had new rules now, and they included being more social. He nodded, got up, picked up his glass, and walked over. The older gentleman stood up and put out his hand. 'Garth. This little lady here is my wife Ruth, and this is Ms Victoria,' he said, gesturing to the ladies, who smiled and nodded their greeting.

'Logan,' he said, shaking the older gentleman's hand.

'We know who you are, son,' Garth said, as Logan sat down beside Victoria. 'Your horse beat us last Saturday.'

Garth's wife Ruth could see Logan's puzzled look, and added, 'We own Society Boy from the U S of A.' Logan nodded, as he remembered the fading horse. 'He is really a dirt horse.'

'That's why we are heading to Dubai with him for the Group 1 World Cup,' Garth said.

'Well, it's very hard for the dirt track horses to handle our tracks, especially the Valley,' Logan responded. 'That turn goes for 600 metres and the straight is very short.'

The younger woman, Victoria, said sincerely, 'My Blue Boy is a very good horse, Logan. I'm sure y'all are very proud.'

If Logan had thought the conversation was going to be all about him, he might have stayed at the bar, but the third red was almost gone and he was going with the flow. 'Thanks. It did hurt to lose him, but everyone knows it was still my polish on the horse. I am very proud of him.'

'Hell yes,' Garth said, and raised his glass in a toast, followed by Ruth and Victoria. Logan lifted his glass and clinked it together. After they all took a sip, Logan chuckled sheepishly. 'It's been a tough week. I've been copping it left, west, and crooked.'

'I bet,' Victoria said sympathetically.

'Well, there ain't nothin' wrong with drowning your sorrows son,' said Garth. Ruth gave him a sideways look and Logan had the feeling that it was Ruth's money, and Garth was a man, like Logan, who felt out of place.

'Hush now,' Ruth said and gave him a look, obviously putting him on notice.

Victoria giggled. 'Yes, y'all behave now, Garth.' Logan had always loved the way the Yanks talked, and Victoria had a Texan drawl.

Garth ordered another round, and that was followed by another two. Garth had done most of the talking, and he told the story of how he and Ruth had met twelve years before. Garth had a ranch in Texas and did cattle drives for tourists. Ruth's best friend had dragged her on the drive, kicking and screaming. Ruth had been a very good dressage rider in her younger days and hadn't ridden for over twenty years. She hadn't been on any kind of holiday since her husband had died four years earlier, and her friends thought the drive would be a great adventure. It was over twelve days and nights, and there were fourteen tourists, three cowboys, and three crew to cook and set up the camp.

On the fourth day, one of the most inexperienced riders got into trouble when their mount got spooked and bolted. The rider was terrified and screamed louder and louder as the horse bolted. Ruth and Garth were the two riders closest to her and, since they were both experienced, they took off after her. When a horse bolts, it basically runs blind until it runs out of steam. The rider was so terrified that she had dropped the split reins as the horse galloped full pelt. Numerous times the horse's hooves had snapped the reins and bridle, and twice the horse nearly fell from the bridle snagging under it.

Ruth had given chase and was a few lengths in front of Garth. They both knew there were fences ahead, as they were following a trail between farm lands. Ruth's horse simply didn't have the speed to get that extra few lengths for her to try to do something. The tourist horses were not the smart or fast type, like the ones the cowboys rode, but under these conditions they still were very dangerous.

Garth saw Ruth drop her head in defeat, as her horse was spent. He knew he had a short burst left in his Texan Quarter

Horse and drove hard with his spurs; but he also knew it was not time for heroics either. He had a lasso but that would only give him one shot and, at flat gallop, he had no time to undo the leather holding it tight on the back of the saddle. He had another plan.

He urged hard and drew up alongside only for that plan to go astray. *No bridle.* He thought for a split second and drove his spurs once more in, and his horse started to accelerate past. As he drew alongside the horse's head, he used his right hand to grab the bolting horse's right ear and pushed back with his left; his body cleared the saddle and stirrups. He jammed his left hand down as hard as he could and he twisted the horse's head to the right. The horse twisted and threw its head up and down as Garth's heels dug into the ground. Its legs came up once more and this time smashed down hard on Garth's right knee, instantly shattering it. By this time, the horse had slowed back to a canter while it fought with Garth's bulldogging style around its neck and head.

Garth had no idea that Ruth had levelled up on the right side, stretched her body out, and grabbed the terrified rider around the waist, pulling her across to her horse. With no experience in this type of riding, both Ruth and the girl came crashing down. The bolting horse, experiencing a shift in weight after the rider was taken off, stumbled and came down on Garth, cartwheeling over him. Ruth had hit hard but was not hurt, and the girl wasn't either, bar from shock. Ruth rushed over to Garth and was horrified to see his right leg was pointing sideways from the knee. He was conscious, but she could see he was struggling to breathe; the weight of the falling horse had broken some of his ribs. Luckily, there was phone reception where they were, so the other tour guide was able to alert a medical dispatch unit. Ruth had trained as a nurse, and it all quickly came back to her. She stabilised Garth before the medical helicopter arrived, then travelled with him to the hospital.

Garth finished the story off by saying, 'Every little lady needs a cowboy.' He had gone from a struggling cowboy rancher to now owning the fourth largest land holdings in Texas. Ruth was the businesswoman, and he was her knight in shining armour.

He then stood and took Ruth's hand. 'Well, Logan, it's been a pleasure to meet you, son, but it's time to go and rest this weary soul.'

'Drunk soul,' Ruth added with a smile.

The two departed and there was an awkward silence, as it was now just Victoria and Logan. Feeling more relaxed after the drinks, Logan ordered two nightcaps. The barman brought them over and sat them on the table. Logan found Victoria quite stunning, and her accent had really hit a spot in his heart.

'How do you know Garth and Ruth?' he asked, as they sipped their drinks.

'I run one of their companies. They have a bottled water business as well—many businesses, in fact.'

'So, you're on a business trip with them?'

'You could say that I guess,' she answered, and Logan sensed an uneasiness in her voice. She bowed her head slightly. 'They brought me along as I haven't been anywhere for quite a while now.'

'What a great employee bonus.'

'I suppose so,' she answered, beginning to fiddle with her glass uneasily. 'I … lost my husband two years ago.'

'Oh shit, I'm sorry,' Logan said, instantly feeling terrible for flirting with her seconds earlier. He opened his mouth, unsure if he should change the subject or not. 'What happened?'

She sensed his discomfort and quickly answered, 'Suicide.'

'Oh, I'm so, so sorry. I don't mean to pry,' Logan gushed, a little surprised by her openness.

'Please, it's fine. Don't feel bad for askin'. My husband was a good man, a very proud American, but he suffered in silence. We lost our business—that is how I came to work for Garth and Ruth. I had a background in accounting and, when our business failed, I needed to take back control of our finances. My husband was never the same man again. He was obsessed with getting back what we once had. He worked too hard and made impulsive decisions. By the end, he had learnt to hide his true feelings so well that I couldn't tell a darn thing, and that's when he was suffering most. He finally snapped when a client's cheque bounced. That started a domino effect. He felt in his heart that he was a failure.' Victoria's voice grew quiet and tears rose up in her eyes. 'He wrote me a note explaining very clearly how he felt about us, about himself, about our life. I never knew. I look back now and realise what an amazing man he was to last as long as he did, suffering alone in silence. He died thinking of everybody but himself. He left behind clear instructions for his effects after he was gone, and he made sure that he took his life in a way that would lessen the burden for the people who found him. My husband was a good man, Logan'

Logan sat back in his chair, letting Victoria's story sink in. After a long silence, Logan lifted his drink and gave Victoria a reassuring smile. 'To your husband—a good man.'

Victoria clinked his glass and added, 'To all good men,' returning the smile.

After a long comfortable silence as the two finished their drinks, they put their empty glasses down on the table—the cue that it was time for bed. 'Victoria, it has been a pleasure getting to know you,' Logan said, as he got up.

'Best of luck to you, Logan,' she answered, rising from her seat and giving him a hug. It was the first time she had openly shared her late husband's story with a stranger. 'Goodnight, Logan.'

Logan realised that Victoria was possibly the most enchanting and beautiful person inside and out he had met in many years. 'Goodnight, Victoria,' he said, and they parted ways.

Logan woke up and looked at his watch. *Two hours to go.* He hadn't slept that great in years. He did feel a bit doughy in the head, but it was worth it. It had been a long time since he had enjoyed the company of strangers.

CHAPTER 9

As Logan walked out of the airport, the cold air hit him straight in the face. It had been over twenty years since he'd been in England. The private driver led him to the car, stored his luggage in the boot, and asked if he preferred the front or back seat. Logan chose the front and hopped in, without giving the man time to open the door for him.

On the way, they chatted about the area. The streets of Newmarket were familiar to Logan, as he had done a short stint in the stables there as a young man.

'It starts here, sir,' the driver said, and Logan looked out to see the new tracks. He guessed the fencing was new, as there were no hedges growing around the day and spelling paddocks yet. Even though the lay of the land seemed quite flat, Logan noticed the grass track had a nice steady incline on the final 400 metres—or two furlongs—of the gallop. He was impressed.

Everything was new, including the house. 'Ma'am has built everything from scratch, sir. Previously it was a paddock full of sheep, rubbish, weeds, and more dead car bodies than horses in work here, sir.'

The driver aimed a small remote at the front entrance gates and they opened smoothly. He drove the last 300 metres at a snail's pace—to be expected on a horse farm. When they arrived at the front door, Logan hopped out and the driver quickly got his luggage and led him inside. The house was beautiful—elegant and charming, without being extravagant. It had a warm and friendly atmosphere. He instantly liked it.

'Logan Weston?'

Logan looked over to see a woman in her late-forties entering the room with purpose. She was average height with a strong build, and was wearing jeans, a tailored shirt, and Dublin boots. *Not extravagant either*, he thought.

'Cynthia Baker,' she said, and stuck out her hand. Logan shook it and found she had a firm handshake for a woman. 'I trust you had a good flight?'

'Superb, thank you, just superb.'

'Only way to fly.'

'Can't argue with that.'

'Can I get you a drink or something to eat before we begin?'

'I'm fine, thank you.'

'Let's take a walk then. I'll show you the farm.'

They slowly strolled around the farm, pausing at each horse for Cynthia to explain its breeding. Logan was also very impressed with the workmanship and detail to safety in the stable complex. Cynthia gestured to a seat outside the barn and they sat to discuss Cynthia's proposal.

'I need a trainer who can provide expert guidance to my boys, but I want someone with a fire burning deep down in their soul. I need someone who will not roll over when things get tough. I like to win, Mr Weston, but if I don't win I will only accept defeat if I know I gave it my best. I met my late husband when he had a thirty-acre farm and fifty-five sheep. He was a good farmer but not business-minded. I turned the farm around and in twenty-three years I transformed a £150,000-debt into the fortune I have today—all while raising two boys. My husband died 18 months ago, killed by a drunk driver. I can't get him back, but I can give my two sons what we have built and give them a chance to succeed in life. I don't feel guilty one bit,' she said sternly. 'I have picked up, gutted, and cleaned more turkeys than any other woman in this world.'

Logan instantly liked this woman. She was driven and strong, and she loved her husband and her two sons fiercely. He admired that quality in any person.

'I want you to help train my boys,' she continued, 'and help me keep them on the right course. If you accept those terms, then the job is yours.' Logan opened his mouth, but he couldn't get a word in. Cynthia was on a roll. 'I am tired of being looked down on by the pompous racing fraternity who have never worked a hard day in their lives. I gather you have met your fair share of these types as well?' Logan nodded.

Cynthia jumped up from her seat, or you could say, her soapbox. 'Mr Weston, do you want to take back the Cox Plate?'

'Yes, ma'am,' Logan said firmly.

'What about a July Cup and Arc as well?'

They were some of the greatest races in Europe. 'Yes, ma'am,' he said again.

'Then find me a winning horse, Mr Weston. Whether it costs three pounds or three million pounds, I will buy it. You get £500,000 per year, plus ten per cent of any winnings and five per cent if we sell a stallion prospected.' Cynthia pointed across the property. 'That house on the left—yours. The black Range Rover in the garage—yours.'

Logan tried to keep a straight face, pretending to mull it over in a business-like fashion, but inside he was yelling, 'Holy fuck!'

Logan took a moment to collect his thoughts before he stood up and said, 'All my life, I have wanted someone to put their faith in me. I never needed half a million pounds, or a Range Rover, or even a state-of-the-art training facility. I just needed someone to give me a chance with a horse with half the quality the other trainers get. I have had the taste of a champion, and I am so hungry to get that chance again.

'You back me like you have just said, and I promise to work with your sons to prove this is the best decision you have ever made.'

They stared at each other for a moment before Cynthia said curtly, 'Very good then.' She stuck out her hand and Logan shook it. 'Welcome to the team, Mr Weston.'

'Thank you, Cynthia. I won't let you down. But, I have to know, why me?'

'Well, we were considering trainers worldwide when I saw a video of you on the news. You knew you would get disqualified. You knew it would be the death of your career. But as a man, you had to stand up for yourself. You walked in a straight line through the media storm that followed, and you never faltered once. When I saw that, I knew you would be a man of your word. My husband was the same. He worked for his family and he died saving my life.'

Logan looked surprised. Cynthia took a sharp breath before she explained, 'My husband, William, and I had finished dinner at a restaurant and had driven out of the carpark when I realised I had left my overcoat with my purse in it on the back of the chair. William stopped the car and said he would turn around so we could drive back to get it—always the gentleman. But I had already hopped out of the car onto the road and was walking over. Tom had texted to see how long we'd be, as he had dropped in for a surprise visit. I was still looking at my phone as I dashed across the road. I should have been more careful, but I was suddenly in a rush to get home. I stumbled and fell down. William jumped out of the car and ran onto the road to help me up. Because it was late there wasn't much traffic, but one lane had to stop to wait for us to move. As William was helping me get back to the car, we heard a loud engine roaring down the other lane. William gave me a hard push and I toppled over onto the bonnet of our car. I didn't know what was going on, but I suddenly heard screeching wheels and the most horrible thud. William was thrown into the air and landed in a heap on the road. Someone who had witnessed what had happened was screaming. The driver of the car was drunk and didn't have their lights on. They were speeding down the road and didn't see us. William died on impact.'

There was a long pause before Logan said solemnly, 'I'm so sorry for your loss.'

Cynthia nodded her head and gave a tight smile. 'Yes, well, tomorrow is a new day.' She quickly reverted to the business-minded lady she had been for the best part of three hours. 'We have built this place in just over fourteen months. I will need you to go to the U.S. tomorrow with Tom. The Keeneland breeze-up sale* starts in three days and we should see what's on offer, don't you think?'

Logan smiled and nodded his head, starting to laugh. 'Yes, ma'am.'

'What is it?' she asked curiously.

'I've only ever dreamt of going there.'

'You're not just *going* there, Mr Weston, you will be *buying* there.'

Logan's smile widened and he tried to stop himself from laughing giddily. 'Just one thing,' Cynthia added, as she led them over to the new house where Logan would be staying. 'Leave the slow ones there,' and she winked. 'I only need fast ones.'

Logan just wished he could call the one person who would be as excited as he would be—his dad, Frank. He had loved the racing game as much as Logan, and he loved his son. Frank always said, 'One day, your whale will come by and you'll get your shot.'

When they walked in, Logan's luggage was waiting in the foyer. The house had been decorated to give an 'English gent who enjoyed sport' type of feel. It was modest and inviting. Logan loved it. 'I trust you will be comfortable here,' Cynthia said.

'Oh, it will do,' he said cheekily.

---

* A breeze-up is when two-year-old racehorses that have not raced perform a gallop before sale. They record the time for their gallop (200 to 400 metres). Trainers and agents watch the breeze-up to determine if they think they can gallop further than the 400 metres on the day, then they bid at auction to buy them. In 2006, a colt made the world record price (16 million) at the breeze-up sale.

'I will leave you to freshen up. You can meet me in the main house in an hour and I will introduce you to my boys. We can start serious talks about our future plan.' As soon as Logan had nodded his agreement, Cynthia marched out swiftly.

Logan wandered around, exploring the house. It had a beautiful view of the track and spelling paddocks. He never imagined that a deal like this would be offered to him—never. Logan had a decent feeling about Cynthia and her boys. Small and boutique, and very selective.

An hour later, Logan had showered and changed. He was quite nervous as he walked up to the main house, as it was now three on one. He was a bit worried that Cynthia's sons may be spoilt brats. But there was no need for concern. Both James and Tom were very similar to their mum—down to earth and hard workers. They both talked openly about how excited they were that Logan had accepted the position. They had done their homework, and Logan was their number one pick.

Logan saw Tom look at his watch. It was 3.45 p.m. Logan automatically said, 'You need a hand with the feed run?' That one comment cemented their faith in Logan. He was a horseman, and a horseman's body clock knows the time to feed. Both boys had learnt the hard way from the start, but their early and late finishing times were herding turkeys.

Cynthia said, 'I must get Jeremy over for dinner. Mike will also need to meet Logan so we can all start getting on the same page.' As Logan quickly learnt, Jeremy was the solicitor for the family. He would have to get the necessary papers signed before Logan headed to Keeneland in the morning with Tom. Mike was their vet, so he would need to talk to Logan about the scoping for wind and X-ray viewing on any possible breeze-up purchases.

'Lovely dinner, Cynthia,' Mike said, and they all raised their glasses and thanked their host.

'Mike, I haven't told you, you are going in the morning to the Keeneland horse sales as well,' Cynthia said quietly, before taking a sip of her drink.

'You can be a right rich bitch when you want to be, Cynthia.' Cynthia raised her glass in agreement with Mike.

'My bags are already packed. The Johnsons have asked me to go and vet for them,' Mike replied, like he just had got one up on her. This made Cynthia quickly put her drink down and look over at Mike. The Johnsons were a thorn in Cynthia's side and were renowned for causing trouble. They had protested to everyone and anyone that would listen about their concerns over Cynthia's raised training tracks, claiming that it would change the flood path in the area, even though there had not been a flood in 187 years. The actual reason was that they didn't want her competition on the racetrack.

'I hope you are bloody well joking, Mike,' Cynthia said.

'It's hunky-dory,' Mike said. 'I sold out to the partners yesterday. I gathered, by Tom feeding me a bit of inside information, you might need a full-time vet in the grand scheme of things.'

'You're quite jammy, Mike.'

'You can't afford me, Cynthia,' he laughed.

'Now you're just taking liberties, Mike.'

Logan enjoyed the British accents and the banter between Cynthia and Mike.

Logan and Tom had instantly gained a mutual respect. Tom was mature for his age and had a level head on his shoulders. James was a nice young man as well, but Logan could see he was missing his father, or there was something else troubling him more so than the fall he had recovered from. Logan instantly thought that a month with old Don back at Scone would do wonders for his confidence. He nodded his head at the idea. Don was the man to make anyone believe. James was to be the stable's number one jockey. He would take a few outside rides every now and then, but he didn't need to ride every day and travel the countryside to make a living. If he only had to ride for his mother, and not worry about an income, James hoped he could focus more than the other jockeys on each ride.

Logan settled in for the first night in his new home for a few hours before he, Tom and Mike boarded the first-class Emirates flight to the U.S. They barely slept, as they all sat reading and going over the horse sale catalogue and marking the pedigrees that suited. But they were also wise not to dismiss a good type or mover, even if its pedigree wasn't up to scratch. Just as in people, the pedigree of your family doesn't always mean success. In the end, they had marked ninety per cent of the horses for closer inspection. No stone unturned. Logan had never been part of a purchase team before. He had never been this excited, and he sensed the other two were quite excited, too. He was sure they were about to make a splash in the sport of kings.

They arrived at 9.30 a.m. at Keeneland, just as Lot 1 was coming up the straight for its breeze-up gallop. If you missed the gallops, you could view them within an hour online; many potential buyers studied them over and over. The advantage of watching them live was that you could see how they coped before and after the breeze-up. In addition, the sound and rhythm of their gallop gave you a clear indication whether they hit the ground hard or soft. A great galloping sound would get any worthwhile trainer's attention.

Logan was in awe. Eight of the top ten trainers worldwide were sitting there in the stands. All the big players in the industry were there. Some had horses for sale, and others were there to buy. Normally, three guys like them would not get a second glance, but Logan was an Internet star. A few whispers started and then a few heads turned. Logan felt quite embarrassed. Thirty lots had breezed up and there was a short break while the track was graded and rolled to make the surfaces even again.

Logan, Tom, and Mike headed down to the cafeteria with the other trainers and grabbed a snack. While they stood in a corner talking about the first thirty lots, a man approached them and slapped Logan on the back. 'Goddamn, if it ain't Logan Weston himself. Woo, you are a star, man! Can I get a selfie? Shit, my buddies won't believe this!' Logan was stunned, but got in a photo with the man. 'Thanks, buddy. Gus,' the man introduced himself, shaking Logan's hand. 'Damn, you nailed that son of a bitch good, boy.' Logan could feel more people in the room looking over. 'C'mon over here, boys. Come and meet the crew.'

Gus ushered them over to a table. 'Logan Weston, this is Alan Paulson, champion trainer, with twelve Grade 1 wins last year; Dexter Fitz, eight Grade 1 wins last year; Denver Hollis, three Grade 1 wins last year, but leading trainer of winners with 426 wins and eighteen million in prize money.'

The men greeted Logan and his group like they were long-lost friends, all because Logan stood his ground and did what so many racehorse trainers would have loved to do in that situation. The last thing a trainer wants is someone improving the horse he just lost. Similar to when a football team's coach gets sacked and the new coach turns the team around and makes them winners.

Logan texted Pete, and was surprised to find he was still up, but that was Pete's business as he had been texting back and forth with Pete back in Australia since he'd arrived to keep him up to date, and Pete sent through: 'Bluey is backing up in the Mackinnon Stakes* on Saturday.'

Logan texted back: 'Not surprised.'

'Any fast ones yet?'

'Yes, a couple of nice ones so far. Only thirty breeze-ups in, and they are grading the track now. Talk later.'

Angus Masters had accepted My Blue Boy for Saturday's Mackinnon Stakes and had written a cheque for $110,000 for a late entry to the Melbourne Cup, as well. Three-year-old horses rarely ran in the Melbourne Cup, let alone a rising superstar that would have a current worth of fifteen million. If anything, winning the Cup would hamper his sire appeal, as Australia still hadn't grasped breeding stayers like European racing had. Australia was focused on breeding sprinters and two-year-olds, and paid ridiculous money for a speedster and a Group 1-winning two-year-old. Masters had also taken Bluey to a private training property, out of the public eye, and had been pouring the work into the horse. He'd worked him hard over 2,800 metres. Most Cup contenders five days out were already well and truly fit enough. Some

---

* The LKS Mackinnon Stakes is a Group 1 thoroughbred horse race over a distance of 2,000 metres, held three days before the Melbourne Cup. Not many Cox Plate runners compete, as the Cox Plate had been their main aim for the spring, but sometimes the odd few have.

would run on Saturday, but they would just need the run to top them off or, on the odd occasion, qualify for the race. In seven to ten days, you can't get a horse fit enough that has been aimed at a 2,000-metre race his whole prep. But, as usual, Angus Masters would not be told 'no'.

The guys settled in for the next thirty breeze-ups. Lot 37 breezed down in 9.8 seconds and looked like he was doing it easy. Heads in the crowd nodded, and Tom turned the catalogue to the back page to make sure it was in the inspection list. The breeze-ups came at no more than two-minute intervals, and Keeneland was running a smart show. There was no idle talk, as this was work, and all three studied the horse and made notes to be compared later that day.

When Lot 41 breezed-up, Tom noticed that Logan had his eyes closed. When the horse slowed down after going past the finish post, Logan opened his eyes and quickly jotted down some notes. Tom watched Logan again when the next lot went. Eyes closed again. This colt ran 10.1. Logan opened his eyes and he already had the catalogue open to its back page. Tom elbowed Mike and motioned over to Logan. Lot 42 approached the 250 metre-mark and, sure enough, Logan's eyes closed. This colt breezed in 9.7— the quickest of the day. Eyes still closed, Logan smiled and opened to the back page.

Tom and Mike smiled at each other. They knew Logan was not there with them; he was in his own world, focused on the sound of the horses. It was no different to a baseball coach hearing a good pitch, or a golf coach knowing the golfer had just nailed a drive down the fairway. Logan didn't feel the need to impress anyone else. He was doing what he had always done, only now he didn't have any other worries in the world so he could focus completely on doing his job. He never had to worry about money again—to a trainer, that was irreplaceable.

Lot 60 breezed and everyone headed back down for refreshments. Tom stopped by some benches outside the cafeteria and said, 'Mike, can you grab us some Coca-Cola and some scrummy fried chicken, please?' Mike didn't even blink an eye when someone as young as Tom asked him to get food. Tom was Mike's boss. Younger or not, Mike knew this.

'Let's go over the notes here. Best way to avoid dealing with your fan club inside.' They all laughed, and Mike headed for the cafeteria.

Mike returned with the drinks and fried chicken. They sat and started comparing notes. Tom couldn't hold it in anymore and he had to ask, 'The Zen, Logan, what's with the eyes shut, do tell, please?'

Logan knew they had been watching him. 'Oh, well I'm listening for their rhythm and their breathing when they ease down.'

'Ease down?' Tom asked.

'If they were holding their breath or running on their last full breath that means they were 100 per cent extended. If I can still hear them making an audible nasal sound every few strides, then they have some in reserve. I would rather buy a 10.8 doing it easy breathing than a 9.8 not making a sound, as they can't go quicker than that. Lot 42 is our horse so far. He breezed in 9.7 and was still breathing in rhythm. He is one that we need.'

Lot 42 was not as regally bred as many others for sale; he had been pinhooked* for the breeze-up by a Group 3-winning son of

---

* Pinhooking refers to the practice of buying a young thoroughbred horse cheaply and re-selling it for a large profit.

Unbridled's Song. He was purchased for $45,000 and the pin-hookers would be hoping to make $350,000.

'What did you have for Lot 53, Logan?' asked Tom.

Logan flicked his book open. 'Hit the ground heavy in front.'

'So did I,' Tom said, with a smile. Logan gave him a quick wink and Tom lit up inside. His father would do that when Tom did something good.

Logan and Mike discussed what they could and couldn't wear with X-ray issues. Mike, now not being tied to a practice, was more relaxed, as he was employed by the same employer as Logan, and Cynthia was prepared to take all risks that Logan, Tom, and Mike agreed on. Many vets had failed so many great horses because they were more worried about getting sued than having the balls to make a decision. Mike felt much happier being a major part of a racing team. He enjoyed the atmosphere of the sales and liked being committed to one stable, rather than spread thin over twenty stables.

After going through some notes, the men joined the group heading back to the stands. Logan stopped at the running rail and said, 'Let's watch from here.'

As Lot 61 breezed, Tom shut his eyes tightly and listened. Logan waited. When Tom opened his eyes, he went to the back page. Logan watched him out of the corner of his eye, nodding his approval. Lot 62. Logan waited. Tom opened his eyes. 'Imbalanced stride, flat to the boards.' Logan winked at him. Lot 63 was scratched.

Lot 64 breezed and this time all three men closed their eyes. The horse went past. 'Wow,' Tom said. Logan's eyes sprung open to find Lot 64 in the book.

'9.1,' Mike said.

'And it wasn't even flat out,' Logan added. All three smiled and nodded, impressed. Logan flicked to the pedigree. Lot 64 was by the champion sire in Australia, King's Speech, who was out of the great sprinting mare Special. 'I broke his mother in as a yearling, she was fast.'

Logan had actually broken in Special when he was doing a stint for a horse breaker.

These days, they can be called a horse 'educator'. He couldn't believe it. She was now eighteen years old and, as a last throw of the dice, they gave her until February to cycle, which put her in the Northern Hemisphere breeding time. She went in foal and produced a bay colt by King's Speech. The owners decided to send him over as a weanling and give him time to grow in Kentucky—and grow he did. He developed into a machine. King's Speech as a sire had sold seventy-one-million-dollar yearlings, and not even a slow one had made it to Logan's stable because he could never afford them. But now he had the firepower behind him. If the inspection went well, this colt was coming home with him.

The rest of the day was spent watching the other 190 breeze-ups, and then inspecting forty-two horses on the short list, which was culled back to sixteen. Lot 64 was still on Logan's radar, and there was a buzz about how easy he had breezed.

The team went back and dined in a private room while going back through the catalogue and re-watching the breeze-ups online. They played the videos over and over and over, but there were still only sixteen on the list. Tom and Logan talked training and did a Skype call with Cynthia and James, where they all viewed the sixteen breeze-ups together.

The finalists were cut to eleven when Mike failed five horses after looking at the X-rays of the horses' joints on the online repository. Even though they had a low tolerance to most issues, there were certain things they couldn't pass, and Tom and Logan accepted Mike's call.

'There are another two we should consider,' Logan blurted out.

'Yes, Logan. Which lots?' Tom asked.

'I don't mean here, I mean back home. Two trained by Masters,' Logan said.

'Your old horse My Blue Boy?' asked Mike.

'I wish,' said Logan. 'I used to watch Angus Masters' track work riders and study his horses in between waiting for mine to come out to exercise in the mornings. He has a colt by the stallion Roman Empire that he paid 1.2 million for. He has had two starts and came fourth and fifth. I know he hates the horse because he sank $400,000 of his own money into him. He's got a super pedigree. I've watched him, and the horse rips and tears everywhere on the track. They even used a hackamore bridle at one stage to stop him pulling, as he had a few victories over riders and bolted a few times. He just hates that horse. He would be four weeks from a start now.'

'The other one?' Mike asked.

'A colt by a nothing-much stallion called Topline. Masters was given the horse by a breeder who is into the line breeding back generations. He boasted in the training hut once that the line breeding is complete bullshit and he takes no notice. I know the owner, and spoke to him at a country race meeting one day just about his theory in the line breeding. This colt would be worth no more than $30,000 on the market, but he goes back to Princequillo and Anne Campbell on both sides and 2 x 3. He will either be a freak or no good. Because he hates the horse, he has the worst track rider on him, and he gets belted and his mouth jerked left and right if he puts a foot wrong. The horse works with head sky high, as he has learnt he has to hold his head up so the jerking is not as severe. He's only had one prep, and I noticed last week he must have been back in, say, five weeks, as he had come from the pre-trainers. I want these two colts more than the King's Speech colt.'

'That bad?' said Tom.

'Revenge?' said Mike.

'No, Mike, karma,' Logan said. 'Both horses have that wow factor. Masters is too blind to see it. His time will come. I want to get those two colts and take them to my place in Scone for four weeks. I have a friend who has 10,000 acres and is due for a muster in the next two weeks. By the end of the muster, those colts will be able to be ridden on a piece of cotton.'

Tom and Mike exchanged looks, unsure what to think of the new plan.

Logan added, 'I want James to come over with me and spend a few weeks there with them. Full days in the saddle with Don. He could learn a lot.'

'Who is Don?' said Tom. Logan had a bad habit that assumed everyone knew as soon as he spoke what he was on about.

'He was my father's closest friend, and he has more wisdom than anyone I know. I think it will do James some good. I can see him struggling without your dad around.'

'You noticed?' said Tom, with a sad expression. 'He's my twin, but I haven't a clue what's going on deep down. I've tried to help but I walk away feeling like a cock up.'

Logan walked over and put his hand on Tom's shoulder 'I lost my dad not long ago, and it's tough. I'm twice your age and

I still miss him every day. Look, don't be worried about James. My place is near Don's farm, and my aunty will take good care of him.'

'I'll need to run this one by mother,' Tom said, thinking it all over carefully. Logan knew Tom would need to talk it over with Cynthia, and also with James, before they could action anything.

Logan said, 'Your mother will know if the time is right for James to get some real-world experience. Tough work will make him a better rider as well. If they agree, then I would like to head back home from here, get the colts, and you and I spend a few days there as well, and we get everything settled and then head back to Newmarket. By that time, the two-year-olds will be back from the breeze-up and we can set a plan.' Logan had hit the ground running, and both Tom and Mike were very impressed so far and loved his confidence of winning the bidding at the sale tomorrow.

Tom listened carefully to Logan, ready to relay the information to his mother and perhaps do some convincing. He got out his mobile and got up from the table to make the call privately. 'Wish me luck,' he said, and winked at Logan. Logan gave him a reassuring smile. Tom didn't seem to have a bad bone in his body. *Very rarely you meet a young man like that,* Logan thought.

Logan woke up early the next day and knocked on Mike and Tom's doors in the suite they were sharing—five-star, of course. 'Sale day,' he called out, smiling like a kid in a candy store with his mum's credit card. They headed down for breakfast, and the spread was incredible. Logan settled for a nice coffee and a small yoghurt. He felt too nervous to eat. His ass was on the line. It didn't matter who had the bigger chequebook, Logan still had to pick the right horses.

Tom walked over, reading from his phone. 'Mother says James will need to get a Driza-Bone jacket and some R. M. Williams boots.'

'Are you serious?' Logan said.

'Yes, and also she says to remind you to leave the slow ones here. It seemed to be turning into her new motto now,' Tom laughed. 'Mary has booked us flights there tonight after the sale, and Mike, you will need to inspect them.'

'You fuckin' beauty,' Logan said, feeling his nervous energy building up with excitement. 'I will call and arrange through an agent I know from Ireland so Masters won't get wind it's me.'

'We're going Down Under, mate!' Mike joked.

Logan made the call to the Irish bloodstock agent. 'Logan, what the fuck ya want, ya thieving convict?' They'd had the running joke since they worked together when Logan was twenty-two years old. Mick was now one of the best, and he had a reputation for buying low-price horses that ended up Group winners, and even champions.

Logan explained the situation and Mick responded, 'Righto. What's the offer?'

'Just buy them, and Tom and Mike will inspect them Friday morning at 9 a.m.'

'And what if he won't sell?'

'Oh, he will. He hates the pair of them.'

'I hate you, but you're not even worth two bob, ya convict.'

Logan laughed and was about to hang up when Mick started again. 'Ya remember that girl you dated? Christine?'

Logan paused, as he knew he was getting set up. 'Yes, I remember', he said with a tone of just get it over with.

'Ya remember her, convict?'

Logan finally answered, 'C'mon let me have it.'

'Well, she said my pecker is bigger than yours …' and then Mick hung up.

Logan laughed hard but knew Mick would get the deal done for him.

Cynthia touched base twenty minutes before the sale started. The team had talked about what they were happy to pay, and Cynthia said she wanted to be online when they were bidding. The list was cut to eight, as on fourth inspection Tom and Logan had dropped three more off, for varying reasons.

Lot 37 was the first on the list and they were on. The sale had started strong, and already a colt by Unbridled's Song had made 2.1 million, and a filly by Eldorado $950,000. Finally it was Baker Racing's turn to bid and try to buy. Cynthia was on the phone with Tom, and the colt opened at $200,000 and quickly ran to $545,000. Tom was stalling, and not one bid from him. Logan was anxious about why they had not bid yet. But he wasn't game to ask. The auctioneer called his second last bid and the hammer was about to drop, and Tom nodded. 'Fresh blood,' the auctioneer called out and rambled on to try to squeeze another bid from the under bidder. '$550,000.' No one else he called. *Whack,* the gavel dropped and the bid of $550,000 was knocked down to Tom.

The bid spotter called out, 'Last buyer: Baker Racing Stables, Newmarket.' Tom was so nervous, he was shaking like a leaf when the sales receipt was getting drawn up. He looked at Logan, and Logan winked. 'Breathe, mate. You did great.'

'Cheers, Tom,' Mike said.

Tom wished his father could have seen his first public auction purchase as a fully-fledged trainer, as he had only ever seen the home bred stock race before his death.

'Don't go too far,' Logan said. 'Only four lots until our next one.' Tom nodded and went outside to make a quick call to his mother. It must have been a special moment for the three, as James was watching live with his mother at the farm at Newmarket.

Lot 41 came in. A filly with a light pedigree that breezed up in 11.4 but she was bred to stay. The team overlooked the time she ran for her flowing action. She had great scope, a good length from hip to tail, was great through the knee, had a lovely deep girth and great shoulder, but she also had a super temperament and kind eye. Her sire, Smart Sense, had won a Derby but had been of the nose for the past three years with not many winners, but he had produced a champion from his first crop and that's very rare. The dam had produced a very talented colt that broke down after only three starts. Tom had been in the stable where the colt was trained while working in the U.S. before he took up training, so they took the punt. Tom was ecstatic when she was knocked down at $75,000.

Logan said, 'Let's go and re-look at Lot 63.' The King's Speech colt was going to be popular, as there was a buzz about him. Talk was 1.4 to 2.2 million. Logan had said he thought a few million, but Cynthia hadn't shown her hand. He inspected great and he had been out so many times he was just taking it all in his stride. Logan had seen this trait in his sire's stock back home. This colt wasn't overly big compared to some of the ones his sire could throw, which was another good sign. Logan knew they all can't be champions. He was perfect. Logan hadn't felt this way since My

Blue Boy. He had inspected over 12,000 horses in his time, and only two had ever given him this feeling.

Tom's phone rang; it was Cynthia. 'Okay, I will put him on.' Tom handed the phone to Logan. Tom signalled to the groom, who put the colt away. In this time, Logan had walked away and was in deep conversation. Cynthia had discussed it with Tom already, but when Logan handed the phone back, Tom pretended not to know. 'And?'

Logan answered uncomfortably, 'She wants *me* to bid next. She said, "Don't get beat."' As Cynthia told Tom earlier, she wanted Logan to have full confidence in his ability and choice, and this would give Logan great confidence in himself.

CHAPTER 10

The colt entered the ring and a hush come over the crowd. The auctioneer started his spiel about the colt, but all Logan heard ringing in his ears was, 'Don't get beat.'

Logan confidently opened the colt at 1 million, and this was short-lived as Alan Paulson hit back at 1.5. Logan nodded 2, and Paulson nodded 2.5. Logan thought, *Oh fuck, what do I do?* He looked at Tom, who gave a subtle nod, so Logan nodded 3. Paulson 3.5. Tom nodded again, but Logan gave the half signal. It didn't matter if he had no budget, he still had a responsibility to his owner to try to get it as cheap as he could. Paulson slightly baulked and then signalled. '$3.8 million,' the auctioneer called out.

Logan knew he had him and fired one straight in at 3.9 and did not look away. Paulson had his last throw—'4.'

Logan took control and called aloud, '4.1!' For so long in his life he wanted to be heard. He wanted to yell, 'This is *my* fucking horse!' Paulson folded and the gavel dropped. Logan couldn't contain his excitement and his face broke into a wide smile. Tom came up for a handshake but Logan grabbed him and gave him a bear hug. When the colt left the ring, Logan got a round of applause. Mike did the Yank thing and gave Logan and Tom a high-five each.

Cynthia watched it all unfold live over the Keeneland live stream, and knew she had the right guy. She wanted someone with passion and heart who could guide her sons. She could tell by the change in Tom's voice that Logan had stepped up to the role already.

The press swarmed, wanting an interview with Logan. He politely declined, instead turning it over to Tom, who conducted his very first interview about the Baker Racing dream and plans. Twenty minutes later, Cynthia and James watched it online and were very proud of Tom and the way he conducted himself, and explained the dream and also the part that Logan and Mike will play.

They finished the sale with two more colts for $97,000 and $355,000. Still on a high, they boarded the Emirates flight. Logan's phone rang as they taxied out the runway. 'Oi, convict.' Logan knew it was Mick.

'Make it quick, I'm taxiing down the runway.'

'Taxi? Couldn't you afford a plane ticket, ya twat.'

Logan just laughed. 'How'd we go?'

'$75,000 and $650,000.' Logan paused as he quickly did the math in his head. Masters had taken a big hit on the colt. 'Ya still there?'

'Yeah, good work. I will call after we inspect tomorrow morning.'

'Don't you go anywhere near the fucking place,' Mick said. 'I don't want you fucking up this deal, and my cut of it.'

'Don't worry, I won't. I know what he's like. It'll just be Tom and Mike.'

'Listen, convict, none of you guys go near there, 4.1 million has got you on every racing channel in the world, you attention-seeking bastard.

'You wait until the money's gone through before you say a word. Masters is a fucking prick to deal with, I'm telling ya. Got me before for $40,000. He is a Grub. I want to chop his balls off and feed them to his cat.'

Logan just laughed. 'Yeah, yeah, I'll call you when the vet check has passed.'

'Righto. Take care, ya ugly bastard.'

Logan sat back in his seat, satisfied. He decided to use his old local vet, who was from the same practice as the Masters vet anyway. He was a bit nervous, but he was now only eighteen hours away from nailing a memorable twenty-four hours.

The plane rose and levelled out. He met Tom and Mike upstairs, and they went over the plan to vet and secure the two colts in the morning. Tom seemed happy with the prices and knew if the colt for $650,000 could win a Group 1 sprint, he could be sold back to Australia for over ten million-plus. They didn't plan to get attached to the colts; they would only ever have six mares to breed per year and would buy the horses in. Logan had seen this plan start out many times: the successful owner wins a Group 1, stands the colt, buys mares to support the stallion, and the journey of endless money pit begins.

They ate dinner and talked about life—and not horses—for a while in the small booth upstairs at the bar. Tom was tired, and after four drinks was about to fall asleep. Mike wanted to watch a movie and get some quiet time, as at home he had five children.

He said that he was enjoying his paid break. Logan said he would sit and have one more. They all said goodnight and would regroup as they disembarked and went through customs.

Logan finally felt like he was living the dream. He simply couldn't believe his luck. He swirled the ice in the bottom of his glass of bourbon and stared off as he thought about all the shit he had been through. The years of suffering and sacrificing and waking up in a panic to check his bank account balance just to make sure he had enough to pay wages on Friday. But those worries were gone now. Now he would be spending $60,000 a year on living expenses at the most, while he earned half a million. It was jaw dropping.

He stared down into his empty glass and considered going to bed when a woman approached his chair. 'I took the liberty,' she said, placing a fresh drink on the table in front of him.

Logan looked up to see an attractive woman in her late-forties. He stood, and she offered her hand. 'Julia Johnston.' Logan melted when he heard a good southern American accent.

'Logan Weston,' he replied, shaking her hand.

'May I?' she gestured to sit down.

'Of course,' Logan said, sitting back down. She didn't sit opposite him, she sat beside him, and Logan supressed a knowing smile. *How forward is she*, he thought? He knew that when women, especially women with money, saw something they wanted, they made sure they got it.

Logan was on a high, with enough liquor under his belt to take the nerves away. Sam had lit a fire inside him that had been dormant for too long.

'So, you dropped over five mil today on a few ponies.'

He was intrigued. 'Were you at Keeneland, then?' he asked.

She took a long sip from her flute of champagne. 'You bought my colt.'

His eyebrows went up. 'If you are on this flight and in first class, I gather it was Lot 64.'

'Good pick, Mr Weston,' she replied seductively.

Two can play at this game, he thought. 'Well, sometimes you see something and you have to have it. And I had to have it,' he said.

'The feeling is entirely mutual,' Julia said, and she tipped back the last of her glass and got up from her seat. She said quietly, 'Meet me in ten minutes,' then she left.

Logan smiled, as he had noticed her when they boarded, and she was in the capsule on his left-hand side, but inside, he was in shock. *Are you fucking kidding! Can this day get any better!* He rose and started walking back to his suite/capsule. He didn't know what it was, but he knew it was a lot better than economy class; fully private, walls closed in. He just needed to freshen up. The barman gave a knowing nod of *you are the man,* as Logan left.

He was still in shock when he knocked on the door. Julia opened the door and he entered and then closed it quickly. For a plane, you simply couldn't get any bigger or better. Not a word was spoken. She untied her robe to reveal a great body for a forty-year-old, that's for sure. She sat back on the side of her bed and reached over to grab his belt and pull him over. She rubbed her hands up his shirt to feel the body shape underneath. She liked what she felt; he wasn't ripped, just toned with a very good set of shoulders. Logan was taller than Julia and still had to have his head slightly bent, as they were in the window area. She unbuckled his new Armani belt—black, and the most country style Armani could make—and slowly pulled down his zipper. Logan sensed he was getting pretty close to being loaded in the barriers. It was going to be awkward but, hell, he wasn't about to say no. His boxers dropped and Julia's face was inches away from what she wanted. She leant forward to give him a little kiss, then seductively looked up and said, 'You are very unassuming, Mr Weston ... but I expect a Group 1 performance.'

The team met after they had cleared customs and headed to the silver services cars pick up. As they were waiting in line, a black limousine pulled up and a very attractive woman opened the door. Logan quickly recognised the woman. As she was getting out, Julia signalled to the driver to wait a moment. She walked over to Logan, Tom, and Mike. She smiled at Tom and Mike, then turned to Logan and handed over her card. 'Great performance. Call me,' she said, and kissed him hard on the lips. She quickly returned to the limo and it took off.

Both Mike and Tom were standing there with their jaws dropped. Logan just smiled and shrugged. 'You snooze, you lose fellas.'

CHAPTER 11

They decided to play it safe and send in Jeremy Stanford from the Flemington practice to check the two colts. Logan wanted the deal to go through smoothly, so he couldn't chance a thing going wrong. Jeremy was very thorough and had checked the last twelve months on their system; there wasn't one treatment out of the ordinary on either colt. They both trotted up sound, flexed well, scoped for clear airways, knees, fetlocks, stifles, and hocks; all X-rays showed not too many issues out of the norm. He did notice the mouth on the bay colt Everest had sore marks, he was extremely tight in the neck and shoulders, and he dropped down when he ran his fingers up his back. Forest Black was a similarly uneasy horse. Jeremy could tell he was a horse who had been mistreated on many occasions. Logan had already warned Jeremy he may find this, and he'd told him to make no big deal of it, just so the sale could go through smoothly. Jeremy finished at 12.30 p.m. and said he was happy; the horses had passed.

Logan called Mick. He answered the phone with, 'It better be good news, convict.'

'Make the deal, you gobshite,' Logan said and hung up.

Mick made a coffee and rang Masters. He said in a casual tone, 'Angus, it's Mick. Jobs right on the two colts.'

Masters paused for a moment. 'You know what, Mick, I think I've changed my mind about the offer.'

Mick held the phone away to stop himself from throwing it across the room. He took a sharp breath and pulled it close again to snarl, 'You fuck me around on this deal, it's off completely, ya greedy fuck. I'm emailing the contract now and you have twenty minutes to sign or I'll buy colts from Maher's yard. Believe me, they are a lot fucking cheaper than your pieces of shite,' and then he hung up. Mick called Masters' bluff and highlighted on the email he would transfer the amount by 3 p.m. They banked with the same bank, so it was guaranteed money in the account by the end of the day. He hoped like hell it worked.

He called Logan and explained the stunt Masters tried to pull. But all they could do was wait and see if Mick's tactics worked. Logan, Mike, and Tom headed to Pete's place to relax and catch up on the latest news. 'Well, Masters has been working Bluey hard each day, and many people think he may already be over the top for tomorrow's Mackinnon Stakes,' Pete told Logan. This time Tom and Mike were the odd ones out as Pete and Logan caught up.

Suddenly, the phone rang—it was Mick. 'Well?' Logan said, as he answered the phone.

Mick was quiet for a second before he mumbled, 'The line must be bad.'

'I can hear you clearly on this end,' Logan said loudly.

'What? I can hardly hear you.'

'I CAN HEAR YOU!' Logan shouted. Pete suggested to head outside to get better reception.

'Ay?'

'I SAID I CAN HEAR YOU, MICK!' Logan was so frustrated he nearly threw his phone. 'ARE WE IN OR OUT? … MICK? … ARE YOU THERE?'

Mick started laughing loudly.

Logan said, 'You're a wanker, you know that?'

'Deal is done, and I've just transferred the money. They are your colts now.'

Logan was too happy to be angry at Mick. He just laughed and hung up. He called a small float company he had used previously and booked both colts to be picked up within the hour and taken up to the farm at Scone.

Tom made the call; they chartered a small plane and headed up to Scone, and arrived by 6 p.m. Aunty Joy met the trio at the Scone airport and was so excited to see her nephew. Logan stepped out of the car and Hank, his little Jack Russell, just exploded with excitement. It took him at least ten minutes to settle down enough to greet the other visitors.

'Not as flash as Newmarket,' Logan said. 'But it's home.'

'Simply fantastic,' Tom said, looking around at the open paddocks, the native trees, and wildlife. 'So, this is Australia. Any sheilas around, mate?' said Mike.

Aunty Joy said, 'It's a great place to just relax. What I love is that Logan can leave most things at the gate and just be himself here.' Mike nodded at that sentiment. With his own business, he knew how Logan had felt.

'James arrives at 10 a.m. tomorrow,' said Tom, as they walked in the front door with their luggage. 'Maybe he will get a Julia,' Mike jibed at Logan.

'Oh, who is Julia?' asked Aunty Joy, raising her eyebrows at Logan. Mike and Tom didn't realise Aunty Joy had got a whiff of what they were on about and they fell quiet. 'Girls can't resist my boy,' she said and winked. 'Mile High Club now, dear?'

Hank interrupted the interrogation about Logan's airborne rendezvous by carrying in his week-old decapitated rabbit to show off again to Logan. 'Hank, for God's sake, give the bloody rabbit a rest.' Logan held his shirt over his nose and started to dry retch at the smell.

'Your dog,' said Aunty Joy, shaking her head.

Logan, quite embarrassed in front of his guests, quickly scraped it up in the closest newspaper he could find. He took it outside, holding his breath, then put the contents in the bin. 'No, Hank!' Logan said, as Hank launched himself in a last-ditch effort to get back his beloved rabbit. Logan was about to the close the bin lid when he spotted the page of the newspaper he had used to pick up the rotten rabbit corpse. He laughed out loud when he read the title of the article: 'Could My Blue Boy be the next Phar Lap?' The headshot of Masters had rabbit entrails smeared all over it. Logan held his shirt over his nose and mouth as he quickly read a quote in the article from Masters: 'My Blue Boy could go on to do great things, and I couldn't pass up that opportunity. Though it is rare for owners to switch trainers so close to an importance race, I just had to put my foot down because Weston just didn't have the skills required to bring out the horse's full potential. Obviously, I do.'

Logan returned to the house, not letting the anger build as he knew he had guests. Aunty Joy was serving up pea and ham soup. She had made it specially, as she knew Logan was on his way back, and it had always been his favourite. Tom and Mike were happy to be eating a home-cooked meal with freshly-baked homemade dinner rolls to dip in the soup. 'Very scrummy,' Mike said, his spoon clinking on the bottom of an empty bowl.

Logan laughed. 'I can't get used to all the different sayings you guys have.'

'I can relate to that, Logan, you wanker,' said Tom. They all burst out laughing.

The chatted until about 9 p.m., then turned in, as the jetlag was setting in. Logan set an alarm for 4 a.m., when the two colts were expected to arrive.

The truck arrived an hour and a half late, and Hank made enough noise to have the whole house up within five minutes. Both colts were unloaded and settled quite quickly into their new surroundings, with horses either side of their yards. Mike ran his eyes over them and took their temperatures. He went back inside when he could smell the bacon and eggs cooking, but Logan and Tom stayed, leaning on the fence watching the colts. 'What's the plan?' said Tom.

'We need to empty their heads of all their bad habits. We need to teach them it's okay to not be perfect; they won't get a belting for misbehaving.' Tom looked a bit puzzled. 'Up until now, they have been reprimanded every single time they put one foot wrong. All great athletes have egos to a certain extent, and so do horses. You, James, and I need to get their spirits back, and it starts from now. I want them to think their shit doesn't stink. I want them to be full of themselves.'

'So they can be wankers and not get in trouble, then,' Tom replied, smirking.

Logan handed Tom the half-empty feed bucket. The colts had just travelled for twelve hours. 'Hand-feed him every bit of grain. In between his mouthfuls, rub him, scratch him, pat him. After six mouthfuls, I bet he doesn't try to bite you. I bet he will rub his head on you. Rub him firm over his eye socket, scratch side to side on his cheekbones, and lightly behind the ear. One of these two horses could be your first Group 1 winner.' Tom knew that he meant it by the look in his eye.

Logan knew both horses were treated as if they had no hope in the Masters stable. When you spend 1.2 million on a colt and he has nothing to show for it, it's easy to hold a grudge against him. This was the case with Masters. He had lost a lot of money on him. Everyone knew he'd been bought at a high price, and Logan could recall the interview on Sky Racing of him boasting, 'Best colt on ground.'

Logan watched Tom feed Forest Black while he fed Everest. Within three minutes, Tom was smiling as Forest rubbed against him, loving the attention. Logan winked at Tom and he nodded, acknowledging Logan's wisdom.

Everest was not coming around as well. Logan couldn't get near his ears because they had obviously been screwed hard many times. Logan had learnt as a young man that if horses were difficult to drench, or if you were doing something with their ears or head, if you lifted their tail straight up over their back it stopped them from putting their head up and being difficult to handle; no harm done or bad memories. There was no way Everest was going to yield easily.

They headed back in and had breakfast. Aunty Joy took Mike and Tom to the airport at Newcastle to pick up James and take them back via the saddlery to get a Driza-Bone jacket and some

R. M. Williams riding boots. Logan went through his things and packed what he wanted to get shipped back over with the horses when they departed.

It was Derby Day in Victoria, and there were six Group 1 races on in the nine-event card. My Blue Boy was in the Mackinnon Stakes at 4.05 p.m. and a favourite at $2.60. The group arrived back with James, and Tom took him for a wander. He showed him the horses and James was impressed to see that Forest Black had warmed up to Tom already.

They all sat in the living room to watch the remaining races. Masters had won the Group 1 sprint over 1,200 metres with an imported English colt called Stop and Go. The owner, David Collins, had just purchased a small farm in the Hunter Valley near Scone for 3.8 million seven months prior, and had purchased fifty-one per cent in Stop and Go after his July Cup sprint win in May at Royal Ascot in England. Collins was a good friend to Masters, and they put the offer forward within an hour after the win at Ascot.

Collins had made his millions in car spare parts and had well and truly been taken in by Masters to help spend it. But this win was the first for an English sprinter, as Aussie sprinters had been winning the Royal Ascot sprints for many years, and this was now a very valuable colt. As much as Logan hated to admit it, Masters could train a horse. If it showed him something, then it got the royal treatment, the best staff, and his full attention. This showed in his stats of having to run 13.1 times to get a winner. Logan's was 3.9 runners to winners, but Logan had never had a Group 1 winner.

It was now 4.05 p.m. and they were at the barrier. They jumped and My Blue Boy was kicked to the front. Logan was a bit amazed, but it was weight for age and he was the only three-year-old in the races and he had the lightest weight, so maybe not a silly move. Nine others in the race were using it as a final hit-out for the Melbourne Cup, so there was no early pace and Bluey just bowled along in front. They rounded the turn and the pressure was building. They spread over the straight. Bluey's jockey LJ just sat cold and even; at the 200 he hadn't moved. Two of the horses he had beaten in the Cox Plate loomed side by side with him and LJ just looked sideways, lowered himself, and urged forward hands and heel. No whip, just four to five urges and it was over. My Blue Boy won by two lengths easing down, proving he was an emerging superstar.

As the others pulled up, LJ kept him going at an even pace for another 400 metres, to everyone's amazement. On returning, the press went crazy. They didn't even ask him about today's win, it was all about whether he was running over 3,200 metres in the Melbourne Cup in three days. Masters had materialised to answer cockily, 'He is in, and now he's an equal favourite. Many said it was one or even two years too early, as he was a late foal and by birthdate not a three-year-old until the 21st of November—'

Back in the living room, Tom asked Logan, 'What do you think?'

Logan didn't want to really answer but finally said, 'He will bust his heart trying, that's for sure. I knew he was very good but that win today was just arrogant. In two runs, he has now beaten eighteen Group 1 winners.' The win stung but Logan did his best to hide it.

Aunty Joy went to buy meat for a true blue Aussie barbecue later on, and Logan sent James and Tom to feed the two colts while he fed the rest of the horses with Mike. Hank hunted for rabbits and kept Tom and James entertained. Logan received some text messages regarding the win, but he only replied to Pete and Neale. Logan was focused on tomorrow and was going over many ideas in his head. He felt Forest was an easy fix, but Everest was still acting with a wall up—he didn't trust anyone, and that wasn't a good sign.

The team rose early and loaded the two colts and two of Logan's old lead ponies on the four-horse angle float he had borrowed for the weekend. They headed to Don's place at the end of the valley, about twenty-eight kilometres from Logan's property. Don had over 1,800 cattle to muster, vaccinate, and cut calves, and had welcomed any help that was offered. The countryside could be steep in many places, so while motorbikes were okay in a few paddocks, Don was still old school and preferred the horseback muster.

They all saddled up. It was the first time James, Tom, and Mike had ridden in the Australian-style stock saddles. They looked a bit awkward, but Logan was sure when they were tackling the mountains they would appreciate the added features that stopped them from falling out of the saddle. Logan gathered everyone around; Don had called in four other stockmen to help them. They went over Logan's plan for the two new racehorses. They were not like the stock horses and were already jogging and continually moving around impatiently. Logan explained, 'The colt James is riding, Forest Black, I want to keep him in the middle of the horses. You guys lean over and pat him and squeeze your horse up to him and make him feel like he's a welcome member of the herd. Just continue to do this the whole day, as often as we can. With this colt,' he continued, patting Everest underneath him, 'do similar things. But I might have to let him have a run first.' The stockmen nodded, understanding what he was on about, but Tom, Mike, and James looked at him curiously.

Fifteen minutes into the ride, Forest Black was coping well and had dropped his head. James had also relaxed and was hardly touching the reins. Tom was impressed with Forest, but looked over anxiously at Everest, who was throwing his head up and down, grinding the bit, and cow-kicking when the other horses came close. He even jacked up and ran backwards so fast that Tom thought Logan was going to get squashed flat if they flipped over.

They came to the north paddock, which was about four miles long and about one mile wide with a few trees. It was used as an airstrip. Everest was reefing and tearing, so Logan just let him go. Everest started bolting, and the others just waited patiently. Everest was quickening, but still flinching, expecting Logan to start jerking his head. But Logan didn't; he sat as still as he could and stood up in his irons. The horse was galloping very close to flat out, but he was not completely in rhythm. It was obvious that the horse had never been allowed to run so freely.

Don said, 'Wow, he's pretty fast.' He looked over at Tom, who had a worried expression, and reassured him, 'Logan's fine. Old Frank, Logan's dad, taught him to do this and he's done it time and time again with second-hand problem horses. He's one of the best. Trust him.'

'I've never seen him bucked off—ever,' said another rider, and the old stockman chuckled.

Everest was now winding down as he was running out of steam. As he eased down, Logan talked to him calmly and rubbed his hand down his mane. 'Steady, fella.' Everest eased back to a walk and was heaving heavily, trying to catch his breath. Logan turned him and slowly headed back towards the group. He just kept walking Everest along at a slow pace, gently pulling on the reins and using his voice and the smooth strokes on his mane to get him to ease down.

'Now that he is not throwing a wobbly, he is pretty quick,' said Tom, as they approached.

'Yeah, he went alright,' Logan said, as he kept stroking the horse's neck. They turned, and Logan just walked beside the group, still talking away to Everest. Slowly but surely, the horse eased in closer to the mob.

They stopped at a back dam and the horses had a drink. Logan rode Everest in further and he pawed and splashed himself to cool down. They walked off and Everest fell into stride with the others. The day was a success and, even though Everest started up again with a few old habits when pushing cattle about, he was seventy per cent better than the first hour of his ride. The real surprise was Forest Black. Not very often do you see a man and horse become one, but James and Forest had. Apart from a few jumps sideways when cattle got too close, the horse was amazing. Logan had also never seen a rider with a better seat or softer hands than James. The day was a huge success and both boys were excited to Skype their mother that night to fill her in on the day's events. Cynthia texted Logan later and thanked him, as it had been a long time since she'd seen such fulfilment in her sons' eyes.

They all went to bed early that night, as it had been a long and tiring day, especially in stock saddles. Mike had a saddle sore rub mark on his ass like a golf ball.

The next day, Logan took a chance and told Tom to ride Everest. After only two hours, Everest started up the same things that led to Logan just letting him go the day before. Logan knew he'd made the right choice when Tom copied what he had done, but this time Everest only went about 600 metres before he eased down. Tom again copied what Logan had done afterwards to ease him down, and Everest came around even quicker this time. Logan was thrilled that the horse seemed to go even better for Tom than he did for him yesterday. Both of Cynthia's boys were very talented riders. James had even chased a few cows on Forest and brought them back to the herd. The two boys had never done any mustering before, only Pony Club, the occasional fox hunt, and track work.

The countryside was truly amazing, and the boys loved the company of the stockmen, especially Don. Throughout the eight-hour day, there was plenty of wisdom to be shared from the experienced stockmen, Don, and old Snowy, who was seventy-three years old and knew more than most about problem horses. He shed plenty of light on how to go about it, as he had fixed many ex-racehorses. Snowy had gone to the knackery sales many times and bought the ex-racehorses, or had been given them, and he re-educated them and sold them on. Some of them went on to be very handy polo and show jumping horses. The boys had many questions and, between Don and Snowy, the questions were answered and solid advice was given.

Mike and Logan agreed on the ride back to the car that it was time to head back home; James could handle things here for another two weeks. Tom rode over and Logan asked him, 'You ready to head back home tomorrow night? James looks like he can handle things from here.'

Tom replied, 'Actually, I thought I'd stay and help James with the colts, then we'll both fly back together later.'

Logan could see the determined look on Tom's face. He hadn't known the boys for long, but he could see the change in them already. They were grown men, but they were still finding their feet after living under the same roof as their mother for so long. Since the death of their father, they had all become incredibly close and protective of each other.

Logan thought that this was probably the first time the boys had been so far away from their mother. *Maybe I shouldn't split them up just yet*, he thought, unsure what to do. 'I'll need to ask Don, since it's his muster,' said Logan.

'His idea,' Tom said, with an innocent smile.

Logan realised he had been set up and he smiled back at Tom. Don had guided Logan through so many times in his life and now he was doing the same for the boys.

'You happy with that plan, Mike?' said Logan.

'Blinding idea, as long as you both promise to come home, and not stay here to become Australian Outback stockmen instead. Your mother would never forgive us, especially if you came home with a sheila,' he said, laughing.

Tom beamed. He may have been twenty-two, but he rode over to tell James the news like he was a little boy with permission to sleep over at a friend's house.

They arrived back at about 6.30 p.m., settled, and fed the horses. The boys had loved the Aussie barbecue the night before, so when Aunty Joy said it was their turn to pick dinner, they had asked for it again and wanted to know if they could throw another shrimp on the barbie. Everyone gathered around the barbecue and Hank was happy to be the centre of attention for a short time again. After wrestling on the grass with Logan, he fell asleep.

CHAPTER 12

Australia comes to a halt for the race that stops the nation on Cup Day, and most shops close for half days. If you don't have a flutter or a bet on, they call you un-Australian. Don had organised an early start for the muster and the guys headed out. A big smile was on Logan's face as the two colts had now accepted the changes and had a totally different attitude. *Being ridden all day has knocked the bullshit out of them, that's for sure*, Logan thought.

Tom and James went with Don and the stockmen to watch the race in the local pub. Logan knew it would give the boys a genuine Aussie Cup Day experience. Logan and Mike went over the plan for the next two weeks and organised the horses' flights back to the UK. It was a long haul, so the boys were to give the two colts some light work on the farm in the days leading up to the flight to keep them ticking over, as fitness helped to fight off travel sickness.

Mike and Logan packed their bags and booked their tickets. Logan was happy, as he had one more leg on his ticket he could use. Mike was downgraded to business class, the poor guy. They'd organised a hire car pick up for 5.30 p.m. for the one-way trip to Sydney to catch their international flight.

As Logan sat in the living room in front of the TV, the knots in his stomach were making him feel uneasy. He was nervous before the Cox Plate and the Mackinnon Stakes, but it wasn't a sick feeling like this. The nation had stopped, and the TAB machines Australia-wide had been going flat out since 8 a.m. taking bets. My Blue Boy was second favourite at 4.50. He looked well parading and had tightened up even more since the run on Saturday. Logan, like many Australians, was not happy with him running, and he was now the youngest horse in seventy-three years to have a start. Social media had been at it again about how Masters was a cruel bastard going for glory and cash, and not the welfare of the colt. Logan had kept his distance from social media.

The red light went on, and they were off. You could feel the whole nation cheering as they headed down the Flemington straight for the first time. LJ had My Blue Boy in third on the fence one back. He had a light weight compared to the others, but still a weight-carrying record for a three-year-old of 52 kg. It wasn't long before, as usual, the Europeans tried to dictate the pace, and three headed the lead with about 2,000 metres to go. They set a solid tempo, and My Blue Boy was now fifth on the fence and going with a solid rhythm and relaxed manner; not ripping and tearing like many others.

Logan had mixed feelings. Like every trainer, he wanted to one day win the Melbourne Cup, but there was no way he would have tried to enter Bluey. He was simply too young.

They approached the 800-metre mark and a few back markers were trying to make their moves. One of the UK raiders had already started to tire. *Very costly exercise to bring a horse out that can't get past the 2,400-metre mark*, Logan thought.

They rounded the turn and the field had strung out over forty lengths. The back markers had no chance today. The two leaders were now five lengths in front of My Blue Boy with Sky Mountain hot on the leader's heels, and he looked full of running. LJ decided to finally make his run. Frankie, 'the world's most famous jockey', had not moved on his mount, Sky Mountain, either. He was two lengths still in front of My Blue Boy and had a clear run to the winning post as the two leaders in front had drifted three off the fence. Frankie made his run as My Blue Boy began his run as well and was now two lengths from Sky Mountain. Frankie turned and saw LJ coming fast. He drove hard, hands and heels, and looked to his right to see horses falling behind. He knew it was the two favourites by the roar of the crowd.

They passed the clock tower and LJ pulled the whip. He gave My Blue Boy three cracks around the backside and urged him like he had never done before, and the horse started to really dig deep. At the 150-metre mark, he was still one length off. Frankie had gone for his whip, but it didn't matter to Sky Mountain as he was flat to the boards. Seventy-five metres out, the roar was deafening. My Blue Boy was closing the gap, gaining with each stride, and LJ had gone back to hands and heels as he knew the whip was not going to get one more inch out of him.

With fifty metres to go, My Blue Boy was a neck away. Sky Mountain sensed My Blue Boy and seemed to lift, and My Blue Boy lifted too. Four strides out, it seemed it was going to be an import winner again. But, in the biggest last-ditch effort, LJ drove as hard as he ever had and they hit the line head and head. The crowd went wild. It was one of the best Cup finishes in decades.

The announcer declared, 'I can't call it! It's a dead heat, or maybe Sky Mountain held on. We're reviewing the footage now.' Everyone held their breath and gave their opinions quietly. Finally, the announcer yelled out, 'And the winner is My Blue Boy!' The crowd exploded with cheers and applause.

At home, Logan punched the air. He loved that horse and his courage to win. A three-year-old horse had never accomplished what he had just done. The camera panned out and saw LJ high in the stirrups saluting the crowd. Logan couldn't take his eyes off his champ. Poor Bluey was spent. To Logan he was Bluey not My Bluey Boy. Trotting back to the winning enclosure, he stumbled. But it didn't seem to matter to anyone that the horse was exhausted, as they had just won the Melbourne Cup. The cameras were now on Masters, who was like a little general in his top hat and tails. He was like a bantam rooster having his first crow and loving the attention he was getting. Angela hugged and kissed him, and held up his hand like he had just won the world heavyweight title fight. In a way, he had. He had kept Bluey going and done what Logan couldn't have done—wouldn't have done. Logan wouldn't have ran Bluey last Saturday either, as he had planned to drop him back to a mile for the Group 1 on the last day of the carnival. *Maybe Masters is a better trainer. He has balls. He wanted something so badly, and he went for it.* Logan shook his head, feeling a little defeated. He knew he had to learn not to hold back so much.

The camera panned back in anticipation of the presentation. As it went past Bluey, Logan saw the horse stumble, then stumble again. *Bluey's never stumbled once in his entire life*, Logan thought, beginning to panic.

'That's not a good sign, Logan. He's not well,' said Mike, very concerned. Logan got closer to the TV and he could see the strapper was pulling on his head to keep it up higher. The horse was exhausted, but there was something else wrong. He looked like he was about to go down. Logan looked at Mike, who shook his head. 'Not good.'

Logan didn't even realise what he was doing, but in a flash he had picked up his phone and called Angela. The camera was on the group and he saw her react. He knew from her expression that her personalised ringtone for him was playing. They hadn't spoken one word since she left, not one, as she had said many things that could not be taken back.

Logan didn't know if she would answer or not. 'Hello?' she said, confused.

'Bluey is about to collapse,' Logan said urgently.

'What? What are you—'

'Your horse, who just won the fucking Melbourne Cup, he's about to collapse.'

She looked around and saw the state that Bluey was in. He stumbled again.

'I can see that something's wrong with Bluey. He's about to collapse. Please, Angela, don't let him die. You at least owe me that much,' he said firmly, and hung up. Logan could see her on screen moving away quickly from the presentation area, but nobody noticed.

'Fuck!' he yelled in frustration, kicking the coffee table away and storming outside.

Mike went to the fridge, grabbed two beers, and headed outside. He knew Logan was right. 'You did the right thing, Logan. You might have just saved that horse's life.'

Logan was pacing back and forth on the front lawn with his hands behind his head, trying to control his breathing. 'That fucking asshole,' he said through gritted teeth. 'He knew the horse wouldn't give in. He's not even three, for God's sake. I bet he's done something to his heart. He looked wrecked.' Mike nodded but remained silent, not wanting to upset Logan further by telling him his own initial diagnosis thoughts—some being dire.

On the Cup grounds, the team took My Blue Boy straight to the swabbing stall and instantly laid him down on the straw bedding. The vets quickly gave him fluids and strong painkillers intravenously. They noted that his heart rate was extremely high, and he took fifty minutes longer than normal to recover. My Blue Boy didn't leave the grounds until 8 p.m. that night, and he went to the Flemington vet clinic for continued treatment. Logan was right in his guess; Bluey had strained his heart. The scans showed a slight bleed around the heart as well. Luckily, My Blue Boy wasn't going to die, but he had just run his last race.

Masters didn't visit the horse until 11 a.m. the next morning. He had played down the trauma to the owners to cover his ass and had been busy with interviews all morning. When he got home, the nanny was taking care of his daughter while Angela slept off her hangover from the celebrations the night before. Being a man who had cheated already on his first wife, he was extremely suspicious of Angela as he was a very insecure soul deep down. Even though they had cheated together. As she slept, he went through her phone. It was filled with congratulatory text messages from friends. Masters noticed the call from Logan at 4.18 p.m. the day before. He instantly went into a rage and stormed upstairs. 'What the hell is this?'

Angela awoke in fright. She had never seen her husband so upset and was instantly scared. She was still half asleep and her head was thumping. 'What's wrong, Angus?'

'What's this!' he yelled and showed her Logan's number on the screen.

'What are doing going through my phone?' she asked, defensively. She had never seen this side of him.

'Tell me what this was about,' he said, shaking the phone.

'Logan called after My Blue Boys win. He said that he could see that something was wrong with him, and he wanted me to get him help. That's all. Then he hung up.' Masters looked again at the screen. It said the duration of the phone call was twenty seconds. Angela realised that a twenty-second phone call was all it took to see the dark side of her husband.

'That's why he called you?'

'Yes. We were preoccupied with the celebrations and didn't see him stumbling. Logan was concerned about My Blue Boy. He … he said he didn't want him to die.'

Logan was right. Bluey had collapsed within seconds of reaching the swabbing stable. They were all so preoccupied, their team wouldn't have had time to make the call to get him out of the enclosure and checked, not with all the commotion and formalities.

'How is My Blue Boy?' she asked.

'He's run his last race. Some minor bleeding around the heart. He could have died from trying so hard,' Angus said, and walked over to slump into a chair in the corner of the room. 'Maybe I shouldn't have run him in the Cup. He's too young. I crossed the line this time.'

Angela had never seen her husband go from rage to defeat so quickly. 'You are the first trainer to win the Cup with a colt of that age,' she said reassuringly, 'and the first ever to win the Plate, Mackinnon, and Cup with a three-year-old. Yes, you push the boundaries, my darling, but you have set the benchmark even higher. He will enjoy the rest of his life as a stallion now. Don't beat yourself up over it. You won the Melbourne Cup, my darling!' She walked over and put her hands on his shoulders and looked him in the eye. 'I love you.'

He leant forward and rested his head on her stomach and she stroked his hair. 'He really saved that horse's life, didn't he?' Masters asked.

She paused and thought carefully about her answer. 'He always put the horses before the people,' she said.

He looked up at her and asked, 'We all good?'

'All good,' she replied. *Some things are better left unsaid*, she thought.

CHAPTER 13

Logan and Mike arrived back in London and were en route to Newmarket. Cynthia had messaged to say they should all catch up at the local pub for a quick drink, as it was now 7 p.m. London time. They didn't really feel like it, but she was their boss. They arrived at the small tavern and Cynthia had just walked in as well. They headed to a booth and Mike excused himself to head to the toilet. He had been suffering an upset stomach for the last six hours and it was time to head to the loo again.

Cynthia sat in the booth and Logan headed over to order three pints. The tavern wasn't full, but around twenty locals were there. Logan had just paid and was holding the three pints when he heard a loud booming voice: "Ere she is, the bitch who got me fired! I worked for you for seventeen years and then I get fired!' The guy was huge and very drunk. He had Cynthia cornered in the booth. She looked mortified to be on the receiving end of the drunk tirade from an ex-employee. 'I fucking worked for you for seventeen years and then you get over 300 million pounds and the new owners give me the sack after six months. How's that fair!'

The bar went quiet. 'You build a horse training complex, and you and your useless boys can't train shit. Money burning a hole in your pocket since your husband died. Bloody dodgy to me.'

Cynthia may have been very tough, but she was visibly shaken. Logan put down the drinks and walked over slowly. 'Alright, mate, you've said your piece. Time to move on now.'

'Who are you, the new lover? You're nothing but a toy boy, mate,' the drunk said, swinging his attention round.

Cynthia said quietly, 'Logan, please, just leave it.'

'It's fine,' Logan said, quickly sizing the man up. The drunk towered over Logan by a good six inches and was nearly double his weight. 'This fine fellow was just about to apologise to you for being so rude.'

'Fuck off,' the drunk spat out. 'This rich bitch owes me.'

That was it; Logan had had enough of this. He stepped up to the guy's face. 'I will give you three seconds to apologise and get out of here.' Logan just stared into his eyes, picking the split second the drunk decided to throw his first punch. The large haymaker swing came from the right and Logan ducked. He came back up and gave the guy a quick combo to the ribs. He went down like a sack of wet sand. No one in the bar said a word, as the drunk had been harassing the clients all afternoon, but the bartender was hoping he would leave eventually.

Logan grabbed a chair, and everyone thought he was going to smash it over the drunk's head. He put it beside the drunk, grabbed him by the ear and twisted it hard. 'Get in the chair.' The man had the wind knocked out of him and he was in pain. He knew he had stepped over the line. 'This lady here is Cynthia Baker. She has built her empire by working fifty times harder than you ever have. It was her money that fed and clothed you and your family for seventeen years. I'm sure her money put your kids through school. This lady helped you and many locals make a living. If she wants to sell her business after seventeen years, she can. In fact, she can do whatever she goddamn pleases with her money. Her late husband died when a drunk like you ran him down, and he pushed her out of the way to save her life, you prick.'

'Logan, enough,' said Cynthia, conscious of all the eyes and ears in the room on them.

Logan dragged the drunk to his feet. 'I'm not done. You apologise to this lady right now or I will unleash hell on you.' At that moment, you could have heard a pin drop in the tavern. The drunk had tears starting to stream out his eyes. Deep down he had been a good man, but he was down on his luck and he had taken to the drink to kill the pain. Logan twisted the drunk's ear and finally he blurted out. 'Cynthia, I'm sorry. My wife left me today because I wouldn't stop drinking. They paid me out £8,000 to leave and I drank the lot. It wasn't the same since you sold it. They didn't like me there. I'm sorry, I'm sorry.' He slumped into the chair and started sobbing.

Everyone sat quietly in the tavern, not knowing what to do. Cynthia slid out from the booth and walked over to the drunk. 'Mr Caldwell, look at me.' He looked up at her, surprised that she had remembered his name after so long. 'I need a groundsman— someone who can muck out stables and work hard. I will expect to see you at 7 a.m. sharp in the morning, and if I smell a drop of liquor on you, you're out. Is that clear, Mr Caldwell?'

He nodded and wiped his eyes and nose, wiping his hand on his pants before he put it out towards Cynthia. She shook it without hesitation. '7 a.m.,' she repeated, and he nodded. He got up to leave and she said, 'Oh, and Mr Caldwell, this is your new boss.' She pointed to Logan and he nodded his head in total embarrassment.

Cynthia slid back in the booth, her hands still shaking slightly, and Logan collected the three pints from the bar. Ten minutes later, Mike returned and said, 'What did I miss?'

'Oh, we just employed a new groundsman and stable cleaner,' Cynthia replied offhandedly.

'Very good,' Mike said, and Logan and Cynthia had to hide the smile on their faces.

Sure enough, at 7 a.m., Jack Caldwell showed up and Logan set him about his work. The five two-year-olds had arrived from the U.S., and they looked superb. Logan, Mike, and Cynthia were extremely pleased with the quality of the horses they had purchased. Four colts and one filly. It was decided they would put two colts in work and the rest out for a spell. The end of the season was coming in a few months but there was one more Group 1 race for two-year-olds, and Logan wanted to get a win with the King's Speech colt, as it would add a large value to his siring price if he was a Group 1 winner as well.

It was the first day the Baker Racing Stables complex would be officially used. The barn was very well built and had lovely stained timber stable fronts. The boxes were a generous 5 x 5 metres, with a foot-thick bedding of straw, twenty litres of fresh crisp water in the corner, and the best horse feed you could buy, covered in fresh molasses. Cynthia had purchased a few yearlings the previous year with Tom and Mike, and they brought six of the ten in for work. 'I want more,' Cynthia said, and Logan turned to see her strolling down the breezeway. 'I want this barn full.' The barn could house forty, but they only had eight in use.

Logan laughed. 'It takes time,' he said.

'Call your Irish friend and find me some more horses today.'

Logan did as he was told.

'Ay convict,' Mick answered.

'We need ten horses by the end of the week. What do you have on your books?' Mick could spot a whale from a mile away and, despite all the shit slinging he could do, there was no one better when you needed to find a horse.

'Where're your stables?' he asked.

'Newmarket. Baker Racing.'

'Right. I'll pick you up in twenty minutes. I'm over here going through some tried horses now.'

Logan got off the phone and relayed the information to Cynthia. She said, 'Very good, Logan. Remember, no slow ones.'

Mick picked up Logan and they headed off. He had a client who had called that morning. 'Caught with his dick in the secretary. Has thirty-four to sell. Eighteen are racehorses.'

'Any good?' Logan asked.

'I wouldn't bang her,' said Mick, and they both burst out laughing.

The package was eighteen racehorses, seven rising two-year-old's that Mick had purchased for him, eight three year old's and four were four year old's . The rest were broodmares. Four of the mares had won Stakes race.

'Are *the horses* any good?' Logan clarified.

'What do you think?' Mick said. 'I have bought every single one for him. We've culled the shit and this is the best of them. I have spent seven years getting this together, and I even helped select the farm and manager, trainers, everything, and the fucking idiot sticks his dick where it didn't belong.' He was pissed off to lose a good client, worth possibly $150,000 a year to him.

They turned into the farm, and it was a very nice boutique place; great fencing and a nice layout. Mick knew every horse and said to the manager they would just walk the farm and paddock's themselves. Logan liked what he saw, and there was a good point to every horse. 'Nice lot of horses, that's for sure,' Logan said.

'I told you, convict, I have culled the shit,' said Mick.

'How much?' Logan said.

'Which one?'

'The lot.'

Now this got his attention. 'You want the lot?'

'Why not?'

'I will put it to them,' Mick replied.

'Cynthia wants instant horses and numbers, and it's a nice group,' said Logan

You better call her up first, convict. Don't let me get this gobshite keen and then it falls through.'

Logan called Cynthia and explained the package. She was very interested and, since Mike was already there doing the IDs on the horses from the U.S., they could both be there in forty minutes.

Logan got off the phone and turned to Mick. 'They're on the way.'

Mick rolled his eyes. 'Fuck off.'

'She's bringing her vet too, so you better go talk to your man,' Logan answered smugly.

'My man? Jesus, why do all you Aussies think you can sound Irish,' and mocked Logan saying 'my man'. 'Alright, I'll go find them now.' He spotted the owner's car driving up to the homestead and headed up to see him.

As he walked off, Logan called out, 'Oi. Get a job lot price.' Mick looked back, confused. 'Horses and farm. And see if the staff could stay on as well, as the horses and farm look superb.'

'Righto,' Mick replied this time and headed off. He wasn't going to take the piss out of Logan as he could smell a big payday. Logan knew he was in business mode. He thought the farm could be a spelling complex for Baker Racing. All the horses had been taken out of work six weeks prior when the husband had been caught. Logan was very keen, as he hadn't seen a nicer group of horses in a long time and he knew Mick was a very good judge.

Cynthia and Mike arrived, and Logan took them around. They were very impressed with the horses, and Mike remembered quite a few as he had vetted them for sales or at the local racing stables.

'I love this farm,' said Cynthia, looking around curiously. 'I love it more than where we are now.' Logan knew what was about to happen. 'I wonder if they would sell the lot.'

Cynthia looked confused when Logan laughed and nodded. 'Yes, ma'am. I have my man asking about that now.'

'*Your man?* Oh Logan, please stop, as you sound utterly stupid. Stay with your *gidday mate,* please.'

'I knew you would feel the same as me about the place,' Logan finished, slightly embarrassed.

Cynthia looked excited, but also a bit embarrassed that in the short time they had known each other Logan had worked her out quite well.

'It will fit the plan. I know all the horses, as I was out here to vet check them all two weeks ago for valuation. They are a bloody nice bunch of horses,' Mike said. 'But why are they for sale?'

Cynthia answered before Logan could. 'I gather he was caught putting something where it shouldn't have been.'

Mick met up with them while they were touring the barns. It had twenty-five stables, was a total of seventy acres, and was managed beautifully. Logan did the introductions and Cynthia took control. 'How much?' she said.

'Twenty-six,' Mick answered.

Cynthia's tone was cool as she retorted, 'No. I'm not the one getting screwed here.' The men laughed, then she continued, 'Twenty-two million and I will take it today.'

Mick didn't hesitate for long. He said, 'One minute, please,' and walked back to the house to pass along the offer. 'Going to talk to his man,' she said. Logan felt even more embarrassed. Mick knew it was a solid offer and would take months, possibly years, to get more. He also knew he may get to keep him as a client as, at that price, he would still have some cash to reinvest and he was sure the secretary would love the horses.

Mick walked back, nodding. 'Job's right.' Cynthia couldn't control her excitement and shook Mick's hand with both of hers. She hugged Mike, then when it was Logan's turn she just said, 'No slow ones, Mr Weston.' For a split second, Logan was a bit disappointed as he had found the place and just put the whole deal together, and now felt a bit left out. Cynthia laughed before she grabbed him, kissed him on the cheek, and hugged him tight. 'Your man, your man. I like your man,' she said. Mick looked at Logan while he was getting hugged and raised his eyebrows as if to say, 'Are you doing her?'

He always has to have the last laugh, Logan thought.

They went and had a look through the main house and the three staff cottages. All were in beautiful condition. While doing this, the owner gathered the farm employees and broke the news. They were a bit shocked, but also relieved, as they were all worried about job security in the back of their mind.

Cynthia, still on a high, texted James and Tom, and told them the news. She knew they would be asleep but she didn't care. There certainly would be some big changes when they arrived home. The barn would be full, and their mother would be moving to the new farm. Cynthia felt good fortune, or so-called luck, had come with the arrival of Logan. She had been putting it all in the back of her mind, but she was starting to have strong feelings towards him. For this, she felt incredibly guilty, as her husband had passed away only eighteen months ago. She knew she had to keep her feelings to herself and push them out of her mind.

The farm would take four weeks to settle, but the horses only twenty-four hours. Cynthia transferred the 12.8 million for the horses to Mick's account that afternoon, as she wanted the stable full by Friday afternoon. Mike was a bit shocked she didn't bother to vet the horses but, unbeknownst to everyone, she had made twenty-eight million on shares in the last year and decided shares couldn't give her this pleasure.

For the first time, Logan felt part of something special. He felt like a key part of the racing enterprise that was being forged. He was finally getting his shot at the big time. He didn't know why he was chosen but he didn't want to question it. Over ten days he had done more than he had ever dreamt of.

At 9.30 p.m., Logan rang Tom. Tom had already spoken to his mother and was extremely excited. 'How are the colts going?' Logan asked.

'Blinding!' Tom said, enthusiastically. 'Today on the muster, James and I decided to just go for a trot side by side. They were very settled so we let them break into a canter and we just let them work along for about a mile.' Logan felt nervous, wondering if they'd been racing them to test them out. 'They were working well and neither were even touching the bit. We both sat down in the saddles and just went, "Whoa, boys!" and they came back to a trot very nicely and then a relaxed walk. We didn't even have to pick up the reins! We stopped and turned around and cantered back to separate areas behind the herd, and both were still unfazed. You were right, Logan. It worked. They have cleared their heads. Everest will eat his whole feed now while I rub his head. He won't leave an oat! Forest has put on weight and you can see it each day. You know how he was, with his eyes all sunken in and a worried, mistrusting look. Well, it's gone! James even cracked the stock whip on his back today.' Tom never took one breath while explaining the day.

Logan laughed. 'Alright, sounds good. And how's Don going? Not sick of you guys yet?'

'James has gotten very close with Don,' Tom said. 'He's like the grandfather we never had, Logan. After the muster this afternoon, Don put him on a colt they had just broken in. He bucked like a bastard, but James rode him and never came off! That stock saddle held him in and he rode like a cowboy. James even went around the big pen and had him going super. Don simply couldn't believe it!'

Logan laughed. He still could hardly get a word in, but he was pleased to hear Tom so full of energy. Finally, Logan said, 'Okay, remember to give them a rest two days before the flight. Oh, and I've organised for Hank to come back with you on the flight.' Logan needed his dog. They had that bond of master and dog, and Hank brought plenty of laughs to Logan's life.

After the call ended, Logan lay down on his bed and finally started to relax. His phone buzzed with a text from Cynthia: 'Boys sound like they don't want to come home.'

Logan replied: 'Sounds that way. Tom says James is going very well.'

'Yes, he talks about a man called Don a lot.'

'Yeah, Don is a great man. Very good advice, kind but hard.' Logan waited, but there was no quick reply. He was buggered so he hopped up and headed to the shower. He thought about the next day. Putting eight into work for the first time in the new setup and the brand new track, and new staff and work riders. He started to feel stressed again. He showered and shaved, ready to start first thing. He realised he wasn't starting at 3.30 a.m. every morning anymore. His official start time was 6 a.m., with the first being ridden at 7 a.m. He laughed to himself.

He put out his clothes ready for morning and lay down on the bed, and what a bed it was! It was king-sized and the most comfortable bed he had ever slept on. Cynthia had spared no expense to ensure the house was comfortable. He rolled over and grabbed his phone to set his alarm. There was a new text message from Cynthia: 'Logan, thank you for the other night. You handled the situation in the tavern brilliantly. You made me feel like someone who is worthy again. You let Mr Caldwell keep some dignity, so I thank you for that from the bottom of my heart.'

He didn't know how to reply. He could see Cynthia wanting to open up more, and he was unsure how he felt about the chance of them becoming closer. Logan had his heart broken so badly by Angela that he had closed himself off. He felt betrayed when Angela turned on him after sharing his life and all his darkest secrets with her. But he knew as well since he had met Cynthia, both their lives had changed for the better. He was attracted to Cynthia, no doubt, but could he see himself falling madly in love with her? She didn't give him the feeling he got when he had first met Angela. It was love at first sight when they met. But Cynthia was attractive in other ways. Her confidence was sexy, and she had an easy power about her. She was optimistic, intelligent, and elegant. Logan found all those qualities very attractive in a woman. Maybe it felt different with Cynthia because she was his boss, a widower, and also that Logan already had a great bond with her sons.

Logan sat with the phone in his hand and finally decided not to text back. He was there for one thing and it was to train as part of a business partnership. He wanted that more than a tricky situation with his boss. *Too much to lose*, he told himself. *Just too much to lose.* At 11 p.m., he realised he'd wasted enough time considering it, and went to sleep.

Angus Masters walked down the stable alleyway at 4.10 a.m., visibly livid. The staff quickly spread the word via text message: 'Code 5!' It was their secret code that meant heads were going to roll. No one knew exactly why, bar Masters and his foreman.

The day before, Masters had bumped into the truck driver who took the two colts, Everest and Forest Black, to Scone. 'Morning, Fred,' Masters said.

'Mornin', Angus. Hey, I spoke to the fella who bought those two colts from you. Apparently, they'll be going to England! The young lad said he's got some fancy new set-up over there. They'd just dropped 4.1 million on a colt at Keeneland last week too. Real nice young fella. He also said that, um, Logan Weston would be training them with him. How's that for a small world, huh!' The truck driver chuckled.

'Well, good seeing you, mate,' replied Masters. Fred carted horses for everyone on different occasions.

Unfortunately for Logan, Tom was green and didn't know that truck drivers were the biggest town gossips, second only to farriers in racing stables.

Masters whipped out his phone and rang Mick in a rage. Mick was fast asleep and his phone was on silent, so it went to voicemail. Masters left him a message that would go down in history as the most abusive outburst Mick had ever heard.

Masters was livid. He didn't have time to spend looking into the sale as it was the eve of the Mackinnon Stakes. He felt set up. Logan knew he would be preoccupied, so he could sneak it through quickly, no questions asked.

'It's fucking war now!' he screamed when he went in his office, slamming the door so hard his foreman jumped to his feet. After Masters had explained, his foreman tried to calm him down. But Masters took it the wrong way and shouted at him, 'Did you know about this? Why the fuck weren't you covering my ass! Why weren't you here when they were vetted!'

'I was at Ballarat races with six of your horses,' the foreman said sternly. 'And you better pull your head in, boss, or I'll walk. You made the deal, not me.'

He was right. 'Fuck!' Masters roared. The stable staff heard this at the end of the barn and a cold shiver ran up their backs. He took a breath. 'David, I'm sorry, I'm sorry.'

'It's okay, boss,' David said. 'I'm pissed as well, but those horses aren't winners anyway. You know that. He did you a favour, if you ask me. Everest is a head case and Forest lacks substance and guts. Let him have those useless horses. You just won three Group 1 races, and the Plate, *and* the Cup with his horse. Let him think he got one up on you. Maiden winners to cup winners? Please, give me a break.'

David was a prick, just like Masters, so they were thick as thieves. David was sprung having an affair with one of the jockey's wives. He got caught when the jockey, Andy Pike, had been stood down by the stewards for not making weight. He arrived home early to find David well and truly saddled up with his wife. David still had the marks on his back where Andy had belted him with an antique jockey whip he had on display. It wasn't padded, like the modern jockey whips. It was worn and tough, and left perfect imprints across David's back, legs, and ass cheeks. The other jockeys joked behind Andy's back that he should have gotten a six-month suspension for excessive whip use.

The trainers' hut was full of gossip, but hushed immediately when Masters and David arrived. Another trainer, Mal Noonan, had heard the gossip from the truck driver too, and the rumour spread quickly. Noonan was a gossip too, so you never wanted to tell him a story that was supposed to be kept quiet. Jim Moodie was one of the trainers who hated Masters and was a mate of Logan's, so as Masters walked by, he said loudly to a nearby trainer, 'Hear Weston is competing in the July Cup?'

The July Cup was a world-renowned sprint race that produced top stallion prospects. Jim knew that Masters had to go overseas and buy the horse he had just won the Group 1 sprint with on the weekend after it had won the July Cup at Royal Ascot this year. It had always been that way. He very rarely trained a good horse from day one. To get the good ones, he just kept throwing money at the owners until they agreed to sell.

'He's gonna win it with some cast-off that was supposedly slow. That'll be a good story for the press!' The other trainers laughed along nervously but stopped as they could see Masters' furious expression as he stood behind Moodie.

Moodie turned around and stared down at Masters. Moodie was twice his weight and a foot taller. 'Problem, Angus?' he said with a smirk. Everyone in the room knew Moodie was intentionally having a jab at Masters with his remark, but he was a man you didn't want to mess with. Masters glared at him before stomping off to the ground level to watch his horse work from there. It was Friday and it was mostly horses working slow today.

Logan rose at 5 a.m. and he was excited. He made a coffee, opened the Bloodstock News and read the racing news for Australia and England. He needed to keep his finger on the pulse again. There were a few emails from back home; one from Neale relaying the story Jim Moodie had told him of Masters' dummy spit over the two colts. It was 5.45 a.m. and Logan couldn't wait any longer. He headed to the stables, checked all the feeds, and went over the horses' legs. The new horse feeds would take some adjusting to, as it was quite different to back home, but Mike and Tom were a good help with the adjustment.

The morning went well, and all the horses behaved well enough in their new surroundings. No horse was within four to six weeks of a start, and the fittest two were the two colts from the U.S. At 10 a.m., the first load of the new purchases arrived. They now had twenty-six in work and had their hands full as they were short-staffed after the instant purchase of a barn full of horses. The staff were buggered by the end of the day, and even Cynthia had lent a hand walking the horses in and out of the paddocks and on the horse walker, plus putting feeds in. The great thing about the private set-up was that it didn't matter if all the horses weren't worked by 10 a.m., as they had all day in the pre-training period.

Mike asked Logan out for a few pints after work. The old Logan would have gone home or stayed on to work more, but he made a promise he would also get a life, so he accepted the invite. They went to the same tavern where Logan had sorted out Mr Caldwell earlier on in the week. He was welcomed with a warm handshake from the puny barman. 'If I ever need a bouncer, I'll call you. You're all right. Drinks are on me tonight.' They all laughed. Mike had now heard the story from the locals about what had happened. The bartender poured them their pints and they took a seat.

Mike chuckled and said, 'Cheers Logan, You're a bit of a hero around here.'

Logan smiled and shrugged it off. 'Yeah, well, at least the guy is a hard worker.'

'He's fucking scared shitless of you, that's why.' They laughed and clinked glasses. 'Cheers.' They made small talk about work and general vet issues that may arise with a few of the horses in work.

'How are your kids?' Logan asked.

'Kids are good,' Mike nodded.

'And Rose, how is she?'

'Alright, I guess,' Mike replied, and Logan could tell he was hesitant when the subject came up, as his whole expression changed.

'Everything okay?' Logan asked.

'Not really. We're drifting apart. We even sleep in separate rooms now. I feel such a cockup. Haven't had sex in two years. Take long showers now,' he said with a smile to try to hide his pain. Logan braced for the outpour. He had a feeling Mike wanted to talk. He felt it in Australia when Mike kept saying how Logan had the life, and he would give anything to swap for a week. A family with five boys aged seven to fifteen was tough. His wife, Rose, was a full-time mother, driving the boys to school, sports practice, and extracurricular activities, as well as cleaning, cooking, and helping with homework. Luckily, they could afford a housekeeper who helped with housework, but Rose wanted to be involved in the boys' lives as much as possible.

Mike felt as though he was always sixth in line when it came to Rose's priorities, and their marriage was being affected. It all came out over seven more pints. Logan changed to mineral water after two pints, as he could see where the conversation was heading. He just let Mike talk and talk, knowing it had been a long time since he had.

Eventually, Logan looked at his watch and said, 'It's eight o'clock. Time to call it a night.'

Mike nodded, slurring slightly. 'I'm fucking pissed, Logan, can I stay with you? My boys have never seen me drunk. My father was a drunk so I've never let them see me drink.'

Logan nodded. 'No problem, mate.' He understood where Mike was coming from.

They hopped in Logan's Range Rover and headed back home. Mike texted Rose to let her know that he was staying on at the Bakers to keep an eye on a sick colt overnight, so he would see her in the morning. Logan thought that a little white lie was okay occasionally, and he knew Mike was just a good guy going through a rough patch. Rose accepted the reasoning without question. Besides, she had five boys to feed and put to bed, as well as three extras staying the night for a sleepover.

When they got back to Logan's house, Mike poured his heart out a bit more and Logan made him drink coffee. He ended up passed out on the sofa, and Logan put a pillow under his head and a blanket over him. He put a bucket beside the couch, plus a few towels just to be on the safe side.

Logan had guessed correct. The next morning, when he got up at 5 a.m., he saw the bucket had been used and the towels saved the polished floorboards. Mike was asleep with the pillow over his head to block out the light in the lounge room that he hadn't bothered to turn off. Logan reluctantly emptied the bucket, rinsed it out, and returned it to its spot beside the couch for good measure. He also put a box of aspirin and a sports drink on the coffee table before he left and headed for the stables.

Cynthia arrived at 5.45 a.m. dressed to work. Logan walked her through the barn so they could both get acquainted with the new stock. He could see where the two boys had got their horse sense from, as she was a natural. Cynthia moved the right way around a horse and never got herself in the wrong spots. That's an instinct you have or you don't.

Logan put her in charge of the ten fillies and was surprised when she pulled out her riding helmet and riding chaps. 'Are you going to ride?' he said, surprised.

'I was an ace rider in point to points as a youngster, Logan. I can handle myself.' He really did admire her. She had the staff cracking as well, as she was a born leader. She led by example, from cleaning stables to hosing the horses down.

After Cynthia had ridden a few horses, Logan quipped, 'Find any slow ones?'

She laughed, thinking how she had not enjoyed herself so much for a long time. 'Slow ones, no. Rubbed arse cheeks and fanny, yes!'

Logan laughed loudly. 'Well, there is one more, and I would like *you* to ride him.' He led out the 4.1-million-dollar colt.

Cynthia was gobsmacked 'Why do you want me to ride him?'

'Because he'll be the best horse you've ever ridden.'

It was like she was handed the key to the most powerful car in the world. She walked up and stroked his head. As she ran her hands over his silky skin, she got tingles all over her body.

Logan thought she might be nervous, so he signalled the groom to bring out the lead pony. 'I'll ride with you. I rode him yesterday and he's lovely. Quite fit, and he's basically had a week off so he must be feeling pretty good.'

Cynthia got a leg up, as he was sixteen hands high and built like a machine. As they walked out to the trotting track, she asked, 'How do you rate him after yesterday's ride?'

'Better than Bluey,' Logan said, and he could see the excitement but also the nervousness in her eyes, as Bluey had just won three Group 1 races, beating the best the world had to offer.

They trotted two laps of the sand track then walked over to the grass. Cynthia was confused. 'The others worked on the velvet track. Why the grass for him?'

'Because you need to feel him, as after this you will be too scared to ride him again without a parachute.' Logan worked off with a huge smirk on his face. Cynthia went all rosy cheeked, as she was now flushed. She had ridden some nice horse in her time, and he felt great, but she honestly thought Logan was talking him up too much.

'When we get up here at the four-furlong marker, I will stride away.' Being in England, Logan had to change from metres to furlongs. 'You wait until I'm about twelve strides in front, then just let him slide a small bit. Don't worry; he's easy to pull up. Ready?'

Cynthia nodded. 'Ready.'

Logan gave the lead pony, an ex-racehorse, his head and he shot forward. The colt sensed he was about to be asked to go and he automatically changed strides, lowering and waiting in anticipation. She gave him an inch on the reins and whispered, 'Go, boy.' That was when Cynthia felt what Logan had told her. He lowered even further and let the enormous stride take flight. He went so quick that, within seconds, it seemed, he had passed Logan.

Cynthia was in shock, but she knew she had to pull him back. She whispered, 'Whoa, boy,' and he came back under her gently, as he had been trained by a well-respected breeze-up trainer who knew they needed to be trained to run more than a furlong.

Logan eased up next to Cynthia and he looked at her, waiting for her feedback. 'You've found me a fast one, Mr Weston,' she said breathlessly. Logan grinned wide and stuck his hand out and they high-fived.

Cynthia was still in shock and hardly said a thing as they headed back to the stables. She was in love. She kept stroking the colt down the neck and rubbing his rump and shoulders. This was her horse and he was going to be a champion in her eyes. When she dismounted, she turned to Logan and said, 'You were correct. Best I've ridden.'

'Well, he's your horse, so I think you should give him a name.'

She petted the colt, giving him a long look before she whispered, 'Warrior King.'

'I really like it,' Logan said.

'So do I.' Cynthia walked the colt, now named Warrior King, back to the tie-up bay to get unsaddled, hosed, and rolled before getting bedded down for the day. Cynthia grabbed a piece of chalk and wrote his name on the door. She suddenly felt jelly-legged and also a bit light-headed; whether it was from the rush of the colt or from being around Logan, she didn't know. Suddenly she felt as though she was blushing even more, so she made her way to her golf cart and headed back up to the house for breakfast.

She remembered feeling this way after a spontaneous, passionate lovemaking hour with her husband many years ago when the boys were not at home. She had literally passed out afterwards, as her husband had been an amazing lover. Her mind wandered and she reprimanded herself for wondering what Logan would be like in bed. She turned her attention back to the wheel and realised she'd driven off the road and was on the grass, heading straight for the rose garden. She quickly corrected her path and worried someone may have seen her near-accident. Luckily, everyone was too busy to notice.

Logan knew he had a possible champion, so he had to keep it simple. He knew that champions made up lengths on great horses just with their raw ability. Fitness and happiness were the keys, and if the Bakers' set-up couldn't give that, then he had no idea what could.

Tom and James headed down with the colts and Hank to the Sydney international airport equine loading area. Both boys were very sad to leave, as both had felt at home with Aunty Joy and had grown extremely fond of Don. In two weeks, Don had changed the boys forever. He had really helped James to get his confidence back, and Tom had never seen him so determined. He was hungry for the very first time in his life.

James had opened up to Don and told him that he felt he was not worthy of his family's success. Don had dealt with many young men who had struggled growing up in their father's shadow. In this case, it had been more his mother's shadow, as it was her drive that made their family so successful. James had turned into an average jockey now. He had a purple patch as a claiming apprentice but now really struggled with his weight and getting rides. Before his fall, he was not even getting rides at the main meetings. Afterwards, people were saying he was already washed up and would be riding jump races soon. He had started to believe what everyone was saying about him. He doubted his ability and his place in life.

The last few months James had struggled with his mother trying to solve all his problems and guide him to take the 'right' path. Cynthia was so accustomed to emotionally supporting the boys after their father's death that she couldn't seem to let go of the reins. Her only intention was to ensure her sons had a successful future, but James had begun to resent her constant control. In a way, the boys were relieved that their mother was moving to the new farm two weeks after their return, and they would be alone in the main house—apart from the housekeeper and cook, of course.

Don had turned both their thinking around, so they could begin to take back full control of their lives and achieve their dreams. They had arrived with broken hearts and left with the life skills to survive anything. But Tom was still wondering why there was one talk he wasn't included in between Don and James. All he knew was that James came back red eyed, but said he was fine.

Logan was pleased the boys were on their way back home. He needed the help, as learning the ropes the English way with twenty-six in work was not a walk in the park. Cynthia had sensed Logan needed help and set out to find him a personal assistant with solid knowledge of the racing game. Mike suggested a young chap that worked in the Hedges stable and texted Cynthia his number. She made the call and arranged for him to drop in for an interview on his lunch hour.

After a straightforward interview in the main house, Cynthia finally said, 'You're hired. When can you start?'

'Monday,' Miles replied.

'Will Mr Hedges let you go on such short notice?'

'Definitely. He'll be happy to see the back of me.'

Cynthia looked confused. 'And why is that?'

'He doesn't like poofs … You don't have a problem with poofs, do you, Cynthia?' he said in a cheeky but matter-of-fact tone.

'I adore them,' she joked back.

'So do I,' Miles blurted out while touching her arm. 'How about Crocodile Dundee? Is he going to have a problem with a poof?'

Cynthia was quite flustered, as she hadn't thought to consult Logan on any of it. She considered for a moment whether he would prefer a hot blonde instead. 'You'll be perfect together, like Batman and Robin.' Cynthia winked and gave a light laugh, hoping to ease the tension. Miles looked somewhat relieved and he laughed along.

Even though it was lunchtime and the staff were all having a two-hour break, she knew Logan would still be working. 'We have twenty minutes. Would you like to meet Logan?'

Miles nodded. 'Sure,' and they headed down to the stables.

Cynthia was correct. 'Here he is … Logan, I have someone I'd like you to meet.'

Logan was shutting the door of Warrior King's stable and turned around. Miles put out his hand. 'Miles Bruce.'

'Logan Weston.' Miles shook his hand with a good, solid grip.

Cynthia said to Logan, 'Miles is extremely experienced in racing administration and planning. He'll be your new PA.'

Logan looked surprised. 'I didn't know I needed a PA.'

Cynthia smiled back at him and said, 'We need the extra help,' in a tone that indicated the subject was not up for discussion.

Miles felt the tension, as it was obvious Logan didn't intend to accept outside help that easily. Miles felt he needed to reassure Logan of his ability. 'Logan, walk with me. You've got twenty-six horses in work this week. In six to ten weeks, some will be ready to jump out and barrier trial. Eight to twelve weeks, ready to race. You'll need to program, research, book jockeys, study the fields and tracks … You'll need help with him,' as he nodded over to Warrior King. 'Special was a brilliant speedster, but we need to get this colt to win over six to eight furlongs instead of the six-furlong sprints. If he can do that, he'll be worth double.'

Logan raised his eyebrows. *This guy had done his homework.*

Miles smiled, reading Logan's mind. 'I make it my business to know everyone's business. My current job is filing and billing clients—fucking boring—so everything I know is from going to the races on the weekends and studying the racing calendar and sales catalogues in my own time. I'm an expert walking the tracks and I'm ready to learn more. More than that, I want to be part of something great. Cynthia has told me a bit about your plans; I want in. Please, Logan, let me help you.' Miles always talked fast.

Logan liked what he heard, but he took a few seconds to think it over. Finally, he shrugged in defeat. He looked at Cynthia. 'Well, it looks like you've already made up your mind, so I'm happy if you are.'

Cynthia smiled at Miles. 'What did I tell you! Love at first sight.' She laughed out loud when she caught Logan's baffled expression.

Miles tried to hide his amusement, and turned to Logan. 'Don't worry, Logan. You're not my type.' This only made Cynthia laugh harder.

Logan felt a bit shell-shocked and couldn't get a quip out fast enough. He just smirked and shook his head as the two laughed together. 'Welcome to the team, Miles. See you Monday morning.' He shook his hand again and went back to his work, and Miles and Cynthia walked back to the house to finalise the deal.

CHAPTER 14

Tom and James arrived in the horse truck with Everest, Forest Black, and Logan's best pal, Hank. It had been a big trip for all five, but Hank couldn't contain his delight when he saw Logan. The colts had travelled very well considering the duration of the flight. They looked a lot fitter than when Logan had last seen them. Both had muscled up and had some great tone starting to appear. *A change of environment and kindness can do wonders,* Logan thought.

'My boys!' Cynthia had seen the horse truck arrive and walked down to welcome her sons home. She cuddled and hugged them both. She put her hands on James's cheeks. 'You look so ruggedly handsome, James. The Outback agrees with you!' James hadn't felt this great in years.

After they got the horses settled, Cynthia and the boys went inside to spend some quality time together. Cynthia wanted to hear all about the muster, and the boys wanted to hear all about the horses.

Hank adapted to his new lifestyle quite quickly, enjoying the tour of the farm with Logan on the four-wheel ATV. When they arrived at Logan's house, the little dog ran from room to room. A little later, Logan looked around for Hank, as he seemed to have disappeared. He found him fast asleep on a pile of dirty clothes in the corner of the bathroom. The smell of his master's clothes had brought the boy undone. He was running on adrenaline until then, and finally felt comforted enough to fall asleep. He barely stirred when Logan picked him up and took him to the couch to sleep there next to him while he watched some races on the TV racing channel.

It was 6 a.m. and all bar one of the twelve staff had arrived. Logan had been down three times during the night to check the two new arrivals. Their temperatures had been fine, and they had both eaten some feed. The English feed was quite different, so it would take a few weeks for them to completely adjust. As usual, Logan had started at 5.30 a.m. Hank received many pats and cuddles from the team as they arrived to work.

They put Everest and Forest Black in the day paddocks for the day and their heads never rose from the lush green pasture. James and Tom felt jet-lagged, but were anxious to see the full stable running. Tom and Logan headed to the watch tower as Logan gave instructions: 'All horses would trot two and canter one this morning.' He and Tom would view and discuss the new acquisitions while they were away. James rode five and was certainly very impressed, but the best was left for last. He was finally thrown up on Warrior King. He was only about three weeks from a trail, as he had the fitness from the breeze ups. He trotted two laps and came over to the tower, where Cynthia was also watching the morning's work.

Logan instructed, 'Work him around from the mile and just let him do some three-quarter from the three-furlong, and run home a bit on the last furlong. But whatever you do, don't let him go too hard.'

James worked into a canter from the mile and was impressed with the size of his stride and his strength. He certainly didn't feel like a two-year-old. At the five-furlong mark, he let his pacework slowly increase, and was at three-quarter pace at the three-furlong marker. He felt the change in the colt and now he was working as straight as a gun barrel. He was up on the bit like a race car in third gear. As they approached the furlong mark, James let the reins slide, but he didn't move. The colt dropped a foot lower to the ground and extended his massive frame and lengthened his stride like James had never felt before. James had felt enough in ten strides and took hold again to get the colt eased down before the finish marker. Logan wanted him to understand what he saw in the colt, and James had thought the same one word — *champion*. The colt eased back to a walk and was so calm and relaxed. He was a four-year-old in a two-year-old body.

James walked back to the tower, and no one said a word, as they were all waiting to hear his opinion. 'What's for breakfast?' James asked casually.

Tom quipped, 'Five Group 1's.'

'Is that all?' James said, laughing. He patted the colt and started to lead him back to the stables. Cynthia, Logan, and Tom walked back alongside him, and they all patted and stroked the horse. Cynthia was beaming with pride. She had worked hard, raised two talented sons, and now they had a future champion on their hands. She picked some fresh grass from the laneway that had never been grazed by horses and fed him a double handful of sweet rye and clover. 'Soon you're going to be spoilt rotten,' she told Warrior King.

Angus Masters boiled with anger—and embarrassment—as the rumours kept circulating about how he had been duped by Logan. Masters vented to his foreman. 'We're going to raid Royal Ascot next year, and any race that fucker Weston has a horse in, *I will win*. I'm going to bury that prick alive.'

Masters could dish it out, but he couldn't take it at all. Jim Moodie had been stirring shit in the trainers' hut all week, telling everyone how Fred's truck had 'mysteriously' broken down. Since Fred was the float driver who delivered the horses to Logan, he reckoned that Masters had been behind the truck's engine blowing up beyond repair. The talk was correct; Masters hired someone to drain the oil out of Fred's truck so the engine cooked. Fred was a struggling horse float driver and he had seven horses on board when the motor blew up. Everyone agreed what Masters had done was unjustified.

When Logan received a text from Moodie about Fred's truck, he immediately felt responsible. Even though there was no proof it was Masters, Logan knew he was capable of doing something like that. Logan made arrangements and transferred money to Moodie's account and asked for it to go towards a new motor for Fred's truck.

Three days later, Moodie called Fred up and asked him over to the trainers' hut. Fred had borrowed a truck, but it was a loan and came at a cost. He was struggling financially and felt at a loss as to what to do. Fred climbed the stairs and entered the tower, looking for Moodie. It was late morning, and the best horses had already worked. 'What do you need, mate?' Fred asked Moodie when he saw him.

Moodie gave him a cheeky smile. 'I have something for you, Fred.'

Fred looked confused. 'For me?'

A few of the other trainers had spotted Fred and made their way over. 'After talking about it, we all feel terrible about what happened. You're a hard worker, mate. You've done good work for a lot of us and, well, we want to chip in towards a new motor for you.'

Fred shook his head. He couldn't believe it. Moodie handed over the envelope of cheques and Fred opened it in shock.

'How much do you need?' asked one of the trainers, who had put in $3,000.

Fred said quietly, 'It's $46,000 to get a new one fitted.'

Moodie laughed. 'Well, get a fresh paint job while you're at it. We all put in what we could, and Logan put in $40,000 as his way of apologising for getting you involved in any messy business. It's about $62,000 total, Fred. How's that?'

Fred was speechless. He held onto the envelope with tears in his eyes. His whole life was horses, and he couldn't have survived without the steady income from driving the float. He was still sharp as a whip and a great driver, and could feel if any horse in the back of the truck wasn't right.

Moodie noticed Masters slip away from the tower and start walking back to the stables unnoticed. *Guilty as charged*, Moodie thought.

Fred shook Moodie's hand and said, 'Thank you. Thank you all so much. Please tell Logan I will never forget this kindness.' Fred made sure he shook the hand of every trainer in the tower who had chipped in, before he left.

Logan and Tom worked really well together, and the stable was running efficiently. Logan had nothing else to do but train the horses and play with Hank, so he felt as though he was living his dream. Within days of being hired, Miles had mapped out all the upcoming trial days and race meetings in the coming months, so Logan and Tom could plan as far ahead as four months. Miles had every horse's pedigree and breeding statistics, their stock's preferred racing styles and tracks, as well as every vet report, uploaded to the system so Tom or Logan could access it at any time. He had also organised a state-of-the-art video camera to film gallops, with GPS tracking to record exact times. Tom and Logan couldn't believe Miles's energy and foresight. Most days he had lunch with Cynthia and, without fail, they would have a sneaky gin and tonic or two.

James had always seemed quite shy, but it increased around Miles. He certainly acted differently and would never fire back at any of Miles's smart-ass comments, like the other staff did. But Logan was warming up to his remarkable assistant and getting used to threats of being 'bitch slapped into next week'. Miles had even taken Logan clothes shopping, as he just couldn't stand his dress sense. Logan had to admit that Miles had a great sense of style, and he felt relieved to have four sets of stylish outfits for important occasions now.

The day of Warrior King's first official barrier trial arrived, and James was legged on. Logan said, 'Just let him get used to racing in the pack, nothing more. You don't have to win, just get him used to the hustle and bustle of ten galloping horses. He needs to get used to clods of grass and dirt coming back on him.'

'Won't happen if I'm out in front,' he said with a wide grin. Logan shook his head and smiled, since they both knew how good he was. There was some talk floating around that the colt was good after his breeze up had caused a stir, along with his price tag.

They jumped and James had him third last. 'Perfect,' said Logan. He was travelling extremely easy as he rounded the turn. James eased him back to last and, even though he was working quite keenly, he came back under James while he was eased back. James brought him to the outside and let him slide, but still had a stranglehold on the colt. With 150 metres to go he was working home and looked like he would run second or third. But, almost as if he knew, he lengthened his stride and won the trial by a nose; hard held by the jockey while the field had been pushed out hard enough. James rode back to the stripping stalls and the colt wouldn't have blown out a candle. Logan just winked at Tom. The media were heading over, so Logan said, 'Off you go, Tom. Your fans await you.'

The racing news went crazy, posting online and all over social media: 'The Best Since Frankel', 'Aussie-bred Colt is the Real Deal', and '4.1 Mil Sounds Cheap'.

At a roundtable discussion, the team decided that Warrior King would start in ten days at Ascot over six furlongs. The tension was in the air, as everyone knew Warrior King was something special.

As Logan and Tom walked back to the barn, Logan put his hand on Tom's shoulder. 'Your first runner will be a champion. Think of that!'

Tom shook his head. '*Our* first runner.'

'He's in *your* name, mate. I just consider myself lucky that your mother got her way with the VRC racing stewards and got my charges changed so I could be here and be a part of the team. But I don't get my licence back for another sixteen months.' Before Tom could speak, Logan said, 'This is a joint effort, I know, but don't feel guilty about being in the spotlight. You've earned it. Besides, if Miles gets half a chance he'll be telling them *he's* the brains behind the whole operation!'

They both burst out laughing, knowing that Miles was actually proving to be the cog that was making the whole machine run smoothly.

James walked in the office and looked around. He was visibly tense when he noticed that Tom and Logan weren't there. 'Oh, hey James.'

'Uh, hi,' James said awkwardly. 'Tom here?'

'No, I actually think he's still with Logan—tugging one out in the stable, I gather, over their little superstar, Warrior King.' He dramatically acted it out with two pumping wrists and laughed at his own joke. 'I swear that horse gets more action than I do.'

James instantly went bright red. He hadn't socialised with Miles much. He kept to himself quite a lot and he'd been so busy with his own training. As a jockey, he had to stay on top of his weight and fitness, time at the gym, and the gruelling sauna sessions. He rarely spoke to anyone on the crew after track work most days until the following morning, so James wasn't used to Miles talking that way.

'Well, you would know what I mean! You rode him. I bet he felt pretty good between your legs,' Miles said, winking. James blushed even more and Miles suddenly realised he was uncomfortable. 'Sorry, James, I'm being a crass poof. Just ignore me.'

'Ah, it's fine,' he said, walking towards the door. 'I'm going to look in the barn. Thanks.' James quickly exited, shutting the solid oak door behind him.

Miles turned and said to the secretary, 'Awkward!'

She shook her head. 'You have no filter, do you?'

'Poor kid. I've made him scared of the big bad poof in the office now.' They both broke out laughing, but Miles knew the way he acted made some people uneasy.

Logan and Tom were exactly where Miles had said—at Warrior King's stable. Tom said to James, 'You have ten days to be ready to ride at 52 kg. Can you do that?'

'I'm 51 kg now.'

'You are?' said Logan, surprised.

'Yes, as of an hour ago.'

'Well done, my brother,' as Tom put his arm around his shoulder.

'No one will be able to get me off this colt,' said James.

'Apparently, two of the top four two-year-olds will be nominated in the race. Brazen Boy won the Group 2 Spring Stakes last start by five lengths over six furlongs, and the filly My Sharona won the same in the filly's division by four lengths. Stiff opposition for a first starter, James,' said Tom, as they all starting walking out. Logan shut the stable door. They all knew the colt was very good, but until you got to the races you didn't actually know how they would cope.

'Up for a pint tonight?' said Tom.

'Yeah, sounds good. I will become a hermit if I don't go out soon,' said Logan. Now the stable was in full swing, Logan had gone back to his old self and life was just work.

James gave his twin brother a filthy look—it wasn't a fair thing to ask in his presence, when he had just made the lightest weight he had been in over twelve months. Tom laughed. 'You can be the driver.' James flipped him the bird and walked off. 'So, I'll pick you up at 6.30, Logan?' asked Tom.

Logan nodded and gave Tom a wink before he went off to walk Hank. He used it as an opportunity to double-check all the horses in and out in the spelling paddocks. He found it very hard to switch off, plus Hank always found at least one rabbit to chase.

Beeeeep went the horn from Tom's BMW 5 Sports AWD. Logan walked out in the new clothes that Miles had chosen for him. 'Looking spiffy,' said Tom.

'Thanks! It actually feels nice to get dressed up and out of work clothes that smell of horses sometimes,' Logan said.

Tom took Logan into town and they headed to a high-end bar that also served meals. Tom was a local and several people said polite hello's, but they all gave Logan a once-over look. He had been the talk of the town on many occasions; first, after the release of the YouTube video, which had now slowed on views but was still at sixty-five-plus million; then when the rumours had circulated about the night at the tavern when he stood up for Cynthia. The word was that he was a tough man not to be fucked with.

Tom ordered two pints, and they looked at the menu. Logan settled on the pork pie with peas and mash, and Tom decided to have the same. 'Logan!' said a voice from behind and it was Mike, their vet. He came over and shook hands with both of them. Logan instantly knew he had been drinking, as he had last seen Mike at 2 p.m. 'You're pissed, Mike,' Tom said with a raised eyebrow.

'I am not!' Mike stood tall. 'We had a vet conference on a new ruling in vaccinations. It was out the back in the dining room, so I'm just having a few before heading home,' Mike replied, beginning to slur slightly.

Logan and Tom exchanged glances. Tom had never seen Mike drunk, unlike Logan, who had the pleasure the other week. 'I thought you didn't drink,' said Tom, a bit confused.

'Well, not in front of the kids,' he replied, moving his arm in a searching sweep. 'No kids here.'

As Mike laughed and looked around for his peers, Logan silently mouthed to Tom, 'He's smashed.'

A lady walked past—blonde, medium height, attractive in a certain way. Mike stuck his arm out to stop her. 'Jo! This is the Aussie guy I told you about.' Jo stopped and looked slightly embarrassed, looking at who Mike was gesturing to. 'Jo, this is Logan. Logan, this is Jo. Oh, and this is Tom. Tom, Jo.' Mike was really hammered and was starting to sway. Everybody exchanged handshakes awkwardly. 'I told Jo that you're a good man—and single too!'

Jo and Logan went bright red, and an awkward silence hung in the air for a few seconds. Finally, Logan held Mike's arm to stabilise him. 'Let me get you a water and a cab home, Mike,' said Logan.

'Shh, shh,' Mike said in a lower voice. 'I can't go home like this.' He stood tall and put his arm around Logan's shoulder. He smelt like a brewery. Logan guessed he must have been throwing them down all afternoon. 'I'll need to sleep on your couch again, mate.' He pointed his finger at Logan. 'That Hank of yours is my friend now.'

Logan handed him a water, nodding. 'Sure, Mike. You have four more of these and you'll be ready to go home.'

Jo liked the way Logan had handled the situation, not fobbing off his drunken friend. Logan found a table while Tom got their drinks. He brought back two pints and a glass of Chardonnay, hoping Jo would stay for a drink and guessing something she might like to drink. Tom nailed it, and she happily stayed. They tried to chitchat but Mike was being loud and kept interrupting. Logan and Tom quickly scoffed their dinner as they kept chatting. Jo and Mike had snacked all afternoon in the conference, so they weren't hungry. 'Righto, Mike,' said Tom, after one too many interruptions. 'I'm taking you home.'

Mike was sensible enough to know that he had to go—and when your boss says it, you don't argue. Even though Mike was twenty years older than Tom, he knew where his bread was buttered. Jo said her goodbyes to Mike but sat back down at the table. Tom winked at Logan and said casually, 'I'll swing by on my way back to pick you up.' Logan opened his mouth to protest, but Tom knew what being a wingman was about.

Logan and Jo settled in, and their conversation came back around to horses, as it usually does. Logan had finished four pints and Jo had stopped drinking after her Chardonnay, as she was on call from 11 p.m. Jo explained that vets hated to be on call, full stop, but 11 p.m. to 6 a.m. was the best shift, as maybe two times a week she got called out, and she had already had those two in the previous two nights. They had only been very minor, and she had been back in bed within two hours.

'I heard about your first night here, at the local tavern,' Jo said, giving him a cheeky smile.

Logan shook his head, sighing. 'Sometimes I walk into a room and it seems like everybody already knows who I am. I blame town gossips,' he gave her a look, 'and that YouTube video.'

'Oh, what video?'

Logan was surprised, as he assumed everyone had seen it, but he explained what had happened. To his credit, he told the story honestly, admitting to his flawed actions and hurt pride. 'I'm actually surprised you haven't seen it,' he said, finally.

'Well, actually, I have. I've watched it about forty times, but I wanted to hear it from the horse's mouth, so to speak.' They both laughed and the tension was well and truly broken.

'So, you're a fighter, not a lover,' she fired at him.

He laughed. 'Sure looks that way, doesn't it?'

'I'm not surprised Cynthia snapped you up.'

'You know her?'

'A little. We hunted a few times together years ago, and when we were younger we rode against each other at point to points. She is extremely competitive.'

Logan quickly glanced at her hands for the first time. No matter how well they look after themselves, a trained eye could spot a woman who was horsey. Logan mused that if he had a choice, he possibly would always choose a horsey lady over any other. He loved the lifestyle. But horses needed constant care, training, and commitment. And he was now at a point where he questioned if he wanted to share his life again with a horsey person. He quickly snapped out of it. He was only talking to a woman at a bar, not planning their future together.

'Any kids?' she asked.

'Not yet,' he answered. 'You?'

'No.' Jo paused for a second before she continued, 'I'm forty-three, so my time is close to being up.'

Logan saw his shot and didn't hesitate, as the fourth pint had kicked in, and he wanted her. 'Seriously? You're forty-three? Honestly, I would have guessed thirty-six, maybe thirty-eight. But not a day older.' She blushed and smiled, rolling her eyes at his comment. 'Seriously! I've known a lot of female vets, and all that hard work often makes them look older, but it must be the reverse with you.' She laughed again and Logan noticed her body language change. She was leaning in towards Logan and fiddling with her hair and her shirt. She wore very stylish jeans, a tailored Ralph Lauren shirt, and a pair of American cowboy boots that she had bought from her trip to the Keeneland sales. Logan's phone buzzed; it was from Tom: 'Need me to pick you up?'

'Everything okay?' Jo asked as Logan considered his reply message.

'Oh, yeah. Tom just let me know that Mike has him cornered. He said it'll be a while before he can talk his way out the door, so I'll need to catch a cab home.' Jo nodded—quietly considering her plan, too. Logan added, 'It's none of my business, but it sounds like he's having a hard time at home at the moment. Growing boys and all that.' Jo didn't really know Mike that well, so didn't comment.

'I can give you a lift.'

'Oh, you don't need to do that, Jo.'

'It's on my way home, honestly. I'm happy to drop you off.'

Logan accepted. *First hurdle passed*, he thought. Jo excused herself and made her way to the ladies' room. Logan quickly texted Tom: 'Negative, ghost rider.'

Tom replied with a question mark, and Logan replied: 'Will fill you in tomorrow. See you at 6 a.m.,' with a wink emoji.

Jo was very attracted to Logan. He was rugged and had a quiet confidence. She thought he looked like an Australian version of Daniel Craig from the latest James Bond movies—not beautiful, but manly. It was the closet she had come to a date in a long time.

When Jo returned from the bathroom, Logan could tell she had applied another coat of lipstick, brushed and put up her hair again, and put on a fresh spray of perfume. She smelt wonderful.

They walked out to the carpark and got in Jo's car. 'Does every vet over here drive an Audi?' Logan joked. Jo laughed and started up the car. Logan could smell the familiar odours of iodine, disinfectant, penicillin, and a mixture of other drugs he knew well from taking care of horses. *For a vet's car, it's pretty tidy*, he admitted.

It was a short fifteen-minute drive to Logan's place. Jo pressed play on her phone to start some music. She turned the volume up slightly to help break the silence. A hit from the Bee Gees blasted out, 'Stayin' Alive'. Jo sang the song word for word as they drove along. Logan was impressed. *Hmm, confident and sassy.*

Jo pulled up to the gates and Logan said he'd walk in.

'Don't be silly. I'll drop you at your door. What's the code?'

Logan smiled playfully. 'I can't tell you. It's a secret.' He unbuckled his seatbelt to lean across to punch it in himself.

Jo laughed. 'What? Don't be silly, just tell me.'

Logan shook his head. 'No, no, top secret, Jo. Close your eyes.'

Jo played along, laughing as she put her hands up to her eyes to cover them. Logan leant across her and typed in the code. Jo could smell him and feel his arm brushing against her chest.

The gate slowly eased open and Logan sat back in his seat. 'You could be a spy,' Jo laughed as she drove in.

Logan directed her to his house and she pulled up into his driveway. 'Very nice,' she said.

'Thanks. Very different to my place back home. Come in, I'll give you the tour and you can meet Hank.'

'Okay, sure,' Jo said, smiling. She turned off the car and they both hopped out. When Logan saw her grab her handbag, it was a dead giveaway that she intended to stay a bit longer. Before Logan opened the door, he could already hear Hank going crazy on the other side. As usual, the little dog held centre stage for about five minutes before Logan could start the tour.

'Wow, it's lovely,' she said, admiring the décor.

'Yeah, it is. I think Cynthia had it decorated to suit the men more so than women though.'

'I like it. I like it a lot.' She ran her hand over the timber kitchen bench top. 'Beautiful timber.'

'It was from the old wool shed here on the farm,' Logan said proudly.

Jo picked up Hank so she could cuddle him and give little kisses as they walked through the rest of the house. *Vets are all the same. Loyal animal lovers, and the female vets openly showed their emotion*, Logan thought. They ended up near the main bedroom and the conversation seemed to end. With Hank in her arms, Logan couldn't figure out how he'd make his intentions known. As they walked past the bathroom, Jo put down Hank. 'Oh, I'll just use your bathroom quickly before I go.'

'Sure thing,' Logan said, as Jo hurried in. Logan felt that maybe she wanted to go now. It was getting late and she was on call. He checked his watch: 10.15 p.m. *There's still time*, he thought cheekily. He wrestled with Hank further down the hallway as he waited. Jo quickly came out. 'Okay, well, thanks for the tour. I'm off,' she said.

Logan got up off the floor and walked over. 'Okay, sure. It's been really nice spending time with you, Jo.'

'You too.' She awkwardly put her hand out to shake his hand, but Logan went for a hug. He knew it would break down the awkward physical barrier. *She smells so great*, he thought, holding her for a long hug. He slowly loosened his grip and they came apart. As he looked her in the eyes, he saw she wanted more. He leaned in and kissed her softly on the lips; once, twice, then a third time with passion. He pulled back and said softly, 'Can I convince you to stay a while longer?'

Jo's cheeks were rosy from the kiss, and she smiled playfully. 'Please do.' They kissed again and the passion had now increased tenfold. Logan broke away and took her hand to lead her to the bedroom. Hank quickly got up off the floor and was walking side by side with Logan—apparently also ready for bed. Logan laughed, scooping up Hank. 'I'll put Hank in a different bed for tonight.' Jo gave Logan's arm a quick squeeze before she sauntered off down to the bedroom.

As she undressed, Jo realised it had been fifteen years since she had gone home with a man on the first date—she'd never agreed to jump into bed so quickly. Logan settled Hank in a different room and soon found Jo under the covers, with her clothes and handbag on the floor. Logan dimmed the lights, preferring to make love with some vision. He got very aroused seeing his lover's pleasure and he hoped it would be the same tonight. He undressed and, like many women before her, Jo was eager to see what she was about to receive. She grinned with a slightly surprised look, as her eyes grew wider and head tilted back with a smile growing that said, 'yes please'.

Jo was horny as hell. It had been three years since she had found out her partner, who was another vet, had been cheating on her. She pulled Logan onto the bed and they started making out like teenagers. Logan liked that she took control. In his time, he had experienced many women who were one way in person and completely different in bed, whether they were shy or extroverted party animals. Others talked the talk, but their performance didn't live up to their promises. The foreplay was kept to a minimum. Time was limited to when she clocked on. She wanted penetration. She wanted the cock she had just laid eyes on and she wanted to be fucked hard. Her last partner had been nothing super in bed—just a missionary type of guy. She pushed Logan down onto the bed. Logan loved the concentrated look on her face as she slowly positioned herself down in the saddle, ready to ride. 'Nice girth,' she smiled, when she had finally got comfortable

Logan rubbed her breasts slowly with the back of his hands—they were softer than his rough palms. He slowly stroked her nipples as she rode him faster and faster. Jo felt her first orgasm in years building up, and she arched her back and placed her hands back on Logan's thighs to support her as she drove down harder. Her breath quickened, and Logan felt she would cum any second. He watched her half-closed eyelids, as she moaned loudly and shuddered on top of him. He hoped Tom and James couldn't hear her all the way up at the main house. Very impressive.

When Logan sensed it had finished, he started rocking his pelvis and driving up into her as deep as he could. She moved her hands to his chest and firmly gripped his body. Her ragged breathing let Logan know that she was enjoying herself. She rocked forward quickly and he thrust hard again. And it was now the second shudder and three hip thrusts again. *Number two*. Logan smiled. Jo leaned forward, as she was trying to catch her breath. She rested her head on Logan's forehead. 'Very nice, crocodile man.'

Logan knew she was jelly-legged after two very intense orgasms like that, and it would have been enough, but he wanted to cum badly. 'My turn.' He rolled her over, and softly kissed her breasts until he felt her heart rate lower again, and then he felt her raise against his mouth. He raised both her legs and put them over his right shoulder, and then raised her back and bottom, and placed a pillow under her back, raising her pelvis off the bed. She looked a bit confused. 'Trust me.' He lowered himself forward and re-entered. She had never been fucked in that position and, on Logan's second thrust, she let out a surprised moan. She signalled not to go that deep again yet. 'Easy.' After composing herself, she smiled up at him, wanting him to keep going.

Smart lady. That was the ultimate compliment to a man, Logan thought.

He slowed down and made precise movements that hit the right spot with every thrust. He knew to raise a woman's body up at just the right angle to achieve an orgasm every time. He was pleasantly surprised when Jo's body stiffened and her body rose higher from the pillow, as an intense orgasm made her jolt. Her face tightened up as well, and her legs stiffened as her back straightened out. Logan watched her with pleasure, on the edge himself. She lowered back down and he waited until she was ready. 'Now's it your turn,' she said breathlessly. He was well and truly ready, and had nearly cum a minute ago but she had beat him to it. He went at the same rhythm until he could see she was ready for number four. He was there, and slowed his motion as he waited. He knew she was a few seconds off, but he was losing his grip and he gave three fast motions. She gasped and he stiffened, then she stiffened again, but this time she trembled weakly and had to release her legs. 'No more, no more. I can't take anymore.' He knew she meant it, and he rolled beside her and caught his breath. Not many guys made sure a lady was spent before they finished, but Logan was an attentive lover. He waited until she spoke first. 'Well, I didn't know that was going to happen today when I had my breakfast this morning, fine sir. You sure know how to fuck, Mr Weston.'

'You aren't too bad yourself,' he teased back.

She went to roll over to kiss him, and her phone rang. The moment she had been waiting for, for a long time was ruined. 'Fuck!' she cursed as she scrambled off the side of the bed to dig her mobile out of her handbag. She pulled it out and shook it angrily before answering it. Logan laughed quietly behind her. 'Hello … Uh huh … Yeah, I'm at home … It's fine … Yup, give me twenty minutes to get there.' She hung up and turned to Logan. 'A colic. I can't believe this—a fucking colic. I haven't been laid in such a long time, and now a colic.' She stood up and started to pick up her clothes to get dressed, then awkwardly closed her legs and ran to the bathroom. Logan laughed as he heard her shout, 'Sorry about that. Great way to ruin the moment!'

Less than three minutes later, she was dressed and Logan was seeing her out the front door. She turned and smiled before she got into her car. 'Thanks for tonight.' She hopped in and quickly drove off. Logan understood the emergency and chuckled to himself. *Well, that's one way to beat the awkwardness the next morning.*

Tom and Logan watched, timed, and assessed the work of each horse. There was some talent showing in the stable, but nothing near the talent of Warrior King. Everest had settled in well, but he still had some bad days every now and then, and could be a prick when he wanted to be.

The flow of horses seemed to stop, and a voice came over the two-way: 'We just need five minutes and the others will be up.'

'All good,' Tom replied. He turned and looked at Logan. 'I pictured you as a stayer.' Logan looked confused. 'Jo was in and out in under an hour.'

Logan laughed and shook his head. *I guess the boys were watching my comings and goings last night.* 'She had a colic. Had to go.'

'Well, when you get time, we need to talk,' Tom said in a serious tone.

Logan instantly felt like he was in deep trouble. 'Okay. About?'

'How you get laid so easy and I haven't been for over nine months! We're training partners, you know. We're meant to watch out for each other!'

They both laughed, then turned as the first horse got their attention back on track. It was Everest and Forest Black. They were about to have their first serious bit of work. James was aboard Everest, even though he preferred Forest.

'Four and two,' Tom said, meaning three-quarter work from the four-furlong marker, then work home the last two furlongs.

'D-Day,' Logan said, as he set the watches and video to play. Logan had put his balls on the line selecting the two horses and he wanted a good result from both of them. More so, he truly wanted to show up Masters. Everyone knew Bluey was always a Group 1 horse in the making, but these two had been labelled as cast-offs.

They worked off, and Everest was being too keen and throwing his head up and down—not near as bad as he was when they first bought him, but still bad form. On the other hand, Forest was working very nicely. They went past the five-furlong marker then slowly increased their pace until they hit the four-furlong marker at three-quarters. They approached the two-furlong post and they quickened again. Forest really grabbed the bridle and extended into a beautiful rhythm, and his breathing was in perfect timing. Everest was staying with him, but he had his head up and his rhythm was all over the place.

Afterwards, the riders headed back up to the watch tower. 'He went well,' Tom said to Candice, who rode Forest.

'He felt super. Great stride and he had him covered easy,' she said, looking at Everest.

James was pissed off, and he complained, 'He can be such a cock some days. He was a shocker. His rhythm was out and he kept changing lead. I just don't know what else I can do.'

'Go around again,' Logan said.

'Me?' said James.

'Yes. But this time just work off at the eight-furlong mark. If he reefs and tears, let him go.'

'You sure?' James asked, concerned.

'Yes, ride him like a stayer on the longest rein you can give him. What do you think, Tom?'

'I agree,' said Tom. 'Just let him keep striding around. If you have to do another lap, just go. Maybe he needs to be worn out again, like we did back at Scone.'

James trotted back down and got to where he was about to work off. Everest worked around with better manners, now he was by himself, but he was still not up to an acceptable standard. If he carried on like that at the races, he would be scratched for being dangerous. Everest sensed he may be asked to quicken soon so he started to reef and tear. James gave him his head and he started to quicken.

He was all over the place at first, but as he cornered he naturally changed legs and gait, and balanced himself. Finally, he found his rhythm and James was on the longest rein you could ride with. He lowered his head to be parallel to his body and this helped his stride lengthen. James was shocked. Everest felt sensational. They ran past the watch tower and James still had not touched the reins.

Everest continued to work but he came back to a slower pace. James was not moving and Everest kept working, and soon enough they were working up to the five-furlong marker again, and the horse was still working very solid.

'He is supposed to be a five-to-six-furlong horse,' said Tom, sounding pleasantly surprised.

'Back home there was a Roman Empire colt that was bred like this bloke,' Logan said. 'They tried him at two, and nothing—then he won a Derby at three.'

James eased him up as he went past the watch tower and walked him back down to Logan and Tom. Neither trainer spoke; they just listened to Everest's breathing. 'He would hardly blow a candle out, Logan,' said Tom, amazed.

All three exchanged a delighted smile. 'I think we have a stayer, boys,' Logan said.

'We have a bloody good stayer,' James said, finally proud of the misbehaving horse. He took Everest back to the stables, and Tom and Logan headed to the office. Now they needed to find a race for Everest, as he just proved to be fitter than they first thought.

They opened the door to the office, and Miles turned and smiled in a devilish way. 'Good morning, *Mr Fuck of the Century*!' he said with enthusiasm.

Logan froze and immediately glared across at Tom. His expression screamed, 'Who the hell have you told!'

Tom threw his hands up. 'I haven't said a word—honest!'

'Calm down,' Miles said, rolling his eyes. 'Jo got the call for the colic from my sister, Tania, last night. I'm staying there with her while her husband's away. Jo and Tania are besties, so I heard all the spicy details. I just assumed you are the only hot Australian horse man in town, and I can see by the look on your face I'm correct.'

Logan was blushing, but a guilty smile crept over his face. Tom started laughing. Miles tapped his finger on his chin dramatically in thought. 'Now, what did she say? Something along the lines of "Cock to die for—best fuck I've ever had."' Tom had lost it and was bent over laughing, and Logan was getting redder by the second. Miles was on a roll, and continued, 'Apparently you're hung like a horse, cowboy.' Miles whipped an invisible horse between his legs and gave a little hop. Logan cracked up at that, and the two trainers roared with laughter while Miles soaked up the attention. 'Maybe you can grab your gear and take me for a ride next,' and he acted out more whipping, seductively biting his lip and growling. Logan and Tom were in tears, and it took them ten minutes to regain their composure. They finally got Miles to be serious and work out race dates for Everest.

As he did that, Logan and Tom talked about his miraculous performance. Suddenly, Logan stopped mid-sentence.

'What's wrong?' Tom asked.

'I've just had an idea,' Logan said slowly.

'Don't hurt yourself,' Miles quipped. 'Whatever will Jo do—'

'Ah. Serious now, mate. Grab your laptop and race schedule for the next two weeks and let's head up to the main house.' Miles switched to business mode and started gathering his things. 'Your mother is home, right?'

Tom nodded. 'Yes, she came in this morning.'

Logan nodded and led the way. He turned at the door and said seriously to both of them. 'Not a word to Cynthia about last night.' Tom and Miles exchanged amused glances but nodded in agreement.

Up at the main house, Logan, Tom, Miles, and Cynthia sat at the dining table. 'This goes no further than the four of us,' Logan said in a serious tone. Everyone nodded. 'I have an idea … Everest is fitter than we first thought.'

Tom shrugged. 'So?'

'Hear me out,' Logan said. 'Miles, what races are on the same day Warrior King will run?' Miles started searching on his laptop. 'We need a maiden, or even open over a mile would suit.'

'There is an open mile that day,' Miles said, still looking at the screen. 'Race two. Warrior King's is race six. Why?'

'I think we should run Everest as Tom's first runner. He's had two starts in Australia with average results and they were over five and six furlongs. Most know Roman Empires are sprinters. I think this horse could jump and run them ragged.'

'Do you really think so?' Tom asked.

'If we just let him go, like James did today, he could do anything,' Logan replied.

'Is he that good?' asked Cynthia.

'We've been treating him like he is a sprinter, but he is just too hot tempered. He's got very good stamina though,' Logan replied. 'So, this is my idea: Let's set this horse up for a massive betting sting. We get Miles to spread the rumour that the Baker's new Aussie trainer is clueless. Find a few of the right people and they will spread it like wildfire. Say he has given the horse five weeks' work and is going to put him over a mile. We should also get Mr Caldwell to say the same at the local pubs so we can get on with the SP bookies. I'll get a few of my Aussie mates to hit him on the online betting, as we can organise a plunge to hit him from Australia, as well.'

Cynthia looked unsure. 'Do you really think he is fit enough for us to pull this off?'

'He is extremely fit, Mother,' Tom said.

Logan nodded. 'He is very fit.'

'What does James think of this plan?' Cynthia asked.

'He can't know about this,' Tom said.

'If he's Tom's very first runner, they'll believe the gossip. They already know that Warrior King is very good, as we have trialled him openly for all to see, so I think we'll get away with it. I'm prepared to put twenty grand on him,' Logan said. 'I may put 100,000 pounds if I can get on, as I would love to take the bookies down and win back our purchase prices.'

Everyone agreed to give Logan's idea a shot. They planned to start working Everest after the staff had gone home so the plan stayed a secret. This gave him a solid fitness work in the mornings then Logan would ride him in the afternoons while Hank had a run around the farm.

Cynthia got to work spreading her money around to be placed on her behalf. Mr Caldwell went to different pubs each afternoon and let slip about the stupid ways Logan was training, and in return Cynthia said she would put two grand on for him. Miles did the same and got the rumours to spill down to the bookies. The plan was to have five bets of £2,000 on the favourite of the race to throw the bookies off the scent of the sting going down and shorten the favourite in, and this hopefully would let Everest ease out in price.

Warrior King had been working superb, and Everest had been working equally as good, but out of sight of everyone else.

Three days out, and Everest worked over ten furlongs twice, barely able to blow a candle out at the end. He was getting fitter by the day, and the freestyle racing allowed him to dictate his speed. It seemed to be the only way to ride him.

Logan was extremely nervous. He had never done what they were about to do of this magnitude, and actually never knew anyone else who had done it either. James knew nothing of the betting, as they needed to keep him clean. The hype was building about Warrior King. Logan made a call to Mick. 'What do you want, you convict bastard?' Logan told him about the plunge that was about to happen. Mick thought on it for a moment before he said, 'If he doesn't win, I'll come and belt the shite out of you and your bloody horse.'

'Oh, he'll win,' Logan said, then hung up.

CHAPTER 15

The day had arrived, and Tom and Logan both agreed either horse couldn't be better. For the first time, Tom packed the racing silks they had designed and made to honour their father. James had really been in the zone, and he felt that it was his comeback to racing. Every morning, after he rode work for Tom and Logan at 9 a.m., he ran for an hour and worked out, then hit the gym with a personal trainer in the afternoon. He was the fittest and lightest he had ever been—50 kg riding weight.

They loaded Everest and Warrior King in the horse truck, and the two grooms took their positions in the front of the horse truck, directly in front of the two colts to keep a very close eye on them both. Logan walked to the truck with Tom and James, but stopped suddenly. He turned around and said, 'I'm so proud of you both. Let's show everyone who we are today. Let's make your father proud.' Tom and James nodded, then they pulled Logan into a group hug.

James hopped in his Lexus, and Logan and Tom got in the truck. Tom drove, and Logan tried to calm his nerves—he felt like he could throw up at any second.

They arrived at the track, and the colts settled quite well in their day stalls. One of the strappers, Sophie, pulled the grooming kit out of the race day bag and set to work on Everest. Logan walked over quickly and shook his head at her. 'No, not Everest. He's fine.'

'But, Mr Weston, I have to groom him up. He's got some sweat marks, and straw in his tail.'

'He's fine.'

Sophie thought he was just being fussy, so she picked up the gear. 'It'll only take a moment.'

'*Don't* groom Everest,' Logan said more sternly. Sophie looked startled at his tone, and Logan felt bad for upsetting her. Beside a select few, no one knew of the sting that was about to take place. He didn't want to create suspicion, so he handed her £100. 'Because, here, I want you to go put a bet on, or you can keep it in your pocket, up to you. You've done great. I'll take care of Everest.' Sophie still looked confused, but, like many stablehands, she was a punter. She shrugged, handed the gear to Logan, and went to place her bet.

Logan could tell that Everest was on edge, but not too bad considering his temper. It was good that the horses knew they were at the races. Warrior King was as settled as an eight-year-old gelding. *That colt never ceases to amaze me*, Logan thought.

Sophie came back, all smiles. 'I put the £100 on him, then I went all up Warrior King.'

'What odds did you get?' Logan asked.

'23/1 on the tote.' Logan smiled, as they were good odds, but he wanted better.

'Take him for another walk, please, Sophie.' Logan wanted everyone to see him looking dishevelled and wild-eyed. It might help get his price out a bit more.

Finally, it was time. Tom came in with the saddle. Logan looked at him and saw he had gone green. Tom was more nervous than he ever thought he could be. 'It'll be fine, mate,' Logan reassured him. 'Splash some water on your face and take some deep breaths.' Logan took the saddle and Tom did what Logan had said. As Logan saddled, he explained, 'It's just fear of the unknown. If he runs a furlong last, I'll look like the dickhead, not you. Don't worry so much, just enjoy this moment—your first runner, Tom!'

Tom nodded, still trying to fight off the nervous sick feeling. He walked over to help saddle Everest, putting his hand on the top of the jockey pad while Logan tightened the girth. Then he stretched both front legs out to make sure the girth had not pinched him. Logan smiled and patted Everest. 'I'm hoping we'll have two winners today,' and he winked at Tom.

Everest headed out to the pre-parade ring unbrushed, with straw in his tail and feet not painted with oil. He was the roughest looking horse in the group, and his price continued to blow out—28/1. Logan could see Everest's nervous tension building, and he went to his off side in the parade ring to help keep him calm while Sophie walked on the near side.

Meanwhile, Miles watched the price in the bookie ring, and had the team in place getting ready to hit the price. He texted Cynthia: 'He's at 31/1!' She was so excited but texted back to just wait until they are near the barriers before saying go. Their patience paid off. Everest hit 33/1, and Cynthia sent: 'Now!' Miles hit send, with one text going to everyone; the team they had assembled hit the local bookies, SP bookies, and the tote, and anyone who would let them on. All in all, £143,000 had been put all on Everest for the win. The bookies didn't know what hit them until the horses were lined up in the gates. The bookies had dropped him from 33/1 down to 4/1 and were shitting bricks.

They loaded in the barriers, and Logan, Tom, Cynthia, Miles, and Sophie all watched from the grandstands. Logan was pretty sure Tom was swallowing so hard to keep down vomit. They jumped. Everest jumped from barrier eight in the twelve-horse field and was like a bullet out of a gun. The field steadied, and James held his balance for fifty metres. When he gave Everest his head, the crowd gasped, believing that the horse had bolted. When they had gone a furlong, the race caller joked, 'This jockey obviously thinks he's in a four-furlong race!'

Everest was galloping along thirty lengths in front. It increased to thirty-five with five furlongs to go. The crowd simply couldn't believe it. The other jockeys were not stressed and now rated him 100/1. Nearly every horse that went at that breakneck speed always caved in and got caught. With four furlongs to go, Everest was still twenty-five lengths in front. The close-ups on TV showed the concern growing on some jockey's faces. With three furlongs to go, he was still twenty-three lengths in front. The race caller said, 'We may have a boil over here.' Everyone loved a frontrunner, and the crowd was captivated.

With two furlongs to go, Everest looked like he was about to tire. Many in the crowd started speculating: 'Here we go, this jockey is about to go for him and there will be no fuel in this tank!' Everest still had twenty lengths on the pack. When James looked around over his shoulder, he couldn't believe how far away they were. As they went past the final furlong mark, he shook up Everest. Everest laid back his ears, lengthened his stride, then lengthened again. James felt him suck the air in, and he was refreshed like he had been having a breather for three furlongs. He kicked, and there was no way they would get near him. Tom, Cynthia, Logan, and Miles knew it, and they started jumping for joy.

When the final margin was posted, James had crossed the line twenty-three lengths in front of the field. James saluted like he had just won the English Derby. The race caller had changed from knocking the early part of James's ride to saying what a wonderful ride it had been. The bookies were in an uproar and had no idea that a combined total payout was to be $4,719,000—possibly one of the biggest stings in history. They had been fooled, and Logan was the mastermind behind it.

On the other side of the world, it was 11.30 p.m. and Angus Masters had just woken up to watch the race. He hadn't really slept, just dozed. He watched everything; the bookies, the race, and the tactics. He knew it had been brilliant, but he also knew he would be a laughing stock. No one had ever got a horse from him before and won a race. He was always too hard on them and they never had an ounce of quality left when he was done. He exploded, 'You sneaky piece of shit!' He smashed the TV remote against the wall.

Angela came running downstairs. 'What's wrong, Angus?'

'What's wrong is your fucking asshole of an ex trained my garbage horse to win by twenty-odd lengths!'

'Really? Twenty lengths,' she said, quietly impressed. She instantly knew she had said the wrong thing and tried to correct it. 'But, like you said, the horse is no good.'

'Well, your fucking ex just proved that theory wrong, didn't he!' Angus roared. 'You probably backed the horse to win as well, didn't you? Texting him again? Plotting my downfall? Was this all just a two-bit plan you cooked up together?' He was yelling so loud his voice boomed through the house.

It was the second time Angela had seen this side of the man she had fallen in love with. But she was tough, and she wasn't going to cop his shit. She stared at him with a defiant look he had never seen before. 'Enough! I don't want to hear another word about what Logan is doing with his life. Frankly, I don't care.' She walked up to Angus and pointed a finger straight at his face. Her voice was quiet, but it had a furious tone, 'And if you ever speak to me like that again, so help me God, I will take your daughter, and half of this house, and half of your damn horses if I feel like it.'

Angus was shocked by the ferocious look in her eye, and his rage halted right there. His wife had never spoken to him like that, but he had never pushed her to her limits before. Despite his big ego, he loved Angela more than he loved himself. He was actually obsessed with her, and constantly worried that she would cheat on him.

'Get a grip on yourself, Angus. You are acting like a child.' She turned and headed back upstairs to bed.

Angus sank onto the sofa, feeling entirely defeated. He realised his jealousy was bringing out the ugly side of him and causing a rift in his marriage. He blamed Weston. *I need to crush him once and for all. I'm going to ruin that man*, he thought.

Correct weight was given, and James came back out for the presentation. It was only a maiden, but the local car yard had sponsored the race, and were on hand to present the sash to the winners. Logan, Tom, James, Cynthia, and Miles were all gathered, laughing and beaming with smiles. Two stewards walked over to the group. 'Excuse our interruption,' said one of them. 'Mr Baker, Mr Weston, we request a meeting with you after the last race of the day, to discuss this horse's reversal of form.'

'Is there a problem?' Tom asked, feigning surprise.

'We have been informed that there have been some large wagers won today, so we're required to investigate,' the other steward said.

'Oh, I see. After the last, then,' Tom said casually.

'Thank you. Best of luck in the two-year-old race, Mr Baker.'

'Thank you, gentlemen. We're looking forward to winning another one today.' The stewards gave courteous smiles and quickly left.

Given the King's four-million-dollar plus price tag and his very easy trial win, as well as Everest's astounding win, Warrior King was now 1/10 favourite. No one could remember a first starter ever having such short odds.

Logan legged James on. 'Stay out of trouble, and just do enough to win. There is Group 1 in three weeks if we can hold him together.' James walked him out on the track and, even though the field had some very smart two-year-olds in the race, the King looked superior beside the others. His sire, King's Speech, was a machine of a racehorse and one of the all-time greats; and his dam was one of the fastest mares Australia had ever seen, and ran five furlongs (1,000 m) in 55 seconds.

James worked the King off and he glided like he was floating on air. The crowd was only watching one horse work to the barriers. They loaded, and James felt a coolness come over him. His vision narrowed and the outside sounds disappeared completely. It was just the two of them now, and he was ready. The gates opened and the King jumped clear by a half-length. James took hold and eased him back to fourth on the fence in the field of fourteen. Before he knew it, they were two furlongs out. He snapped out of his tunnel vision when he heard every rider starting to go for their mounts. He hadn't even moved, and when they passed the one-furlong-to-go post, there were still three in front of him.

On the sidelines, Tom screamed, 'What's he doing! Let him go!' With 150 metres to go, Logan couldn't breathe.

James let his grip go. 'Hah! Go, King!' In a split second, the King dropped down and drove forward like a Formula One car racing a sedan. In eight strides, he had them and won by three-quarters of a length. Logan let out a ragged breath and turned to Cynthia and Tom. 'Jesus, that kid nearly killed me.'

They all shook hands and hugged, but this time Cynthia held Logan for a second. 'No slow ones, Logan,' and she planted a kiss on his cheek.

The press swarmed Logan, which made him very uncomfortable, as he wanted Tom to take the interviews. Tom understood the viral video made Logan a great media story. Logan insisted on not making a comment, and said the team's spokesperson, Tom Baker, would field any questions.

After the last race, Logan and Tom sat down for a meeting with the stewards. After thirty minutes, they seemed satisfied that no wrongdoing had taken place. In fact, Logan got the feeling they enjoyed the whole story and also the bookies crying poor for once. Many stewards seemed to think that bookies were just thieves with a licence.

The English Racing Post didn't battle alongside the rest of the media; they didn't approach at the races for an interview at all. They went one better by driving straight to the Baker property and waiting for the team to return home. Cynthia was first back and they approached her politely at the gate. She was on a high, so she invited them in, gave them a tour of the farm and racing set-up, and even did a short interview while they waited for the boys.

Tom, Logan, and James all arrived home together and washed up quickly before their interview. They sat side by side on the couch and presented as a close team, passionate and determined. When the interview was released, it was recognised by many in the public as one of the best racing interviews in many years. Everyone was warmed by the story of the team's success, and the personal triumphs and tragedies of Logan and the Baker family.

Cynthia sent an invite around for a celebratory event at the main house. Miles arrived with the staff in tow, including the two strappers for the King and Everest. Mike was also there to celebrate. The champagne popped and the laughter seemed endless. The stories seemed to get better every time they were told. The fact the stewards saw no reason to pursue their investigation was a huge weight off Logan's shoulders.

After many drinks, Logan found himself in the cellar looking for another bottle of Red. He was enjoying himself so much that Tom said he would cover the morning duties so Logan could have the day off. *Well, if I don't have to get out of bed until noon, I can have another drink, or five,* Logan thought happily.

He heard someone walk into the cellar and he turned to see Cynthia. She quickly cornered him, and when he realised she was as drunk as he was, he felt very awkward. 'So, you and Jo I hear?' Logan crossed his arms defensively. 'What? Can't I ask, Logan? Everyone else talks about it. Apparently Jo's been saying you're the fuck of the century.' Logan had sensed many times that Cynthia was interested, but he knew if he gave her an inch she would take a mile. He was already so intertwined in her family; it wouldn't take much. But he also knew she was still mourning her husband. Sure, she was tough, but in his opinion she wasn't ready for a serious romance just yet. He thought the only way to counter was to be blunt. 'We're fucking, if that's what you're asking.'

'Just fucking?' Cynthia asked, hastily.

'Yes, just two adults fucking,' Logan said casually and his body language closed her off. There was a slight pause and Logan went back to reading the labels on dusty bottles on the shelf.

'So, you're not in love with her then?' Cynthia asked, quietly.

Logan prickled at the question. He turned back around and gave her a firm look. 'Do we have to have this conversation tonight, Cynthia?' Logan was a bit pissed off at Cynthia's line of questioning, and he was drunk enough to be blunt. She was his boss, but he was through with people prying into his personal life for their own interest or gain. He was humiliated when news spread about Angela's affair, and the media just wouldn't let it go, even in the last few days.

'Are you?' Cynthia asked again, wanting to know the answer.

'Just fucking. That's all.'

'So, she's not the one then?'

Logan paused, as this was a dangerous question to be answered. He walked over to her, giving a slight smile. 'I'm not going to move in with her, if that's what you're thinking.' He put his arm up on the sandstone wall behind her head and lent in, speaking softly. 'Besides, I want a woman who drives me wild; who makes every guy jealous; who I think about 24/7. I want someone who can fill my mind, and my heart, and my soul. But until I find that someone, I think it's fair to be able to fuck whoever I want, no strings attached, don't you?'

Cynthia's cheeks started to go a light pink, and she didn't say anything. She felt weak at the knees and lent back against the sandstone wall. That was the answer she had wanted to hear, and it made her want him more. All she wanted to know was that Logan was still looking. She just gave a slight nod, looking away from his gaze.

Logan grabbed a bottle and said, 'Now, let's go back up to the party,' and started to walk back up the stairs. Cynthia lingered for a moment, wondering if she could give Logan everything he wanted, before she followed him up the stairs.

Throughout the night, Logan's phone kept ringing with congratulatory calls. 'Logan speaking.'

'Logan, my boy.' It was Don. They spoke for twenty minutes about the races and the boys, and Logan could hear how proud Don was of their accomplishments.

Finally, Logan said, 'We'll all come back soon to visit you, mate.'

Don chuckled, sensing Logan's homesickness. 'Logan, you're exactly where you're meant to be. I don't want to say too much, but take care of those boys. James is going through a tough time and, well, he'll need your support when the time comes.'

Logan was confused but he said, 'I will, Don. I promise.' Don had to go and they said their goodbyes. Logan looked across the room for James and saw him enjoying himself. He quickly dismissed Don's comment; in his mind, James was flying along just fine.

Logan's phone rang again. 'Logan speaking.'

'I know that, you dumb gobshite.' It was Mick. 'I just dialled your feckin' number, so I know it's gonna be you, ya twat.'

'How'd you get on?' Logan said smugly.

'Look, mate, I'm on the way to the hospital.'

'What? What happened?' Logan asked, concerned.

'I tore the hole out of four bookmakers, so I'm visiting them in hospital to give them all a box of tampons for their rings.' His cackling laughter didn't stop for a good minute. 'You're a good man. You're a cabbage, but you're a good man. Anyway, I'll call you in the morning. I've got a solid stayer that's for sale in the U.S. Might win you that Melbourne Cup.'

'Do you ever stop selling?' Logan asked.

'I'd sell you, if I could get more than a bitch price for ya.' Mick cackled again and hung up. Logan never managed to get the last word in.

As he walked back over to speak to the boys, Mike grabbed him by the arm. He was smashed. This concerned Logan, as in the short time he had known Mike he had gone from hardly drinking to getting hammered on many occasions. Mike slurred in a terrible Australian accent, 'G'day, mate! You're a right beauty, mate!'

The last thing Logan wanted was a drunk hanging off him pretending to be Aussie. Logan turned him around and sat him down on the nearest chair. 'G'day, Mike. I think you've had a bit too much to drink, mate.' Logan took the glass of red wine from Mike's hand.

'Aw, don't,' Mike moaned. 'Who are you, my wife?' Mike looked sad and suddenly got quiet. 'She hates me. All I've done, and she hates me.'

Logan wasn't in the mood for a pity party. Sophie was sitting nearby, and Logan said to her, 'Can you keep an eye on him while I get him a coffee?'

Sophie was pretty full as well and she leant over to hear Mike's sob story.

Logan headed over to the kitchen to make Mike a strong coffee. Tom put his arm around Logan as he walked by, and hooked James on his other arm. 'We did it, boys! Woo hoo!' he yelled out. Everyone around him echoed back the 'Woo hoo!' and raised their glasses.

Logan slipped away to put the kettle on. As he waited for it to boil, he watched everyone still celebrating. He looked down at his phone, flicking through his messages. He had invited Jo to the party but hadn't heard back from her all day. *Could Cynthia have said something?* he thought, remembering their strange encounter in the cellar earlier in the night.

He quickly made a coffee and walked back to put it in Mike's hand, who was being comforted by a very confused drunk Sophie. He headed out the back door for some fresh air and decided to call it a night. He was happy they won, but he wasn't a partygoer and his mind was still racing. *Is Jo just a fuck? We get on great, but it's not like we've gone out on a date since we met at the bar. How do you tell if you love someone, how do know if you don't love them?* he thought. Logan had enough to drink and he was confusing his thoughts. *I do really like Cynthia, but she's my boss. And it just doesn't feel the same as when I first met Angela. But everything has changed since then.*

He walked in his front door and Hank was asleep on the couch. He roused when Logan gave him a pet, but he was just too comfortable to get up. Logan drank two glasses of water, popped three painkillers, had a mouthful of green grapes, and walked to his room. He was buggered. When he turned on the light, he was startled. 'Jo?'

Jo was laying on his bed naked and with her legs in a very inviting position. 'I've been waiting for over an hour for you to come home, Logan.'

He leaned on the oak doorway arch, liking what he saw. 'You missed the party,' Logan joked. 'There was champagne.'

Logan felt that they were matched well sexually. They had only slept together seven times, but both their appetites for passionate, satisfying sex were identical. As with all sexual partners, you gradually get more comfortable and trusting, and Jo was ready to skip a few levels.

'What a shame. Champagne makes me so horny,' Jo purred. She gave him a shamelessly lusting gaze. 'I dropped in for a shag, if you're not too tired.'

He laughed, undoing his winning tie that he was still wearing from the races. 'It would be my pleasure.' He walked over to the bed, taking off his shirt, then his slacks and boxer shorts. As he approached, Jo opened her legs and he knew exactly where to begin. Logan delivered the third winner for the day. Afterwards, Jo grabbed him firmly by the hair and urged him up 'Shag me baby,' she smiled. 'C'mon cowboy, shag me.' He was surprised at how quickly she had recovered, and he was glad there was a lot more on the table that night.

Champagne may be an aphrodisiac, but Logan found red wine could certainly delay an orgasm. Jo certainly didn't mind, and Logan added three more winners to the day's score before he got one for himself.

Logan lay beside Jo, looking up at the ceiling, and caught his breath. *What a day*, he thought, shaking his head in disbelief.

CHAPTER 16

Logan's body clock woke him up at 5 a.m. The only thing covering him was a twisted sheet, and Logan shivered in the cool morning air. His head wasn't too bad, but he had some slight pain down below. The night had been sensational, but he was sore and red. Blurry eyed, he got up and pulled the sheet over Jo, who was still asleep, and picked the doona up off the floor to cover her.

He showered, got dressed, and went to the kitchen to make coffee. Jo had been on call all week, she had said, and had a terrible run of call-outs after full workdays. He decided he had the day off, and she did as well, so if she wanted to sleep that was fine by him. The questions Cynthia had asked had been bugging him. He liked Jo. She was easy to be around and there was a great chemistry between them. *But is she the one?* He couldn't put his finger on one bad thing about Jo, but he knew she didn't bowl him over like he wanted to be. He quickly snapped out of it, as she hadn't asked for one thing more than what they were doing now. *Don't rock the boat. If it isn't broken, don't fix it*, Logan thought.

After he finished his coffee, he quietly slipped outside. As he opened the door, Hank raced out and over to the spelling paddock—his favourite place to poo. Logan started walking over to the stables, even though he knew Tom would have everything fully under control. He guessed they would only ride two, and the rest would have an easy Sunday off. When Logan spotted Mike's car out the front of the barn, he quickened his step. *Why is Mike looking at the horses so early this morning? Maybe something has happened.* The thought made Logan pick up the pace, and he jogged the rest of the way.

Logan rushed into the barn and headed straight for Warrior King's stable, looking around for Tom or Mike. 'What is it? What's happened?' he said as soon as he spotted Tom, who looked baffled. 'Is it the King?'

'What?' Tom said.

'Or Everest?' Logan said, sidestepping Tom and heading for the Everest stable.

'Logan, nothing has happened. Both colts are out in their yards for the day in the sunshine like we spoke about last night.' Logan stopped and turned around, and Tom looked at him carefully. 'Did you have a bad dream or something?'

Logan shook his head, still confused and looking around for Mike. 'Well, why is Mike's car out front?'

The amused look on Tom's face disappeared, and he turned back to what he was doing. 'I drove it down from the main house this morning, so he could, well, make a quiet getaway later.' He signalled with his head to the upstairs living quarters, where Sophie and Mary lived. Mary was the next in charge to the foreman, fifty-two years old, and lived for only one thing; and that was work. Sophie was Everest's strapper, twenty-two and attractive, and a good work rider, but that was about as far as she intended to progress up the ladder.

Logan had calmed down and it finally clicked. 'Are you serious?' Tom nodded but didn't say a word. 'The bloody dickhead! Jesus, we don't need this! We can't have this bullshit interfering with our plans, or him getting distracted. Tom, we need a new vet.'

Tom replied, 'You're being a bit harsh, don't you think?'

'He stuck his dick where it didn't belong! Now what? She'll fall in love with him and he'll get all gushy over getting affection for the first time in ages. He's a well-off bloke, so who knows what Sophie wants out of it. Maybe a meal ticket and the chance to be with a vet. His wife is already at the end of her tether with him. Can you imagine how this will go down? She's been running herself ragged raising his five boys, and he goes and fucks a twenty-two-year-old. She'll throw him out, and he'll be living here with Sophie, and he'll slowly lose everything—wife, kids, house, car. He'll have child maintenance to pay. He could even lose his clients over this.'

When it sounded like Logan had finally finished, Tom said, 'Jesus mate, sounds like you've seen this before.'

'At least three times over the years. My dad's best mate lost his practice, over what? Temptation.' Logan paused for a moment. 'He gets one chance, Tom. One fuck up and he's gone. We have two very, very good horses here, and there is no room for error.'

Tom thought about it for a moment and finally nodded. 'Okay, but I think we should try to at least get him some help.'

Logan sighed. 'Fine. That silly, reckless bastard.' They walked the rest of the barn, talking about finding someone for Mike to talk to. He was a great guy, but they had seen him getting worse over the last few weeks. He had started drinking more and more, and not going home as early. His mistake, if you can call it that, could impact his life and his family for a long time to come if he wasn't careful.

Finally, Tom said very cheekily, 'Know any good vets?'

Logan laughed. 'Don't go there, Tom. Don't go there.'

Logan's phone rang, showing an Australian number Logan didn't recognise. 'Logan Weston speaking.'

'Logan, Darcy Brooks.' Logan was surprised. He knew Darcy. His father was MJ and owner of the biggest and best thoroughbred farm in Australia. They stood King's Speech. Darcy was a trainer and had won Group 1s in three different countries. He also had access to some of the best bloodlines in Australia. 'Great win yesterday, mate.'

'Thanks, Darcy.' Logan had never received a call from Darcy before and was surprised when he actually said abruptly, 'What can I do for you, mate?'

'Well, that's the reason for the call, Logan. We were blown away with Warrior King's performance, and, well, how would you feel about selling the standing rights? Or, even better, fifty per cent?' Logan was quiet, formulating the correct response. Before he could reply, Darcy added, 'Written guarantee the horse stays with you, of course.'

Logan's eyebrows rose, and he added this extra factor into his response. 'Darcy, I appreciate the call, but I'm just an employee now. I'll have to talk to the owners, the Bakers, before making a decision like that.'

'Logan, we know you're at the helm of that ship. You retrained Everest and selected Warrior King, and I also know that it was you who made My Blue Boy into a champion. Give yourself some credit, mate.'

It was a very nice compliment, but Logan replied, 'I'm sure you can understand why I'm hesitant, Darcy.'

'Look, mate, I'm no Angus Masters. The guy's an asshole, if you ask me—or anyone else.'

Logan had heard about the $250,000 dispute from Pete. Masters claimed that the Brooks family had sold him a yearling with medical issues. Most yearlings are sold with X-rays of twenty-four to twenty-six joint shots, to give the buyers a chance to see possible soundness issues. Many horses overcome X-ray issues, as most times it is the vets who fail them. Masters bought the colt out of the ring without a prior inspection. He put a bid in knowingly and without getting him vetted and got the colt at $250,000. Only then did he review the copy of the X-rays and baulked at the medium risk issues on the report. He was lazy and overly ambitious with the sale, and it bit him in the ass. With the medium to high-risk X-ray report, it made the yearling much harder to sell and find owners with the high price. Many had proven to be great horses with bad X-rays but Masters had now changed his mind. So, he turned around and blamed the Brooks family. So they took the horse back off him and put it into work. Darcy won three straight with the colt in the city. Then an offer came in and he was sold to Singapore for $650,000.

Darcy continued, 'We're not trying to screw you around, Logan, we just want in. He's only won one race, but the old boy King's Speech has only got one more breeding season in him, if we're lucky. If you can win a Group 1 over there and back here, then we have it made.'

Darcy and MJ Brooks had been very good to Logan over the years. They had never given him a horse to train, but they always showed the yearlings willingly to him at any sale, and showed a respect to the little battling guy. Many stud farms snubbed buyers with low budgets, but Darcy and MJ always showed whatever horse Logan wanted to see.

'Thank you, Darcy. I'll speak with the team and get back to you as soon as possible with an answer.'

'Oh, and just one more thing ... No agents. Especially that Irish bastard. He overcharges me every time.'

'Sure thing. Bye.' Logan laughed after he hung up. He knew Mick was one of the best, but he wasn't scared to charge for his time. You could spend three million dollars, but he would charge the twenty-eight-dollar currency exchange fee to the bill.

Logan got Tom, and they headed up to the main house. Cynthia had stayed the night, as she had too much to drink. She was standing in the kitchen holding her aching head. Beside her half-made cup of coffee was a packet of painkillers. Tom kissed her on the head and she groaned. 'Good morning!' Tom laughed, and they spoke about the party for a while. When there was a pause in the conversation, Logan got down to business. He explained the offer and talked them both through a few different scenarios.

Cynthia changed to business mode. 'This is a business as much as it is a hobby. I certainly see more going out than coming in. I know that was never the case at the start, but we have a colt that you,' she pointed at Tom and Logan, 'paid 4.1 million for, and we won over three million on the punt yesterday. If I have the possibility of getting five-million-plus for fifty per cent and still full control, it would be a smart decision, I think. Besides, we won't ever stand stallions.'

Both Logan and Tom nodded in agreement, since they knew the breeding game was harder than training.

'What's a good price, Logan?' asked Tom.

'I'd go for five million for fifty per cent, and an additional 2.5 million for each Group 1 win. Remember, we would still own the other fifty per cent. We win three Group 1's, that's an extra 7.5 mil, plus prize money. It's win-win.'

'Do the deal, Logan,' Cynthia said, having slumped into a chair, still holding her head.

Logan nodded and added, 'I would also recommend that Tom takes this one. This is his team, and your business, so he should learn to seal a deal.' If any deals were going to be struck, he knew it had to be done by Tom and Cynthia.

The deal took two days, but they finally agreed on the terms of the sale of Warrior King.

Tom was very excited to tell Logan the deal also included a lifetime breeding right for Logan. This happened a lot in Australia; trainers got one free service per year, and sometimes it was a very fruitful payday. Warrior King's sire, King's Speech, had stood for $330,000 per service and could mate four mares per day at one stage in his prime. If it all turned into a fairy tale, Logan would have money coming out his ears, as he also got a percentage of the selling price of any colts sold. He now had a bank balance beyond anything he'd ever dreamt of. Logan would have been lucky to spend £200 per week on living expenses. Money was there to be enjoyed, and though he never wasted it, if he wanted something, now for the very first time, he could just buy it. He had deposited a cheque for £660,000, courtesy of Everest.

The deal would be finalised when Darcy arrived and did his inspection with a vet of his choice. The good news was, he was already on his way over. The team was extremely excited.

Back in Australia, Moodie was at it again in the trainers' hut; back to his old tricks of stirring up shit. As Masters climbed the stairs, Moodie pushed play on the TV, re-watching the recording of the win by Everest for the racing archives. Masters was still pissed off from watching the race live days earlier. Fuming, he took up his spot on the far side of the tower. He turned his head and looked at his track work pad and pretended to focus his binoculars on a horse working. Masters still had a few friends in the hut, but the majority had been burned by him before, so they were happy to play along with Moodie's jab at him.

Moodie spoke loudly to another trainer. 'Over four million they won on the punt! And, just quietly, Logan rang me personally to tip me in and I won thirty-five thousand. Well, apparently, they worked him on cattle for two weeks in Scone before he departed. That seemed to get his head right, by the look of his last win. You know how you can tell a top trainer? A truly amazing trainer? Dedication to horses. Getting the best out of them. It's just amazing how Logan could improve a supposed off-cast, in under six weeks too! Yeah, it sure will be interesting now he has an open chequebook. I wonder how many more winners he'll train! The owner has already made over eight million dollars since he started. Now word is Darcy Brooks and MJ have bought fifty per cent of the superstar, King's Speech colt, which Logan bought for 4.1 million. Logan will need security guards soon, with all the money he's making. You know, I always liked him. He's a good bloke. He deserves it.' Moodie decided he had rubbed the salt in enough, and he looked over his shoulder at Masters, to make sure he wasn't barrelling across the trainers' hut for a fight, before he got back to work.

Masters was furious that Logan was now being supported by the biggest and best breeders in Australia. Masters had MJ as a client years ago, but he had screwed him on the sale of a colt to Hong Kong, when he pocketed an extra $150,000 right from under MJ's nose. With the latest argument over X-ray issues, MJ had him blacklisted.

Masters only lasted another ten minutes before he returned to the stables. He'd had enough of Moodie's loud mouth and the gossiping trainers in the hut. His staff were on high alert and were not surprised when he exploded for three tiny flakes of mud poultices that hadn't been washed off a two-year-old colt's front shins. He pulled up the strapper and ridiculed her in front of all the employees in the barn. 'Do you understand how a hose works? You turn the hose on, you aim the water at the mud, you rub your hand on the horse's leg. It's not fucking hard!' Masters angrily swiped at the mud on the horse and it jumped. 'You can't even hold the fucking horses still,' he yelled at her. 'Was I that fucking desperate for staff when I hired *you*?'

The strapper had tears running down her face, and Masters rolled his eyes at her. He turned and walked away, kicking a feed bucket and splitting its side.

CHAPTER 17

Cynthia sent her driver to pick up Darcy from the airport. Darcy had arranged with the Thomas and Associates Vet Practice for their top soundness vet to inspect and X-ray, scope, and trot up, plus watch the colt work. For five million of the fifty per cent sale, they wanted to be thorough.

Darcy arrived shortly after 9.30 a.m., and Logan greeted him with a firm handshake. They spoke briefly about the trip and Logan was happy to have a fellow Aussie present. They immediately felt closer, being two Scone country boys in an environment that was vastly different from back home, and it made them feel closer than they would have if they were back in Australia. Darcy had flown business class and had slept most of the way, so he wasn't feeling too jetlagged.

They went inside the main house, and Logan introduced Darcy to Cynthia and Tom. Cynthia wanted to meet Darcy to make sure they would get along, as it was a big deal taking on a partner, but she knew MJ had made more successful stallions than most.

'When does your vet arrive?' Logan said, looking at his watch.
'Ten o'clock.'

'Let's all head down to the stables, shall we,' Cynthia said,
taking the lead.

As they walked to the stables, a black Audi pulled up and
Jo stepped out. She had dressed up a bit more than normal, and
looked smart in a dress shirt, vest and tailored well-fitting jeans. She
greeted everyone and introduced herself to Darcy, taking him aside
to have a quiet talk. Cynthia whispered to Logan, 'who did she
dress up for Logan? He is rich and younger than you.' Logan shot a
glare and shook his head, and Cynthia put her hands up in defence.

Darcy was delighted when he inspected the King and was
shaking his head in awe of the colt's substance and strength. The
King had a huge overstep in his walk, like most champions. Logan
and Tom gave Jo and Darcy space to do a thorough vetting. After
twenty minutes, they had wrapped up and were ready to see some
track work. 'I'm happy just to see a trot and canter,' Darcy said.

Logan nodded and prepped the King, while Tom took Jo
and Darcy to the tower to watch. Logan rode the lead pony and
the best work rider rode the King. They trotted two laps of the
sand warm-up, which was a good mile and a quarter. 'We'll work
off from the mile and do three-quarter from the three-furlong
mark. Let him dash up the last furlong. He needs the fitness work
anyway.' Logan's lead pony was a ten-year-old ex-racehorse who
had won £300,000, so he was no slouch. They worked side by side,
and the old lead pony was loving it. Tom knew they were going
to work, and he stepped back to watch Darcy carefully, who was
filming the colt on his phone. In three strides, the King dropped
Logan and his trusty steed, and scorched the grass. Darcy watched
through his phone, glancing at the numbers ticking over as it

recorded. Tom realised he was counting. The King was hard held and still ran a scorching 10.2 seconds for his last furlong. Darcy turned, and hadn't noticed Tom watching him. He was shaking his head, with a big smile on his face. 'That's incredible!' He walked over and shook Tom's hand. 'Bugger what the vet thinks, I'm in.'

Logan and The King arrived back at the base of the track work tower. Darcy gave the colt the biggest rub on the head and looked him in the eye. 'So, this is what an English champion looks like.'

Tom texted his mother: 'Deal is done. He's on board.'

She replied: 'Good Lord, let's all go out to lunch to celebrate.' Cynthia had talked herself into a negative state of mind that the deal would fall through.

Logan was a bit surprised that Darcy approved the deal without Jo's final opinion, as she still had to closely view the X-rays, but she didn't make any objections. Darcy walked Jo to her car and they talked for a good 30 minutes, which Logan found odd. Logan could see they were making fast friends by their body language. He wasn't jealous, or maybe he was. Darcy was a strapping young guy—but that's what he was, young. He was twenty-eight and she was in her early-forties. Finally, they shook hands and Jo drove away.

Tom, Darcy, Logan, and Cynthia all headed out to lunch together. Darcy Skyped MJ over lunch so he could join in on the celebrations. Darcy had sent him the track work film on the way and he was equally impressed. Logan and Tom talked training methods and future plans with Darcy, and he was eager to see what else the King was capable of.

Cynthia caught Logan on his way back from the restroom and had a quiet word with him at the bar. 'Blinding result Logan, you well and truly aced this one.'

'One day I might get the way you Brits speak,' Logan said back, as he was not up on the term *blinding*.

'Our lives have turned the corner since you agreed to come on board; my boys have not been this happy for a long time.'

'They're good kids—sorry, *great* kids. Two very honest and smart young men.'

'Logan, you really look out for us. I just want to make sure you know I appreciate that very much.' Cynthia placed her hand on his forearm gently. 'I really mean it, Logan.' Logan looked into her eyes and could see her words were sincere. Logan felt like he was more than just an employee, like he was a close part of Cynthia's family, but he wasn't sure if he wanted to get too close.

Lunch finished and they all shook hands again before they went their separate ways. When Logan and Tom arrived back at the property, they checked the horses and went through the daily afternoon trot ups to survey each horse. Both Tom and Logan were excited, as two fillies they had bought in the farm package were showing huge potential and both look like Oaks fillies.

Logan texted Darcy and asked if he wanted to catch up for dinner, but Darcy said he was having dinner with a client before he headed home on a red-eye flight from Heathrow. *Shame*, Logan thought, *it would have been nice to talk shop with an Aussie for a change*.

Later that night, Jo dropped in for a visit. She had texted Logan after 11 p.m. to see if he was free. Logan opened the door. 'You look very nice,' he said.

'Thank you, I have been out to dinner,' she replied. Logan found it hard, but he didn't ask any more details. Besides, they weren't exclusive or in a relationship, so it would only make their arrangement awkward.

Jo put her arms around Logan's neck. 'Fancy a late-night shag?' Logan quickly realised that it felt different. It was still as passionate, but Jo held him tighter, kissed him longer, and caressed him slower. They made love—not just fucking this time—for longer than ever before. Jo told him straight out many times she had never had sex like it, and Logan would say it was some of the best sex he'd ever had, too. Once they had finished, she lay in his arms instead of dashing off to the bathroom. He kissed her head gently. 'You alright?' he asked.

'I'm actually really good.' She rolled over and propped herself up on one elbow. 'I got a job offer today … Big money, new car, my own house, and only thirty-five horses to care for.'

'Wow, that's great. It sounds like Mike's job.' Logan laughed. 'So where is it?'

'A placed called Scone,' she answered, and there was silence as the penny dropped.

'Dinner,' he said quietly. 'With Darcy?'

She nodded, and Logan could feel the distance between them already. Jo said quietly, 'I leave Friday.'

The mood turned, and Logan felt suddenly awkward. 'That's … quick.' Jo nodded as she felt she had just betrayed Logan. 'I don't do sad goodbyes,' he joked. 'I really wish you the best, Jo. I know you will love my home town.' She smiled, and they hugged. She gave him a final kiss before she got dressed and left. Logan knew he would miss the sensational sex, and it felt like a chapter of his new life was closing. The news was still a massive blindside but he didn't mention it again.

Logan lay in bed and reflected on the women in his life. Sam—his first love, first kiss, and first sex. Twelve other girls while he travelled as a young man during his first time away from home.

Then there was Angela—his true love. *She was the one*, he thought. But he felt different now. Her actions over the last two years, and especially her public comments recently, had dulled the feelings he still kept close to his heart. Everyone's true colours eventually come out and reveal themselves. Did she actually change, or was Logan now seeing what everyone else saw all along? He had never asked his friends what they thought of her. If he asked Pete or Neale now, they wouldn't have a nice word to say about her, after all the pain he had gone through.

Who is the perfect woman? Had he met her yet? How did he really feel about his boss? Cynthia was attractive in many ways. She was smart, driven, tough, confident, powerful, kind, and a fiercely loyal and loving mother. Logan wondered if maybe it was fate that had brought them together. *I'm exactly where I'm meant to be,* he thought, remembering what Don had said to him. For the first time in his life, he was not under one bit of pressure. Just him and a bank balance now pushing over the one-million mark, the best horses and set-up money could buy, and he felt like he really belonged there.

Logan rose at 5 a.m. with a clear head and not a worry in the world, apart from the horses. He headed to the stables with Hank beside him and met Tom on the walk down. 'You got cuckold old boy,' said Tom, trying to break the tension.

'That sly dog. I could see he was infatuated with her,' Tom said.

'They had dinner together last night,' said Logan. 'He brushed me off for her.'

'But does he have the moves like you?' Tom laughed, but continued 'He's a younger, better looking, richer Group 1-winning trainer.'

'You finished?' Logan lashed back.

'He had a lot smaller feet than you,' Tom laughed.

Logan laughed and gave Tom a playful shove. Hank thought he could join in and grabbed the leg of Tom's jeans and tugged on it, giving a playful growl.

Tom and Logan were surprised to see Mike's car parked at the barn. Logan instantly got concerned. 'If he's screwing around again, he is done.' They both walked into the barn and the lights were already on. Normally Logan was always the first there and turned them on in the morning. Mike walked out of the King's stable. 'Morning, lads,' Mike said. They both looked a bit puzzled, and Logan was frowning. Many horses get banned substances given to them by crooked staff, or vets even in some cases. He instantly went on the back foot, putting his hands up like he surrendered. 'I'm just here doing my checks. I know that I've let you guys down the past few weeks. I'm part of this team and I want to be here as much as you guys.'

As Mike explained, he had stopped his world crashing down on him, not by running and hiding, but by arranging a retreat with his wife. They arranged for a family member to babysit the boys, and they flew to stay in a remote cabin in an area well known for camping, fishing, and hunting. They had two days alone together to work things out. His wife admitted to having a brief affair with their son's rugby coach the year before, at a time when things were heading south in their marriage. Her unbearable guilt made her focus on the boys and push away from Mike, as she couldn't bear to tell him what she had done. Mike told her what had happened with Sophie, and eventually they agreed that they should see a marriage counsellor. It was tough, but they were giving it another shot. They were booked twice a week now, and actually planning on having weekends away with no kids every so often, to stay in sync with each other's needs.

Tom and Logan were relieved. 'How are the horses?'

'I just checked their shins and legs for any soreness and heat.'

'And?' Logan prompted.

'The King's legs feel great. He flexes very well.' Mike went through and took all the horses' temperatures, felt legs, and flexed a few joints. When Charlie got in at 6 a.m., he trotted up a couple for Mike to check soundness. Mike scoped three fillies that seemed to be getting snotty noses. He said he would scope them after work as well, and pull some bloods. Tom and Logan liked what they saw. Mike's slip up may have been a blessing in disguise, as he seemed back to being focused on his work.

Logan and Tom waited in the watch tower, waiting for the first work riders and their horses. 'You date much, Tom?' Logan asked.

'Since father died, I haven't really felt like it,' Tom replied. 'Mother might be tough on the outside, but I've heard her crying in her room for months. It's hard. We were all so close. I don't think I'm ready to let someone new in just yet.'

Logan nodded. 'And James?'

'He dated for two years, and they broke up two years ago. She broke his heart, and he hasn't had a date since, as far as I know.' There was a pause, and Tom realised the conversation was maybe more about Logan. He asked, 'You okay with Jo leaving?'

Logan shrugged. 'I'm fine. It was just sex, that's all. We got on great, but it was just a sundown to sunup thing, nothing more than that.'

The first horse arrived, and Tom gave the exercise orders. Miss Jasmine, a filly they purchased in the package, was showing huge promise. 'This filly goes very well,' said Tom. 'I think we better get Miles to start looking for a race. She could be group class.'

Logan winked at him. 'Good call.'

Forest Black galloped, and James was on board and with a smile from ear to ear. As he rode back to the stables, he called to Tom and Logan, 'This horse is ready. He is fit. Let's get him to the races. I feel like riding another winner!'

Logan and Tom had taught James about what feedback they needed to fine-tune the horse, and Logan felt that he had become a very reliable judge. He always gave them a clear idea of how the horses were really going.

At 9.30 a.m., Logan walked into the office to go over the morning's gallop and times, as Miles entered them into the system. Logan's phone rang while he was in the bathroom. It was Mick. Not wanting to let it ring out, Miles answered. 'Good morning,' he sang into the phone.

'Convict?' Mick said, slightly confused.

'Oh, playing that game, are we? Well, how about I put you in a stockade and paddle that lovely ass with a bat. I hear you like that, pretty boy,' joked Miles.

Mick didn't miss a beat. 'And I heard you like to sit down to take a piss, Miss,' Mick fired back.

'Oh, honey, I can't! It takes two hands to hold my hose. Ask your brother. And while you're at it, tell him to stop calling me.'

Mick was still cackling down the line when Logan walked back in. Miles handed him the phone. 'It's your boyfriend.'

'Hello?' Logan said into the phone.

'Convict,' Mick said, still snickering. 'I like that one.' Logan looked at Miles, who had gone back to work, wondering what he'd said. 'Look, I have two at Saratoga in the U.S. you need to look at. Both stayers and have European pedigrees, but they are racing them on dirt. Stupid Yanks will never learn.'

'I'll talk to Cynthia and see if she's interested in them.'

'She any good?'

Logan was a bit puzzled. 'Who?'

'Ya boss. Ya riding her yet?'

'Pull your head in, mate. She's a lady and a nice person.'

Mick knew he had pushed it too far. 'Got carried away. Sorry.' That was something you hardly ever heard from his mouth, so Logan knew he meant it. 'They are both worth the look.'

Logan smiled. *He always has to have the last shot.* Logan managed to get in, 'I'll let you know.'

But, for once, Mick didn't have the last shot. He said, 'Bye, bye, bye,' like a little kid ending a call with his grandmother. Logan laughed, as for an instant no BS came out of his mouth.

At breakfast, Logan discussed the horses and watched the videos of their races with Tom, Cynthia, James, and Miles. Miles ran pedigrees and performance, putting together stats on their sires in the U.S. and England, and turf versus dirt. 'They are worth a look,' he said. Miles was a pedigree buff and statistics genius. When it came to research, Logan had never known anyone to be so quick and thorough. 'One of them is entered in a 2,000-metre dirt race this weekend.'

'If we book a flight, you and James could go today and be back by Tuesday,' Cynthia said. 'Warrior King and Forest Black are in next Saturday.'

Logan looked at Tom. 'Your call. Are you okay with us being away leading up to your first Group 1 race?'

Before Tom could reply, Miles looked up from his screen and said, 'Don't worry. I'll hold Tom's hand for you.'

Logan supressed a laugh as he said, 'In that case, I think we're going, James.' Miles reached across the table and gently squeezed Tom's hand, and they all burst out laughing.

'I will get my PA to book you boys a flight to New York,' Cynthia said, starting to type away on her phone.

'Do you need me to babysit Hank?' Miles asked Logan.

'Actually, that would be great, thanks,' Logan said.

'Do you have silk sheets—in case I get lucky?'

Logan and Tom shook their heads, and Logan said, 'Just please don't traumatise my dog.'

'Actually, he might be perfect for picking up hot guys at the dog park,' Miles mused, lost in his thoughts, as everyone dispersed.

Tom and Logan walked through the barn and talked about every horse. Everest was jumping out of his skin. They had entered him in a mid-week ten-furlong race the following week; it seemed like a weak field and good placement. 'If he works well tomorrow, and I mean works super, then maybe we try the ten-furlong next Saturday,' Tom said. Logan knew it would be tougher opposition on the Saturday, but he felt the horses were easy Saturday class.

Logan nodded. 'I had that in the back of my mind as well. He's doing really well and may need the racing more than training.'

'I've found a lovely old gentleman who has 1,500 acres about thirty miles away with cattle. I might throw Everest and Forest Black on the truck and take them over next Wednesday, then Friday again for an hour or so each time to freshen their heads up.'

Logan loved the idea, and it showed him that Tom was always thinking ahead. He winked at Tom. 'Sounds good to me.' Tom knew he had done well.

Logan and James had to pack and get everything ready before their flight. James made sure he packed his gym gear; since he wouldn't be riding each day, he would have to work harder at the gym instead. The plan was for James to ride each horse; just a trot and canter, on Friday morning, then fly home on Monday night. Logan was keen to go to the races at Saratoga over the weekend, as he always said, 'You can never stop learning.'

Logan was happy Miles was staying at his house, as he hated Hank being at home alone, even though the staff would have dropped in to feed him. After all, Hank was Logan's closest mate.

There was a knock at the door. Logan gathered it was Tom finalising their plans before they left. 'Come in, I just need one sec.' Logan walked out of the bathroom with a towel around his waist and was surprised to see Cynthia. 'Oh, shit, sorry, I'll grab some clothes.'

'I won't stay long,' she said, staying in the doorway. Logan thought her admiring gaze was too obvious, and he'd noticed her looking at him many times before.

Logan quickly turned and ducked into his room. 'One sec.' He liked Cynthia, and she was easy enough on the eye, he just didn't know the risk was worth the reward. Besides, he was living the dream and didn't want to change a thing. *One wrong move and you could be out on your ass in a second,* he reminded himself.

He quickly got dressed and walked back out. 'Sorry about that, I thought it was Tom. What's up?'

He could tell by her body language it was something difficult for her to say. She was fidgeting with her hands and couldn't quite get the words out smoothly. 'When you get back, maybe we could—one night—possibly … do dinner. Yes, go out—to dinner. If you would like to, that is.' Logan didn't know what to say and he was silent for a moment. Cynthia quickly added, 'If you don't want to, I understand. I'm your boss—the boys' mother and—yes. Okay, well, I better leave you to it.'

Logan replied, 'Sorry, all I'm focused on right now is sorting out Saratoga and next Saturday, then … we'll see.' He felt shit about fobbing her off. He needed to save her pride. 'You have me scared to buy a "slow one" so I'm trying to stay focused'. He felt he'd levelled the playing field again.

She nodded slowly, averting her eyes. 'That's fine,' she said. 'Safe trip.'

Cynthia quickly turned and walked out, shutting the door behind her. Logan wandered over to the window and watched her walk back up to the main house. She didn't turn her head once to look out over the garden or the horses, like she usually did.

Hmm, she said fine, that's a bad sign, he thought.

CHAPTER 18

Logan and James arrived and checked into their very flash Airbnb house for the weekend. It was a well-kept home, with eight bedrooms, and was walking distance to the track. That was the reason it was chosen. It was spectacular in its grandeur. Logan was gobsmacked at the rooms they had; no expense had been spared.

The plan was to meet the trainer at 5.30 a.m. at the track the next morning so James could work both horses. Even though they flew business class, they were both a bit stuffed from the flight, so they went to their rooms to get settled. Logan felt like he had been going a hundred miles an hour from the day he arrived at Cynthia's door; even though he had help, his mind never stopped. He thought of their trip as a perfect chance to relax and take some time off. The bed was very comfy, and there was a collection of movies. Meanwhile, James quickly unpacked, then went for a run. He then found a gym nearby and hit it hard, as he was going to have to work harder than ever to keep his weight down this week, as Forest Black would get a very light weight.

Cynthia was on Logan's mind, and she had been the whole flight. *What if it works out?* he thought. She had everything he would ever want. He wasn't being shallow, just realistic. She had more money than they'd both ever need, and that was the main downfall of his last major relationship. He only had $27 to his name when Masters swooped in and took Angela away, with promises of an easy life. When she walked, Logan didn't try to fight for her. She didn't even move out to be by herself for a while. When most couples split, they live separately, communicate, and many retry. Not Angela, she moved straight from their home together into Masters' house. Within two days, she had an X5 BMW, new designer clothes, new hair; she named it, Masters bought it for her. Logan, in the meantime, had been left with $228,000 in bills. But he knew he would get there one day. After a while, he realised that he had made some stupid decisions that led to his situation, including going into huge amounts of debt to purchase My Blue Boy and other yearlings on spec that year. But he would do it all again to get a champion.

Now he had a woman chasing him with a bank balance so big he could get any horse in the world. On paper and pedigree, Cynthia was the perfect partner. If she were a horse, Logan would have rated her extremely high, but he'd never been in this type of league with horses or women. He felt like a fish out of water.

Ding! It was a text on his phone from Cynthia: 'You get there okay? x CB.'

'Aw, man,' Logan said to himself. He flicked his phone up and it landed back down on the bed. *I have no clue what to reply. The message is fine, but the kiss symbol? That's putting me in a weird position,* he thought. Finally, he replied: 'All good. Going to bed early, feeling off from the flight.'

Cynthia replied: 'Oh dear, hope you feel better. Talk soon! x CB.'

He showered and stretched out on the luxuriously soft bed to watch TV. He ordered an exquisite home-cooked meal delivered, while poor James was probably having steamed veggies and water—he couldn't afford to indulge and put on weight.

Angus Masters had been on the phone, booking a trip to Newmarket for the Tattersalls December sale. He had arranged a group of owners to go and buy stayers for the Melbourne Cup. He had told his foreman privately on the phone afterwards that he had secured the group to fund his spending spree. Angela overheard him bragging that he was going to outbid Logan on every horse he bid on at the sale in the coming weeks. She confronted him and told him how ridiculous it was, which instantly sent him into a rage. Angus accused her of being on Logan's side. In his anger, he snarled, 'Don't forget, you were *broke* when I met you! I took you in and gave you everything you have. You were just a loser like him until I came along.'

His words cut her to the bone. He was right. She had nothing, but since then she had made a home for them, and they had a beautiful baby girl together. This side of Angus terrified Angela, and she worried one day he would finally snap. She hoped her method of not copping his shit would work, and she threw him out of the house. He stayed at a nearby hotel for the night and, by the apologetic text messages he was sending her, finally started to calm down.

Logan may have been in Saratoga, but Tom gave him minute-by-minute updates about the morning's work. Everest worked super, and Tom and Miles agreed he would race next Saturday in the ten-furlong. Forest Black worked even better, and it was the surprise of the morning. He seemed to have finally overcome his field shyness and was now loving people's attention. He had gained forty-two kilograms, and was going to race at 522 kg, and that was a serious horse weight. They aimed at a seven-furlong race first-up for him. Tom texted Logan to let him know that, based on the morning's work, he rated Forest better than Everest.

Tom was very surprised with Miles's abilities. He was an excellent horseman. The horses were drawn to him, much like they were to Logan, and he had a knack for soothing their unique natures. He also took his self-assigned role as temporary assistant trainer very seriously. He walked through the barn inspecting the horses thoroughly, and ensuring jobs were completed to perfection. *Very Logan-like,* thought Tom. But when Miles started barking orders at the staff, Tom had to reign him in. 'Miles, ease up. You're scaring the staff.'

'But it's so fun. I've never been in charge before. I love it.'

'You're not in charge.' Miles looked a little disappointed and Tom laughed, putting an arm around him. 'What I mean is, you're a great help, thank you, but just be careful or they'll all revolt and lock you in a cupboard.'

'Listen darling, you think I'm scared of a cupboard? I came out of the closet a long time ago.'

Tom had breakfast with his mother and they discussed the upcoming races. Cynthia reflected on how the planets had finally lined up for them all. Logan and Miles, plus many of the other great staff, had really got the family rolling again and given them a purpose. Logan was the captain of the ship, Miles seemed to have that way of holding everything together, and James, Tom, and Cynthia all grew fonder of both men every day.

Logan and James met in the hallway outside their rooms at 5.15 a.m. It was a seven-minute walk to the track, they were told, but they did it in five. James used the walk to loosen up. After a brief introduction, James was legged up with another work rider. It was just a trot and canter, as the gelding was racing tomorrow. Logan positioned himself down near the running rail, and pulled his binoculars out and studied the gelding. He was big, very scopey, and still looked like he hadn't fully matured. Many stayers didn't hit their primes until they were five years old. He worked okay; good stride, well behaved, correct in the legs. James came back in and hopped off. The groom took the gelding, Jimsnotmyname (all pronounced as one word), back to his stall to be cooled down.

They had five minutes until the next horse came out. While they waited, James and Logan discussed Jimsnotmyname. 'What did you think?' Logan asked.

'He needs the chiropractor badly,' James said. 'His stride was rough and unbalanced. It was like riding a steel drum. Besides that, he felt like he was only working on three cylinders.'

'Is he worth a punt?' Logan asked, leaving it to James to make the call.

'Great, so it's now my ass on the line,' he said, with a smile. 'If he runs in the first three tomorrow, he is, because he'll be doing it running with only sixty per cent of his ability.'

The next one was a four-year-old mare, My Mistress, by Everest's sire Roman Empire. Jet black with a star. Her head was very similar to the Halo sire line, and she was a mirror image of her sire. She had cut her leg as a two-year-old and missed twelve months. She had three starts and ran a fast-closing second in her last race. She was due to race in a week's time, and the trainer was happy if she worked four and two; meaning she would sprint home the last furlong.

Logan legged James on, and he spoke to her trainer, and was accompanied by another work rider for the gallop. Logan noticed her feet were huge and round. Most American gallopers had more box-type feet and more heel. Hers were like most Australian race-horses. Her feet didn't suit the dirt, as they didn't sink in like the other horses, and she may struggle to get a grip on some dirt tracks. She worked solid and had the upper hand of her galloping opponent, which Logan thought the trainer had set up. Everyone was aware that the Bakers had a big chequebook, and were hoping for overs. James came back in with a poker face on. When the others were not looking, he winked at Logan to secretly confirm she was good. They politely thanked the trainer for his time and told him that Mick would call if they were interested. When they got well out of earshot of the track, James told Logan, 'Felt ace, she can't grip on the dirt. I'm sure her stride will change if we get her on grass.'

When they got back to the house, they ate breakfast. Logan felt guilty for the full plate of pancakes and steaming coffee, while James had egg white on one slice of wholemeal toast and a cup of green tea. They planned to meet at 11 a.m. the next day to go to the races. It had been ages since either one of them had free time on their hands. James was going for a six-kilometre run and hitting the gym and sauna. He said he might do a bit of sightseeing later or go to the racetrack tack store to look at gear. He loved the American-style racing wear. Logan was going clothes shopping and getting some new shoes, maybe some cowboy boots. He said he might even have time to get a haircut before taking in the latest Tom Cruise movie.

'If you want to catch up for dinner, just shoot me a message later,' Logan said. 'I've got no plans yet.'

'I think I'll probably just have an early night,' James replied. Logan got the feeling that James wanted to do his own thing for a change.

They split up after breakfast, and Logan hit the shops. He bought a new Armani suit, smart shoes, got a haircut, and found a western store and bought two pairs of designer lizard-skin cowboy boots. He walked out halfway through the movie, as he forgot how much he hated science fiction. He texted James at 6 p.m. to see where he was, but James said he was going to bed, and that he'd see him in the morning.

Cynthia had texted Logan a few times, but he didn't open them. He responded to one work text and left it at that. She wasn't letting up though, and he was starting to stress about what he intended to do when he got back.

He parked himself at a table at a quiet restaurant, had dinner, and ordered a drink. He called Pete, as he was always up for a chat no matter what time it was, and caught up on all the local racing news and gossip. He mentioned the talk between the trainers of Masters losing it in the trainers' hut after Everest won. Logan rang Aunty Joy and talked to her for half an hour. He was surprised to hear that she had her gall bladder removed the previous week and didn't tell anyone—not a soul. She was as tough as nails. Logan was relieved she was well and everything on the farm was going smoothly. Since Logan had taken Hank, she'd felt lonely and bought a husky-cross called Tess. She said she had never had a kinder dog in her life.

Logan checked emails, and Miles had entered four for the races the following Saturday: Warrior King, Everest, Forest Black, and the filly Hamper Queen. Logan was a bit surprised at her entry, but Tom said she had been jumping out of her skin. When Logan read the track work times, he knew why they had entered her over six furlongs.

He had spoken to Mick and said they would wait until after the race tomorrow before making a decision on the gelding, depending on how he performed. They would then arrange a vet to look at them both, or just the four-year-old mare, as they were very keen on her.

By 9 p.m., Logan was stuffed and he decided he needed to go to bed so he didn't have to keep seeing the texts from Cynthia come in. She had been texting unimportant questions about work just to get him to respond. He thought she was acting like a teenage girl, and it was making him uncomfortable. When he was with Jo, there was no issue.

Logan woke at 4.30 a.m. Even on the other side of the world, his body clock seemed to adjust. He wished he could train it to let him sleep in sometimes. He lay in bed, wide awake, thinking about the two horses they may purchase. He knew he wouldn't be able to get back to sleep, so he decided to walk down and watch the morning track work. It would be a good opportunity to see the way the Americans trained. He shaved, dressed, and walked out his door.

He stopped at the top of the staircase, considering whether he should wake up James to come along. James's door clicked and opened quietly. *Oh, good, he's up anyway*, Logan thought. But the young man tiptoeing out of James's room wasn't James. The young man closed the door behind him and turned to see Logan on the stairs. He smiled and walked over. 'Good morning, Mr Weston,' the man said quietly. Logan looked immediately puzzled. 'Jake,' he said, putting his hand forward. 'We met yesterday.' Logan shook his hand slowly, still confused. 'I rode the other horses out with James,' Jake elaborated. 'I work for Mr Hay, the trainer.'

Logan was still trying to put the puzzle pieces together in his head. 'Jake, yes. Good morning.' Logan noticed that Jake was maybe twenty-years-old, very good looking, fit, about 5' 6", and was dressed like he had been nightclubbing. Logan was standing there stunned, when Jake said, 'Have a nice day,' and quickly walked down the stairs and let himself out the front door.

Logan went downstairs and made himself a coffee as he processed what had happened. *Was that a walk of shame? Is James gay?* He remembered that James was quite uncomfortable around Miles when he was making lewd jokes, but he never took it to mean anything. Neale's brother Robert was gay, and he and Logan were best mates throughout school. Unfortunately, Robert had died in a car crash in his early-thirties. Logan also had another good friend who was gay. He and his partner had made Logan godfather to their children. A lady had carried the twins for them, a girl and boy, and they were now thirteen years old. Logan was stunned that he didn't notice. James always kept to himself, but Logan assumed it was because he was so busy getting his riding back on track. Besides, it had only been five weeks, even though the boys and Cynthia had become very close in that time. He suddenly realised, *Maybe James has been struggling because of this. Have I put my foot in it by bumping into Jake?* He decided that he wouldn't say a thing about it. He abandoned his idea to walk down to the track and instead went back to his room to go over Miles's updates and respond to some emails until breakfast.

At breakfast, nothing seemed unusual. James gave nothing away, and Logan certainly wasn't going to bring it up. James and Logan walked to Saratoga for the day's racing. They talked along the way about the horses. James seemed to have a spring in his step, which Logan hadn't seen before, as James was normally quite reserved. Logan smirked, as he supposed it was no different to him getting some.

The members' room had invited them to the exclusive lounge and dining area. James ran into some friends, and Logan felt like the odd one out, and excused himself by saying he'd like to see how Jimsnotmyname handled waiting at the track before his race. When Logan got down there, he could see that the gelding was happy and calm and walked the pre-warm-up area extremely well. He decided to head back up and get a spot to watch the race.

CHAPTER 19

Logan rode the escalator the three flights up to the members' area. The whole time he was fixated on this woman in front of him in a crowd of people. Elegant, tall, lovely figure, beautiful floral dress, matching shoes and hat, slender neck, toned legs and arms. In his eyes, Logan had never seen a more beautiful woman. He was so taken, he was mesmerised and completely in a world of his own.

The escalator finished, but Logan didn't step off in time. He stumbled and the binoculars he was holding flew out of his hands and skidded across the floor in front of him. It all happened in a split second. He landed flat on his chest on the floor. If it had been a lady, someone from the crowd of onlookers might have stopped to assist, but Logan was no lady. Besides, he was already quickly getting to his feet. He brushed himself off and looked around, trying to see where his binoculars had gone, quietly cussing under his breath. Finally, he noticed them about nine feet away; some people were stepping over them. He weaved through the crowd and reached down to carefully pick them up, flipping them around to look for damage.

'Not broken, I hope,' a woman's voice said behind him. The voice was familiar, but he couldn't work out from where. He turned around and saw that it was the graceful woman he was busy watching when he fell on his face. 'A bit far from Australia, aren't you, Logan?'

So how do I know her? He tried to remember her name, but his mind was blank.

'I'm going to walk away if you can't remember my name,' she said with a cheeky grin.

That voice and accent, he knew it, but he gestured that he was thinking and just about had it. His mind raced as he looked at her beautiful brown eyes. There was a long silence, and she shook her head in disbelief, about to turn to go.

He snapped his fingers. 'Victoria!' She smiled and nodded. 'We met on the Emirates flight.' Then Logan did something he had never done in his life: he spoke without checking his words first. 'You were the most beautiful woman I'd ever seen in my life.' Victoria was taken aback by the sincere tone behind his comment and she blushed. 'Until today, when I saw you again in the crowd.' Logan went bright red and looked shocked at himself. 'Oh, I'm … I'm so sorry. I shouldn't have said that out loud.'

'Because you didn't mean it?' she asked.

'No, no—'

'No you didn't mean it, or no you did?' she said in a matter-of-fact way.

Logan felt his mind being twisted and tripped up, and he looked at her blankly. He couldn't put one right word in place. 'No, I mean—' he stuttered.

Victoria burst out laughing and gave him a hug, taking him by the arm. 'Quit while you are ahead, Down Under man.' He laughed along, letting out a relived breath for being let off the hook. 'So, are you here to watch the races?'

'What races?'

'Today's races,' she said, supressing a laugh.

'Oh. Today, yes, sorry.' He felt silly, as she could clearly see he was caught off guard by her beauty—like a love-struck teenage boy.

She slipped her arm around his. 'Well then, shall we go and get a seat?'

He nodded and tried to compose himself as they walked together, imagining an invisible hand slapping him across the face to wake him out of this dream. 'Actually, the real reason I'm here is because I'm looking to buy a horse. He is in this next race.'

'Oh? Garth has a runner in the next as well, the favourite, Bluestown Tune. He couldn't attend today, so here I am.'

They settled in the grandstand in the members' area. They made small talk, and Logan quickly explained to Victoria how his life had been turned upside down and how that led to him being there. The horses entered the pre-race enclosure. Victoria's horse looked superb and Logan could see why he was favourite. 'Very impressive colt,' he said.

'Garth paid $750,000 at Keeneland for him two years ago. He won his first two races. They think he may be a Derby colt.' Logan could see why. His sire, Spiritual Song, had a stint in Australia and covered three seasons of mares. But his progeny didn't suit the Australia conditions and were dirt track horses, so he never returned for another season.

Jimsnotmyname came in, looking relaxed, and Logan leant forward in his seat to study him. 'Your horse?' Victoria asked.

'Yes,' Logan replied.

'Good?' Victoria asked, since she wasn't a horsewoman. Being the finance manager for the cattle and bottled water business, and close friend to Garth and Ruth, she had limited experience judging horses.

'He needs the chiropractor and a turf surface.'

It was over so quickly, and Logan spent more time watching Victoria than the race. As Bluestown Tune neared the finish, she yelled and rode him home in her seat like a hard-luck punter. When he crossed the finish, she jumped up and down and jubilantly hugged Logan. The bookies were correct, and Bluestown Tune officially won by four lengths and now was on the radar as a real Derby colt. Logan was happy that Jimsnotmyname ran second, considering the issues he and James believed he had. Victoria went into the enclosure and did the trophy presentation, and was as jubilant as Garth would have been.

They were escorted to the winner's lounge and they shared the bottle of expensive French champagne that was placed on the table. Logan hadn't laughed and smiled so much for as long as he could remember. Logan was surprised, since the last time they had spoken Victoria had shared the sad story of her husband's suicide. He remembered her as being reserved and shy, but now she was joking and laughing. Logan couldn't believe the size of the smile on his face. She had a wicked sense of humour, and Logan couldn't tell if sometimes she was serious or pulling his leg.

They finished the bottle, and this normally indicated it was time to vacate and make room for the next group of winners. They headed back to the members' area and settled into a table overlooking the pre-race parade area. Victoria excused herself to the ladies' powder room and Logan looked around the bar. At home he would know ninety per cent of the participants, but here he didn't know anyone. Then he spotted James in a small group of young people. Logan hadn't thought about James since he ran into Victoria. James must have been looking for him, too, as he was scanning the bar. They locked eyes and James smiled and gestured him over. Logan got up and walked over to their group, as James was stepping away.

'What did you think of the run?' Logan asked.

'Pretty good, considering,' James replied. 'Has Mick called yet?'

'Not yet. I'm sure he will soon though, so we should make a decision.'

One of the young men from the circle of people James was with turned to see who James was talking to, and Logan nearly died when he realised it was Jake. 'Oh, hello again,' Jake said, giving a friendly smile.

'Hi,' Logan said, feeling awkward.

'Have you met?' James asked, looking a little confused.

Logan scrambled for words, and they both replied at the same time: 'At the track,' Logan said, while Jake replied, 'This morning.'

James quickly realised what had happened, and his face drained of colour. Jake was a proud gay man, and he looked between Logan and James, not sure what to say. Logan saw the guilt and the embarrassment wash over James, and he felt terrible. Up until then, James had been a man on top of the world. The silence was extremely awkward and the tears were building in James's eyes. Logan put his arm around James and whispered, 'It's all good, mate.' James looked up at him, and Logan squeezed him in for a hug. 'It's all good.'

There was a pause, and Logan decided to quickly change the topic to brighten to mood. 'Anyway, enough about you.' Logan laughed. 'I met someone! She is incredible.'

'Who?' James said curiously.

Victoria was heading back over to their table, looking around for Logan. 'Over there.'

James and Jake whipped around to see. 'She's beautiful!' James said excitedly.

'Shhhh!' Logan hissed quietly. 'Not a word.' He waved over at her. 'Victoria!' She turned, smiling, and walked over to the group. Logan did the intros, then ordered two bottles of French champagne for the table. The conversation was full of laughter and smiles, and boasts about some winning bets, as well. James had never seen Logan so relaxed and happy. Logan called Tom to tell him to go ahead with the deal with Mick.

The group decided to kick on and headed to a bar that Jake recommended. It was a gay nightclub and a first-time outing to this type of club for both Logan and Victoria. James had decided that if he drank straight spirits, he would gain less weight. But it also meant he got drunk very quickly. He was always quite reserved at home, so Logan couldn't believe how funny he was when drunk.

On the way back from the bar, James and Logan ended up in a quiet corner for a drunk heart to heart. 'Well, that looks serious, what's going on over in the corner?' Victoria asked.

'Well, Logan caught me leaving James's room this morning,' Jake said, quite drunk himself.

Victoria shrugged, as if to say *who cares*.

'Well, no one knows that James is gay.' Jake knew what James was going through, as he went through a similar thing at the age of sixteen.

Victoria's mouth opened, as the penny finally dropped. She had just assumed they were a couple. Victoria looked over and Logan was giving James a big hug, patting him on the back as he spoke to him. She started to tear up seeing the emotion in Logan's expression. 'That's so sad. I didn't realise.'

Logan and James walked back over to the group and James raised his glass. 'I'm James and I'm gay.' Everyone raised their glasses, clinked, and downed their drinks. As if on cue, the DJ put on Queen's hit 'Crazy Little Thing Called Love'. Logan grabbed Victoria's hand and they hit the dance floor, and James and Jake followed. Victoria was pretty impressed with Logan's moves, and they danced for another three songs. They could both feel the chemistry, and though it was only 10 p.m., they said their goodbyes. As Logan said goodbye to James, he gave him a wink. James smiled, feeling reassured that everything was going to work out fine.

Logan and Victoria arrived back at her hotel, and he walked her to her door. No words were spoken; she simply led him by the hand. He knew what was on her mind. Before she had opened the door, he turned her around and placed his right hand on the small of her back and pulled her close. He inhaled her scent; the scent he wanted to remember forever. He placed his hand softly on her cheek and she rolled her head closer to his touch. She hadn't been touched intimately for so long, and Logan felt her trembling. He could see it in her eyes: the fear of the touch of someone else; the anticipation of feeling wanted, possibly loved, again.

He moved in closer until their lips touched. Her lips were soft and plump. Logan went slowly, and the sensations kept building. This was their first kiss and he wanted it to be something he would always remember. They kissed for minutes, and finally she broke away, whispering, 'I think y'all need to come inside.'

Logan smiled but he shook his head. 'Not tonight. I want this to be perfect. No rush, just perfect.' She frowned like a spoilt little girl, kissing him so passionately he thought he might change his mind.

'Breakfast at nine, then,' she said.

'Nine, then,' he said, and winked. She felt it hit her heart and flutter through her body.

Logan lay in his bed, horny as hell, but satisfied in many ways. To him, Victoria was perfect. She was funny, sincere, and intelligent, and he was highly attracted to her. From her elegant beauty, to her dress sense, to the way she carried herself, she was a true lady. This was different for him. Not taking anything away from the other women he had been with, but Victoria was the first real lady he'd been with in many ways. *And she's the most beautiful woman in the world*, Logan thought, as he fell asleep. Meanwhile, unknown to Logan, James was arriving home with Jake. They stumbled through his door and out of their clothes. It was on, and the raw emotion James had experienced 'coming out' was followed up by holding nothing back—two extremely fit young men going for it all night.

Logan sat opposite Victoria in a booth in a small café. She wore a simple outfit of jeans and boots, hair pulled back in a ponytail, and very little makeup. She looked stunning, and Logan found himself staring at her. 'What?' she asked.

'You are just so bloody beautiful.' She blushed and leant over the table. He prepared for a kiss and leant forward, puckering his lips. But he felt her finger wipe the egg yolk drip from the side of his mouth. He was gone, just like a kid with a new toy. She liked to see that side of a man, though she knew he would be as hard as granite in many ways.

Victoria took control for the day. She asked him questions about what he liked to do, then decided that they wouldn't do any of those things; they would do something new. First, they walked through the art gallery. Logan had never set foot in a gallery. Victoria had planned it would take an hour, maybe two hours tops. She was wrong. Logan seemed to turn into another person. He loved guessing why they painted or sculpted that certain way, and admiring the different methods and applications involved in each piece. This impressed Victoria, as she had been a lover of the arts all her life and appreciated the sacrifices artists endured to bring their work to life. They walked hand in hand, and occasionally Logan would raise her hand and kiss it. The art of a gentleman had never been wasted on him. His father was tough from a young age and ensured Logan showed the utmost respect to the women in his life. His mother was the only other woman in his life Logan would call a true lady, but he was four when she died. His father never got over her death and told so many stories of the woman she was. Aunty Joy was a lady in many ways, but she was the type of tough woman that would rather call a spade a spade.

Logan checked his watch, and this made Victoria stop. 'What's wrong?' he asked.

'You'll have to go soon,' she said sadly.

'Tomorrow morning.' He saw the look in her eyes, and he kissed her hand gently.

She got very close to him and whispered, 'Take me somewhere, Logan. Make love to me.' Logan took her hand and they walked to the exit. Across the road was the Hilton. They walked into the foyer. 'What are you doing?' she asked.

'Let's not lose the moment,' he said, and winked. He paid $675 for the best room they had.

He could feel her hand shaking in the lift. Her late husband was the only man she had ever been with, and she was terrified at the thought of being a letdown.

For the first time that day, Logan took control. Logan doubted himself when it came to many things in life, but love-making he knew and exceled at it. He was a confident lover and, from the compliments he seemed to always receive, he knew it was his time to shine.

He started everything very slow. He kissed her gently, lightly just touching her lips. He placed his left hand just behind her ear to cradle her head; his right hand on her waist. They hadn't even made the move to the bed, they were just standing in the middle of the room. Victoria anticipated the next move, and went to make a move, and Logan whispered, 'Not yet' softly, sending shivers down her body as he continued at the same slow, teasing pace.

He moved from her mouth to her neck, just above the collarbone, and kissed it softly, then moved to the sensitive skin just under her earlobe. Victoria loved it. Her emotions were running wild, and he sensed this at the slight buckle of her knees. This signalled Logan to move them closer to the bed. With an easy one-handed movement, he unbuckled her belt and opened the top button of her jeans. He lifted her shirt and she raised both arms up so he could pull it over her head. Another swift move, and he removed her bra to reveal two beautiful full-sized breasts. She wiggled her body and her jeans dropped to her feet, and she stepped out of them. Logan took a step backwards and admired Victoria's beauty. She didn't seem self-conscious about her body. She worked out three times a week and worked hard to stay in good shape. There was no doubt he liked what he saw, and the bulge in his jeans was noticeable.

It was her turn. She stood and undid his shirt buttons one by one. Victoria ran her hands down his toned chest, admiring the physique of a man who liked to take care of his body. She reached down to unbutton his jeans, but they had tightened from the extra pressure and she fumbled with her long nails. Logan took care of the holdup himself, unbuttoning his jeans and letting them fall around his ankles. Since he'd mistakenly packed more socks and less underwear, he sprung out instantly. 'Oh my,' Victoria whispered. She looked up at him and he grinned at the surprised look, as it certainly wasn't the first time he had seen that reaction.

Logan lowered Victoria onto the bed and suspended himself above her. They kissed passionately and explored with their tongues. She ran her hands over his muscly back and arms, and down his body. He was extremely hard, and she felt him rubbing her leg every now and then. He lowered himself down her body, softly sucking and circling her nipples with his tongue, left then right. He moved to the side and cupped her breast softly and continued kissing and sucking at her stiff nipples. He moved his left hand down, and she subconsciously raised her backside; he slipped her underwear down and over each ankle. Without her noticing, he put two fingers from his left hand in his mouth to make sure they would slip in easily.

Logan parted his fingers slightly and moved them between her legs, slowing moving them up and down her moist lips. He applied pressure gently to the outside of the G-spot area, hitting the spot every few strokes. She started to arch her back as the arousal built up with each stroke of Logan's hand. His hand dipped lower and he inserted two fingers, curling them up towards the middle of his palm. This was a move he often found worked; the pressure on the inside from his fingers and outside with the middle of his palm.

He kept teasing her right nipple with his tongue, and increased the pace with his hand. Her breath quickened, and he rose up to kiss her deeply. She returned the kiss, hard and passionate, then pulled back to gasp and take some heavy breaths. Her hips rocked desperately, and Logan gave three quick hard thrusts with his fingers. She tensed up and her hand clamped down hard on Logan's. Her back arched, and Logan's fingers were trapped. She rocked forward, moaning, then collapsed back, shaking her head side to side. She finally caught a breath and whispered, 'Wow, I needed that.' Logan was smiling, watching her as her chest heaved up and down. She gave him a cheeky smile. 'I'm done.'

'Really? I haven't started,' he said, kissing her as he moved on top. She was so wet, and the tight feeling added to his sensation as he rocked slowly to ease in his girth. Her eyes opened in surprise and she gasped. He had seen this before, and he smiled down at her, lowering his head to her breasts and lightly rolling his tongue and teeth over her nipples. When he stopped and looked at her again, she whispered, 'Easy, boy.' He wanted to make love to her; this wasn't just a one-night stand.

He started long and slow, then raised his body up higher and pushed in deeper. Victoria had closed her eyes and was biting her bottom lip. Her head turned side to side slightly and she moaned, wrapping her legs tighter around his waist. She sucked in some sharp breaths, and Logan felt that she was close again. He quickly moved back and raised both her legs over his right shoulder. Victoria opened her eyes, unsure of this new position and feeling herself lose her momentum, but Logan drove forward and her legs went tight again. She gasped, as she had never felt this type of sensation before in her life. Logan kept up his rhythm, long and slow, but now another inch deeper. Her eyes closed tighter and her breathing gave away her next building orgasm. Logan gave a few hard thrusts, and her body arched so hard that he popped out. She rose up off the bed like she had been electrocuted before collapsing back down.

Victoria thought her heart was going to burst and she was gasping for breath. She was fit; *But not sex fit*, she thought. She didn't speak, and Logan just watched her. She smiled, but she was like an athlete trying to regain control on her body. Her pelvis was still twitching and she could feel tingling between her legs. She put her hand down and touched the sensation gently, curious and surprised.

Logan got up and grabbed a water out of the bar fridge for her. He was still hard and she finally got a decent look. It was very impressive, maybe seven inches, but thicker than she imagined, and the end was like an over-sized fireman's helmet. 'I might have to call y'all the Thunder from Down Under, with that weapon,' she joked. Logan grinned; compliments were always welcome.

Victoria sipped at the water, then placed it on the side table. 'Now, what can I do for you, Mr Thunder from Down Under?' He lay down and she knew it was her turn. She rolled on top and slowly eased her way down, bracing herself with her hands on his chest. Her hair fell forward down over her breasts, and Logan thought she looked spectacular. He cupped her breasts softly and they bulged out over his palms. She slowly eased up and down, feeling him getting even harder. Slowly he was building, and so was she. She looked at him and said, 'Now it's my turn,' moving from the sitting cowgirl position to squatting, still leaning forward. Logan was impressed with her balance. Her muscles instantly tightened and his sensation grew. With each movement up and down, she tightened her muscles.

She knew he was close, as he was raising his hips to meet her halfway. He couldn't hold any longer and as he came he drove his hips upwards. Victoria changed her position and pushed down on his cock as he bucked hard. This was enough to trigger her third orgasm, and she shuddered and rocked forward on her hands. Logan realised and gave a few small thrusts upwards. Victoria raised her hips slightly and whispered, 'Stop, no more.' She touched his lips and leant down to kiss him softly. They stayed in that position while they both caught their breath. Logan broke the silence. 'You were amazing.'

Victoria smiled shyly. 'I'm out of practice. You're the one who's amazing.' She slipped down beside him, placing her left hand on his chest, which was still rising and falling faster than normal. He kissed her head, and she moved her hand through the hair on his chest. She reached down and pulled the sheet up over them. *Good sign,* he thought. *Settling in, and not dashing off awkwardly to clean up.* Her scent was just beautiful. The softness of her skin and the gentleness of her hand. In comparison, like many people who worked with horses, Logan wore the wears and tears of his profession—his rough hands and bumps and scrapes. Victoria was delicate and unmarked, and he liked it. He felt so at peace in the moment, he quickly fell asleep.

They napped for almost an hour. When Logan woke, he slipped into the shower, quickly followed by Victoria. She admired his body as she washed him. She realised he was three inches taller without her heels on. They took their time washing and touching each other before returning to the bed. Victoria positioned herself on top and set the pace—no sex, just kissing and caressing. She was still too sensitive. It wasn't until 3 a.m. that Logan was able to make love to her again. 'I have to get back to my room and pack as I have a 7 a.m. flight' he said softly.

It was hard to say goodbye, and neither really knew what to say. *Will we even see each other again?* Victoria thought. She was in the U.S., he was in the U.K. They were adults and knew that even though the chemistry was electric, it wasn't an easy situation. For once, Logan was so unsure of himself. He didn't know if Victoria felt what he did, and he was too scared to admit it, but she had touched his heart and soul. Never in his life had he connected with such a woman. Her beauty, class, style; her softness and her humour. Logan was lost for words.

While Victoria was getting dressed, Logan grabbed the pen and paper from the hotel room and wrote a message on it. As they shared a final kiss goodbye at the door, he placed the note in her hand. 'This is for you … But I want you to wait a week before you open it, in case your feelings change in that time.' Then Logan turned and walked to the elevator.

She didn't wait a week; she barely waited one second after the elevator door closed. She unfolded the note to read: 'I think you are The One.' She held the piece of paper to her heart and leaned back against the door jamb, her smile breaking into a joyful laugh. She looked at the note and, without thinking, ran to the elevator. She didn't know what she was going to say, but she knew he couldn't leave without knowing she felt the same way. The elevator seemed to take forever, and when it opened she jumped in and hit the button for the foyer impatiently.

When the doors opened, she could see Logan slowly making his way through a group of early morning check-outs with suitcases standing around the lobby. She yelled out, 'Hey! Thunder from Down Under!' Almost at the door, he turned, and so did the crowd waiting in reception. She didn't care—this was her romantic moment. He stopped, confused, and she ran over to him and slapped the note to his chest like she was pinning it to his heart. 'So do I,' she said breathlessly. He looked down, still confused, suddenly realising it was the note he'd given her. He looked into her eyes and she stood up on her tiptoes—having forgotten her shoes in the hotel room—to kiss him passionately. 'So do I,' she said again, and she slipped out of his arms and walked back towards the elevator.

CHAPTER 20

Logan and James settled into their business-class seats for the flight home. They'd hardly slept the two previous nights, and now the weekend was over, it was time to refocus on business. Logan sensed James needed to get it all off his chest before they got home. The seatbelt sign had hardly been off for a second, when James climbed into Logan's capsule. For over two hours, James opened up about his struggles keeping his sexuality a secret, and seeing a therapist. Logan had no idea how tough it had been for him. James said that Don was the only person he'd actually told— though he suspected that some of his friends had guessed already. This sparked in Logan's mind the memory of his call with Don: 'James is going through a tough time and, well, he'll need your support when the time comes.'

James said, 'I'm sure mother and Tom should be okay with it. But it was hard growing up. As much as I loved my father, he was always very homophobic.' He opened up about how much it hurt that his father refused to believe that someone could be born gay, instead claiming it was a terrible choice. This drove James to keep it more supressed and, over time, he suffered in silence, unsure if his family would ever approve.

'In a way, I'm happy he's not here to be a part of this. I don't think he would have ever forgiven me, and it would have hurt so much to be the one who created a rift in the family.' Logan was taken aback, and heartbroken that James felt that way about his own father. He didn't see James any differently. If anything, now he saw a young man who had lifted a huge burden off his shoulders and had finally opened his heart. He had a full life ahead of him with so much potential. Logan was so fond of the two boys. He couldn't believe it, but they felt like his long-lost little brothers.

They landed at Heathrow, and Logan couldn't wait to get home and see the horses. No one was at the stables, but Hank greeted him enthusiastically as he walked into the barn. Logan knelt down to give Hank a big wrestle. He had missed him. But Hank had just rolled in fresh horse shit, and Tom cracked up laughing as he walked in the stable barn, as he knew it must have been Logan when he noticed the lights on. Logan was wiping his hands with a towel.

Logan asked. 'How are the horses?'

'Great! Come take a look.'

Logan walked into Warrior King's stable to admire the 4.1-million-dollar colt. He pulled his rugs off. 'Improved?'

Tom simply nodded.

Then they walked into Everest's stable. Logan rubbed his hand down the horse's skin. Even though it was getting cold, his skin was like silk. Logan ran his hand down his backbone, over his rump, up and down his neck. Everest didn't flinch a whisker with any unease or soreness. When they got him from Masters, they could hardly touch him anywhere without some kind of reaction. 'Perfect. Feels good. And he's tightened up.'

Tom nodded and said, 'Wins again.'

'That's a bit cocky mate,' Logan replied. Tom smiled.

Logan walked the rest of the barn, and Tom hung back a few strides. Hank darted into each box when Logan opened the doors to see the horses up close. The horses had grown accustomed to Hank and completely ignored him as he darted underfoot. When they got to the end of the barn, Logan turned to Tom and said, 'And Miles? Did he do a good job?'

'Yes, I did!' Miles called out, as he swaggered down the barn. 'I'm in and you're out, Mr Aussie. I'm the number one trainer around here now. Even your dog prefers me!' He laughed confidently, baby-talking at Hank and patting at his legs. 'Show Logan our trick, Hanky!' Hank's ears perked up, and he bolted down the barn. He jumped up at Miles, who caught him in his arms. Hank executed the trick perfectly, and Miles smirked at Logan. 'See?' Hank gave Miles a big lick on the lips, and that's when Miles realised he had just been eating fresh horse shit. Miles almost dropped Hank flat on the ground, trying to get away as quickly as possible. 'Oh, yuck! Bad dog. You can have him back, Logan!'

After planning the morning gallops with Tom, Logan retired to his house. He bathed Hank, unpacked, and put on a load of washing. His phone dinged with a text from Victoria: it was a photo of her reflection in her bathroom mirror at home, with a love heart drawn with lipstick around her head, and a message: 'From the #1 xxx.'

He smiled; in fact, he hadn't stopped smiling since their day at the races. She was in his mind every second. He replied: 'Who's this?'

The reply was a photo of her cleavage with no message.

He replied: 'I won't forget those in a hurry. I'm back home; all is good here, horses look great, just one thing missing—you.'

Logan's door knocked. He looked at his watch—9.15 p.m. *Maybe Miles has left his teddy here,* Logan joked to himself. But it was Cynthia, and she was drunk. 'Can we talk?' she said, trying to act composed.

'Sure,' Logan said, unenthused at her state, and he ushered her into the kitchen and plonked her on a seat. She was stumbling and Logan had to support her. She was hammered. He wondered how she had even made it to his door.

'James is gay,' she said abruptly.

'Yes, I know,' Logan said calmly. He crossed his arms defensively, unsure of her tone. She was his mother, but that didn't matter. He was going to support James. God knew that kid deserved it after everything he had gone through.

'He's *gay*,' she said again. James and Logan hadn't been home long, so Logan gathered he must have sat her down straightaway to get it over and done with. He decided to cut her a little bit of slack, and was sure she wouldn't remember all of this in the morning anyway. 'What did I do? What did I do wrong?'

Drunk or sober, he wasn't going to let Cynthia turn this around and make it about her. Logan snapped and he said gruffly, 'This isn't about you, Cynthia. It's not about your parenting at all. James didn't decide to do this to you; he was born this way. He is a great young man with a huge heart, and he is your son. And I promise you, if you turn him away over this, you will lose him forever.' He paused, waiting for his words to sink in before he added, 'And me.'

She looked up at him and the expression on his face told her that he was dead serious. He continued, 'I'm starting to love those boys like they were my own little brothers. James needs our support right now. He needs his family to accept him for who he is.'

Cynthia put her head in her hands and Logan could tell she was crying.

He walked over to her seat. 'Come on, I'm taking you home.'

She pulled herself closer to him, whispering, 'Let me stay here with you.'

'I'm taking you home,' he said sternly.

"Wait, please wait, I need to talk.' Logan put coffee on and for the next 40 minutes Cynthia dropped the bombshell on Logan. She finished with, 'never tell the boys.'

'I won't say a word, Cynthia. Not a word, never say a word to anyone.' Logan lifted her up, as it was now time for her to go.

Cynthia rose up and landed a surprise kiss on his lips. She was off balance, so Logan kept hold of her instead of pushing her away. He slowly eased her back, shaking his head. She slurred, 'What? Don't you want me? I thought you liked taking women to bed, and I hear you're a stud.' She leant against him again, touching his chest. 'You can take me to bed, if you want. I'm good in bed,' and she purred and scratched at his chest flirtatiously. 'I'm like a tiger.'

Logan laughed, gently easing her back and moving her towards the door. 'Yeah, I bet you are, tiger. But you need to go home.'

She arrived having a breakdown over James being gay, the next minute she dropped a bomb on Logan that gobsmacked him, and now she tried to make a move on him. Cynthia was hammered.

He helped her into his car and drove her up to the main house. 'You can stay with the boys tonight,' he said. She had closed her eyes, so she probably didn't even hear a word he said.

Logan got her out of the car and walked her in the side entrance that led to the kitchen. James and Tom were there, and both turned, looking worried. The two boys rushed over and took her from Logan. 'I'm fine, I'm fine,' she said, staggering and catching her balance on the back of a breakfast stool. She straightened herself up, focused on James, and walked over to him. She stood in front of him with her hands on his shoulders to keep her balanced. 'I love you,' she said, pausing as tears rolled down her face. 'I don't care if you're gay … I was surprised, but I want—I want you to be,' she pointed an unsteady finger at his chest, 'happy.' She broke down into tears, and Tom rushed over to help James support and hug her. She kept saying 'I just want you to be happy,' as she cried on James's chest.

Tom gave Logan a nod and mouthed, 'We've got her,' and Logan took off, knowing it was his cue to give the family their privacy. He had had his fair share tonight, that was for sure.

Cynthia dragged the boys down to the floor as she collapsed, sobbing as she told them everything she had been keeping inside— her husband's death, her sister's death, feeling utterly alone, the pressure of running the family and finances, and holding it all together for them, her feelings for Logan. She had finally let her barriers down. But she didn't say one word about what she had told Logan. The two boys stepped up to the reverse of roles and comforted their mother. They were ready to help her pick up the pieces and be a part of her healing process.

CHAPTER 21

Angus Masters had a son on the way. Angela was pregnant with their second child, so Angus had been doing his very best behaving himself. He had curbed his obsession with Logan in her view, but deep down he was going to take him down.

He had been making headway in leaps and bounds. He had now set his sights on an assault on Royal Ascot. He had secured ten stables at Newmarket, three staff, and was sending his second-in-charge foreman Blake Robertson to oversee the training of the team. He was arriving on Friday for the weekend's meeting, where Logan had entered four runners—two of them previously trained by Masters. The following Tuesday and Wednesday, he hoped to purchase tried stayers at the Tattersalls Racehorse in Training sale, which had become a popular hunting ground for many Australian trainers. The last three Melbourne Cup winners had all come from this sale. He had five million to spend, which four clients had pooled at his request.

No Australian trainer had secured stables and done a full prep from an English base before; all opted for the flight three to four weeks prior. Masters was a great trainer, as his record showed, but horses were a dime a dozen to him. When they broke down from being overworked, he just got a new one to replace them.

Warrior King, Everest, Forest Black, and the filly Miss Jasmine all worked superbly. Tom and Logan both agreed that all four would go to the farm on Thursday to wander around the cattle and freshen their heads up for an hour.

Mike pulled bloods and shot some X-rays of Warrior King's knees and fetlocks to make sure nothing was changing, as he was still a baby—even though physically he was mature for his age. Logan and Tom were pleased that Mike and his wife had worked things out. Mike was on the ball and checked every horse personally every day, visited Cynthia's spelling farm to cast his trained eye over all the spellers, and worked extremely close with the farriers and also the horses' chiropractor and masseur. Many vets are against animal chiropractors and masseurs, but Mike knew if they could help just that one bit more, it was worth doing.

Cynthia rose at 11 a.m. with the world's biggest headache and nearly died when she faced herself in the mirror. The night's events were foggy but she recalled over the next few hours how everything had quickly unravelled.

When Cynthia went downstairs, James was making a snack of chicken soup before he headed to the gym. He still needed to strip two kilograms before the race. They went for a walk around the farm so Cynthia could get some fresh air, and they spent hours talking. James even missed his personal training session. Tom and

Logan spotted them siting in the shade, deep in conversation. 'Looks like progress,' said Logan.

Tom nodded. 'Mother was a real mess last night. Things came out we never knew. We talked until 2 a.m. before she passed out from exhaustion.'

'She'll be okay. She's a special person, your mother.'

Tom paused for a moment before he said, 'Well, we found out she likes you.'

They both laughed awkwardly. 'Yeah, about that ...' Logan paused. 'I met someone at Saratoga.'

'Really? Who?'

Since they had twenty minutes to kill while the horses walked on the water walker for the afternoon exercise, Logan told Tom how he met Victoria and about their amazing time together.

'When will you see her again?' Tom asked.

'Don't know,' Logan answered softly, staring off into the distance.

They stood in silence until Tom handed Logan a lead rope to grab Warrior King from the water walker. Logan scraped the water off him, and put his boots and bell boots on, and put him in the sand roll. He bucked and kicked and rolled over three times. He was fit, and Logan admired the colt's strength. He was ready. Everest was full of himself, but Forest Black was the opposite; the fitter he got, the more relaxed he was.

Logan, Tom, and Miles reviewed the race entries and discussed the next few weeks of racing. It was getting close to Christmas and there would be a few runners each week. Many of the horses they took over in the package deal simply needed some more time to train. Even though some were three and four years old, they had never had a serious prep. A few went shin sore, and Logan had already sacked three, as they had shown nothing in a few gallops. Unless they were potential Stakes horses, they would be sacked. Cynthia had made it clear that Baker Stables was for winning races, not feeding horses.

James finished his conversation with Cynthia and arrived at the office with red, puffy eyes, as he had been crying. They all politely ignored it and got down to business, going through the form and race replays of the runners their four horses were up against on Saturday. Miles was a gun when it came to this and had everything ready, from form to the possible race pattern, to where James should expect to be in the fields. When they had gone through everything thoroughly, Logan leaned back in the comfortable leather chair Cynthia had chosen for the office. 'We just have to hold this together for 72 hours, boys.'

Miles stood up and stretched. 'Well, I'll see you boys tomorrow. I have to go get ready for my Grinder date tonight.'

James looked interested. 'Well, give us a look.'

Miles looked puzzled but he pulled up the photo on the guy's dating profile and showed it to James.

James gave it a look and nodded, smiling. 'Very nice! Have fun.' Miles looked at Logan, feeling as though he was missing some piece of the joke, so James added, 'Oh, I'm gay.'

Miles looked surprised, and Logan stood up and slapped him on the back, laughing. 'Sorry you had to be the last to know, mate.'

CHAPTER 22

Victoria and Logan called each other every night. She was smitten and so was he. They texted all the time. Logan sent selfies of himself and the horses. He had never been a selfie person before, but the distance made it necessary.

On Thursday morning, they trucked the horses out to the farm. This was completely new to the King and the filly Miss Jasmine. But the horses really enjoyed the walk and trot with the cattle and sheep. Everest started out shaking his head up and down being toey, but he soon settled and even put his head down to munch on a patch of clover and rye. For a riding horse this was frowned upon, but Logan was sure at 60 km/h, he wouldn't do it when it counted.

Finally, they loaded the horses back into the horse truck and left the farm. About three kilometres from the stables, in a back-street of town, suddenly a four-year-old child came running out on the road in front of the horse truck. Logan hit the brake pedal to the floor and knew the horses would scramble as they tried to regain their footing. Tom and Logan got out of the truck to see that, luckily, the child was unharmed. The very shaken mother held her child and couldn't stop apologising to Logan. Logan was quick to brush her off and rush to the back of the truck, where Tom had dropped the loading doors.

'Fuck,' Logan shouted, when they saw that Warrior King had gone down and he was still tied up with the bungy strap not breaking. Tom and Logan didn't need to say a word; they both swung into action. Logan raised up the King's head with all his strength while Tom undid the tied-up bungy rope. They both grabbed the head collar and a hand full of mane each and pulled his head and neck anti-clockwise to have him facing outwards and looking down the loading ramp. Tom quickly grabbed the lead rope and clicked it to the head collar. Tom pulled softly on his head to motion to get up and Logan grabbed his tail to help get him up. But the King couldn't get up. He seemed to be in shock. The other three horses had managed to stay on their feet and were whinnying, sensing the panic. Tom pulled on his head, but still he wouldn't get up. Tom and Logan both looked at each other with worried expressions. He could have broken anything—knees, cannons, stifle, pelvis. 'Try again,' Logan half shouted. Tom pulled his head and motioned—nothing. 'Again,' Logan said, and this time Logan slapped him over the ass very hard with an open hand. 'Get up, get up,' and he slapped him once more. The King lifted himself up on wobbly legs and stumbled down the ramp. By now there were cars lined up behind them on the road, heads sticking on the side windows, wondering what was happening.

Tom led the King straight into someone's front yard to get him off the road and onto grass. Logan and Tom frantically checked his body, but they couldn't see any breakages. His knees had a small bit of skin off and he was covered in horse shit from where he fell, as he always did one as soon as he loaded on the float. 'He seems okay,' Tom said, relieved.

'Yeah, can't *see* anything,' Logan said, still a little apprehensive. He took a deep breath, as his heart was racing fast. 'Alright. Put him back on. You'll need to stand with him the rest of the way.'

Tom nodded, pocketing some of the grass from the lawn they were standing on. He knew that the unsettling experience could make the King scared of being in the horse truck, so he had to calm him down and show him the truck was still safe. They loaded him back on and Tom stood with him, speaking to him calmly and feeding him little bits of grass as Logan drove the rest of the way slowly.

Logan rang Mike on the way and let him know what had happened. When they arrived at the stable, it was all hands on deck. They took the King straight to the wash bay and they washed him down. There were many little nicks from the fall, but he had fared pretty well. It was too close to the race to administer anti-inflammatories or a precaution of antibiotics, so they decided to cold-hose all four legs at once to pre-empt any swelling. Logan was so thankful for the state-of-the-art set-up, as they had a freezer that water ran through for hosing on the horse's legs. Like many horses, the King hated the ice boots and tended to panic when they put them on. He remained relatively calm while they worked hosing all legs. Luckily, the others didn't have a scratch on them. Cynthia had bought the best horse truck on the market, and it had just paid for itself twice over.

Then it became a waiting game. Every two hours, the King's legs were hosed with cold water, and they set shifts for every four hours during the night. The other three horses were hosed twice, and were hand-walked and fed fresh-picked grass for an hour longer than normal to help calm their nerves.

Tom had called Cynthia, and she was in a complete spin. She insisted that their new partner, Darcy, was told what had happened immediately. Logan called Darcy, who was back in Australia. It was 6.20 a.m. in the morning there. 'I've put you on speaker, Logan,' Darcy said.

'Hi, Logan,' a familiar female voice said.

'Hi, Jo,' Logan replied. He had heard through the grapevine that the two were officially together. Darcy was a lot younger, but Logan wasn't going to judge.

'Now, tell us what's happened,' Darcy said.

Logan explained the incident, the King's current state, and the measures they were going through. Finally, Darcy said, 'Well, if you and Mike can't get him sorted, I don't think anyone else could. Let me know if anything changes.' They said their goodbyes and hung up.

Logan headed up to the main house to assure Cynthia that everything was under control. Cynthia may have lived forty kilometres away, but she was at the boy's house every day. She still had her office and PA there. After Logan had settled her down about the King, they talked briefly about James and the other night. Finally, Cynthia said, 'Logan, I have to apologise to you for my behaviour.' Her tone was business-like and distanced. 'My advancement ... it was out of line, very unprofessional, I'm sorry.' Her cheeks had gone bright red.

Logan nodded, trying to ease her discomfort by not making a big issue out of it. 'No harm, no foul. Whisky can give you courage like that.' It took a moment for Cynthia to realise that

Logan had tasted what she'd been drinking when she kissed him. Before he left, Logan said, 'Let's focus on Saturday's races.'

'I want four winners, Logan,' Cynthia said, back to her old self again.

'All four. No slow ones.' He winked at her and left.

Logan called Victoria and told her all about the day's drama, and they talked for a while longer afterwards. 'So, what are you doing for Christmas?' Logan said.

'The answer you want to hear is "Coming to Newmarket to spend it with y'all," isn't it?'

'Well …'

'It can be arranged,' Victoria said coyly.

'Text me the dates you're available and I'll book the flights,' Logan said, showing his eagerness. 'First class fine by you?'

'Is there any other way to travel?' Logan just melted at her accent and the way she spoke so confidently, but with a subtle humour. Sometimes he struggled to work out if she was being serious or making a joke.

When they got off the phone, Victoria saw that Logan had already sent her a photo of his big, love-struck grin.

Logan and Tom took turns hosing the King during the night. At 6 a.m., Mike gave the all clear with the flexion test; noting that there was only very slight swelling on both knees. James hopped on and gave him a light trot and canter. 'He felt fine,' James said on his return. 'Sound.' They all agreed they had dodged a bullet but continued the hosing for good measure.

As the day of the race approached, the pressure was building. This was their first chance to win a Group 1 race. Logan was getting nervous, and Tom felt it too. Even Miles was a bit tense, and his smart-ass comments were down by eighty per cent. On the other hand, James was focused and in a good headspace. He headed to the gym for his last hard sessions so he could scrape in for weight.

Logan decided he wanted a brand-new suit for race day and Miles took him to the best tailor in Newmarket. Logan wanted everything new—a fresh look. He trusted Miles's styling and accepted the smart new look that was picked out for him. Dark blue jacket and slacks, polished tan shoes, new cufflinks, new tie. No expense spared on this outfit. It was a neat £2,800 at the till. For once, Logan didn't have to worry about his bank balance. He was extremely happy and thanked the tailor before they headed for the door.

It opened, and in walked Angus Masters and two of his clients. They both stopped dead in their tracks and stared. Masters knew he would run into Logan eventually while he was in town, that was a given, but Logan had no clue he would be running into Masters.

'Logan,' Masters said, giving him a nod. Logan didn't reply. He headed for the door and roughly brushed past Masters, looking dead straight. Miles, being Miles, gave Masters and his clients the once-over out of curiosity before he followed Logan out. Just as the door was easing shut behind them, Logan heard Masters give a scoffing laugh and say loudly to his clients, 'I didn't even know he had changed teams! Now he's riding that bitch.'

Logan and Miles had only taken a few steps out the door when Logan whipped around. Miles was rolling his eyes, but quickly saw that Logan was barrelling back towards the door. He jumped in front of him and blocked his path. 'Don't! Logan, don't. It's not worth it. I'm not bothered. Let's go.'

Logan sidestepped Miles and pushed through the door. He barged past both Masters' clients and thundered towards Masters. Masters wasn't expecting Logan to charge back in and he stepped back too quickly, falling over the tailor's stool behind him. He fell flat on his ass on a pile of material and sewing instruments. The tailor's prickly pincushion drove sixteen needles close to an inch into his arse cheek. He rolled onto his side and yanked it out, crying out in pain. Logan had closed the distance between them quickly and stood over him. When Masters made a move to get up, Logan stepped the lizard-skin cowboy boot down on his forearm to keep him pinned to the floor. Masters' two friends were stunned and didn't move an inch. They had seen the video of the fight and knew Logan could throw a punch. Besides, they were only along for the ride and Masters was the one with the smart mouth, not them. They didn't want any trouble.

'Get off me!' Masters screamed.

Logan rolled his foot forward and pushed down harder. Masters cried out in pain, grabbing Logan's boot to try and pull it away. He looked over at his cowardly friends for help, but they weren't moving. Miles had walked back in after Logan and was standing there, looking just as clueless about what to do.

Logan motioned to Miles. 'This is Miles. He is my racing manager, and a good friend of mine. As you have guessed, he is gay. He is also a human being who deserves respect. Unlike you, he is not a complete asshole. And I think you owe him an apology.'

Logan pressed down harder, and Masters blurted out, 'I'm sorry, I'm sorry. I shouldn't have called you that. I'm sorry.'

Miles looked unsure but said quietly, 'I accept your apology.'

Logan lifted his foot, and Masters rolled over onto his side to grab his aching forearm. Before Logan could react, Miles had walked beside him and stamped down hard on Masters' wrist. Masters gave a high-pitched yelp, and Miles hissed, 'Who's the bitch now!'

Miles spent the rest of the afternoon dramatically retelling the story of the horrible encounter to anyone who would listen and explaining how Logan had swooped in and heroically saved the day. 'I bet that Masters guy didn't know *he'd* be the one with an ass-full of pricks!' Miles had repeatedly joked about Masters landing on the pincushion. Miles had never had anyone stand up for him so valiantly before. He had been threatened many times by homophobic people, and once was even assaulted when he was eighteen years old. Logan was his hero, and he spent the afternoon jokingly calling Logan his brave Romeo.

Logan slipped out of the barn and went for a walk. He was shaken to the core. Masters haunted his thought. He really did hate him. He hated everything about him. He brought up too many memories and too much pain. He couldn't let it go. He may have finally seen the real side to Angela and let his feelings go, but losing Bluey and losing those three Group 1's had scarred his ego beyond repair. On the outside, he may have appeared cool and calm, but on the inside he fought back the feelings of self-doubt every day to stop them from enveloping him.

Logan called Don and, after talking it through for forty minutes, he started to feel much better. Don broke things down, compared the last two months to the last ten years, reminded him that there would always be bumps in the road, and Masters was just a bump. Don told Logan that he was sure he would have to encounter him a few more times yet, so he needed to prepare for that.

Logan got off the phone and walked through the barn to check again on the horses. Mike had done X-rays of the King's knees again and all was clear. Tom had put a mud poultice of natural ingredients on his knees and cannons. Logan would do the 10 p.m. hose and Tom would do the 2 a.m. one.

Logan's phone pinged. It was from Tom. It was a YouTube video with the title 'Weston wins Round 2!!!'

CHAPTER 23

The high-end tailor had security cameras all over his shop—four different angles, all with sound. He had saved the recordings, originally to report it to the police, but his son had a better idea. After editing the shots together, he uploaded it to YouTube. It showed the whole scene play out clearly, starting with Angus's comment and finishing just after Miles's sassy stomp. Logan groaned. He didn't want the attention, especially this close to the race tomorrow. He texted out to everyone close to contact him on his personal number only; his work mobile would be off.

Victoria sent through a message immediately: 'Remind me to never piss you off!'

Both Pete and Neale called Logan quickly afterwards to laugh about the whole thing. Pete told Logan, 'Everyone at the track knows he is still obsessed with you.'

When the video was sent to Masters, he erupted with rage in his hotel room. He ended up in a heated exchange with Angela that ended with her hanging up on him.

That night on the phone, Victoria read out the video comments to Logan: 'Oh, what about this one! "You're a good person, Logan. That guy is an asshole." Aw, that's sweet.' Ninety per cent of the comments were on Logan's side, and the rest were mostly online trolls trying to stir the shit even more. Victoria finally managed to get Logan to laugh about it, which relieved the stress a little bit.

Finally, it was race day. Mike, Logan, Tom, and James inspected all four horses. All four seemed one hundred per cent fit and healthy; blood counts were spot on, they all trotted up well, and all four trotted two laps of the track. They had thirty minutes in their paddock before coming back in for a hose down and shampoo, then twenty minutes under the infrared lights to help dry them and warm their muscles.

Forest Black was in race two, barrier eight, at $6.50.

Everest was in race three, barrier eleven, at $2.20, favourite to win.

Warrior King was in race five, barrier five—Logan's lucky number—at $1.90, favourite to win.

Miss Jasmine was in race seven, barrier two, at $11.20, pretty good odds. There was a filly in the race that had won her last four races that was 6/4.

Logan headed back home, with Hank at his heels, to get dressed for the races. Victoria texted, as she knew he would be too busy for a phone call, and wished him luck. She had just had a haircut and it was quite short. Logan loved the new spunky look. He replied, then put his phone away. He needed to get in the zone. He was very focused on his work, and Victoria understood that.

Tom had invited his new girlfriend Lily to watch the races. It was their first official outing as a couple. Her family, the Henry-Mays, also had a large turkey breeding enterprise and could have bought Cynthia out three or four times over. Tom was very quiet about his private life. Apparently, they had been dating for weeks, and no one knew a thing. Logan instantly liked Lily. She was switched on, confident, and presented herself as a no-nonsense type of girl. Tom was a good-looking young man with plenty to offer, and Logan instantly saw the connection between the two. Tom didn't have time for a needy girlfriend, as he was very focused on his work. *He could become the youngest man to train a Group 1 winner at Royal Ascot in almost eighty years,* Logan thought, smiling proudly at Tom.

Miles headed out to the track early with James to walk the track. There had been four millimetres of rain overnight and eleven millimetres on Monday. The track was going to be rated a dead four (good to firm); it had been broadcasted on the 9 a.m. turf talk and stewards' report. Logan thought it would be perfect for all four runners.

The horses arrived at the track and all four settled in well to the tie-up stalls. Forest Black was first up, and it had been decided he would start over seven furlongs. They were hoping he would run well and gain experience from the run. He was very fit, and Logan would not be surprised if he won, but he was being realistic as the field had three other maiden starters, and the talk was the two from the Talisman Racing stable were pretty smart.

Cynthia looked beautiful. Logan actually gave her a kiss on the cheek and said, 'You look stunning.'

It was time. Tom brought the saddle over, and he and Logan saddled Forest Black up and eyed the competitors in the saddling enclosure. Both the Talisman Racing colts looked extremely good. O'Brien's colt looked smart and so did Angus McCarthy's. But Forest Black certainly held his ground in the field on presentation. The plan was to let him jump and settle mid-field if possible and run home.

They all loaded in, and the gates sprung wide. He jumped well and James eased him back. He was running sixth, three back and one out with cover. James had him extremely relaxed and he had his head down and was striding beautifully. The field started to quicken three furlongs out and he kept his position. At the two-furlong marker, two colts powered past from the Talisman Racing stable and he looked as if he was struggling and hesitating to go through the gap. James quickly felt the resistance, eased him back, cleared the heels, and switched to the middle of the track. He balanced Forest and gave him three smart whacks around the tail. Forest laid his ears back and lowered his body and went after the leaders. Stride by stride, he clawed his way forward. With seventy-five metres to go, it looked like he had no chance and would run a very solid second, but James gave him one more around the tail. Logan yelled 'Run, Forest, run!'

Run he did, and it was a head bob at the line. Logan and the team were ecstatic! They didn't care if he had won or not. He had shown true grit. The race caller said the developed print was a short half-head. 'The winner of race two is Forest Black, ridden by James Baker and trained by Tom Baker, and he has paid $4.80 on the tote.'

Miles was the most excited, and he was bragging that it was the work *he* had done in Logan's absence that had turned the horse around. 'Because, as you know, I'm the number one trainer around here.' They all laughed.

Everest was up next. The team was confident, even though he was now in a Stakes race. Tom and Miles had changed him to the Stakes race when the nominations came out, with only a handful of runners looking like they would accept to run it. He was rock hard, fit, and they all seemed to think he had improved more. Tom got the saddle from the weigh-out room and they saddled him up. He was a bit on the toe, so Logan asked Sophie to walk him to help calm his nerves. The plan was the same as last time; let him jump and set his own pace. The clerk of the course rode past indicating they were to head to the saddling enclosure for the jockeys to mount up. As they were walking from the back ring to the front, the number two horse just stopped and wouldn't budge. It had a bee in its bonnet and had decided it was not going out. Everest was doing his best to behave as they waited.

'How are you, buddy?' a familiar voice said, then made a click-click-click sound, which was used to urge a horse forward. Everest started to stir, getting uneasy again.

Tom was behind Everest and snapped at the man trying to stir up the horse, 'I don't need your help mate; stop stirring up the horse, please!'

The man clicked at him again. This time, Tom didn't get a word in as Everest laid his ears back and lunged at the man. Everest had recognised his old trainer—Masters—and he bit down hard on his arm, which had been resting on the fence rail. Masters jumped back and hollered, 'You bastard!'

And just like that, Everest seemed to calm down and regain focus. Number two had been coaxed along by the clerk of the course, and the horses all started to move forward again. Tom saw Masters holding his arm and realised he was the man riling up the horse. 'I guess *he* hates you too,' Tom said over the fence. 'Add me and him to the list. I imagine it's quite long now, you twat.'

The race began. Everest jumped and James let him find his own stride. That worked out to be a twelve-length lead after two furlongs. James didn't fight him; it was about him finding his own rhythm. Four furlongs out from the finish, he was still eight in front and travelling well, but the other jockeys were not falling for this trick again and they started to make their own moves. At the two-furlong marker, they still had four lengths to claw back but they seemed to be struggling. Then, with just one furlong to go, James let the hand brake off and Everest quickly put another four lengths behind him. The race wasn't the day's draw card, but the crowd got extremely excited as they witnessed an incredible horse in the making.

The official margin was seven lengths, eased down on the line and a race record. James gave his second whip salute to the crowd. It was his first Stakes win and his twin brother's first Stakes win and second double. Now the smile was wide on the team, but it was made even better when Tom told them what had happened before the race. Logan had won with both Masters' ex-horses and he was there to witness it—while nursing a bite on his arm. Logan had never witnessed such jubilation at a winner's presentation. It was not just a team, but a strong family unit—Logan, Tom, James, Cynthia, Mike, Miles, and the strappers.

But there was no time to waste. Logan quickly brought James and Tom back to earth and set their sights on the next race. He gave them a pep talk—'Focus, and stay grounded.' Tom brought the saddle over, and they saddled the King. Logan had a deep feeling they were about to witness something extraordinary from this colt. He had never been fully extended, but this was going to be a test. There were the best two-year-olds in Europe in this race. His first start was over six furlongs and this was over seven furlongs, and with the uphill rise, more like a mile.

As they left the saddling enclosure, Logan noticed Masters from the corner of his eye. He could see he was captivated with the King's size and strength. James rode out on the track and bounced up over Warrior King's neck. The racetrack had brought the docile King to life, and he felt huge and powerful. Logan received a text from Darcy wising him luck. They had paid a handsome sum for a fifty per cent share in a colt that was possibly going to do something super on this royal track. $1.40, he was on track, as the bookies were not taking a chance. They didn't want to be skinned alive again by Baker Stables.

Logan had been nervous in many races, but he had never had such a champion in his care. James loaded him in the barriers. The starter had them all in, and hit the buzzer. The gates flew open and he jumped a half a length slower than the field. Within three strides, he had got squeezed so bad that James was thrown back and they both nearly fell. The King knuckled and banged his nose on the ground. James lost his right stirrup and the King got back to his feet. They were a good fifteen lengths behind. The field were three-quarters full speed and the King was basically in a trot. The race caller said, 'Ladies and gentlemen, I would say the favourite Warrior King will be retired from the race.' It was like James had heard the disappointment in the crowd. He placed his foot back in the stirrup and drove the King in a forward momentum. James gave him his head and let him find his rhythm and balance; he felt fine and sound. The caller was amazed. 'Looks like Warrior King is not giving this one up without a fight! He certainly is a Warrior, ladies and gentlemen, but unfortunately he is currently forty lengths behind.'

They passed the five-furlong marker, and Logan was just gutted. An hour and a half ago, the team was on fire, and now it was like a swimming pool of water was dropped on their heads. James worked out that if he increased his tempo just slightly more by the four-furlong marker to home, if he was fifteen lengths off, he may have a chance if the King could sustain the run. He was still a two-year-old and he was a mature colt, like Everest, but he knew he was something out of the box. He increased the tempo and, just like James had hoped, he was closing the lengths. James gave him a very slight breather and the others kicked. With two furlongs to go, the caller said, 'It looks like Warrior King's run has just ended.'

James sat lower and urged on the King. 'C'mon, boy! Pss, pss!' He drove him hands and heels, pushing him out. The King lowered and James drove hard. He passed one, then two. With 150 metres to go, he had four lengths to get back on the leader. James knew he was giving his all—he felt it—but in that split second he gave him one around the backside to see if there was anything left.

The caller yelled in excitement, 'The King has grown wings!' The crowd were all on their feet. The colt had nearly fallen, was forty lengths behind, and now he was within winning distance. James couldn't believe it! The King lengthened and lowered, and he ground back the advantage. He was neck and neck. On the last stride, James pushed down hard on his neck and the King stretched it out as long as he could, like he understood. The crowd roared as the horses bolted across the line. The race caller yelled out, 'What a finish, ladies and gentlemen! I think Warrior King has missed to Tempest Two by a nose!' Logan and Tom hugged. What a race.

The team stood close to each other, almost holding their breath as the finish was played back up on the big screen in slow motion. It showed the last few strides and it was official—the crowd erupted with cheers—Warrior King had won by a whisker. 'Ladies and gentlemen, this is what racing is about. I think today we have witnessed the next champion of Europe.'

James rode back and everyone cheered him, as it was a performance that was worth a standing ovation. The race caller announced, 'Warrior King completed his last three furlongs in 32.8 seconds. There has never been a horse to ever break 33.2 up the rise.'

James saluted the judge and unsaddled. Cynthia and Tom came running over, and James burst into tears in their arms. It was a very surreal moment for the three of them. Logan shook James's hand and gave him a big hug. They couldn't hear a word over the applause from the crowd, so Logan gave him a wink and nod. Miles bear-hugged James and was so caught up in the moment, he planted a big kiss on his lips. James blushed deeply and Miles stood back, shocked at what he had done. Cameras were flashing all around them. 'Oh, uh, sorry.' But James just grinned and took Miles's hand, then his brother's, and raised their arms up to the crowd. Tom joined in and took Logan's hand, who took Cynthia's, who took Mike's, and so on. The team stood there, their arms raised up together like they had won at the Olympics as the crowd cheered.

As the team walked over to the presentation, Logan laughed and shook his head at Miles. 'You always have to be the centre of attention, don't you, mate?' Miles was pale with guilt, 'Fuck, what did I just do?' but James gave him a smile to let him know it was okay.

They held the presentation, then the pressed swarmed. Logan told Tom he was going to load up the three colts and head home. 'I'll send a driver back to get Miss Jasmine after her race.' The King was absolutely buggered. He had tried harder than any other horse that Logan and Tom had ever seen before.

'Just one more, boys,' Logan said, winking. The chance of winning four races today was very slim, but the bookies had slashed her price to $2.80, favourite. Logan loaded the three colts and a strapper to feed the King fresh grass to keep him calm for the short trip home.

Tom took the reins and Miles replaced Logan to help saddle up Miss Jasmine. Tom gave him plenty of shit about helping James come out to the world, and even though Miles felt incredibly guilty about the incident, he stood tall and said quietly, 'Gay pride, my friend.'

Tom legged James up and knew he didn't need to say a thing, as James was in a very rare state of focus. The day looked as if it would end with a fairy-tale finish, but with just three strides from the winning post, Miss Jasmine was caught right on the line by the second favourite. The mood in the crowd went flat. James was their new hero, but it just wasn't to be.

'A treble with a Group 1 and Group 3 is pretty bloody good,' Tom told a deflated James, as they packed up their gear.

James said quietly, 'Bollocks Tom, I really wanted to win it.' He felt as though he had let the whole team down.

Miles could see the sadness in his eyes, so he said reassuringly, 'It would only have been icing on the delicious three-tier cake we already have.' James nodded sadly, and Miles put a comforting arm around his shoulders. 'And you can't eat cake anyway, you fat bitch.'

James scoffed and looked up at Miles's cheeky smile in shock. He gave Miles a hard shove and the three of them cracked up laughing.

Logan had sent back a lead horse in the truck so Miss Jasmine had some company to keep her calm on the drive home, and they loaded her in. As they left, the press were all over James and Tom. It was extraordinary. It was their second-ever race day and they had won the two Stakes races and showcased a potential champion. Tom suggested a 9 a.m. press conference, tour of the facilities, and a four-way interview with Cynthia, Logan, James, and himself. The members of the press were disappointed, but they also were very keen to get an interview with the Aussie behind the success.

Angus Masters was the press's next target but he had no issue telling them to fuck off. The YouTube video was well over two million views by now, and inside he was simmering away. He had to keep a calm face as he had clients accompanying him who were going to outlay a decent amount of money on some exciting new staying prospects. Adding fuel to the fire was the wins by Everest and Forest Black. Everest was extremely promising, and Masters knew Logan must be thinking of the Cox Plate next year. After seeing that performance, Masters knew he would be hard to run down. He decided to lay low and told his two travelling companions that he was going to spend the night going through the sales book and doing form. Part of this was true—he was going to review what had been sent to him by his racing manager.

Logan's phone rang. 'Convict.'

'You know, it would be nice if you could just say hello for once,' Logan grumbled.

'It's convict or gobshite. Up to you, but I know which one I would prefer.'

Logan just laughed and shook his head. He didn't get a chance to ask what the call was regarding before Mick said, 'The King. The sheik wants to buy him.'

Logan was silent. He knew this would happen. The King has a sensational pedigree and had now won a Group 1 with possibly the best performance ever on a racetrack, worldwide. He could go to stud now and dual-hemisphere for 50,000 euros and $85,000 Australian, and, if his fertility rate was good, earn upwards of sixty million in his first three years.

'Don't do this to me,' Logan said quietly. 'Please, mate, I'm begging. I can't lose this horse. He is a once-in-a-lifetime horse.'

For once, Mick didn't fire back with a comment; he just said, 'I'll ring Cynthia myself, then.'

'Do what you have you have to do.' Logan wasn't mad. He knew Mick had the needs of his client to look out for.

Logan hadn't even had time to let the thought of losing the King set in, when his mobile rang five minutes later. It was Cynthia. He froze and his stomach knotted. He felt like he was going to throw up. He sat down on the closet feed bucket, answered the phone, and braced himself. 'Cynthia.'

'Logan. I just got off the phone with your Irish friend.'

Logan didn't say a word.

'He offered fifteen million for the fifty per cent we still own. He said if I was interested, then the sale would go through another agent, as he could not be the one to take a "once-in-a-lifetime horse" from a good friend—his words.'

Logan felt good knowing that, but he still didn't know if she was going to sell. He was holding his breath, waiting for Cynthia to continue.

'The problem is, when I signed the deal with your Aussie mates to sell fifty per cent, the arrangement stipulated that he couldn't be resold again while racing, and that he couldn't be sold to an opposing stud farm for standing rights, either.'

Logan was slowly processing what Cynthia had said before she added, 'Logan, the King is *our* King and he's not going anywhere.'

Logan let out the breath he'd been holding, and Cynthia chuckled quietly. 'As you Aussies say, "She'll be right, mate." Now go throw his bloody rug on and come up to the house. We need to celebrate!'

CHAPTER 24

Logan had turned his work phone back on, and it had not stopped for more than a minute between calls. Finally, the call he had been waiting for came through. 'You must be pretty proud of yourself. Congratulations, Logan,' Victoria said.

Logan grinned like an idiot. He had not stopped thinking about her all day. 'Cynthia just got offered fifteen million for our half.'

'Really?' Victoria said. Logan had talked about his horses endlessly, and Victoria knew he wasn't in it for the money. His passion was horses, and she knew how much he loved them.

'But he's not going anywhere,' Logan added. 'Cynthia told them he's not for sale.'

Victoria exhaled. 'That's a relief.'

Logan grinned, overjoyed that she understood him so well already. Deep down, he was madly in love with her and had pictured their life together. When the truck pulled up, Logan had to say his goodbyes.

The team unloaded Miss Jasmine, and Mike checked all four horses thoroughly. After giving the all-clear, he headed home to change. Logan had the staff pick fresh rye and clover and place it in the corner of the stables. The water troughs had the temperature set at eighteen degrees at all times. Each stall also had a surveillance camera, and Logan could actually log on and scroll through the live feeds whenever he pleased. As well as this, they had full-time security. Both security guards were retired horseman and knew the horse would get sick before they knew it themselves.

As Tom settled in Miss Jasmine, Logan came around to check over her legs. 'She ran super,' Tom said. 'She will be a Group filly in the making.'

Tom nodded and wrapped him up in a bear hug. 'We did it, mate. We bloody well did it.'

Tom teared up. 'What a day.'

Both Tom and Logan were horseman first and, they ignored all the competitive bullshit that came with racing, which people like Angus Masters fed on.

They walked down the breezeway and talked and laughed, as the grooms shook their hands and congratulated them. Everyone gave Tom and Logan a hug, and a few of the women landed some kisses on their cheeks, as well. Logan looked across at Tom and could see that it was really starting to sink in.

Everest was bright-eyed and loving the attention and pats from passers-by; Forest Black was standing asleep in the back of his box; and the staff briefly gathered to admire the King. He was the most valuable two-year-old in the world and possibly the best racehorse in all age groups; only time would tell. The King didn't seem to care about the attention. He had eaten all his fresh grass, had cleaned up his feed and was sound asleep. The staff went home to change for the celebration dinner and drinks that night, so Tom and Logan were the last two in the barn. They watched Warrior King sleep and quietly talked about what was next for him.

They heard a car pull up outside, and Cynthia, James, Miles, and Mike walked into the barn. They had gone home and dressed for the party. Cynthia walked with big strides, back straight; she had a powerful aura about her. 'Here comes the commander-in-chief,' Tom whispered to Logan, jokingly.

Logan knew that Cynthia had never been prouder in her life. 'Gentleman, thank you very much for giving me the most beautiful afternoon of my life.' She looked radiant. 'I'm not just proud of my two boys, I'm so very proud of us all. Today, we proved to the world that we are to be taken seriously.' They all nodded. Still on a roll, she continued, 'Moving forward, we take no prisoners. If the horses are not up to scratch, we don't waste our time on them— cut them loose. Only fast ones.' She paused to let the words she had said so many times to Logan before sink in, then she smiled and added, 'Now, let's celebrate!'

Everyone gave a little cheer and started to make their way up to the main house. As they walked back towards the cars, Cynthia said to Tom and Logan, 'I just bought Livingston Farm.' They looked a bit confused. Livingston Farm was where they had been taking the horses to work cattle, and to ride and relax. It had been an integral part of the horse preparation. 'I purchased the property, and the cattle as well, from Mr Livingston,' she said matter-of-factly. 'Mike is moving to the house there. Maybe that will wear his bloody kids out,' she said more quietly, laughing.

Logan couldn't help but find this powerful, in-control side of Cynthia very attractive. Victoria had a similar side, but subtler. He missed her and sent her a text with a sad face emoji: 'I wish you were here to celebrate with me.' He was like a love-struck school boy.

She replied: 'Go and enjoy the night. I'm having a low-key celebration here in your honour.' She sent a photo of her on the couch eating salmon and pasta, with a white wine spritzer in hand, watching an old midday movie with her two cats, Ralph and Tiger.

She had told him right from the start that she was 'low maintenance'. And Logan had to admit that she certainly was.

CHAPTER 25

Winning with Everest and Forest Black was every bit as satisfying as Logan had hoped—even more. He knew he shouldn't be smug, but he couldn't stop grinning. He imagined Masters' face seeing his two ex-racehorses winning. After Warrior King's win, Logan felt like he was about to be woken up from a dream.

The whole team and all the staff had assembled for the celebration of the day's triumphs. Logan didn't need a party to celebrate the victory. Truthfully, he wished he was on the couch with Victoria watching a movie, decompressing. The build-up to this moment didn't start just from the day Cynthia had hired him, it had been a lifelong quest. He was always extremely competitive and, up until now, he had tried so hard to win the Group 1's but never achieved it. He considered the reasons why he'd never managed to do it before: *Overthinking things. Being pigheaded. Not doing things the right way. Doubting myself.* The fact was, he had never been given the chance to just train and have no other pressures, plus now he had horse quality equal to the best of the best trainers.

Training with Tom had made him pull back and focus, giving only the best of himself. He wanted to teach Tom how to do things the right way. Tom was almost a faultless human being; his manners were impeccable and his outlook on life was very similar to his own in many ways. For someone his age, he got what life was about, which was very rare in a young man. It had given him huge amounts of confidence, and now they both bounced ideas off each other, and Logan felt that he was learning and changing into a better trainer, too. Being paid 'a shitload', in Logan's terms, helped as well. He had not checked his bank account for over seven weeks. He never worried about a thing other than the horses. *And it all started with punching Masters in the face.*

Cynthia stood up on a chair to make a speech to the party. Her speech was proud and very thankful—maybe dragged on a minute too long, but she had just won the biggest race of her life with a horse that showed endless potential. Logan knew she was going to celebrate this win, and by the amount of drinks she was finishing, he knew she was going further into dangerous territory. After one alcoholic drink, Logan wandered into the kitchen to get a soft drink. He was still buzzing from the win and alcohol would only dampen it.

Miles and James were in the kitchen, laughing together, when Logan walked in. 'Hey, champ,' Logan said to James, pouring himself a glass of coke. 'A+ performance on all four rides today, mate.'

James smiled, but didn't get to comment before Miles quipped, 'I'll tell you in the morning if it's five for five,' shooting James a flirtatious look.

Logan burst out laughing. James rolled his eyes at Miles, and they all went back in to the party.

Everyone was reliving the wins and, after a while, Logan realised he was too tired to be around so many intoxicated people. He quietly said good night to Tom and told him that he was slipping away from the party. Tom understood, as he was about to do the same with his girlfriend.

Hank was happy Logan was home. Logan wrestled with him on the floor until his wrist couldn't take any more scratches and chew marks from Hank. He texted a few times back and forth to Victoria, and even sent a video of the wrestling session with Hank, which she adored.

When there was a knock at the door, Logan already knew who it would be. He hoped he was wrong, but when he opened the door, Cynthia was standing there. 'You didn't say good night,' Cynthia said. 'You didn't say good night to me.' She was hammered and was trying to act sober leaning against the door.

'You're right. I was tired so I slipped out. I should have said good night. I'm sorry.'

'Maybe you should make it up to me,' Cynthia said, giving him a seductive look as she ran a finger down his chest.

Logan took a deep breath and went to turn her down again, when Hank flew out the door, barking. 'Hank?' In the moonlight, he could see Hank was racing towards the barn. Logan gently pushed Cynthia back and grabbed his shoes from beside the door, rushing to pull them on.

'What's wrong? Where are you going?' Cynthia demanded.

He didn't have time to explain; he just took off, sprinting as fast as he could after Hank. The last time Hank had acted so strangely, they'd caught some teenagers breaking into their shed at home. Hank had disappeared into the barn, and over his heavy breathing Logan could hear him going off, barking and growling.

As he got closer, Logan saw the beam of a flashlight darting around inside. He lengthened his stride, then he heard the loudest yelp he had ever heard from Hank—just one, then silence. 'Hank!' he yelled.

Logan hit the lights at the barn and he could see Hank sprawled out on the ground, motionless. As he ran further in, he saw the door to Warrior King's stable was open, and a dark figure raced from behind the tack room door and sprinted out towards the end of the barn. 'Stop!' Logan called out. The intruder stumbled and fell hard onto one knee, but quickly got back to his feet. The man was smart enough to hit the light switch at the end of the barn as he raced out. It was the central switch, and the barn was flooded with darkness. Logan was blind for ten seconds before his eyes adjusted, and he quickly found the barn light and switched it back on. He slowly stumbled over to Hank and sank to the ground beside him. He looked over into Warrior King's stable to see a stiff, lifeless body; with fesses out behind him, eyes glassed over. Logan had seen many times before how a horse looked when it had been put down.

Logan put his hand on Hank's heart, his eyes already filling with tears. 'Hank?' he said hoarsely. There was still a strong beat. He said his name over and over, but there was no movement. He was out cold. 'Don't you fucking die, you little bastard. Don't you fucking die!' Suddenly, Logan felt the rage swell up inside him. He gently scooped up Hank, hurried to the end of the barn, and looked out into the darkness. He heard a car start up outside the property fence and quickly drive away. *Whoever that is, I'll kill them*, he thought, hugging Hank's motionless body closer to him.

As he walked back through the barn, his mind raced. If Hank died, he would never forgive himself. He gently placed Hank on top of a straw bale and just waited. Tears were streaming down his cheeks, and he couldn't even see Hank clearly. Then he felt a soft lick at his hand and he looked down to see Hank's tail slightly wagging. Hank was slowly coming around. He knew Hank was going to be all right, and Logan gave a relieved laugh, kissing his head. 'Good boy, good boy,' he kept saying.

Cynthia had finally stumbled down into the barn, confused and angry. When she walked over to Logan, who was standing at the door to Warrior King's stable, she screamed in horror at the dead body. Logan ignored her and rang Tom.

Tom was in bed with his new girlfriend, but when he heard his phone go off for the third time, he answered, already wary. 'What's wrong?' He assumed his mother had made a move on Logan again and needed to be dragged back home.

Logan spoke through gritted teeth, 'Get James, Mike, and Miles and get down to the barn *now*,' and he hung up. Tom knew it was much more serious. He scrambled out of bed, ignoring Lily's confused questions, threw on some clothes, and ran across the hall to bang on James's door. 'Down the barn now, both of you. No questions, get moving.'

When everyone arrived, bleary-eyed, Logan took them to Warrior King's stall. Miles put his arm around Cynthia, who was shaking like a leaf. Their immediate shocked reaction slowly lessened as they realised, just as Cynthia sobbed, 'It's not him. It's not the King.'

Though it was a striking resemblance, the person who had targeted the King, and as far as they knew had succeeded in killing him, had instead put down a colt called Polish Navy. Logan nodded and said, 'With the tour tomorrow, I knew the press would be snapping photos and getting underfoot, spooking the horses. I thought the King deserved a day off. I put him in Polish Navy's stall after everyone left, to go out into the paddock with the others tomorrow instead.' He turned back to the body. 'With a rug over him, he's the spitting image.' They all looked at the body in silence. Polish Navy was a beautiful big horse and hadn't even raced yet. He had taken the hit for the King.

'I've already called the police,' Logan added calmly. 'James, put Cynthia to bed please. Tom, please find security—and fire those useless prick immediately.' The horse dying was bad enough, but the intruder had nearly killed Hank.

When the police arrived, Logan was sitting in Polish Navy's stable, watching Warrior King sleep. Hank was asleep at Logan's feet. The police went over everything, and finally left at 2 a.m. Logan was still too wound up to go to bed, so Tom sat with him in the kitchen and they talked until the sun came up, drafting the press release for the morning.

At 6 a.m., everyone gathered in the kitchen to go over their plan. Cynthia looked like death warmed up, and sat quietly, looking very sorry for herself. It was decided that Tom would handle the press and be the one to release a statement, standing alongside the sergeant from the local police station.

Mike checked Hank over and did a full vet check, then followed up with X-rays of his ribs and legs. He was fine, nothing broken, but he was still sore and felt sorry for himself. Hank had never been allowed on the bed, let alone in it, but now he slept under the doona beside Logan's pillow. Logan would have to sleep in whatever spot Hank had left spare in his new domain.

When Logan called Victoria to tell her what had happened, she was furious. She was more concerned that Logan could have been hurt, or even killed, if he had intervened earlier, but Logan dismissed it. As bad as the situation was, Logan knew there was work to do that was more important. He wasn't going to be so easily knocked off course.

Tom, Logan, Miles, and Mike headed to the Tattersalls Racehorse in Training sale. They had forty-eight horses they were interested in. Logan turned his phone off, as the press was going wild after the tragedy last night, and it had quickly spread worldwide. The Australian investors, Darcy and MJ, were very relieved that the King survived and arranged to speak with Cynthia about her security measures moving forward.

The Tattersalls sale started with a few days of inspections and vetting. Despite the incident, business had to go on as normal. Mike knew it was a serious day and had only been drinking soda water during the celebrations. He didn't need a throbbing head while he was bending down and flexing legs. The day was long. Normally it would take a few hours to see all the horses, but everyone wanted to congratulate them and also offer their sympathy. Logan and Tom were both irritated. They both loved animals, particularly horses, and Polish Navy was a lovely-natured horse. It wasn't fair. Though he didn't say it, Tom suspected that Logan was the target, more so than his family. There was not a shred of evidence at the scene and the local police seemed useless.

Tom and Logan had just finished looking at Lot 52, when Logan noticed Masters and his two backers in the next row over, looking at horses. His blood started to boil inside, as just being in the guy's presence got to him. Tom noticed Logan had a lock on someone, and quickly realised it was Masters. Masters was looking over the shape, type, and athleticism of a three-year-old gelding. He wrote notes in his catalogue, as all buyers do. The catalogue is the buyer's bible. He moved to the front to inspect the legs. When he dipped, he reached down to his left knee in pain, quickly straightened, then continued his inspection. Tom and Logan locked eyes, thinking the exact same thing. Logan had recounted to the police how the intruder had briefly fallen to one knee before running out of the barn, and he didn't remember Masters having a limp at the races the day before. They both knew it didn't prove anything.

'Let's call it a day,' Logan said, and Tom agreed. They all headed home. Tom and Logan didn't say a word to Mike or Miles, as they didn't want to run around slandering and accusing Masters without solid evidence.

Logan called Victoria, Neale, and Pete and told the story. Neale and Pete were not surprised, as they thought it was something that Masters was capable of, and they also knew about his obsession with Logan. 'Take the prick out,' Pete said in a serious tone. 'The fact is, Masters is obsessed with you, and the more you win, the more fuel it adds to the fire. Take him out.'

Neale had a different opinion: 'You're finally in a perfect position in your life. Let it go; don't stuff it up on a hunch.'

The next day, they had twenty-eight more horses to look at. They already had six on the shortlist, and a three-year-old colt sired by Brigadier was the number one pick. He was unraced, as he had fractured his splint bone on his first prep and was given twelve months out. In the meantime, the two owners had a falling out and put him up for sale. They had paid £960,000 at the same venue, but the yearling sale was two years prior and his value had surely dropped, most would have thought. Brigadier was one of three of the best stallions in the world, alongside America's Eldorado and

Australia's King's Speech (the sire of Warrior King). Logan and Tom wanted the colt, as he was the perfect stayer type.

The team inspected the final list of sixteen horses again, and passed Masters and his backers in the process, as they seemed to be on a few of the same horses. Logan was completely focused on the horses and pushed Masters to the very back of his mind. Logan knew he would get square. He owed it to Hank and Polish Navy, but today was about buying horses. He knew the chance he had been given, and he wasn't going to disappoint the team. The sale was due to start at 1 p.m. The Group 1 win had opened up a whole new world for him. Many trainers worked their whole life to be successful but never achieved a Group 1 win of that calibre. Logan felt he had finally proved he had what it takes to rub shoulders with the racing elite.

If anything, Masters was the one who was uncomfortable. The new 'Round 2' video had gone wild. He felt repeatedly humiliated by the video and there was no way of taking it off the Internet. But Masters was very arrogant, and wasn't going to do anything about it. He had decided to kill Logan's prize horse, but had once again been bested by Logan. He was initially furious that he'd killed the wrong horse, but was nonetheless chuffed he had got away with it. He thought he was untouchable.

Cynthia texted Tom: 'If you want it, buy it. No limits; no slow ones. Don't hold back. We won't be put down by anyone or anything. Tell Logan I have employed four security guards. Two are full-time in the barn. This will not happen again on my watch!' She was furious about what had happened, and she was feeling sorry for herself for getting drunk again. She decided she would do her best to stay sober, focus on the business, and lay low at her farm for a while.

The list was now cut back to six with Mike ticking off medium to high-risk for racing. There were two mares, as well as one listed Stakes winner. She wasn't going to be cheap, and Logan valued her at 400,000 pounds, as she was just about turning four and had plenty of racing left in her, with only five starts to date. But the Brigadier colt was the pick. Both Tom and Logan wanted him, and they had been given the green light by Cynthia. The value of the King, and also Everest, had skyrocketed, and it had been Logan who had the final say on them both. He was coming home, that was a given. MacDonald, the sheik's man, was there, along with all the big guns, as the previous year's sale had produced six Group 1 winners and a Derby and Oaks winner from the sale of just 180 horses.

Logan, Tom, Miles, and Mike took up their seats. Directly across the auditorium, Masters was ready to duel. The Stakes-winning filly was the first on the list at Lot 32. Logan could see Masters was on her with his body language. He had bid many times against Masters back at the Magic Millions and Inglis sales in Australia. He had never won a bidding duel yet. It was all about to change. Tom realised the stare-down was on. 'You want me to bid?' he asked, wondering if Logan could keep his cool.

Logan replied, 'I got this,' with a quick glance over the shoulder at the team. Tom looked at Mike and Miles and gave a nod like they were backing Logan up in a fight.

Masters opened the filly up at 100,000, and Logan smashed it straight back with 150. Michael Squire from the Australian Sky Racing network instantly noticed the duel about to erupt and hit record on his phone camera. Masters hit back 200. Logan locked eyes with Masters and nodded. The auctioneer called 250. Masters nodded 300. Back to Logan, who didn't hesitate with

350. MacDonald dropped a bid on behalf of the sheik, 400, before Masters could nod. 'Fresh blood!' the auctioneer called out. Masters hit down at 450, only to be quickly trumped by Logan at 500. MacDonald nodded 550 and Masters hit again at 600. Logan nodded 650. MacDonald waved he was out, and the auctioneer looked at Masters. His backers leant in and Logan knew he was done. 'Is there anymore?' the auctioneer called, still clearly looking at Masters. But he angrily signalled he was out. The gavel dropped, and Tom slapped Logan on the back with a congrats. But Logan had locked eyes with Masters, and held the stare until Masters broke away to pacify his visibly unhappy backers.

Michael Squire uploaded the video to the Sky Racing Facebook page: 'Round 3: Weston vs Masters. Weston wins bidding duel on Stakes filly. Score: 3-0, Weston advantage.' Within minutes, the views were climbing, and Michael could see a few phone screens in the room playing the video, as he was also sharing with Racing UK's live site. Miles was one of them, and he turned his phone sideways and nudged Logan in the ribs. 'You always have to be the centre of attention, don't you?' he whispered; a dig that Logan had said to him many times.

Logan just laughed. He loved the fact that he had beaten Masters, but he wasn't a fan of the following he had created based around their rivalry. He looked at the steel-killer look he gave Masters at the end of the video and was quietly impressed by the rugged determined look. 'Send me that, would you,' Logan said to Miles. Logan forwarded it to Pete, Neale, Aunty Joy, and Victoria.

Miles nudged Logan as he spotted Masters watching the video. He was squirming in his chair and he looked over at the team. Logan raised his glass at him and the others followed suit. It was game on. Logan told Mike and Miles his theory about who killed Polish Navy and made them swear they would not say a word.

Lot 62 was a bay gelding called Naturalism. The bidding opened at 50 and Masters went head to head against MacDonald. MacDonald had the bid at 350, and Master was baulking at going again; the hammer was ready to come down. The horse had okay staying form but, even though they had an open chequebook, Logan and Tom had valued the gelding at $250,000. They liked the horse, but he was overpriced. 'Tom,' Logan said out of the corner of his mouth, 'whisper in my ear and nod your head. Quickly, do it now.' Tom was confused but quickly did it. Masters was watching him, and Logan knew it. He feigned as if he was about to bid, and Masters took the bait. He raised to 400. To Masters' surprise, Logan just moved his hand to his head and rubbed it. He shot Masters a glance, laughed, and mouthed the words, 'Gotcha.' The team worked out quickly that Logan had just faked he was going to bid, and Masters, with his ego, paid $100,000 more than he wanted to. The hammer dropped, and the team laughed and clinked glasses, as that one was for Polish Navy.

Masters held a smile, as if he meant to win at that price, and worked his backers up with excitement, too, so they were none the wiser. It was now only four lots until the Brigadier colt. The team quickly huddled to talk about their approach. They knew he could make well over 1.5 million, as all the right buyers were on him. 'We need to set up another bidder to take over from us. We need to drop out midway, to throw the others off the scent,' Logan said softly.

Miles said, 'Leave it to me,' and he slipped away while the bidding continued. He returned to his seat as the colt came in. 'The guy in the blue Ralph Lauren jacket over there will start bidding for us when we stop. Unless I take my hat off, he won't stop.'

'What did he want for it?' Tom asked, expecting he had struck a deal for cash.

'Oh, nothing. He was happy to do it.'

Logan pretended to scan the crowd and looked over at him subtly. He didn't look familiar. He wondered who he was and why he had agreed so easily.

Masters was on, as he did his usual pre-bid moves. MacDonald opened at 500,000 and Masters went hard. Logan joined in at 1 million, and Masters stayed strong. Logan whispered to Tom, 'He's got balls, I'll give him that. Masters jumped to 1.3 million. Logan went 1.4. Masters didn't hesitate and went 1.5. As they had arranged earlier, Tom put his hand on Logan's and pretended to whisper as he shook his head. He played the part very convincingly, Logan thought. Masters grinned. He knew Tom was, for all intents and purposes, Logan's boss. He thought, *Fuck you, Weston. I'm winning this one.* As the call came for final bids, Logan kept up their act, whispering back at Tom, gesturing as if to convince him to keep bidding.

Miles's man raised his hand. 1.6 million. With fresh blood, the crowd got more excited. Masters wanted the colt and went again at 1.7 million. The blue coat gestured and the auctioneer called out, '1.75 million.' Masters was deaf to his backers, as the bidding continued. But, finally, at 2.85 million pounds, Masters was forced to cave. The gavel dropped and the crowd went hushed as the man in the blue jacket rose to speak to the staff member holding his sale docket. Everyone was wondering who he was. The woman looked slightly confused but took the docket up to Logan and Tom. It was clear now that the man was bidding on behalf of Baker Stables.

Tom signed the docket, and Miles went to shake the man's hand to thank him. At the very least, Miles said he'd buy him a drink. 'Nonsense. It was thrilling! Thank you. I've never bid so much money in my life!' Michael Squire had been recording the whole scene as it played out, and was loving the drama and tension. Logan looked at Masters fiercely, then raised his hand with his thumb out, then turned it down, just like in the movie *Gladiator* with the Aussie actor Russell Crowe. The new Facebook post read: 'Weston slays Masters!'

The team agreed they were done, as they had bought the two they really wanted. Logan and Tom made their way to the sale day office to sign the two purchases out and make arrangements for transportation. Meanwhile, Miles and Mike made their way to the gents. Miles was washing his hands when Masters walked in. Masters was furious and barked, 'You fucking fag. Think you're top shit. Well, you're not so tough without your boyfriend to back you up, are ya?' He shouldered Miles hard into the wall and was getting ready to drop a right to his chin, sneering at the frightened look on Miles's face. Miles was completely shaken. He had never had a fight in his life. He quickly slipped out of Masters' grip and made a quick exit. As the door was closing behind him, Masters yelled, 'Run, you cock sucker!'

Masters walked over to the trough, unzipped, and took a spread stance. Mike was still in the cubicle and had heard the whole thing. He didn't flush, just quietly opened the door and peered out. He saw Masters standing alone at the trough. Mike had been a good striker in his local soccer team until he had injured his right knee in his twenties and had to give the sport up. Mike never even hesitated and took two big strides towards Masters and drove his right foot as hard as he could between his legs. Masters was lifted a few inches off the tiles, then came crashing down in the urinal trough, his whole left side getting covered in his own piss. Mike quickly limped out the door before Masters could spot his face. Masters guessed that it was Miles but had no proof.

Mike hurried to the car, where the team was waiting. Miles was on the verge of tears and obviously hadn't said a word, as Logan and Tom were talking excitedly in the front seat. As they drove away, Mike patted Miles's shoulder. 'You okay?'

He shook his head and suddenly burst into sobs as he told the story of what had happened in the bathroom. As soon as Logan heard Masters' name, he calmly pulled the car over. Miles finished, and Mike kept patting his back to comfort him. Tom was shaking his head, and Logan sat in silence, gripping the wheel. He contemplated going back, but didn't want more trouble and media attention. *Why can't he just back off!* Logan thought furiously, feeling guilty for bringing Miles into it.

Mike said quietly, 'I have a confession.' Everyone looked confused. 'I heard every word he said to you, Miles. After you left, I crept out of the stall and saw him standing there alone. I punted him and I legged it.'

'You *what?*' Miles asked.

He lifted his right leg, and Miles could see his foot was already starting to swell in his shoe. 'I kicked him as hard as I could. I swear he got at least three inches of air before he landed in his own piss. I think I might have broken my foot doing it too, so … could we please make a stop at the hospital?'

Logan and Tom exchanged concerned glances before they burst out laughing. Mike and Miles cracked up, too. Miles leaned across and hugged Mike. 'You maniac!' he said, laughing.

Mike was right. At the hospital, they did a few X-rays and confirmed that he had broken his foot in two places. Miles stayed with him, wheeling him around the hospital and treating him like the hero he was. When they were done, Mike's wife came to pick them up. Coincidentally, Masters was taken to the same hospital and discharged around the same time as Mike. He froze when he saw Miles in the car park, helping Mike into the car and packing in his crutches, and he quickly realised who had landed the winning kick. In his situation, most people would admit they were in the wrong, but not Masters. He felt they had tormented and humiliated him in front of the industry. In his eyes, *he* was the one who had been hard done by. He couldn't even concede that his jealous and spiteful actions had been the cause of the backlash he was receiving through the media. He was the kind of man to believe his own bullshit.

CHAPTER 26

Masters spent the next week keeping a low profile while he set up his stable. He was no dill when it came to training. It was true that he was hard on the horses—'Bone and muscle,' he always boasted—but he had won many Group 1 races. He was very particular about how things were set up and the daily procedures. Staff hated when he would try something new, as he would go over and over the most minor details, until he was happy they understood what he wanted done. His horses worked with GPS systems on their training gear, so he could log on and watch their track work times, heart rate, and recovery times all from Australia. This was another important tool that helped him fine-tune their training.

He had made friends with a few local trainers. You either liked him or hated him, but Masters always attracted the so-called 'groupie' trainers with his success. Many groupies had never won the big league races but loved having the connection to racing elite. They were hangers-on and fed off the scraps of the top-class trainers. When their stables were full, groupies took casts-offs just for the training fees it generated.

Masters took charge of ten stables, and within four weeks the Australian shipment of seven would arrive to go with the three purchased at the Tattersalls sale. He was very serious about his Royal Ascot tilt. He was sending two Group 1 winners over, and three other Stakes winners to boost the stable quality, and was going to spend the final six weeks training before the carnival started. Many thought this was stupid, since the Australian racing prize money was double to triple that of the Royal Ascot meeting, but he wanted to conquer the most prestigious racing week in the world. Royal Ascot was the Everest of the racing world.

The social media sites were loving the stoush between the two men and were continuously asking for comments and interviews, but both kept replying, 'No comment at this time.'

Masters boarded his flight from Heathrow to Melbourne and vowed that the next time he set foot on English soil it would be to destroy Logan. He would enter as many horses as he could in the same races as Logan to beat him and win back the dignity he felt he had lost with Everest and Forest Black.

It was only three weeks until Christmas, and Logan couldn't wait to see Victoria. He was mad about her and the feeling, he hoped, was mutual. The racing tapered down, to start back up again in mid-February, building up to Royal Ascot.

It was 7.15 p.m., and Logan and Hank were both confused and worried when the security guard pulled in the driveway. 'What's wrong?' Logan asked immediately, thinking the worst.

He gave a polite smile. 'I have a visitor who insisted on seeing you, Mr Weston.'

The visitor stepped out of the passenger door and hurried along the driveway to greet Logan. Logan's heart almost leapt out of his chest when he saw Victoria, and her smile gave him goosebumps. 'I was talking to you half an hour ago. What're you doi—' and before Logan could finish, she wrapped her arms around him and kissed him.

The security guard placed her bags at the door and left. Logan looked at her pile of bags, which were clearly for more than a few days. 'Are you going to tell me what's going on?' he asked with a matter-of-fact look on his face.

'I gathered you've had a tough week and, well, I thought you might like some company, so I took some indefinite leave,' she responded. 'I'm following my heart.' She stared into his eyes and they embraced. Logan kissed her as if he would take her right there on the front step.

She pushed him back gently, blushing. 'I've been in human soup for over twelve hours on the plane, I feel disgusting.'

Logan chuckled. 'Fair enough. How about some champagne, a hot shower, then … well, whatever you want,' he said with a cheeky wink. He picked up her bags and took them inside as Hank jumped into Victoria's arms. Hank was a good judge of character, so Logan knew she was a keeper.

They enjoyed two glasses of champagne and some cheese and nibbles that Logan hoped weren't out of date. Victoria said she was impressed with how comfortable and stylish his bachelor pad was.

Logan took her bags to his bedroom and very quickly cleaned up the bathroom, even though it was pretty tidy, anyway. He was still surprised that she had just rocked up on his doorstep, and he was nervous about them living together so suddenly, even it if was for just a few weeks. He got a clean towel for Victoria and hung it beside the shower. They had only ever spent one night together, so they were both slightly awkward in their actions.

Victoria undressed in the bathroom and opened the shower. Nothing had been spared with the design and fittings. The shower was double the normal size, with the widest showerhead she had ever seen. She thought the water must have been filtered, as it felt very soft.

Hank lifted his head at a noise in the bathroom and trotted towards the door, pushing it open with his nose. He quite often did this when Logan was using the bathroom, as he liked to know what was going on. Logan followed, to usher him out. Victoria turned and noticed them. Hank was wagging his tail. 'Sorry,' Logan said, 'maybe he thought you called him.'

'I was actually calling for you.'

'Oh shit, you need a towel,' he said, embarrassed.

'You already gave me one, remember?' He felt the redness growing in his face, as she had now turned around and he could see her clearly through the glass screen. 'I need help washing my back.' She gave a cheeky smile. Logan didn't need to be asked twice.

'Welcome to England,' he whispered.

The next morning at track work, Tom and James saw the glint in Logan's eye. They had seen it before, so they knew exactly what it meant. 'You get lucky?' asked Tom.

Logan couldn't contain his grin. He was so happy when Victoria arrived out of the blue. He was more than smitten. He wasn't going to say it yet, as he preferred to play his cards close to his chest. 'Yes, I had company last night, and she is still here.' The grin broadened. 'Victoria flew to see me, and I guess she is staying for a few weeks.'

James was excited because he really liked Victoria. They had so much fun together in the short time they had spent with her at the races and the gay nightclub. He also thought she was a good match for Logan.

Tom smirked and asked, 'Which one was better, the King's Group 1 win, or your night with your surprise visitor?'

Without hesitation, Logan answered, 'Well, I didn't have to share *that* win with you last night.' They all laughed. The two boys and Logan were growing closer every day. Tom knew at some stage Logan would meet someone who could mend his broken heart. He may have enjoyed the single life so far, but Tom could tell he was a deeply loyal person and missed having a life partner, for better or for worse.

'I better warn Mother,' James said. Logan knew she may not take it that well as, drunk or not, they did have chemistry. He knew how keen she was, and if he had given the green light it would have already been on.

'That's going to be so awkward,' Tom said, and Logan went red in the face.

'Tom, I will sort Mother out; it will be fine,' James said. 'I'll organise dinner tonight and we'll get it over and done with.' They all agreed, before turning their attention back to the horses. James got legged up on the first ride of the morning, and Tom and Logan walked towards the tower to watch him ride.

CHAPTER 27

They had turned out twenty-two horses for a two-week break over Christmas and New Year's. They had a good indication of the quality of horses they had. They believed they had possibly four new Stakes horses, plus the King, Everest, Forest Black, the two new ones from the U.S., and also two others from the breeze-up sale, all showing serious potential. The two new purchases from the Tattersall sale were given two weeks out as well. Early to mid-January, it would all start again. The King, Everest, and Forest Black were going to get to the last week in January, and if they lost any tone or muscle they would be put on the water walker each day. It was agreed Logan would take off the first seven days, since it was his birthday on the 24th anyway, and come back to work on the 26th of December, and Tom would take a week off.

Dinner was at Charlie's. Charlies was a simple place, but the food was the best in the Newmarket area. Logan was surprised when Cynthia sat next to Victoria. After 40 minutes, he knew he hadn't a worry in the world, as both ladies had hit it off like long-lost friends. Victoria straightaway knew how to take Cynthia and her controlling ways and took the mickey out of her in a polite way, which Cynthia found very amusing. Logan had noticed Cynthia only had a very close-knit group of friends and, in some ways, she may have needed a fresh friend. The two girls had finished three bottles of champagne and were both well and truly drunk. Victoria's nervousness had gone completely. Miles joined in on the joking and teasing, so it ended up being a hilarious night for everyone.

At the end of the night, Logan took Victoria home. She had been whispering lustfully in his ear on the way home, but, by the time Logan brushed his teeth and came back to the bedroom, it was Hank who ended up being the lucky one. He had snuggled up beside her in bed, and she had passed out with her arms around him. Logan pulled her boots off one by one, and suddenly noticed that she was missing her middle toe on her right foot. He looked at it carefully and could see that it had healed over a long time ago. He couldn't believe he hadn't noticed before. He gave both her feet an affectionate squeeze. The missing toe was just another mysterious part of her. To him, she was the perfect woman. Perfect for him. Perfect in every way.

Hank let out a small growl when Logan picked him up. He had never before done that, and Logan scolded him on the way to his spot on the lounge room sofa. 'Just remember that you're number two around here, mate. I'm not going to share the number one spot with a Jack Russell.'

Logan returned to bed and slipped in beside Victoria. It was cold, so he cuddled in. Victoria stirred and rolled over. She just stared straight at his eyes. The light from the moon trickled into the small gaps in the shades. He kissed her softly, and she whispered,

'I love you.' He knew that was the reason she had rocked up un-announced on his doorstep. He knew she was still intoxicated, but he also knew there were no boundaries right at that very moment. He didn't know what to say, so he kissed her again then rested his forehead on hers. They stared at each other between slow gentle kisses. Victoria closed her eyes and drifted back to sleep.

Logan rolled onto his back and stared at the ceiling. He knew he loved her as well, without a doubt. He knew she had never been with anyone since her husband had committed suicide, so was it possible that she just fell for the first man to take her on a date? What should have been a very joyous moment was now filled with self-doubt. *Am I actually good enough for her? What do I really have to offer her? Besides, she lives in the U.S. and I'm here in England.*

These thoughts were interrupted by Hank's barking. Someone was at the door, and Logan hoped it wasn't true as he opened the door, but, yes, it was Cynthia. The boys had gone to bed, and, by the looks of her, she had kept drinking. 'Jesus. What are you doing?' Cynthia only had a nightgown and slippers on, and it was nearly freezing outside. He escorted her to the sofa, wrapped a throw blanket around her, and grabbed his mobile. He was not having her here; he was not playing these games anymore; he was done. No matter how friendly they were, he was not going to bring Victoria into it like this. He called the security guard on duty, then Tom. 'Cynthia needs to be taken home immediately, please.' They knew the drill.

'I approve,' she slurred. 'Beautiful woman. You've done well. Smart lady, very smart lady.' She pointed at her chest. 'Maybe not as business-savvy as me, but still well done.'

Logan heard the security car approaching, and he helped her to her feet. Cynthia turned and wrapped her arms around Logan, trying to land a kiss on his lips. He twisted away from her and opened the door as security walked up to the front door.

Logan heard a noise and turned to look towards the bedroom. But it was only Hank trotting back through the open door to return to his spot beside Victoria. Instant relief.

'Time to get you home, ma'am,' security said, giving a polite smile.

She turned and said, a little too loudly, 'I bet she isn't as good as me in bed. I'm like a tiger,' and she motioned a claw with her hand. 'These lips, baby, these lips are amazing.' Logan struggled to keep a straight face, as she couldn't get her finger to her lips after three attempts. Together, Logan and the security guard got her into his car. 'But she's a good girl, she's a good girl,' Cynthia finally said.

Logan shook his head. 'Goodnight, Cynthia,' he said, and the security car took off. He walked back inside, closed the door, and stood quietly. He couldn't hear Victoria, so guessed she was still asleep. He breathed out with relief.

When he got back into bed, Hank was there, but this time he had buried himself deep under the blankets so he couldn't be dislodged easily. Finally, after putting Hank back on the couch, he closed his eyes to sleep, when he heard Victoria whisper, 'Like a tiger, huh?' He opened his eyes to see that Victoria had rolled over and was motioning her hand like Cynthia had.

Logan went bright red. 'Oh God. You saw that?'

She giggled. 'Most of it. Well done fending off that kiss.'

He shut his eyes, aggravated. 'I'm so sorry. We were never a thing, believe me. She just—'

'Can't resist you.' Victoria pulled him close and kissed him. 'Neither can I. So you better make love to me before she comes back.' And that he did, ever so slowly, as he didn't need to get up for track work in the morning.

Victoria woke with a cracking headache, but she had a warm fuzzy feeling inside because she could hear Logan cooking breakfast for her. Logan made eggs benedict and was complimented for serving them with headache tablets on the side. Victoria decided the morning was to be spent in bed, and this suited Logan too, since the weather was typically English—cold and wet.

Cynthia spent three early hours hugging the toilet bowl, then disappeared into the spare bedroom to endure painful, dizzy sleep.

Angus Masters had spent two days mapping out the Royal Ascot program; setting time frames for each horse; studying the English weights and ratings, so he knew the requirement for each horse to be qualified in the lead-up races; evaluating local feed and supplements content to choose a locally available brand; and researching jockeys and their strike rates so he could speak with their managers. He spoke to four Australian jockeys about the possibility of basing them in England for six weeks for the carnival and lead ups. LJ was his number one pick. LJ had won two Group 1's in the last two years at Royal Ascot for English trainer Howard Parker. Masters and LJ had combined to win eleven Group 1's in the last four years. Masters had also set up cameras that could be controlled from his phone so that he could view every single horse from Australia while in their stable. Much to everyone's surprise, he also set up four cameras in the stable courtyard so he could view every angle of each horse when they were presented in the afternoon in their walk and trot-ups soundness test. He had covered every base.

He had even bought a sofa couch, so he could sleep at work if needed to watch the English track work. It had crossed Masters' mind more than once that he was spending more time with his work than he was spending with his pregnant wife. With her increasing morning sickness, back pain, and wild mood swings, Masters was spending more and more time at the stables. Angela wasn't pleased and knew he was avoiding her. She had even started to worry that he was screwing a stable employee.

Logan knew nothing of the extent of Masters' plan and was enjoying the pleasure of helping Victoria relieve her headache. The distraction was a very pleasant change. For once, Logan even stopped thinking about the horses.

Logan lay beside Victoria while she napped again. He still couldn't believe how the turn of events had changed his life forever. Money was no worry. He now had over 1.1 million in the bank earning interest. He owed not a cent, had his dream job, had a team of talented and passionate people to help him, and now had a girlfriend who was simply perfect.

They didn't go out. Logan made dinner then they watched a movie on TV, cuddling on the couch with Hank in between.

CHAPTER 28

Victoria decided that it was time Logan actually went into London, so they organised a private driver to take them. Besides Newmarket and the races, Logan had never ventured outside of the farm or airport. He was happy at home with Hank and the horses. He had no hobbies besides the horses, lived for his work, and was in work mode basically 24/7.

They may not have known each other long, but they both already knew the small things about each other. Logan knew Victoria had done it tough many times over, like he had. He knew she would often go without and have to save to buy quality goods. Victoria knew Logan enjoyed living a simple life, didn't have the need to buy lavish things, and was satisfied wearing the same clothes and shoes as long as they were in good condition and comfortable.

They were dropped off right in the middle of the most exclusive shopping district in London. Victoria was as excited as a child in a candy store, but she was very self-conscious around the swanky stores and wealthy shoppers, so she wouldn't let Logan take her inside. She felt so out of place. Her bank balance was sitting around $30,000 and she owed $567,000 on her mortgage. She was actually struggling and was thinking about putting her house on the market so she could downsize.

They stopped and looked at the display in a jewellery store window. The rings on display were simply stunning, and Victoria singled out a princess cut ring. It wasn't the biggest or the flashiest ring there, and Logan loved how modestly stylish it was. Just like Victoria. Logan grabbed her hand and took her towards the door. 'We're going in.'

'No, no. That's okay, I'm happy just looking,' she protested.

Logan squeezed her hand. 'It'll be an adventure.' He winked, and she let him take control.

'Can I help you?' a staff member in his mid-forties said.

'Yes, thank you. The princess cut in the window, fourth row, third across from the left. We'd like to have a closer look, please,' Logan said with a smile.

The man looked over his glasses at Logan at his clothes—jeans, a sports coat, cowboy boots, and a cap with a racing logo on the front. He gestured to a counter with a display of smaller, lower-end rings right beside the door. 'Perhaps I can find you something suitable from *this* selection,' he said with a condescending sneer.

Logan instantly disliked the man. He was actually pretty pissed off but wasn't letting on just how much. He had been spoken down to by snobs so many times at the horse sales and races. But the so-called 'social royalty' were blind to the fact that the sport had changed drastically. The average Joe was winning nearly as many of the big races as the royalty now, being part of syndicates. Logan had worked his way from nothing and wasn't about to have a 35,000 pound-a-year employee spoil what was about to happen. The man judged a book by its cover by assuming Logan couldn't afford the ring in the front window, and Logan decided the man had just talked himself out of a commission on the sale. Logan immediately looked around for another staff member and caught the eye of one who was walking past. Logan spoke up, 'Excuse me.'

The man stopped and quickly turned, looking between his co-worker and Logan. 'Yes, sir?'

'I would like to buy a ring from the front window display, and it appears this man can only sell rings from this counter,' Logan said, gesturing to the cheaper rings. The man who first served Logan went to speak, and Logan put his hand up. 'I'm not interested in those rings. You had your chance, mate,' and his strong Aussie accent came out. 'As I said, I would like to see the princess cut in the front window, fourth row; if you have an issue with showing me, then I'm happy to take my business somewhere else.'

The new staff member gave Logan a genuine smile and nodded. 'Of course. My sincerest apologies, sir. I'd be happy to help you instead.' Logan looked at his name badge—Alistair, Manager.

Alistair gave the other man a stern look and told him to find another customer to help, nodding towards some people milling around the door. The man made himself scarce. Alistair took Logan and Victoria over to a counter and laid out the counter display pillow in front of them. He unlocked the window display behind the counter, pulled out some white gloves from his pocket, and put them on swiftly. Victoria stood there dumfounded, still holding onto Logan's hand. 'Thank you, Alistair,' said Logan, as he carefully placed the ring on the display pillow.

Victoria was still in shock, and Logan took control. He picked up the ring and slid it on her finger, guessing it would probably be the wrong size. But it fit her perfectly. Victoria was stunned and could do nothing but stare at it, slowly moving it side to side so the light could capture the beauty and clarity. She still hadn't said a word, and Alistair took the chance while she was distracted to gently place the tiny paper price tag beside the display pillow, on Logan's side. Logan had already gathered it would not be cheap. He couldn't stop looking at Victoria's happiness as she admired it on her hand. Logan shot Alistair a look that meant, *Really? After you almost lost the sale completely?* Alistair looked embarrassed and slipped over to the register quietly to see what the best price he could do was.

'What do you think?' Logan asked Victoria.

She laughed. 'It's gorgeous but—'

'I love you, Victoria. I want you to stay here with me,' Logan said, and Victoria looked up at him, finally realising what was happening. He took both her hands in his. 'When I saw you that day at the races, I literally fell on my face in love with you.' Victoria laughed, in shock, starting to tear up. 'To me, you are perfection. And now I *know* that you are the one. I want to spend my life with you, and I'm hoping you feel the same way. If you do, I think you should marry me.'

'Yes, yes, yes!' Victoria said, laughing, crying, and jumping in his arms.

A few people had turned around in the store, and Logan heard a collective, 'Aww!' and some clapping. The staff member who had been rude to Logan looked floored.

After their happy moment, Logan moved over to the counter to finalise the sale. Victoria was still stunned and wiped the tears from her face. Alistair had cut Logan a considerable discount to make up for the lapse in customer service, hoping it would encourage his return business. Logan didn't blink as he signed the receipt for £275,000. For the first time ever, he didn't need to worry about money. Victoria decided to wear the ring out of the store. As Alistair handed Logan the receipt, he said, 'I do hope you come see us again soon, Mr Weston.'

They walked out onto the street into the cold weather. Logan wrapped Victoria in his arms and squeezed her. Victoria was still looking at her ring and squeezed Logan back. 'I love you, Logan,' and she started to tear up again.

Logan winked at her. 'I know, you already told me.'

She punched him softly in the chest. 'I was drunk! It doesn't count.'

'Yes, it does,' he whispered, and picked her up and kissed her like they were twenty years old.

When he put her down, Victoria looked around. 'So, what do you want to do now?'

'How about we go to Paris for lunch?' Logan said, and before Victoria had answered he had hailed a cab.

Inside, Logan called Miles, as he knew one of his best friends owned a small charter service with planes. 'As quickly as possible. We need to be there for lunch,' Logan said into the phone.

'Jesus, aren't you a big spender today. What, did you propose or something?'

Logan paused, as this caught him completely off guard. 'How did you know?'

'Are you serious? Congratulations!' Logan needed to play it down, as he wanted to tell them all together. 'Yes just walked in and bought a ring, proposed, she said yes and now we are off to Paris for lunch.'

'Did you not get laid this morning, you cranky little shit,' Miles served back, thinking it was just a gee-up.

'Thanks, mate. Hey, do you mind—'

'Yes, I'll take care of Hank, don't worry. Have fun, you two!'

Miles texted through the number, and Logan and Victoria flew to Paris. They spent the next 72 hours as blissfully as any two lovebirds could. They explored Paris, and Logan happily spent the £25,000 he had been discounted on the ring, with not one care in the world. They decided to find a marriage celebrant and say their vows, and would have a party to celebrate after Royal Ascot Super Saturday when all the Aussies were over. This was about two people who fell in love at first sight, not about meeting everyone else's expectations.

After the ceremony, Logan called the house to tell Tom and James the news. 'You what?' Tom said. 'Hold on!' He gestured over to Miles, Mike, and James as they were around the kitchen table, discussing the plan for the Christmas break. 'Get over here! Logan has an announcement.' Tom spoke back into the phone, 'All right, you're on speakerphone. Say again.'

Logan blushed with embarrassment at the sudden attention. 'We got married!' he said, and the phone erupted with hoots and cheers. Logan put them on speakerphone so that Victoria could hear the cheering.

Miles quipped, 'Honey, I hope he bought you a real diamond!'

'Nine carats,' she replied, and there was silence on the other end of the phone.

'Fuck me,' blurted out Miles. 'I'm just picking my jaw up off the floor. Well done!' Miles said, laughing.

They all said their congratulations. 'Welcome to the family, Victoria,' Tom finally said, before they said their goodbyes.

Logan knew they would all be talking about how out of the blue it was, but he also knew they would be extremely happy for them both.

Logan and Victoria hadn't even worked out which side of the bed was his and hers. Most of the time they slept in a tangle of arms and legs. 'Will you be happy living with me on the property? Or should we think about moving?' Logan asked after another marathon love-making session.

'As long as Cynthia keeps her distance, and there are no more surprise midnight visits, I'm happy.' They both laughed, then Victoria added, 'I know you need to be close to the horses.'

They flew home late on the 24th and had a very quiet Christmas and endured the miserable English weather by staying inside. Logan needed to switch off, and Victoria knew the remedy—movies and sex. Now that they were married, it was important to Logan that they got to know everything about one another, so they talked endlessly—sometimes until two in the morning.

Christmas lunch was at the main house and was low-key, with only the close family. Cynthia and Miles got very drunk and started a good-intentioned lecture about rushing into things—aimed at Logan and Victoria's marriage. But they still slurred about how happy they were for them and how they would support them. Logan took it on the chin, choosing to nod and smile instead of to argue. After all, they were right. But he knew Victoria was the one, so he didn't hesitate to marry her.

When Logan and Tom went for a walk through the barn later in the afternoon, Miles took the opportunity to corner Victoria and ask her what Logan was like in bed. Victoria laughed and kept her lips shut, but Miles kept trying to wear her down. Eventually, she got tired of it so decided to just shut him up with something. 'Let's just say he is a very satisfying size.'

Miles leant back in his chair and said in a very frustrated tone, 'I knew it!' There was silence, and Victoria thought both Miles and Cynthia looked envious. At least Miles owned it by saying, 'Well, I'm incredibly jealous, but I'm very happy for you.' He leant over and kissed Victoria drunkenly on the cheek, and Victoria played along by patting him on the back sympathetically.

Cynthia, meanwhile, stayed quiet. She finally said, 'I could have had him if I wanted, you know. But it's just not professional, so I turned him down.'

Victoria's eyebrows raised, but she quickly regained her composure. By now, Logan had come clean and told Victoria about the many drunken encounters and awkward moments he'd had with Cynthia. And Victoria had seen it with her own eyes once. She simply said, 'Yes, Logan is always saying how much he respects your professionalism.'

Word had filtered back through to Masters about Logan's marriage courtesy of Miles's Facebook post. He brought it up over Christmas dinner. Angela had been suffering terrible morning sickness that seemed to carry on through the afternoon, and her mood was not good. She had even been too sick to leave the house, so they decided they would do Christmas with just the three of them and the housekeeper/nanny. Masters arrogantly pushed his phone in her face with a Facebook photo of Victoria, like he wanted a reaction. 'She looks great for her age, doesn't she?' he said with a hint of sarcasm. As any sick, self-conscious, pregnant woman would, Angela burst into tears. As always, Angus took it the wrong way and thought it meant that she was still in love with him. That wasn't the case at all. Angela felt that his comment was a dig at her appearance, and thought that was why he had not slept in their bed for weeks—especially since all he seemed to want was sex. It didn't matter if she had just spent ten minutes hugging the toilet bowl with morning sickness, he wanted sex. They argued about his constant absence, but Angus made it all about how hard this pregnancy was on *him*.

The noise made the nanny come to the dining room, but she soon retreated when she saw the look Masters shot her. He grabbed his car keys and stormed out, leaving Angela slumped at the dining table in tears. He drove straight to the Hyatt and booked a room. He got his room key and just sat at the bar, fuming. He had nothing to do, so he scrolled through his phone. He thought about the assistant foreman, Sandra, from Barn B. They always flirted when the others were not around in the barn, and she was one of the best at getting the gallops perfect. She was twenty-two years old, blonde, very fit, and had tattoos on her left shoulder and back. She had a naval piercing, and a previous boyfriend had bought her breast implants, she had told Masters. She was a knockout, with a glint in her eye that said, 'I can steal your husband if I want'. Masters also knew she was switched on and was ready to play the game. The chance of making it big-time in training was slim-to-none for most females.

After the third whisky shot, he muttered to himself, 'Fuck it,' and sent a text that was short and to the point: 'Hyatt Hotel. Room 312. I have your Christmas bonus for you.' He instantly felt regret after he had hit send. He had crossed the line. If Sandra showed anyone, and it got back to Angela, he could be ruined. He downed the last of the drink and nervously watched the screen. His phone buzzed and his heart felt like it was about to burst. A photo came through of her breasts squeezed into a tiny bra. It read: 'On my way. Merry Christmas to you.' She lived about ten minutes away. He downed the fourth whisky and headed up to his room to quickly shower.

CHAPTER 29

Masters didn't know, but Sandra became a professional escort at seventeen years old. At twenty-one, she had extorted enough wealthy married men to quit the business and take up an easy job riding horses. She had even ended up in hospital after a few extortion attempts when her targets had flipped out and bashed her. But she felt Masters was a target worth pursuing.

When she walked in, she didn't even kiss him, just went straight for his cock. Masters didn't realise what was about to hit him. Her 'designer' handbag had a hidden camera in the side, and Sandra told him she liked doing it with the lights on. She rode him reverse cowgirl, then straddled his face, screaming as she faked multiple orgasms. Angus felt no remorse, as he climbed back on for a second go. She told him she had never been fucked like this before, while he took her from behind. She moaned so loudly, Angus worried the room next door would call the front desk to complain.

Angus looked like he was slowing down, but Sandra wanted more incriminating footage for the blackmail reel. She started talking dirty to him, making up stories about the hot girls she had fucked, and he got very hard and came again after only five minutes.

In the early hours of the morning, she said she wanted to do it again before they had to go to track work. Angus was struggling to keep it up, so Sandra made up another story about fucking three guys at once, and Angus came again ten minutes later.

Sandra showered and left. Angus turned his phone back on and saw he had 22 missed calls from Angela. He listened to the voice messages—it was the nanny. She had taken Angela to the hospital. He panicked, running to the bathroom and throwing up in the sink. He cursed himself in the mirror and kept listening through the voicemail messages. The final message said that Angela was okay, but she had suffered an anxiety attack. The doctors were worried about the baby, so they're keeping her overnight. The nanny left the hospital name, ward, and room number, and asked Angus to come as soon as possible.

Angus immediately called the stable foreman and said he was not coming in, and he told him what was going on. He rushed home, changed, and sped to the hospital. Angela was asleep; they had given her something to calm her down. The nurse made him sit in the waiting room with the drunks and drug addicts, as Angela had asked for no visitors.

His phone buzzed. It was Sandra. The message read: 'I just want to thank you for the great fuck—I mean three fucks last night. Hope your wife is all right. Kiss kiss.'

Angus felt the vomit rising and staggered over to a trashcan to throw up into it. Luckily, he wasn't the only one puking in the waiting room, and the drunks thankfully hadn't recognised him from YouTube. He quickly clicked on settings and blocked her number, then deleted all her messages. He was screwed. He hoped that if he didn't reply, she would leave it at that and realise it was just a one-off thing. Otherwise, he knew it could turn nasty quickly.

Masters was allowed to take Angela home later that morning, around 9 a.m. She was still slightly sedated, and they talked calmly and cleared the air. He kept picking up her hand to kiss the back of it, telling her how much he loved her and how sorry and stupid he had been acting. He blamed stress, saying that his clients were being difficult, and the business was to blame for his behaviour. He did really love Angela. He loved her so much that he never wanted anyone else to ever have her, but in his head he justified his own need to fuck someone else.

They arrived home, and Angus's phone rang. It was a number he had not seen before. 'Hello, Angus Masters speaking.'

'You fucking blocked me! You fuck me like an animal, and now you fucking block me!' Sandra screamed down the phone.

Masters was standing close to Angela, and quickly reacted, pretending he was talking to a colleague. 'What do you mean he's not taking the ride? This is bullshit. Hang on.' He turned to Angela. 'I have to sort out a jockey for Saturday. I'll just be a minute.' He quickly walked outside to take the call.

'Do you want me to tell your wife?' she screamed.

'Whoa, whoa, whoa,' Masters said quietly. He had never seen this side of Sandra. The truth was, he didn't know what game she was playing.

'Or maybe I should just show her the video I took of us fucking last night.'

Master was stunned, and he spluttered out, 'You videoed us?'

'That's why I left the lights on, baby, so your wife could see you eating my pussy. Where should I send the video?' She rattled off Angela's email, personal mobile number, and their home address.

Masters' heart was pounding, and he scrambled to think of what to do. He only just managed to whisper, 'What do you want?'

'Meet me tonight at your office and we'll talk. 6.30 p.m. Don't be late,' then she hung up.

He was spooked, real spooked. He thought maybe it was best to just come clean.

CHAPTER 30

It was 6.30 p.m. and Sandra opened the door to the office. Masters sat at his desk. They were alone in building. He pointed to the seat. 'You wanted to talk, so let's talk.'

Sandra sat with a smug look on her face, as she knew she had the upper hand. 'I want $50,000 or I'll send this video to your wife, and everyone else you care about.'

Masters had spent the whole day thinking about what she really wanted. He thought it was about her job, but it wasn't that complicated. He had seen Sandra driving a small sports BMW, and he knew she lived in a big apartment building in a nice area. He knew from her wage that she couldn't afford either, so it clicked that she was hustling him for money and had clearly done it before. If he gave in now, she would only keep blackmailing him for more money. No, instead he was going to use her to his own advantage.

'Just fifty grand, and I'll go away.'

'I have a better deal for you, Sandra,' Masters said calmly. Sandra looked confused, as he leant back in his chair and pulled open the top drawer of his desk. He pulled out a .44 Magnum handgun and gently placed it on the desk, resting his hand on it. The superior look dropped off her face.

'Do you know what I learnt today?' he asked her. 'Jamie Lee Walsh.' Sandra flinched when she heard the name of her younger sister. Masters rattled off their home address.

Sandra was fighting to keep her anger from rising up. She was incredibly protective and proud of her little sister. Masters could see the tears building up in her eyes. She knew she had been trumped. 'I always knew you were a cunt!' she snapped, wiping away a tear, as Masters just laughed.

'This is my offer: $75,000, and six months in Newmarket on full pay.'

Sandra shook her head, confused. 'I don't understand. What's the catch?'

'It's simple. I'm hiring you to fuck over Logan Weston's farrier. This is just business, and one cunt talking to another cunt, it seems.'

Sandra thought it over, glancing back at the gun. It was this or nothing—or worse. Finally, she nodded. 'I can do that.'

'When the time is right, I will fill you in more.' Masters said. 'I'll book your flight and arrange an apartment in Newmarket.' He got up from his chair, holding the gun in his hand. 'Just one last thing.' He walked over to Sandra, who didn't say a word or move. He undid his belt and dropped his pants. He was already rock hard. He grabbed her by the hair, and she didn't argue.

Sandra swallowed, returned home, and packed her bag for London.

James and Miles took a holiday together over the break and headed for a drive around France. Every day, James grew more confident about being openly gay, helped along by Miles, who never gave a damn what anyone thought of him.

James was a fitness freak and was helping Miles get into shape. They worked out hard, took PT sessions together, and Miles had even cut down on sugary drinks. He was still hooked on energy drinks, but he managed to limit himself to one a day.

Their romantic holiday was slightly dampened when James lost it at Miles for harping on about Logan's 8-inch cock. In fact, the exact measurement seemed to keep growing each day. James felt sick at the thought of Logan's naked body. Logan was more like an older brother or a father figure than a sex object to him.

Miles managed to make it up to James, and he even let slip that he was falling in love with him after one hot and sweaty afternoon session.

Tom's relationship with Lily was also going extremely well. It seemed everyone had someone but poor Cynthia. Deep down, she was miserable, lonely, and still in mad lust with Logan. She thought he was extremely handsome, rugged, and, as she told Miles, 'very shaggable'. She realised that now she had no chance with him.

Cynthia decided to solve the problem and went online to a site Miles had told her about. She had never used a vibrator before. She took over an hour to choose and decided to buy not one but four. One with a rotating head and vibrating clitoral stimulator; one with rapid fire pulses with variable speed; an 8-inch one with a suction cup that said it was perfect for in the shower; and one that was small and powerful for clitoral stimulation. Embarrassed, curious but excited, she paid extra for next-day delivery.

Victoria had flown back to America on the 28th of December to pack up her house and put it on the market. Her clothes and belongings were sent to England. The hardest decision she had to make was to leave her two cats, Ralph and Tiger, with her good friend Emily. They were brothers and eleven years old—too old to risk the big move to England. By the way Hank chased rabbits, Victoria couldn't bear the thought of him ripping them to bits, too.

Newmarket was now home. Garth and Ruth threw her a beautiful send-off and gave her so many well wishes. She had gone through hell already in her life, and both Garth and Ruth had finally seen a glint of life coming back in her eyes. She was crazy in love and had a nine-carat ring on her finger that proved it was mutual. She settled into the first-class seat heading back to her new home and texted Logan her love. He always made sure she was taken care of.

CHAPTER 31

It was 7.10 p.m., and Victoria and Sandra stood almost side-by-side in the customs line at Heathrow. They had even made idle chitchat. Victoria was speaking to the woman who was sent on a mission to England for one reason and one reason only—to take down her husband. Neither knew what was planned for the week of Royal Ascot. Sandra told Victoria she was from Melbourne, but Victoria didn't think to mention her husband was from Melbourne.

Logan had his head buried reading the racing post out the front of customs when a shiver went down his spine, like someone had just walked over his grave. He looked up to see a woman turning away from him. *Had she been staring at him?* He was a YouTube sensation and his combined videos had over 96 million views, so he thought maybe she had recognised him and stared. *Or do I know her?* He watched her walk away with an odd feeling, as if something was wrong.

When he turned back, his new wife was walking up to him. Logan jumped up to greet her, but she gave him a jokingly stern look. 'Caught you! Window-shopping is fine, my love, but y'all just remember what you have is one of a kind,' and she winked at him. He lifted her up, and they shared a passionate kiss.

Logan put her down and Victoria asked, 'So, do you know her?'

'Who?' he asked, taking her bags.

'That woman you were looking at. I talked to her in the queue. She said she was from Melbourne.'

He turned back around quickly, but she'd vanished. 'No, I don't think so. I thought she was staring at me, but I assumed she was just a big fan of my work,' he joked, laughing. Victoria shrugged, and they headed to the car park.

Logan hated the city. He had hated going into the city in Melbourne, and now it was the same in London. As they drove back to their quiet home, Logan updated Victoria on all the horse-related news and plans. He told her that he was due to go back to Australia to the yearling sale on the Gold Coast but had eventually decided not to. He started to explain the whole preparation and planning for the Royal Ascot meeting, but she had switched off. She loved him so much, but she had no idea what he was talking about when it came to horses, especially when he was getting into the nitty gritty of training them.

When they got home, Hank was extremely happy to see Victoria and started running around the house, bouncing off furniture. Logan cracked up laughing at Hank's hilarious antics. Hank was always there with Logan every step of the way.

Victoria jumped in the shower. Afterwards, she flopped down on the bedspread in her towel, completely exhausted. It had been a frantic and emotional experience packing up her house and leaving her old life behind. She never knew her decision to arrive early before Christmas would have ended with getting married and moving halfway across the world.

Logan had given Hank two bones and locked him in the laundry to chew quietly and calm down. He walked into the bedroom and saw Victoria spread out on the bed and he laughed. She laughed too and said, 'I think I need a nap.' He had other plans and crawled up the bed, lifting the bottom of her towel. Victoria gave a cheeky smile. 'I didn't realise first class service continued at home as well.' She could see his erection through his pants. 'Happy to see me?' He couldn't help but smile at her. Logan started to undo his pants, and Victoria yawned dramatically. 'I'm too tired now. Maybe after a nap.' Victoria saw the disappointed look on his face and she winked. 'Welcome to married life, darling.'

Meanwhile, at her house, Cynthia struggled for ten minutes to put the batteries in the correct way in her new toys, then settled down on her bed to experiment. It was very lucky that her PA didn't open the parcel, as she usually organised her mail. At 9.45 p.m. she lay gasping on her bed, thinking, *Best £170 I've ever spent*. It had been the first orgasm since her husband's death—actually the first four. She pulled the bottom drawer out of her bedside table and hid the toys carefully, so the housecleaner wouldn't see them when she was tidying up.

CHAPTER 32

January, February, and half of March passed. Sandra had been slowly working on the farrier, Bill Smart. He was forty-six years old, married, had two boys, and lived in Newmarket. They hadn't had sex yet; actually, nothing had happened. He was shoeing her riding horse. The horse was all part of the plan. Every four to five weeks, he would have to shoe him. She even pulled the shoe off twice just to get him out.

The weather was warming slightly, and the last time he came to replace the lost shoe on Jasper it was late afternoon. Sandra had dressed up in skin-tight jeans, black knee-high boots, and her leather jacket. She had her hair down and put on some pink lipstick. She left her top buttons undone to help set the bait. Bill was immediately interested, and she knew it.

Bill's home life was quite normal. His boys were eight and ten and were always riding at a show or competition every weekend. His wife, Emma, was mad about pony club and was on as many committees as she could be. Bill worked a lot of Saturdays, as he was always plating up the racehorses before they raced. His sex life was about average—once a week; sometimes twice if Emma came home drunk from a committee meeting or a girls' night out. Bill kept to himself quite a lot but had a few close friends. Just an average routine that consisted of working hard and supporting his family. Emma always insisted they volunteer at the pony club, as she was the club president, and he lived a busy life. So when Sandra talked about wild and kinky sex, compared to his three to five per month in the normal missionary position or maybe doggy if she was drunk, it was very appealing to him. He was bored and couldn't see anything changing in life anytime soon. Emma kept joining more committees, which meant he would be getting even less sex.

She told him how disappointed she was in English men. None of the ones she had met were wild or kinky enough, she had told him. Bill had Jaspers front hoof out the front, clinching the nails down and rasping the excess toe off to finish the foot. Bill was staring at the black leather pointed toes of her long black boots while she was complaining about not being satisfied enough. He imagined she must be wild. He placed Jasper's front hoof down, stood, and straightened his back.

A lot of guys have egos about being good in bed. Farriers are well known for flirting with the equestrian women, as, well, they spend most of their days with women stablehands holding horses for them. Bill winked at her and joked, 'Maybe you just haven't found the right man yet, luv.'

Sandra knew she had him on the hook. 'I have a high standard of how I like to be fucked. Do you think you can deliver, farrier boy?' She walked two steps forward and placed her hand on his bulging crotch. It was always hard to tell, as the farrier apron straps always pulled in tight and accentuated the crotch anyway.

Bill shrugged casually and turned to gather up his tools. He packed everything in his bag and placed them and his anvil in the back of his 4WD.

Sandra asked, 'So how much for the repair?'

Bill went to climb in his 4WD. 'You know my number. We'll work out a payment then.'

'I might just do that,' she answered. He was in—hook, line, and sinker.

Bill drove off with a smile and a hint of guilt that he would need to contemplate. He knew Emma was more interested in her own commitments and the boys' lives than his. It had been years since she had dressed to the nines and made him feel like he was the only man in this world for her. Her idea of wild was a glass of wine in bed, or spontaneous morning sex before the boys woke up. He drove away feeling alive. Sandra was twenty-two and clearly wanted to fuck him. It did wonders for his self-esteem.

Sandra texted Masters to say she had her ducks in a row.

He was flying over at the end of April after the Easter carnival in Sydney was over. Royal Ascot had been brought forward by two weeks as the course proper was to undergo a complete revamp, and the work needed to be carried out before the winter set in. Masters' team of ten had all been making progress. They had worked out the few minor issues with the feed and training and were adjusting well.

Logan and Tom also had the team running smoothly. Warrior King had strengthened and developed into a superstar. He was only doing three-quarter work, but he was bigger and stronger, and the riders were giving very positive feedback. Everest had also improved along with Forest Black and the new horse purchased from the Tattersall sale. They had called the 2.85-million-euro colt Trumped, because Masters certainly was. Slipstream, Trumped, and Everest were ahead of the others by two weeks. Trumped was going to be aimed at the Derby, as the whole program had been changed to suit the rebuild of the Ascot track. The Super Saturday in Australia, Dubai World Cup, and the Breeders Cup meetings had proven so successful the English racing officials had bowed to the pressure to give it a go. The program was now with the combined races moved from Epsom to Ascot. The Royal Ascot meeting had the following races that were to be targeted by the Baker Racing stable:

English Derby, 2,400 metres, which Trumped was entered in.

English Oaks, 2,400 metres, which a filly called Slipstream that was showing promise was entered in.

The July Cup, 1,200 metres, which possibly Forest Black would be entered in.

Shergar Stakes, 2,400 metres (for three-year-olds and up), which Everest was entered in and was already one of the early favourites.

And the world's richest race, the eight-million-pound Queen Anne Stakes, 1,600 metres (for three-year-olds and up), which Warrior King was entered in and was already the favourite at $2.50. Logan thought of entering Forest Black in the Queen Anne as well.

It had been kept very hush-hush, but My Blue Boy had been given nine mares to serve as a test, and it was confirmed that he was completely infertile, which was a major blow. The owners had the choice of taking the infertility insurance of five million or racing him again. They sent him to the best vet in Australia, and all the tests on his heart came back clear. Not one thing was wrong with the horse, so they put him back in work. He had been back in work and was up to three-quarter pacework at a private pre-training facility and was better than ever, Masters was told. He was aimed at the Queen Anne Stakes as well. It was going to be a showdown.

Masters called a press conference to announce the news. He had seen how good Warrior King was, but he knew Bluey was just as good. He wanted to beat Logan with his old horse, and he had plans in place to ensure his victory. He had Sandra, and he also had an ex-mercenary on the books for good measure. He knew he couldn't fail. Sandra had called him a cunt and he was.

Social media went crazy with the news My Blue Boy's comeback would be a clash against his old trainer at the Queen Anne Stakes. Masters was arriving with him in the last week in April to have one run over 1,400 metres as a lead up.

Like many people, Logan was shocked at the news, as he thought the horse was finished after his last win. He knew how good Bluey was, and the trainer gossip was he was working phenomenally in his prelim work. The King was by far the best he had seen, but My Blue Boy had done what no other horse had achieved at three years old. He had very mixed feelings.

Logan, Tom, James, Mike, and Miles all sat and went through the lead up programs. They agreed that all the horses would race second and third up in the Super Saturday. It was planned to utilise the new farm Cynthia had purchased for fitness and relaxation and doing cattle work for two to three hours to build strength, stamina, and getting used to carrying weight, as these were keys to success. The staff would ride in normal jumping saddles, and the strappers were the ones who would ride, not the everyday work riders. It was Logan's way of saying thank you to the ground staff, and they also weighed more than the track riders. Logan, Tom, and Cynthia would even ride the horses when they could. Working them on cattle was a great way to freshen their minds and fine-tune their reflexes from the sharp turning and stopping required.

Tom had sensed the changed in Logan. He was back to being the same person he was before the Group 1 win. He had the eye of the tiger look more than ever. Victoria hadn't seen this side of Logan yet, but was very impressed with his focus during the day and his attempts to relax when he got home to spend quality time with her. Victoria had uprooted her life for Logan, but he was currently their sole provider, and she knew this so she gave him 100 per cent support. Logan had insisted that, for the time being, she enjoyed the break from the rat race and focused on settling in to her new life in Newmarket. Logan really enjoyed the company and just knowing someone was there to be with him. Hank adored Victoria and she spoilt him whenever she could. Although, he took a while to get used to the new little doggy coat she had bought him, but he eventually grew to love it. It was a lot easier to wash the horse shit from the coat than washing and blow-drying Hank every few days.

The pressure was building, and Miles was complaining about the mood swings James was having while building to peak fitness. He had started with another personal trainer and dietician. He was the lightest he had ever been, but they were hammering him extremely hard. Miles knew how serious and strict James's life had to be, so he grew to accept his moods, and they both agreed not to talk work when spending time together, if possible.

The Super Saturday was the 4th of June. Normally the crowds would spread the five days of racing, but now it was all to be one day with another three Group 1's two weeks prior in the lead up day on the 21st of May.

CHAPTER 33

Logan looked at Tom again for the fourth time that morning. They both knew they had some serious chances with the way the horses had galloped. Everest was the only problem, as he was simply too keen, so Logan and Tom decided he would go out to the cattle farm for Thursday's gallop. They had done it before, and it was time to do it again. One paddock was thirty acres with a slight rise of forty metres over 3,000 metres. The surface was a natural pasture, and Logan had organised the farmer to slash it to seven inches. Then he would go out personally and mow the final cut on the zero-turn mower to five inches to get the best possible surface. Tom knew it was Logan's way of relaxing, by spending four hours on the mower.

They had been putting the miles into Everest, Trumped, and Slipstream with plenty of trotting and cantering plus the water walker each afternoon for fitness and cooling the joints. Logan had made up rugs with the same material as wetsuits to put on the horses' backs. He left no stone unturned, and Tom was amazed, as every day he would strive to be a better trainer. Trumped was going to have to win, just like Slipstream, in a maiden, then both win their second starts as well to gain starts in the Derby and Oaks.

They arrived at the farm for the Thursday relaxation work. Logan told James to hop on Everest and he legged him up onto his back. James hadn't put his feet in the stirrups, luckily, as Everest reared up as straight as a horse could without falling over. Logan jumped back and James looked concerned. Logan shook his head as he told James, 'If he keeps acting like a dick, just let him go on the gallop. You have 3,000 metres. Just like back at Don's, let him find his rhythm and clear his head—*hopefully.*' Logan jumped on the lead pony, as he wanted to make sure Everest didn't do anything stupid. Cynthia was on the King, and she and two riders took Warrior King, Trumped, and Forest Black out for a trot and canter around the cattle.

Everest was bouncing up and down on the spot in anticipation. James patiently sat while Logan came in beside him and grabbed the rein right up close to the bridle and took control. Everest started to settle and seemed happy to trot beside old Creamy, the lead pony. They came to the paddock where Logan had spent almost five hours mowing the previous day. Logan led the way and was aiming dead square at the middle of the strip. James shortened his reins on the rubber grip slightly, and Logan let old Creamy work into a canter. 'You right?' he asked James.

'Yes,' and he bounced up over Everest's neck as Logan released the rein. He bounded forward, dropped his head momentarily, and James thought he was going to get bucked off. He sat back in the saddle for a few strides and pulled his head up; the horse was just feeling so fit he was jumping out of his skin. Everest was running completely free and was loving it. James got up over his neck, and Everest balanced. He let the reins slide, as he had done this many times before, and the horse gathered momentum and kept increasing his gallop. James didn't resist. He gave him his head and rested his hands four inches in front of his saddle. Everest reached a perfect cruising speed and kept it going longer than James had anticipated. They were now at least 2,300 metres up the rise, and only had about 700 metres left before they crashed into the middle paddock fence. 'Steady, boy, steady. Whoa, boy,' he said in a calming and soothing voice. 'Whoa, boy, whoa.' Everest started to ease, and James kept soothing him. 'Steady, boy.'

Everest had eased backed, and James was back in control, pulling him up before the fence. Logan couldn't believe the horse's stamina, and he met James about halfway back. James had let him trot back, as he wanted Logan to hear his breathing. 'Wow, he would hardly blow a candle out,' said Logan.

'He felt enormous, Logan.' James beamed. They both walked back down to the paddock the others were in, and joined in for thirty minutes, just pushing the cattle from corner to corner and back again. Stop, turn, go, and so on. Warrior King had his ears pricked and, when close enough, did his best to nudge and bite the cattle on the back. Even in cattle work, he knew he was boss. It was decided Warrior King, Forest Black, and Trumped would work up the rise in single file at a steady canter. Logan rode halfway with James, and both were surprised that Everest didn't get too fussy when the others worked past. Warrior King looked as if he had improved even more. Cynthia's smile, and her constant talking of how he was doing this better certainly gave them confidence.

Tom drove the truck home with Cynthia and the staff, while Logan and James stopped in at the bakery to get coffee and bacon and egg rolls for everyone after the late morning ride. As they walked to the car along the pathway, Logan got a shudder through his body, as if someone was watching him. 'What's wrong?' James asked as Logan twisted around.

Logan turned and saw the same blonde girl from the airport walk into the bakery. He shrugged it off and told James, 'Déjà vu, I think.'

Sandra was about to put her plan into action in two days' time. Saturday was pony club day and Emma would have the boys at some show. Bill would be flat out until about 11 a.m. replating racehorses' shoes, then he normally spent another three hours shoeing pleasure horses for cash. But he wouldn't be shoeing pleasure horses this Saturday, Sandra knew. She had been slowly working away at Bill, teasing him by telling him she wanted a man who was not just a one-hit wonder. She wanted it all night and every morning, and needed someone who could give her orgasm after orgasm. Bill didn't realise that she was throwing the challenge down and setting the bait. He quietly had grown infatuated with Sandra and constantly thought about her. He had always been very strong from the back-breaking work he carried out each day, but he had started to work out to increase his stamina. She had manipulated his mind to the point that when she knew the moment she gave the green light, he would be in.

Sandra sat and ate her croissant and black coffee at the bakery. It was time to take the second step. Masters had paid her $50,000 upfront and the other $25,000 would be paid only if the plan was a success. Sandra didn't even know what he would have to do, but she was aware that Masters had hired a mercenary as well. She had been texting Bill and finally closed the deal: 'Free at 2 p.m. this Saturday to pay you for all your hard work. Hope you can keep up with me, farrier boy.' She sent through the address of her apartment and the same photo that she had sent to Masters back in Australia. The question was, would he actually risk his marriage?

Until Sandra had come along, he was happy enough in his life and mostly satisfied in bed. 'That's life,' he had always thought. He knew all married men complained about wanting more. Deep down, he resented Emma for being completely dedicated to pony club. Their two boys were very good riders, and this made her the envy of the other mothers on the committee, so she involved herself as much as possible to push them. But the obsession with the boys riding was driving them apart. She blew all their money on shows, lessons, new riding gear, and new horse rugs, and that was all she ever talked about, as well. She would bitch on the phone for hours each night about other mothers and the kids who were spending more money than she had on better horses just to win a £2 felt ribbon. Bill couldn't remember the last time he and his wife took a break and went away somewhere and fucked all weekend. This was all he could think of now; he wanted dirty, wild sex, and he was working out just how much sex he was missing out on. Sandra had manipulated his mind to think that's how his life should actually be.

Sandra wasn't surprised when the reply came through: 'Prepare for the fuck of your life. xx Farrier boy.'

It was 1.55 p.m., and Sandra had dressed the part. Black overcoat, sexy lacy bra with suspenders, her black boots, and no underwear. She tightened the belt up, put one more layer of lipstick on, and pushed play on the hidden video cameras and the cameras set to take photos at thirty-second intervals. She had set up two: one in the bedroom and one in the open lounge room/ kitchen area, as she had no idea how it would play out. She was actually very nervous about making sure everything went to plan, but she was also excited and very horny.

She heard a knock at a few minutes past 2 p.m. She was very surprised when she opened the door, as she had never seen Bill out of his farrier clothes. He was actually very attractive in a rugged way. No words were spoken as he walked in confidently, and she closed the door. She walked past him towards the kitchen and he grabbed her waist from behind and pulled her closer to him. She didn't resist, and he kissed her neck, just below her earlobe. His hands slid under the overcoat and over her skin. She went weak as he nibbled at the sensitive spot on her neck. *He's very good*, she thought. *Hitting all the right spots already.*

She took two steps forward and placed her hands on the kitchen bench. Bill knew that he was in the right spot when his hand slid between her legs. No panties; and she was wet. He gently pushed in two fingers, as his other hand unclipped her bra and moved to squeeze her breasts. He had always wanted to see what she was hiding in that leather jacket she always wore. They may have been fake, but they felt amazing to him. He quickly undid his trousers and let them slip down his legs to the floor. He moved both his hands to her waist, and she lowered her body down onto the kitchen island bench. He squatted down slightly to get the right angle as he guided his cock inside her. She had always wondered how big he was, as she thought the farrier apron exaggerated the bulge size. She was wrong. Bill was huge. She had never had a cock that big in her life, not even in her professional life. She gasped and moved her hands over the bench to get a better grip. 'Oh fuck,' she let out, as he drove the full length in.

Bill started with long and slow strokes, and Sandra hoped the tenants next door were out, as she couldn't help but moan loudly. He took her ponytail in one hand and gently pulled it back as he increased his pace. 'You like it like this?' he asked. She did, and she nodded even though he had her head in full control, holding her hip with his other hand to keep balanced.

Sandra arched her back as he drove in faster and faster. The pressure built quickly, and she surprised herself as the words, 'Oh, fuck, I'm cumming,' slipped out of her mouth. Bill drove two quick deep thrusts in, and she pushed back against him hard, shuddering. He stopped as she held the sides of the bench and caught her breath. Her legs were shaking from the orgasm; the deep penetration had taken it to another level of stimulation.

She slowly regained her breath and muttered, 'You didn't warn me about your cock.' Bill smiled; he was not done yet. Round two. He re-entered her and he started moving again at his long and slow pace, moving his hands up under her jacket and up and down the curve of her back. He loved her toned body. Emma was toned when they first met, but after two children and not enough time to work out, she had lost her figure. Sandra lowered her head and gripped the bench again. Bill pulled almost completely out then slowly drove in as deep as he could, long and slow. He moved his hand down and over her waist, finding her clitoris and starting to massage it with his fingers. It was an awkward position to keep up, but it was working. He felt the tension building again, and Sandra was moaning and bucking back against him. He grabbed onto her ponytail again and started the deepest penetration he could. The second orgasm was better than the first. When Bill stood back, Sandra slipped off the bench and onto the floor. She turned around to lean against the bench with her jacket open, bra half hanging off, and her eye shadow and lipstick smudged. It was the most erotic pose Bill had witnessed.

Still completely hard, he positioned himself in front of her. The sight of the most impressive cock she had ever laid eyes on was too much to resist. She rose to her knees and grabbed it in both hands, opening her mouth. For two minutes, she sucked and jerked better than she had ever done and kept full eye contact as he came in her mouth.

Bill caught his breath and offered a hand to help her to feet. 'I think that about covers shoeing your horse for one afternoon. Maybe we can trade again sometime.'

She knew she had to keep him hooked. She got closer and looked him in the eyes. 'Me too. I'm very impressed with this, farrier boy,' she said, rubbing at his cock. Bill didn't know what to do—stay or just go. Sandra knew she had to keep him keen and the desire burning. She looked at her watch. 'Oh no, I have to get ready. I have a date tonight.' She pulled her coat shut and walked towards the door, opening it. Bill scrambled to pull up his pants, giving her a shocked look. Sandra added, 'We're going to Arnolds in London for dinner, so I have to look nice.' Arnolds was one of only two restaurants in the city to be awarded the 5-star rating. 'Then we're staying at the Four Seasons for the night.'

Bill walked through the door and stood there, feeling, well, he didn't know how he was feeling, actually. He had never been in this position. 'So, that's it?' he asked.

'I told you I'm not easy to satisfy. You didn't think we were exclusive, did you, Bill?' She put her arms around his neck. 'Look, if he doesn't fuck me well enough tonight, I'll give you a call.' She kissed him long and wet on the lips, turned, and went back inside and closed the door. Bill drove home utterly confused. He hadn't had sex that good ever in his life, but she was seeing other men too. What did it mean?

Meanwhile, Sandra looked over the recordings and photos. It had worked perfectly. She got her blackmail, and she got inside his head just as she had planned. But she had also just had the best sex of her life.

CHAPTER 34

Trumped and Slipstream had their finals gallops on Wednesday and were both exactly where Logan and Tom had hoped before their first start that Saturday. Trumped didn't seem to have a quick turn of foot like the filly, but he could really wind up and seemed to sustain the run for a longer amount of time than the normal horse.

They were about to load the horses on the float and head to the races, when Logan's phone rang. 'Convict.' It was Mick. 'You there, convict, or you building another boat to escape because you ate someone's sheep, ya thieving bastard?'

'I'm here,' said Logan in a defeated tone, as he knew he would never get the last laugh in.

'Good. I want first offer on the standing rights on Trumped. What made you call a horse after that gobshite?' Mick knew the colt was good, as Logan had indicated he went alright after he had his first gallop. High-price colts always attracted great interest.

'I haven't even started the colt yet, for God's sake,' Logan replied.

'Don't you take the Lord's name in vain! He's my father, you know.' Logan just laughed and rolled his eyes. 'Don't talk to any other bastards until you give me the first crack. I want first offer on standing rights.'

The staff had brought out the two horses to load on the truck. 'I've gotta go,' Logan said.

'I get first crack, Logan! You owe me this.'

Logan scoffed. 'Owe you? All I've done is make you money this past four months. How exactly do I owe you?'

'Because of your new wife.'

'What about her?' Logan asked, wondering how he was going to cross the line.

'Well, if she met me she would leave you tomorrow, so you owe me for keeping my distance. No one wants a thieving convict.' Logan laughed and hung up. Mick was on the money, and Logan's phone didn't stop ringing.

Miles was a nervous wreck, as he was so worried that James would have a fall and get hurt. 'I'm in love, I'm in love,' he kept telling everyone.

Trumped jumped away slow in the maiden over 1,400 metres. James sat quiet as he tailed the field at Epsom. At the 800-metre mark, he was full on running. Tom commented through his binoculars, 'He is travelling well.' They came around the turn with three furlongs to run, and James eased him to the outside. There were four well-bred colts in the race among the field of twelve, and James wasn't overly confident. He was now running eighth with two furlongs left. They had never pushed Trumped out fully, so they didn't know how good he could be. James started to get a bit desperate, as he wasn't quickening like he had hoped. He hated to use the whip on any horse, especially two-year-olds. He gave four hard backhands around his rump and drove hands and heels. Finally, he was starting to respond and, at the 300-metre mark, he was four lengths from the leader.

All of a sudden, the leader started to drift out rapidly, and the rider of the horse who was at his hindquarters had no choice but to check his mount and pull the right rein while sitting back. James had to check Trumped back hard as well, and the two horses almost clipped heels. James lost momentum for three strides, and all looked lost. He urged once again, and he felt Trumped dig deep and noticed he had laid his ears back. James looked quickly to his left and the running was clear. He drove hard towards the inside rail as the leader was now clear, and the jockey had straightened the colt. He rode as hard as he ever had in his life. On the post, he looked over and he couldn't believe he had got so close.

Victoria, Logan, Miles, Cynthia, and Mike had all been on their feet like it was the richest race in the world. The judge called for a photo finish. Everyone held their breath and patiently watched the big screen for the replay. 'Paper Rock Scissors has held on to beat Trumped, and Smooth Style has held on for third,' the announcer called. The team was extremely deflated. The Derby was more than likely out of the question now.

James came back to scale, and Tom and Cynthia knew the look. He was fuming. When he stepped on the scales, he announced to the steward present, 'Protest, sir.' The siren sounded, and the caller announced a hold on all bets. James was sure the interference caused by the winner had cost him over one length, when he hampered the fourth horse that was at the time in front of him.

The winning margin was only a nose. In racing that was less than six inches.

The team huddled as Logan made the call. 'You, Tom, and your mother go in.' Tom went to protest, but Logan insisted on his choice. 'Cynthia, if you get the chance to speak on behalf as the owner, set them straight. He took the other horse out, and it took our running and we lost momentum and only ended up being beaten by a nose.'

Logan was correct, and in a matter of minutes the siren sounded to announce the protest being upheld. The rider was given six meetings for not stopping to straighten his mount immediately.

But there was no time to celebrate, as Slipstream was in the next race over the same distance. There was no issue with her, and she romped in by four lengths, beating Miss Swede. She was now on the line for equal second favourite for the Oaks, as her time was also a second faster than Trumped's. They had a very serious filly on board. The stable now had twelve runners in total for nine wins. It should have been eleven wins, but the wet tracks hampered the two runners over Christmas, and they had to settle with a second and a fourth.

Victoria invited everyone home for the celebration. It was their first official night with guests as a married couple in their home, and she had been preparing for weeks to have everyone down. After their win, it was the perfect time. Hank was happy, as the celebration included half a barbecue chicken that Logan had picked up on the way home as a treat.

Across town, Bill the farrier couldn't get Sandra out of his mind. He couldn't believe she was going to spend the night with someone else after they had fucked. He didn't seem too worried that he had just betrayed his wife. Over dinner, Emma talked about the day's pony club competition. The boys seemed more interested in the latest Pokémon games than the ribbons they had won. On and on Emma went about the day's triumphs and the bitchiness of the other mothers. Twice she asked if he was okay, as he was unusually quiet. When he replied, 'Fine' for the second time, she didn't bat an eyelid. She thought he was just tired from shoeing all day. She had no idea he had the best sex of his life behind her back and was infatuated with Sandra.

He tucked the boys in bed and showered as normal. He had already showered once when he got home and had hidden his sex-stained clothes in the tool shed to wash later when Emma was out. He hungered for the next time. *Sandra is like a drug*, he thought. *Only once, and now I'm addicted.* He lay in bed, and Emma came in from the shower. She started talking again, but this time about how it was time to get the boys in the hunting clubs with horses and hounds, and how they should think about selling the ponies to buy horses more suited to jumping. She went on about the connections they could make from hunting. Bill had finally had enough. He exploded. 'All I ever hear is fucking pony club, shows, and now hunting! Every living minute is about the kids riding, the kids winning, the other mothers being nasty to each other. You spend every goddamn cent I earn with my head lower than my ass all fucking day, getting the shit kicked out of me. You stopped working because you are so bloody obsessed with the kids' ponies, but you're the one training them, not the kids. They ride them once a week at best. You do everything, and you override my decisions about how they should be doing more and taking on more responsibilities. They are not the Royal Family, you know. Maybe they could feed and do their boxes one morning, and you actually give me more than two minutes of your time once a month.' Emma's jaw just dropped. She had never once seen Bill explode like that, not ever.

Bill got out of bed started to get dressed. 'I'm over it, Emma. I'm your husband and I deserve more than just working until I die to support you.' Emma didn't move. No one had ever spoken to her like that. As he stormed out, Emma realised that she had turned into the exact same person her mother had been, and she didn't like it.

Bill slammed the back door, got in his 4WD, and drove away. He was furious, but more with Sandra than Emma. He drove to Sandra's house and sat outside. He went to text her and stopped. He had already acted out in anger and was not going to risk losing Sandra too. Thoughts raced through his head as he sat there, and he wondered if he and Sandra could be together if he left Emma. Since they first met, he had never stopped thinking about her.

CHAPTER 35

Masters and My Blue Boy landed at 4.30 p.m. on the 26th of April. Flights had been a hassle to get, but they were finally here. Masters had also brought his two new purchases. His original horses had gone awry, as he had worked them too hard, and they both broke down. So Masters did what he was good at— he bought more horses. His backer had bottomless pockets, so he had bought a sprinter called Shark Tank who had won three Group 1 sprints. He was a grey gelding with no stud value, but the offer of three million for a gelding was too good to refuse. He also bought the Group 1 Caulfield Cup winner, Maximus. He felt he was ready to lower the curtain on Logan. He also had the stable ticking over well at Newmarket.

Masters' team settled the horses and found that all had travelled well. No irregular temperatures, and all three had eaten on the flight. Masters wasted no time and texted Sandra the address of the fully furnished cottage he had rented for his six-week stay. He may have been jetlagged, but he had one thing on his mind.

Masters didn't know, but Sandra had been hustling another man, an Englishman she'd met while there. He was fifty-four and had a thing about her dressing in a school girl outfit. He had already forked out over £20,000 for jewellery, clothes, expensive restaurants, and hotel rooms in London. She had even made him beg and call her 'mistress' while secretly recording. She had planned to use the videos and photos to scam him for more money later. She knew anyone in politics would not want that sort of thing to get out.

Sandra arrived at Masters' cottage wearing the same outfit that worked so well for Bill. Masters smiled as he opened the door, and this time the only gun was in his pants. She played him again. This time she faked three times. The only time she actually orgasmed was when she was thinking about Bill.

Masters pulled his pants on and poured two glasses of whisky. 'On the morning of the 1st of June, I want you to drop the bomb on the farrier. A simple short message telling him that you need a favour. And send just one photo, and tell him about the videos. You are going to give him a bottle of hoof dressing. On the 2nd of June, he will be plating up or at least checking the runners' shoes. All he needs to do is put the dressing on the hooves and on the coronet bands. That's all you want. And that's all I need. The hoof dressing contains enough illegal substances to get him banned and rubbed out for positive swabs for ten years.' Masters had a chemist create a mixture of the most common illegal substances, but he had also had cocaine added in, so the animal welfare department would tear Logan apart. He would never train for anyone ever again after they announced *that* was administered to the horse. 'After you drop the hoof dressing off, you are to lay low with a, let's say, friend of mine. Once the positive swab comes out, you will be paid the balance and you can go.'

Sandra looked concerned. 'What about Bill?'

'Well, it's your job to make sure he doesn't talk, isn't it? That's what the videos are for. You're a smart girl. I'm sure you'll work it out.'

Within three days, My Blue Boy, Shark Tank, and Maximus were jumping out of their skins. All had put back on the weight lost on the flight over. New surroundings had done wonders to freshen up the horses and their trainer. For once, Masters was keeping a low profile.

The 21st of May had three Group 1 races; six-furlong, seven-furlong, and ten-furlong races; plus a Group 2 for colts and geldings over ten furlongs; a Group 3 over nine furlongs for fillies; and two listed Stakes races. Masters hated that he had to adjust to the term furlong in England.

It was all systems go for Logan and Tom. Every horse was working a treat. Everest was going to the farm every second day. Logan was excited as Aunty Joy, Don, Pete, Neale, and a couple of old school mates, Marc and Shaun, were making the trip to Royal Ascot. Aunty Joy had been calling everyone to come.

Victoria was taking the Super Saturday at Royal Ascot very seriously. Cynthia had taken her shopping and carved up a solid six hours in some of the best boutiques in London. Now she was not working, Victoria had taken to jogging with James in the mornings after track work. Hank joined in most mornings, too.

James was a person who valued routine, especially on race mornings. At 6.45 a.m. he would run for an hour—same time, same running distance, same route. Then he would have a hot bath and sweat it out for an hour. If he was coming in underweight that allowed him to have a small breakfast, so he was strong enough for the day's racing.

The first two weeks of May went very smoothly both in the Baker racing camp and the Masters camp. Neither men had crossed paths. The team met in Logan's office and all discussed the nominations for the upcoming Saturday races. Everest was in the Group 1 over ten furlongs; Forest Black, seven furlongs; Warrior King, the sprint over six furlongs; Trumped, the Group 2 over ten furlongs; and Slipstream, the fillies' race over nine furlongs. They also put a few of the up-and-comers in the listed races to judge their future potential.

Forest Black was up against My Blue Boy in the seven-furlong race; Everest was going to have to take on Maximus in the ten-furlong race; and the King would take on Masters' grey flash, the winner of three Group 1's, Shark Tank. Logan hoped he had the hometown advantage. It wasn't only Masters who he had to worry about. The best of the best from around the world would be there. 'It's not going to be a walk in the park,' Cynthia said, with a hint of nerves. The Australian owners would be there, and Logan had learned that Darcy and Jo were now living together.

Logan had gone quiet, and it seemed a normal habit every night before the races. As per his ritual, he walked down through the stables at 8.30 p.m. Even though they had a full-time employee, a semi-retired horseman, on the lookout for colic and horses getting cast, he still did his nightly walk-through. Hank always walked with him, and now Victoria had joined the ritual. Logan looked over the door, and sometimes went in to check their feed and water or check their legs for heat. Hank would also go in looking for horse shit to roll in—to Victoria's utter disgust. The ritual officially ended with Logan scrubbing the horse shit off Hank in the bathtub and Victoria blow-drying him afterwards. Victoria had given up Hank wearing his doggy rugs.

Mike pulled the bloods, and Bill the farrier came to adjust a few shoes. Logan had been pissed off, as the horses had been shod later than he had planned. A miscommunication between Tom and Bill had resulted in the horses not being re-shod in the fronts when out spelling over the Christmas break. They were now going to have run on Super Saturday five weeks in their shoes, instead of the normal three to four weeks. Logan preferred not to plate up for race day, but with the work out on the farm the shoes were wearing quicker than normal. He personally booked Bill to replate or shoe Super Saturday's runners at 9 a.m. Thursday 2nd of June.

CHAPTER 36

The Super Saturday lead-up was finally here and Masters was about to have his first English runners in just under three hours. He had been asked by the daily racing post for an interview that morning. Ego had got the best of him and he accepted. Nothing was held back, and he spoke about the rivalry and how he planned to take Logan down with the firepower he had brought over. His final comment was, 'In the Queen Anne, Logan Weston will fall on his own sword. My Blue Boy won't be beaten, and Maximus will crush all the competition.'

Half an hour later, it hit YouTube. Miles couldn't help himself; he loved being involved in such high-stakes drama, and he thrust it under Logan's nose as they settled the horses in to the race day's tie-ups. Victoria quickly pulled Miles aside and gave him a good grilling about his stupidity.

As James was walking from the jockey and trainers' car park with his saddlebag, Masters drove up beside him. 'Heading to the ladies' room, Baker? I hear you fags sit to piss. There are real jockeys to ride against today, you realise!'

James kept his cool and eyes straight ahead. 'Maybe I will use the women's changing room today. It doesn't stink like BO, and we can all gossip about cakes and boys between rides. Good luck in the race. I hear you need it.' Masters didn't have a quick comeback and James slipped through some parked cars to get away.

He was about to burst out crying when he heard, 'G'day, James.' He quickly turned, and there was Don. They didn't shake hands; they hugged. Don was the first person James had ever confided in about being gay, and he had kept in contact with him ever since. Many times, he had called Don when he was down and had received support and often some solid advice.

Don was looking over James's shoulder. 'If not for my bad hip, I would have gone over there and punched that prick right in the mouth.' James wiped the tears from his cheeks. 'Big day ahead. Don't let him get in your head,' Don said as he put his arm around James, and in they went.

'I thought you weren't over for another week or so,' James said.

'Needed a holiday,' Don replied.

It was Don's first time to Ascot, and he was in awe. 'The Everest of racing,' he said, as he stopped and admired the grandstands. He stood there in his blue sports jacket, blue striped shirt, white moleskin pants, and R. M. Williams boots—as Australian as you can get—and took it all in. Then he turned to James. 'I didn't come all this way to see you quit.' He gave him another hug. 'Give 'em hell, boy.'

Logan was saddling Trumped when he heard, 'Your father would be proud of you, son.'

He didn't even lift his head; he just shook it and laughed. 'I'll just be a minute, Don.' He was concentrating on saddling up, and Tom was on the other side.

'Saddle up, son. Don't mind me,' Don said.

The strapper walked Everest past, and he suddenly stopped. He turned his head and pulled the groom towards Don. Sophie struggled to hold him back. 'Hello, mate. How've you been?' Sophie let him go and he buried his head into Don's chest.

Don scratched his cheekbones and rubbed his forelock. Sophie was amazed. 'I can't even brush him without getting attitude.' She quickly handed Don the comb. 'Here.' Don happily took up the job. He felt like a rock star. He hadn't felt so alive in years, but he was now fighting prostate cancer. Only he and his doctor knew. The trip was just what he needed. He didn't need treatment for another six weeks, and he was feeling the best he had in over a month.

Logan was very proud to introduce Victoria. Don gave the wink of approval, and after meeting Cynthia and Miles he was escorted to the private box Cynthia had booked for the two-day carnival.

Tom legged James on Trumped. The first thing he asked was, 'You see Don?'

Tom nodded. 'Yes, he's up in the box with Mother.'

Trumped was up against the identical field for the lead-up to the Derby. He needed the win to gain a start. The margin was four lengths pulling away on the line. He was now in the Derby and third favourite. 'He was good, real good,' Logan told the press in his first ever interview. It was shaping to be one of the best Derby's in years. Logan and Tom were beaming. Cynthia couldn't hide the emotions today, and she teared up talking about her two boys.

James followed that win with another, but his ride with Slip-stream was extremely hard-fought for nearly two furlongs. Baker Racing now had a filly in the Oaks as well. The moment was spoilt when the post-race interview only asked about the rivalry between Logan and Masters. Logan finished the interview with a very blunt, 'I will tell you in forty minutes.' Masters was watching the interview, and he knew he had got under Logan's skin. Logan said to Tom, 'Remind me to leave the rest of the interviews to you. I hate that shit.'

It was now Everest versus Maximus. Ten furlongs, Group 1 and £500,000 up for grabs. Everest laid his ears back when Masters walked past with Maximus's saddle. Luckily, Mike grabbed his head in time and held him back.

Tom and Logan huddled with James. Cynthia decided she was too nervous to be any use today with decision-making. 'He is very fit. I'd say fitter than we think. These are the best horses he's faced. They'll think he will fold up against them, but you know how to ride him.' Logan patted James on the back, and Tom legged his twin brother on.

Maximus was a come-from-behind stayer, and James knew he was on the best horse in the race, closely followed by the four horses from France from the Lester stable. Two had won two Group 1's at ten furlongs.

James jumped very fast and was in front by four lengths after two furlongs. At the six-furlong mark, he was ten in front, and he was bowling along beautifully. Maximus was sixth and about fourteen lengths back as the field was packed tight behind the tear-away leader. Touchdown, from the Lester stable, was second and travelling well. James decided to pour the speed on from the four-furlong mark and make the last 800 metres a real staying test.

Masters had flown his best jockey, LJ, over to ride the two-day carnival for him. He knew he was going to have to withstand a long run, and Masters had told him to be no further back than six lengths. He argued. He didn't care if he was a back marker. Masters insisted, saying, 'Do not give Everest more than six lengths, or you won't ever run him down.'

James gave the full throttle, and Everest gave them a galloping lesson and won, easing down by six lengths.

When LJ dismounted in the second-place winner's stall, beaten by six lengths, he knew he was going to cop the blast every jockey hated to get. James couldn't help it and, as he walked past Masters, he scoffed quietly and muttered, 'Loser'. Masters was choked up with anger and was extremely close to lashing out at James.

His foreman could see the expression on his face, which he had seen many times before. He grabbed Masters' arm and Masters tensed, ready to throw a punch until he realised who it was. His first defeat by Logan with his own ex-racehorse. It couldn't get any worse. The press went crazy and, for once, Masters kept his mouth shut.

Logan and Victoria had a break between runs and decided they needed a quick fifteen minutes away from everyone. Logan got the shudder again and turned, and there she was again in the crowd—the blonde woman he had seen at the airport and the bakery. They kept walking but Logan turned again to get another look at her. She was meeting with Bill, their farrier, and had dressed to impress. As a farrier, it wasn't unusual that he would be at the races. *They look like old friends. So maybe I've just seen her around the stables then*, Logan thought, trying to brush away the bad feeling he had about her.

The next race was Warrior King versus Shark Tank. Shark Tank was a leader, and Warrior King came from behind. The King looked enormous. He had grown, strengthened, and improved. Shark Tank was small in comparison, but he was a triple Group 1 winner. Masters told LJ to lead—no matter what—and dictate. James knew how hard the six-furlong uphill was at Ascot. Many champions came unstuck in the last 100 metres up the rise. History doesn't lie; Shark Tank faded with 100 to go and ran fifth. Warrior King won by five lengths going away from the field. He was a freak. To do that to a Group 1 field of the best-seasoned sprinters was breathtaking for a three-year-old. That made two Group 1 winners, Group 2, and Group 3 winners in one day.

Now the real test was Forest Black versus My Blue Boy. 'Go put your house on him,' Masters was telling everyone. Logan hadn't laid eyes on his ex-racehorse for over six months. He had chosen him, broken him in, and taught him to be the horse he was. To add salt to the wound, a pregnant Angela waddled up alongside her husband. Their eyes met and she gave Logan a shy wave, which he returned just as timidly. Masters had been treating her terribly. She felt so alone. Even though she was due in five weeks, he made her fly over for the carnival, as he said he didn't trust her. He was worried she would pack up and leave while he was away.

'Is that her?' Logan was startled by Victoria speaking; he was embarrassed she had caught him staring at his ex-wife. 'She's pretty. Maybe I'll go over and thank her.' She kissed him on the cheek and then rubbed the lipstick off. 'She did us both a favour. Don't you agree?' She hugged in closer to him, subtly squeezing her breasts together with her arms. Logan looked at her and was instantly distracted. She had learnt he was a boob man and knew that a top that flattered her cleavage would keep his eye in check all day.

Forest Black had huge potential, but he was a bit untapped and overshadowed in the Baker stable. My Blue Boy could race anywhere in the field and that's exactly what LJ did. He sat right outside James in third spot. He also knew how tough his mount was and rode as close as he legally could without copping a suspension. James was worried he was going to hit the rail as he felt Forest melting under the pressure of My Blue Boy bumping him as they galloped inches apart. Then LJ gave the full bore and left Forest Black in his wake. He demolished the field and won by six lengths. The colt Greenwood from the U.S. ran second, and Spartacus ran third for the sheik. Forest ran on for fourth, beaten by eight lengths.

Masters ran out on the course and met his colt. He had taken the spotlight well and truly off Logan and Tom. Many thought his performance matched or bettered the King's. Times for the last two furlongs showed Masters' horse was the faster of the two. As James walked back past Masters to the jockeys' room, Masters smirked. 'Someone get boxed in, did they? What a pity.' James kept his cool and kept walking.

Logan knew he couldn't win but was disappointed in the horse. 'He just gave up after he was squeezed.'

James agreed that he was intimidated by the tight racing and suggested he spend more time at the farm doing cattle work and working in a mob to prevent it in future. 'Maybe we take him on a hunt so he gets used to a mob of horses.' Logan nodded and said they'd talk about it later. He never made decisions on race day.

The mood was sombre even though it had been an amazing day. The gloss had been taken off with the disappointing run of Forest Black and the fact he was trounced by My Blue Boy.

The two Group 1 races they won were worth £680,000 just in winners' cheques. Logan's percentage from both wins was £68,000 and, given the stud value of both colts, plus Trumped's value,

Logan's bank balance would be looking pretty good very soon. They returned home and had a few drinks at the main house. It seemed like everyone was going to kick on for a while yet, but Logan and Victoria decided it was time to go. Cynthia was hooking into the alcohol, and Victoria joked about how they were overdue for another unexpected visit.

At 7.30 p.m., Victoria fed Hank dinner, then dragged Logan to the movies, which he went kicking and screaming to. He was able to switch his head off and they watched the action movie, ate popcorn, and cuddled like teenagers.

When they got home, Logan put Hank in the laundry so they could have some uninterrupted 'alone time'. Logan realised it was the fourth time in a week. Logan didn't know, but the health kick they were both on also had added supplements to increase libido in women and men, Victoria was told.

They showered and Victoria washed her husband down. 'Why're y'all still moody as hell?' she asked.

'Just hate being beat. Especially by that asshole.'

'Well, darlin', if you win the eight-million-dollar Queen Anne, you can get two blowjobs.' Logan was shocked; he was still getting used to the prim and proper Victoria saying it straight sometimes. 'What? Can't a lady talk like a guy sometimes?'

Hank decided it was long enough and started to howl.

Cynthia had snuck off to her car to drive home, even though she may have been borderline over the limit. At 7 p.m. she had switched to sparkling mineral water, after James told her to pull her head in when she asked a simply too-private question about Miles. Two wrong turns later, she was in the small industrial area of Newmarket. She was lost, but soon spotted a neon sign:

'Adult Store'. She pulled over. She was curious about the new world that had been opened up to her. Loving the vibrators, she had grown more curious about what was on offer. She still hadn't had sex for nearly two years and was missing the touch of a man.

She went in to browse, then found a vibrator/dildo called 'Max Douglas'. The label said: 'Have you ever wanted 10 inches?' She blushed, but the temptation was too strong. She took the monster to the counter and didn't say a word. The cashier was used to being discreet and put it in a plain brown paper bag with no logo. He threw in some free lube, and she turned bright red, paying and quickly leaving.

She got back in her car and placed her handbag and the brown paper bag on the passenger seat beside her. She fiddled with the GPS and finally set off in the direction of home. The red and blue lights shocked her as she looked back in her rear-view mirror. 'Oh fuck ... fuck, fuck, fuck,' she said to herself. She pulled over and a male police officer walked up to her window as she was lowering it. 'Good evening, ma'am.'

Cynthia nervously shot her answer back quickly, 'What's wrong officer? What have I done wrong?'

His calm tone didn't falter at her response. 'Ma'am, I saw you fail to come to a complete stop at the stop sign back there.'

She was flustered but relieved. 'Oh ... Yes, sorry. I've have never been this way through town before. I'm lost, and I must've been looking at my GPS.'

'I need to see your driver's licence, please, ma'am.' As Cynthia reached to quickly grab her wallet from her bag, she fumbled and knocked the brown paper bag off the seat. It made a thud as it hit the floor. She looked highly suspicious, as she jolted to pick it up, and the officer gave her face another look. 'Have you been drinking tonight, ma'am?'

Cynthia stuttered, 'I stopped at 7 p.m. and have been drinking sparkling mineral water ever since.'

'That's not an open container of alcohol?' He nodded to the bag.

'N-no.'

He put his hand out, gesturing to see it, and Cynthia reluctantly complied. He looked in the bag cautiously and read the label at least twice. Cynthia was turning bright red. 'It's a gift for a friend,' she quickly added, trying to diminish her utter embarrassment.

The officer handed the bag back without a word and took her licence from her hand, then walked back to his car. He got in and started typing her details in to check her driving history, retelling the story to the other officer in the car. Cynthia watched them in the rear-view mirror and saw them both suddenly burst out laughing. They laughed for a good few minutes, looking as if they were in tears. Finally, the officer got out and walked back up to her window.

Cynthia was fuming, and she snatched her licence as he handed it over. She held her tongue, as she hoped she would get away without being breathalysed. She glared at him and he couldn't help breaking into another soft chuckle. 'My apologies for the laughter, ma'am.' He tapped the tag on the right side of his chest, which read: 'Senior Constable, M. Douglas.'

Cynthia's jaw dropped, then she burst out laughing too. She could see now that he was red in the face from blushing. 'Have a good night, ma'am. Drive safe.' No ticket, no breathalyser, she was sent on her way home.

Mike, Logan, and Tom had checked all their runners for soundness, aches, and pains. All had pulled up well. Forest Black had a slight bruise on his near fore heel, as he must have overreached at some stage, but Mike had to press quite firmly to get a reaction of pain. All the horses had the day out in the yards, as the sun was simply beautiful. It was only thirteen days until the showdown.

Sandra had Bill hooked and had just given him the best night of his life. He was actually the best sex she had ever had. Bill's wife Emma spent a lot of time thinking about Bill's outburst, and she knew he was right in many ways, but she simply couldn't let her lifestyle go. She was addicted to the drama of the pony club life. She enjoyed being kingpin in the local district. Bill was sleeping in the spare room, with only Sandra on his mind.

Masters was all smiles after his first Group 1 win at Royal Ascot. He told the press, 'Yesterday gave me a lot of confidence moving forward. My horses performed well, and we will be even better prepared for the Super Saturday.' He explained how they thought Shark Tank had actually got his tongue over the bit and possibly choked down. It was decided a tongue tie would be used on the next start. Maximus had a good blow after the run and would take a lot off the race. My Blue Boy had licked his feed bin clean and was feeling so well he nearly got away from Masters when they posed for photos with the press interviews.

As well as Masters' plan to take Logan out of the picture, he also had one to remove James. No other jockey had ever sat on any of their horses in a race. All good jockeys could adapt, as they were professionals, but if James was taken out of the picture on the morning of the race it would throw them off their game. His mercenary had been watching the training facility for three weeks. He knew every move in and out. Logan and Tom had no idea the old abandoned farmhouse 300 metres from their front gate had the perfect view of the stable and was being occupied daily by Joseph Jackson—ex-sniper, ex-seal, ex-FBI, and now rouge mercenary. For £50,000 he was prepared to take James out with one shot. Masters had thirteen days to ensure both his plans were a success.

Don was staying with the boys and was extremely impressed with the training set-up. Miles had cooked up a huge spread for breakfast and Logan had piled up his plate.

CHAPTER 37

The social media and press were building the meeting to be the showdown of the heavyweights. It wasn't just Masters versus Logan; the Queen had her Group 1-winning filly Dual Choice; the Sheik had three champion runners from Dubai; plus two from Ireland and two from France. The Derby and Oaks were normally the main feature, but not this year. The Queen Anne had been elevated to the highest prize money ever in England's history. Eight million pounds, and 5.4 million to the winner.

Sandra sowed her last seed with Bill. She gave him another wild night and added extra kinkiness that blew his mind. Emma didn't like the fact Bill was going on a so-called 'boys night out', playing cards all of a sudden. Masters arranged his so-called 'safe house'. He also updated his hired mercenary Joseph Jackson on his plans for the Saturday morning. Angela had been feeling sick and staying in bed most days, so he didn't have to worry about her tagging along and getting in the way.

Tom and Logan watched the King and Forest Black do their final work at 7 a.m. The King had the upper hand anyway, but he worked better than ever. Neither horse would have blown out a candle, though the team acknowledged they would be more confident if Bluey wasn't in the race.

In the last-minute nomination change, Tom made the call to switch Forest back to the 1,200-metre sprint. 'I think he will run super up the straight. He can sit back to either side and get a trail, then peel out. The last three have been run up the middle of the straight and won by late swoopers,' said Tom. Forest Black's fourth placing to Bluey in the Group 1 was enough for him to scrape into the field for the sprint.

'I think you might be right on the money, Tom. Good call.'

Tom and Logan worked extremely well together, and Miles was a huge part of the process, as he knew the racing patterns inside out. He was standing close by and heard their conversation. He repeated Logan sarcastically, 'Yeah, good call, Tom.' He rolled his eyes. 'Who do you think told him about the fucking race pattern? I don't see you two reviewing race videos all day and night. I don't have time for anything else at the moment. All I do is gather data for you two, and you swoop in and take all the credit.'

Logan walked over and put his arm around him sympathetically. 'Sorry, mate. We appreciate what you do for the team. Seems like we're all just very tense at the moment.'

Tom smirked. 'Yeah, you're very tense, Miles. I think you need to get laid.'

Miles snapped, 'Yeah? Tell your brother that!'

Tom laughed and replied, 'Cut him some slack. He's doing whatever it takes to stay in the zone for the race.'

'Well, *my* zone hasn't been hit for almost four weeks!' Miles said dramatically.

'God, you have no filter,' Logan said, and walked away laughing.

They took Everest, Trumped, and Slipstream to the farm for the longer gallop. This time James rode all three in gallops. Everest moved like the machine he was—a winning gallop. Slipstream was also very impressive for a young filly, though she still had to mature a lot more. Trumped worked like a potential superstar. James struggled to hold him slow enough and his time was still better than Everest's. 'Make room on the mantel, brother. There will be a Derby trophy there Saturday night,' James said.

'Fingers crossed,' Tom replied.

Tom fired a question to his brother. 'If I had to choose between him and Warrior King over ten furlongs—.' Tom hadn't even finished his question and James had answered, 'I would pick this guy to outrun everyone.'

Logan chimed in, 'That's a big call to make.'

'Have I been wrong yet?' James said with a wink, then trotted Trumped back down to the truck.

It was like the witty Irishman was telepathic. Logan's phone rang and he held it up to Tom. 'You want to talk to him?' Logan asked, and Tom shook his head.

'You have to give him an answer sometime, and you know Mother would be happy to sell fifty per cent for the right price,' Tom said.

Logan hit accept and the strong, loud accent came down the phone: 'You still in bed with Miss America? You know, she keeps calling me. Unlike you.'

Logan just started smiling. 'I've been busy.'

'You know I have a friend in immigration. I could deport you and have you sent back to convict island.'

'Is there a specific reason you're calling?' Logan said assertively.

'Listen, you gobshite, you know I want in on Trumped.'

'Yes, but I don't need you wasting my time this morning. Trumped is going to win the Derby and you don't have a client with deep enough pockets to afford him.'

'Fuck off,' Mick said, scoffing.

'He will win the Derby,' Logan said again. 'Are you listening? You can't afford him.' Then he hung up. Tom looked in disbelief and Logan told him, 'Relax, he's just trying to get the price down so he can get a sale. For once, let's make the bastard work hard for his commission.

Tom said, 'Just don't piss him off too much. He's one of the best agents in Europe and has some of the biggest clientele in the world. Smart arse or not, he's still very good.'

Logan nodded. Mick was the hardest-working agent he had ever come across. His phone rang again and Logan looked at Tom with a smile, as he answered it and put it straight on speakerphone.

Logan quickly said, 'What's the offer? No fucking around. I'm seriously busy today.'

Mick switched into business mode. '6.4 million for fifty per cent, another two million if he wins the Derby, one million for any other Group 1s, and two million if he wins the Queen Anne next year, if you can train him to win over a mile.'

Logan looked at Tom. Cynthia had made it clear that if they ever needed to make a decision, and both Tom and Logan were in agreement, then she would accept their decision. They did the calculations quietly: 6.4 million now, another two million after Saturday, and they still have fifty per cent.

'Before we agree to anything, who's the buyer?' Tom asked.

Mick replied, 'Japanese billionaire. He's building a new farm and wants a foundation stallion when he is done. You guys have complete control on his racing, Mr Tanaka has made that clear.'

Logan was about to speak, but Tom said, 'We get Saturday's prize money and the trophy. After that, it's 50/50. In exchange, tell Mr Tanaka we would be honoured if Trumped could wear his racing silks on Saturday.' Logan looked floored and patted Tom on the shoulder and winked. Another great call.

'Done,' Mick said without hesitation. 'I'll send a vet over in two hours to X-ray, check soundness, and pull bloods. Nice doing business with you, gentlemen.'

'Logan. Logan. Logan.'

'Yes Mick.'

'Don't forget to buy the top hat and tails, ya penguin,' and he hung up to finalise the deal by the end of the day.

That was how the racing game has worked for decades. Stallion stations would take huge risks buying colts before they even performed at the Group 1 stage. Only about twenty per cent of deals ever came off better, and possibly ten per cent made a return on their money within five years. It's only a lucky few who get lucky. In his prime, Warrior King's father was mating four mares a day for about three months at $330,000 a pop.

They loaded the horses and headed back to the stables. Logan did his normal detour to the café/bakery and now they sold barbecue chickens. It had become a ritual now on the way back from the farm gallops. Logan had a pie and coffee, and Hank got barbecue chicken along with the staffs' food. Logan walked in the café/bakery, picked up his order, and turned to walk out. He almost ran into the woman behind him, and she caught the three bacon and egg rolls in the brown paper bag from falling to the ground.

'Thank ... you,' Logan said, quickly recognising the woman he couldn't stop running into everywhere he went.

Sandra didn't answer, just smiled and handed him the bag. She stepped forward casually to the counter, pretending to look up indecisively at the menu and take interest in the cashier as she ordered. In her mind, she was screaming, *fuck, fuck, fuck!* It was only one more day until she sprung the plan on Bill. She couldn't attract attention to herself. Logan thought for a moment about asking her if he knew her from back in Australia, but she was busy ordering so he left.

As she handed the money over for the coffee and croissants, her hand was trembling. 'Morning,' came a voice from behind, and Sandra jumped, nearly spilling her coffee everywhere. It was Masters and Angela; they had heard the coffee was good, and luckily they had somehow missed Logan by seconds.

Masters looked smug and happy with himself as he played the perfect husband in public. He even pulled Angela's seat out and took her order up to the counter. Sandra was using serviettes to clean her hands and wipe her coffee cup.

The door opened, and Bill walked in. He recognised Masters immediately, but Masters had never met him before so he had no clue who he was. He saw Sandra and Masters talking and walked over. 'Sandra,' he said, looking between the two. He wondered just how many men she was still sleeping with.

She looked nervous. 'Oh, hi, Bill.'

There was an awkward pause, then Masters put out his hand. 'Angus Masters.' Bill shook hands and made sure to give Masters an extra firm grip. Bill had very big strong hands; just like his cock.

Sandra chimed in, 'Oh, sorry, Bill! Angus is my old boss from back home.' Hearing his voice, Angela had turned to look at who her husband was speaking to. Over the last six months, she had been less and less to the stables. The staff turnover was always huge; when something went wrong, Angus would fire the first person he saw. The three of them stood there awkwardly. 'And what do you do, Bill?'

'I'm a farrier.' The penny dropped, and Masters nodded slowly, then clapped his hands together. 'Well, it was nice seeing you Sandra. Bill.' He nodded at Bill, then headed back over to the table to wait with Angela for their coffees and food.

When Masters walked away, Bill said, 'I need to talk to you.'

She quickly placed the napkins in the bin. 'I'm running late, sorry, I have to get going.' She quickly headed for the door, looking very flustered.

Bill rushed out onto the path to catch up. 'Is that him?'

'Who?'

'Angus Masters. Is that the one who takes you into town, buys you everything, and has the small cock?' He was pissed off. He knew Masters and heard all the rumours about him flying off the handle and being an arrogant prick. 'He's an asshole. You should dump him.'

'He's just my old boss. I rode work for him back home.'

Bill looked at her like he thought she was lying. Masters was exactly like the type of guy he had pictured in his head, just shorter. 'Why do you stay with them? Just be with me.'

She was fumbling in her bag for her car keys, shaking her head. 'You're just a good fuck, Bill. That's all.' The truth was, she was starting to really like Bill. But this was a job, and she feared the consequences of failing. She jumped in her car, ignored Bill, as he kept speaking through the closed window, and drove off.

Breakfast was quiet. Angela got the feeling the pretty blonde woman was more than just an ex-employee, and she sulked in silence. Masters buried his head in the nominations for Saturday's fields. Nothing was nominated that was a real surprise to him. The only change was that Logan had dropped Forest Black to the six-furlong sprint against Shark Tank. He welcomed the entry, as he was sure he had his horses right for the race. At the Masters stable, there was a last bit of fast work that morning. Bluey worked super, but it was Maximus who really hit the line hard full of running.

What Logan didn't know was Masters had Tom Rolf enter Mayday for the same race as Everest and Maximus. In Europe, it is allowed to have a pacemaker entered to make sure the race is run true. Masters had paid the entry fee for Mayday and also guaranteed £30,000 if he took on Everest stride for stride from the start, so Maximus could sit back and have the jump on him at the end. He was sure Everest would bolt or, at least, rip and tear trying to keep his lead. He also had a plan that he and Joseph only knew about—for James on race morning.

Cynthia took the news about Trumped very joyously. She was enjoying the partners. Everest would be next. There had been nibbles for him from the U.S., as his sire, Roman Empire, had been the champion sire there and in Australia. A deal probably would have been done already, but he had a dam line that had three disappointing sires that had gone to stud in the first three dams and he had been overshadowed by Warrior King and now Trumped.

Sandra was sick to her stomach with what she was about to do. Bill had been ringing her all night. He was knocking on her door, but she had already moved to the safe house—a cottage four miles from Royal Ascot that was hidden from view behind a mass of trees in the corner of a farm. It stunk and was old and creepy, but it was only for a short time.

On the morning of the 1st of June, Sandra sent the text to Bill with the photos and the video. She explained in text she was sorry but this was a job. Just as Masters had instructed. They were planting evidence as well. She outlined the instructions very clearly: 'If you make contact with anyone else about this, your wife will receive the photos and videos I have attached. I have her number and your address. Two bottles will be delivered to your house today. The package is marked as an urgent delivery from Blacksmith and Co. You will put the bottle marked 'The Good Oil' on the following horses trained by Logan Weston tomorrow morning when you reshoe them: Forest Black, Warrior King, Everest, Trumped, and Slipstream. No others. You will paint their feet and also allow the oil to penetrate their coronet bands* on all four feet. Use the plastic surgical gloves provided. Take the 50 ml bottle labelled 'Vitiam GF' and place it in the toilet system in the men's bathroom. When the positive swabs are announced, the images and videos will be destroyed. Do not contact me until I contact you again.

She could hardly hold her hand steady as she hit send. She hoped Bill would use common sense and not try to contact her or find her.

Bill heard his phone ding and looked down as he was driving between shoeing jobs. He saw it was a long message from Sandra

---

* The coronet band is like the base of your fingernail.

so decided to pull over to read it. He hadn't even reached the end of the message when he had to jump out of the car to throw up. He knew he was screwed. He knew the risk he took and thought it would go bad eventually, but not like this. He sat back in the driver's seat with his door open, as his stomach was still churning. He read the message again and again for another fifteen minutes before he decided to text his last two clients to cancel, saying he pulled something in his back. He drove home shakily and parked in the driveway, walking straight to the shed. Emma was out; he suspected she was buying more riding gear. He paced back and forth for a while, going over every different scenario in his head.

His phoned buzzed. It was another text from Sandra. He had to sit down to read it. 'When the job is complete, there will be £25,000 cash delivered to the address of your choice.' This added even more scenarios about how it would play out. It was a shrewd move by Masters. He knew Bill had everything to lose and nothing to gain, and a farrier would be lucky to make 50K a year, so he put the £25,000 kicker in there for insurance.

Bill thought for a while and decided that maybe he could do the job, then come clean; give Emma £25,000 for riding gear and horses. Maybe she would forgive him and give their marriage another shot. He started to convince himself she was as much to blame as he was. *If she had been a better wife, I wouldn't have strayed,* he told himself. He knew many guys who had got back with their wives after they had cheated.

'Fuck it,' he said, deciding to stop feeling sorry for himself. He went into the house and found the box that had been delivered sitting on the kitchen bench. He thought about the worst thing that could happen: *I get warned off and lose my wife and home. Well, fuck them all.* He was getting mad. He always hated the rich pricks that he worked for. Even though they drove expensive cars and lived in mansions, they still never paid him on time or offered him extra cash for being able to come reshoe their horse at the drop of a hat, if required. He knew Logan wasn't like that, and he really admired the story behind his success, but he thought Cynthia was just another rich bitch in a big house with too much money. *Fuck her.*

CHAPTER 38

It was Thursday and only 48 hours until race day. James had to get down to 51 kg to ride Forest Black and he was always riding well at 52.5 kg. He was as fit and as lean as any jockey in the competition but now it meant lettuce leaves and green tea to help strip the extra 1.5 kilograms, since they decided to swap Forest Black after his poor run a fortnight prior.

Miles was moody as hell in the office. 'What's wrong with you today?' Logan asked him.

'Nothing a hand job wouldn't fix,' he scoffed. But he wasn't smiling. He chomped down on a cream bun he had bought at the bakery out of anger, when James turned him down again earlier that morning. 'I can't wait until after Saturday,' he sulked.

Logan smirked at him. 'Substituting sex with cakes, huh?'

Tom walked in the office just as Miles was wiping the cream from his lips. 'My brother finally gave in, did he?' Miles's jaw dropped and Logan laughed. Tom turned to Logan and said,

'Mother and I are heading to meet Mick and Mr Tanaka to sign the papers and get his racing silks. I'll be back soon.'

Logan was happy, as he was about to receive five per cent of the 6.5 million. His deal had been ten per cent of the prize money and five per cent of any sale of colts for stallion potential. He had already pocketed his commission for Warrior King, now Trumped, and possibly Everest soon.

'All good. Bill will be here soon to plate up,' said Logan.

'Watch the King. Last time, Bill got the shits with him, as he leans real hard when he pulls the foot out the front,' Tom told Logan.

'All good. I'll ask Matt to hold him.' Matt was a stablehand and was a gentle giant. Logan liked him, because he was strong but also very patient with the horses. It also stopped the farriers from giving the horses a smack up the ribs when they were playing up while getting shod.

Bill had just pulled up at the front gate and was getting buzzed in by security. They now had a guard at the front gate around the clock, and also another two in the barn. He had installed cameras in every stable, so the guard could sit in the office in the barn and watch every horse, and it was all recorded. Even the feed rooms and vet rooms were monitored.

Bill backed his 4WD into the opening next door to the farrier bay. He unpacked the tools from his farrier box and set out his anvil and forge. Matt went and checked the list. As he got to the King's box, Logan came walking down. 'He's still eating.' He looked at Forest Black next door. 'Take him in the meantime.'

Matt led Forest Black down, and Logan followed. Logan saw that Bill had all the aluminium plates out and everything laid out, ready. He saw the hoof oil bottle with a strange label. 'Is that a new brand?' he asked.

By that time, Bill had Forest Black's near fore up between his legs and had his pinchers pulling in a forward motion taking the shoe off. 'Yeah, supposed to be great to promote hoof growth. Some new formula.'

Farriers nearly always used a lacquer or oil after shoeing to help give a better final finish. Logan picked up the bottle and smelt it, but it didn't smell any different. Masters had added the illegal substances to a normal bottle of hoof oil and made a new label. The smell of the hoof oil could even hide the smell of petrol. He labelled the mixture 'The Good Oil' and added the slogan 'Promotes hoof growth'. He thought he had been very smart with the name.

Logan put the bottle back down and left Bill to his work. He went back to the office and started to go through the field with Miles. It was 10 a.m. and the final fields had been declared, and the barriers selected. Logan was disappointed they didn't have the famous barrier draw like they did at home for the big races.

Hank woke up from his bed in the corner of the office and wandered out, as he heard a visitor. He'd only been gone a minute when Logan heard him barking loudly in the barn. Logan clicked his mouse and viewed the barn security cameras to see that Hank was directly across from the farrier bay and barking like mad at Bill who was now at the anvil. Logan watched and at first was amused. Bill put his hand down to soothe Hank, but he circled around and kept barking. 'Hank doesn't seem to like Bill today,' said Miles, watching over Logan's shoulder.

Logan shook his head. 'I can't shake this weird feeling I have today. My gut is telling me something is up.'

'Pre-race nerves. Maybe you need a hand job.'

Logan shot Miles a look and walked over to the office door. 'Hank … Hank.' He whistled, but Hank wouldn't budge. Logan walked down just as Bill was finishing the last foot with the hoof oil. Bill looked totally different now than he did when he arrived. He was sweating and looked like he was going to be sick. Logan was about to ask him if he was coming down with something, when Matt walked Forest Black out in front of him.

'Trot him,' said Logan. Bill turned around, as he felt like Logan questioned if he had pricked the foot on the horse with the nail too deep.

'Sound as a bell,' Bill said, as he grabbed the broom and swept up the manure and hoof clippings. He offered Hank a piece of clipping, as everyone knows dogs love chewing on horse hoof clippings. But Hank growled at him and wouldn't come close. 'Gee, he's cranky today.'

Logan didn't say a word, as he turned around and walked back up the barn. Matt walked past with the King. He walked lovely and loose as he went past. Logan ran his hand over his supple skin.

Logan walked into the office, clearly agitated. Hank had followed and guarded the door, not barking, but clearly pissed off. Miles gave Logan a concerned look. 'Gee, you and your dog are acting crazy today.'

'Something feels off.'

'You need to get out of the barn. Go for a relaxing drive; get some air. Look, the King has ripped his good rug. How about you drive in to Newmarket Saddlery, and pick up the new one. Take a half an hour break. Take your dog too.'

Logan nodded, grabbing his keys. He was hungry anyway, as he had skipped breakfast. He had received a text from Victoria that she had joined Cynthia and Tom for lunch with Mick and Mr Tanaka. Victoria was fluent in Japanese, and they thought it would make the transaction go smoothly, as Mr Tanaka insisted they have lunch after signing the deal. Garth had been raising Wagyu cattle and selling directly to the Japanese for many years, and Victoria had learnt as part of helping with the contracts.

Logan drove out to the saddlery and picked up the rug. 'Do you have the hoof oil called The Good Oil in stock?'

'You mean McCarthy's farrier oil?' asked the cashier.

'No, no, it's a new type. It's called The Good Oil. The slogan said, "Promotes hoof growth."'

'Oh, no, I don't think so. Let me see if we can order it in for you.' She grabbed the mouse and started to search on her system. 'Funny, it's not in our system at all. Let me see if you can buy it online.' She went into Google.

Logan's bad feeling froze him on the spot and he couldn't even manage to thank the woman before she shook her head. 'No, nothing at all comes up about hoof oil. Valvoline car oil is as close as it gets.'

'Fuck,' Logan whispered. He dropped the rug and took off running straight out the door. He hit the car remote to unlock and startled Hank as he jumped in. Logan turned the car on, sped out of the car park, and started swearing loud enough to make Hank jump in the back seat. 'You lying fucking asshole!' The Good Oil is what John Laws would say when trying to sell fucking car oil. John Laws was the golden voice of Australian radio and would promote car oil on his morning radio show. He hit Miles's number—no answer—then tried the office, but Miles was up at the main house apologising to James for being a little shit.

Logan swerved through traffic and rang the security hut, then cursed himself for not thinking to call the security guards before. 'Yes, Mr Weston.'

'Open the gate. Open the gate *now*.'

'Mr Weston, where are you?'

'Open the fucking gate!' The guard hit the button and the gate started to slowly open as Logan roared up to it. Logan felt as though it was the slowest gate he had ever had anything to do with, and he cursed Cynthia and the guards and the gate. He pulled to a screeching halt in front of it and waved his hands at it as though that would make it move faster.

When there was an opening wide enough for the car to fit through, he floored it. The tyres squealed, and the engine roared loud enough to alert James and Miles, who were in the kitchen talking. 'What the hell!' said James, as they rushed to the glass sliding doorway and saw Logan's car tear up to the barn.

'Let's go! Quick!' Miles took off running, and James followed.

Logan unbuckled his belt and pulled into the stable walkway, leaving the car still running. Hank knew something was up and excitedly bounced out after him. Logan rounded the corner and caught sight of Bill putting the sanding block down on his farrier box. The next step was to apply the oil.

Hank had darted in front and startled a relaxed Warrior King by barking right at his feet at Bill. The King had been playing up, and Matt had worked his magic, stroking and patting him on the neck and head until he relaxed. Warrior King got startled quickly, and he pulled his front foot back hard over Bill's leg—545 kilograms pushing down on his knee. 'Christ! Argh! My knee!' he hobbled forward and turned to see Logan in full flight right at him. *Whack*, then an *oomph*, as Logan crash-tackled Bill to the ground.

This had bent his knee back the other way, and the crunching they heard was his meniscus snapping. 'Argghh, my knee,' Bill cried as he rolled around on the ground.

Matt kept holding the very startled King, who was wild-eyed and snorting. Hank was bouncing around and finally lunged to latch onto Bill's jean leg. 'Hank, that's enough.' Logan grabbed him by the back of the neck to make him let go. Logan went over and took the King from Matt. 'Follow me,' he said, and they headed back to his stable. The King pranced down the breezeway, snorting and jumping with tail up over his back. He snorted so loudly that the whole barn came alive with fit racehorses rearing and kicking out. 'Hold him here until he settles,' Logan said, handing the King back to Matt, then he pulled the door closed on the stable.

He walked back up the barn towards the farrier bay. By now, James, Miles, and the security guard had arrived. 'Why the fuck did you tackle me like that!' he screamed at Logan. 'Get me an ambulance,' Bill screamed, holding his knee in pain. He was going as white as a ghost.

Logan pointed to the security guard. 'You. Wait outside.' The guard looked from Bill to Logan but didn't question the instruction. He knew something was going down, and it wasn't good. He was employed to watch the horses, not whatever this was, so he quickly left. Logan turned to James and Miles. 'Sit him up. We need to ask him some questions.' They dragged Bill over to the wall and propped him up. James put a rug over him, as he was in shock and getting the shakes. Logan gave Bill a few minutes to settle, as he was still crying out in pain.

'What's in the hoof oil, Bill?' Logan asked calmly. Miles looked confused and went to speak, but Logan put his hand up. 'Shut up. For once, just shut up.'

Bill looked at the three men, then paused. He finally said, 'I don't know what you're on about.'

Logan looked him in the eye. 'Really, Bill? Going to play that game?'

Bill was in so much pain, but he did his best to lie. 'You're fucking paranoid. Just like your dog. I need an ambulance,' he said, rolling his head back in pain.

Logan walked closer, then drove a kick sideways into Bill's knee at half force. Bill screamed in pain, and Miles couldn't hold back. 'What the hell are you doing?'

Logan picked up the hoof oil and crouched down right in front of Bill, who was moving his head side to side in agony. He couldn't even speak it was so painful. 'Tell me what's in the hoof oil,' Logan asked him again, trying to stay calm.

Bill shook his head, sweat pouring down his face, and grunted, 'It's just normal hoof oil.'

Logan nodded, then motioned for James. When he awkwardly walked over, Logan handed him the bottle and said, 'Open it.' James complied, and Logan put one hand against Bill's forehead to keep him still, and the other was locked on his jaw. 'If there's nothing wrong with the hoof oil, then you won't mind if we pour it down your throat.'

James was shocked, but he stayed quiet. After Polish Navy was killed, James believed that anything could happen, and he trusted Logan's instinct.

Logan gripped Bill's head tighter. 'It won't hurt you, Bill, bar a case of the runs.'

Bill was choking up with pain. He shook his head again and Logan wrenched his jaw open. James moved closer and feigned beginning to pour, being careful not to spill any in his mouth, as he really didn't want to hurt Bill.

'Don't, don't,' Bill cried. 'I'll tell you.' Logan and James stood back, and Bill hung his head in defeat.

'Tell us everything,' Logan said.

For the next half an hour, Bill spilled his guts about everything. Miles filmed the confession, the whole story, on his phone. The ambulance arrived ten minutes later. Miles called Emma so she could meet Bill at the hospital.

Mike was called in to take bloods from both Forest Black and Warrior King and deliver them to the laboratory for testing. Logan phoned Sir Ivan Humphreys, the most well-respected and trustworthy committee member on the board of English racing, and gave him a brief rundown of their situation. He decided to bring the two head stewards in and also the head of the London Police Department, who was a close friend to Sir Ivan and had shares in many good racehorses. They all met in a motel room, as Sir Ivan knew it was serious, and anyone could have been watching. This was the case, as Joseph had seen Logan and the ambulance arrive and had warned Masters that something was up. The chief of police combatted this by organising a broadcast over the local radio news that afternoon to throw them off the scent: 'A local female horse rider was taken from a racing stable by ambulance today after getting kicked in the stomach by a horse and bursting her appendix. She was taken to hospital and is recovering well.'

Bill kept his mouth shut with Emma; as far as she knew, he was accidentally kicked by a horse. Both their phones were being tapped by the police, and their house was being watched as well. Bill had said he didn't know who Sandra was working for, but he did mention running into her talking to Masters at the bakery.

They all assumed it was Masters. Phone records showed nothing, as the numbers listed belonged to pre-paid over-the-counter numbers. Masters had used many different numbers to contact Sandra. They also never exchanged text messages about the job; only calls.

Mike phoned Logan. 'He's positive.' Logan didn't say a word. '*Everything* is in his system. I've never seen anything like it. We'll know in a few days how he reacts to the substances, but he is definitely out. I'm heading back over now to run some fluids into him. I want us to be as prepared as possible for the worst.'

'Thanks, Mike,' Logan said, and hung up. He put his head in his hands, letting the situation sink in. All the dreams and effort down the drain because of Masters' obsessions with him. They had no solid proof yet, but Logan knew it was him.

The committee members and the police chief told Logan to carry on as normal. They were not to arouse suspicion. The police kept Baker Stables under constant surveillance hoping to catch the culprits if they had anything else planned. Bill was also told to keep his mouth shut. Detectives were monitoring all his contact in and out. Surgery was scheduled for 8 a.m. in the morning to repair the torn meniscus.

Matt and the security guards were briefed and told not to speak a word about it to anyone. The only positive was James could actually have a proper meal, as he didn't have to drop the weight anymore.

Logan was extremely restless, and he left it to Victoria to entertain Aunty Joy and the boys who had made the trip over. The guys were disappointed, but they understood. Aunty Joy didn't blink an eye. She and Don went to London for the day, and by 6 p.m. she was in bed.

The team spent Friday on high alert. Mike had been taking every precaution necessary, and Forest showed no signs of illness, yet. The chemist who made the cocktail for Masters said there would be little negative side effects; if anything, they may even race better. Masters wasn't worried about the horses' health, only that they were to produce a positive swab and that Logan was barred for life.

Everything was packed for the races. Logan had gone through all the tack bags, and he gave the staff the afternoon off, to their amazement. Cynthia gave them all £200 each and told them to buy a new outfit for the races. The staff thought there was something going on, but they didn't ask questions. Back at the barn, it was all hands on deck. Miles and James were walking the horses in and out of the day paddocks and sand roll for the afternoon. Cynthia and Victoria were cleaning stables. Tom made all the feeds for that night and the morning. Mike and Logan went through and did all the treatments and soundness checks. Don was on the broom.

At 6 p.m. they were finished. Cynthia and Victoria got Chinese takeaway and one BBQ chicken. They sat down in the stables, and Miles brought the plates and cutlery from the office kitchenette down. The girls had bought some beers, since champagne wasn't the appropriate drink for the occasion.

Don looked around the stable, as he said, 'I came halfway around the world to watch you guys tomorrow. This afternoon showed why you are the most dominant training operation going in the world at the moment. There are no egos in this team. Everyone just puts their heads down and does what needs to be done. Yesterday could have been much worse. He could have ruined what you have going here.'

Logan's gut had been telling him something was going to happen, and it did happen. Luckily, they were able to shut it down before even more damage was done.

Don continued, 'In an instant, you have pulled together. Tomorrow is your day. Best of luck. Cheers.' Don raised his beer bottle up, and they all clinked their drinks. They packed up the leftovers and everyone went home. Logan and Victoria walked back up to his house, and Hank waddled after them, completely stuffed with chicken.

The others had all driven off, and Logan lingered for a moment to look back at the barn. 'What's wrong, darlin'?' Victoria asked. He looked like he didn't want to share his thoughts. 'I can't help you if you don't talk to me.'

'It's not over. I know he's going to try something else,' Logan said.

'Like what?'

'If I knew that, I'd be a mind reader, wouldn't I?'

Victoria stared at him for a moment before she replied, 'Don't you get goddamn shitty with me Logan Weston. I'm here to support you.'

She was right; he shouldn't get snappy with her. 'I'm sorry,' he said, taking her hand and walking up the pathway, both deep in thought.

At 9 p.m. Logan finally surrendered to fatigue. He had caught up quickly with his fellow Aussies and they understood his early departure. Victoria had his clothes laid out for tomorrow. Everything was ready. Hank got to sleep on the bed as Logan's head wasn't about to switch off, and he wasn't in the mood. Logan's mind raced all night, just like everyone's on the team, trying to work out the next step. Bill had admitted to everything. He had no photo of Sandra's face, but from her description Logan asked if it was the woman he was with at the races, and Bill nodded. If they accused Masters without solid evidence, he would feed the media the whole conspiracy about Logan trying to bring him down, and it would be even harder to prove he was guilty in the long run.

James couldn't sleep either. It was up to him now to steer the horses and make the right moves. There had been talk about a pacemaker being entered in Everest's race. What would he do in the Queen Anne—go to the front or ride behind My Blue Boy? He watched the clock, waiting until he could get up and go for his morning run. It was the only real time his head switched off. It was just one foot after another. He got up and inspected the clothes he had laid out for the next day. He had a blue pinstripe suit and smart dress shoes; two sets of riding silks, jodhpurs, and jockey pads; the saddle weights; two whips; one helmet; and two sets of boots. He had cleaned it all perfectly. Standing there, looking over his racing clothes again, only wound him up more.

Tom had two sleeping tablets at bedtime and was out of it. Cynthia had downed a bottle of Chardonnay and taken her battery lover to bed. She would have traded places with Victoria in a heartbeat. Victoria knew how lucky she was. Logan was the glue that held it all together. She just hoped his gut instinct about tomorrow was wrong.

CHAPTER 39

Logan woke at 5 a.m. and headed to the stables. Tom was already there and answered Logan before he even spoke: 'They all ate and no temps.' Logan hardly smiled, even though they were the exact words he wanted to hear. It would be a big day.

As usual, James didn't risk riding track work on race day. He texted Tom at 6.30 a.m. to say: 'Everything all good at stables?' Tom replied with a thumbs-up emoji. James laced his shoes and put two running suits on. He still needed to sweat off half a kilogram, which was standard on race day morning. A run, hot bath, then sauna would easily strip the weight. The team had discussed everything the night before, but Logan was still worried. The plot had failed and stopped with Bill, who had got Forest Black but no other horses. So, what was his back-up plan? James punched the code in the electric gates and headed out for his pre-race run, not even thinking he may be a target.

Normally, the excitement would be electric on race day, but the team had mixed feelings. Scratchings had to be done by 7 a.m. for Super Saturday, which was earlier than normal and would give the emergency runners a chance to get ready for a start. Tom had made the call at 6.30 a.m. to the racing office and scratched Forest Black with an elevated temperature. At 7 a.m., Sandra and Masters listened in. The only scratching for the whole day was Forest Black. Within seconds, Masters was on the phone. He knew something had gone wrong. The ambulance was one, but Bill had confirmed in a text with a thumbs-up emoticon that the job was done; he had hoof oiled all the horses. When they followed Emma to the hospital they knew something was amiss and his 4WD never leaving the farm was another solid clue. Joseph also had told Masters something was up as he had spotted unmarked police patrol units circling the farm as well. But there was no way he could find out why they had scratched him. Masters made the call as his gut feeling told him Bill was lying. If Bill hadn't oiled the horse's feet then Logan's horses were running to win without a positive swabable outcome. He told Joseph to go ahead: 'Activate.' This was the code word. Masters' backers had bet extremely large sums of money at fixed odds last night. He had too much to lose without taking the second precaution of taking James out. Masters just hoped Logan's horses were selected randomly for pre-race swabbing when they arrived at the track. Stewards were entitled to select any horse for a pre-race swabbing and if any irregularity showed the horse would be scratched before the race.

By now, Joseph knew James's whole schedule. He had three other mercenaries to help him carry out the kidnapping. James was going up one of the back lanes behind the farm. There were two houses within a kilometre and the rest was farmland. There had been an extremely heavy dew and he was running on the road, as usual. The van was within 200 metres, and they opened the side door, ready to grab him.

James was running with his earphones in, listening to music, so he didn't hear them approach. Within seconds, two men had jumped out, thrown a black bed cover over him, and started to drag him into the van. He struggled, but a punch to the stomach winded him. He knew it was futile to fight and would only get him hurt, so he settled down and let them lift him into the van. It seemed like minutes but was actually 16 seconds. He was driven straight to the safe house where Sandra was based.

The van parked in the garage and the car lights were turned off so they were in darkness. The bed cover was taken off James and they put a hood over his head before he could see anything. He was told that if he removed the hood, or tried to run or call for help, he would be shot between the eyes. He nodded. He didn't need to be told twice. 'If you sit here and behave yourself, at 6 p.m. you will be released unharmed.'

James just nodded. He heard all the men get out of the van and lock it. They hadn't tied his hands or legs, so he was able to lay down on the floor. He realised his heart was still beating fast from the adrenaline, and he focused on his breathing. He shut his eyes and told himself that everything was out of his power. *If they wanted me dead, I would be dead already,* he told himself. *If I just do as they say, maybe I can go home afterwards.* He knew the men were obviously being paid by Masters, or whoever it was that was orchestrating this plot, and the less they had to do for their money, the better. *All this for a horserace,* he thought miserably.

Miles set off the alarm bells at 9 a.m. James hadn't come back from his run. He had already driven along the route James always took and didn't see him anywhere. When he returned and burst into tears, it sent everyone into a spin. Don pulled Logan aside for a lecture. 'You have a job to do. Assume the worst and act accordingly. If he has been kidnapped, there is nothing you can personally do. You have two hours before you need to be at the races, so find a jockey.' Logan knew he was right.

The detectives watching the house set about searching for James immediately. They had not taken any notice when he left that morning and decided to keep an eye on the stables rather than follow him as he went for a jog. Logan was literally sick in the stomach for not thinking that James could have been in Masters' sights. Considering his vital role and strict routine, he made an easy target.

Normally, Logan would have asked Miles to help him pick a jockey from the best of what was left on offer, but he was a mess. Victoria went and helped him pack up James's riding gear and get it ready to take to the races, just in case a miracle happened. Logan enlisted Tom to help him search, and finally they organised a backup jockey, just in case. Daryl Simcock would ride all four races for them if James didn't show up. He was past his prime, but he was still able to land at least one Group 1 every year. 'He's the best of what was left,' Logan said and exchanged a concerned look with Tom. Tom did his best to push the worst-case scenarios from his mind as they prepared to leave. As twins, they were extremely close and shared everything. Tom had recently told James how he had broken up with his girlfriend Lily, and no one had a clue, as he was extremely private.

Don got Aunty Joy and the boys in the cars. They were all just gobsmacked at what was unfolding, but there was nothing they could do, and they were told that everything would go ahead as normal. And the fact was, James could have just decided he didn't want to ride and could have been having a meltdown. Everyone was dressed in their best. Logan had never worn a top hat and tails and wasn't in the mood when he was struggling with the vest to adjust the sides.

Victoria organised for the housekeeper to stay at the house in case James came back. Miles gave her his phone number and told her to call him immediately if he got back.

When Cynthia arrived, completely clueless about what had been happening, Victoria took her aside and sat her down. They could no longer keep her in the dark. To everyone's surprise, Cynthia just nodded. She didn't shed a single tear, just said firmly, 'He'll be fine. My boys are strong. James will be fine.' She had faith that James understood the possible situation: the win, the money—it wasn't worth his life. She hoped he could stick it out until the races were over. In her heart, she knew he was alive and that he would come home. By now the English guard was on the case, and they couldn't do anything more than wait.

At 11.25 a.m. they all arrived at the races. Everest, Warrior King, Trumped, and Slipstream. The team had been bigger six weeks ago; now down one more with Forest Black scratched. But there was still a very good chance of winning four Group 1 races in one day.

The program had race one as the Oaks, with Slipstream; race five as the Derby, with Trumped; the Shergar Stakes at race six, with Everest; then the main race was the eight-million-pound Queen Anne Stakes with Warrior King.

'Ah hell,' Logan groaned. The Australian co-owners of Warrior King had arrived and were heading their way with Logan's ex-lover Jo in tow.

Tom turned to Logan. 'You saddle up. I'll take care of them.' Logan ducked away unnoticed, and Tom acted like the professional he was.

The clerk of the courses called five minutes until the race one starters needed to head out. The Queen and His Royal Highness had had just finished their entry down the course proper and were making their way to the royal box.

Slipstream looked superb. She was fit and hard. They had poured the work in and she was ready. As they entered the outside ring, Logan's phone received a message. He prayed it was news on James. It was Mick. 'Convict—or should I call you Penguin—filly looks great.' Even at that very shitty moment, Logan still smiled. He just could never get the last laugh.

The team gathered, and poor Daryl was very awkward when discussing tactics. Tom had explained what was going on and accepted that he would be the rider for the rest of the day. 'Just do your best, Daryl,' Tom said, his voice shaky.

As Logan, Tom, and Cynthia went to leave to go up to the box that Cynthia had reserved, she squeezed Tom's arm and whispered, 'He'll be fine. Your brother will be fine.'

Logan greeted his aunty and friends who had made the trip. There was still no word on James, and that quickly dampened the mood. Logan was about to have a chance at winning one of the world's most prestigious races, and he could barely focus. The first race jumped. Daryl was trapped three wide on Slipstream. When he decided to kick forward to try to get in, the inside runner kicked up, and he decided that was where he had to be, four back and three deep; sometimes that just happens. 'No hope,' Logan grumbled.

They rounded the second turn and straightened for home, and she was now six wide. The crowd started to roar as Miss

Swede, who Slipstream beat by four lengths last start, had kicked clear. Daryl gave two back handers with the whip and she seemed to dig deeper. The final few strides it looked like she was going to get there. Logan dropped the binoculars and started to ride her. Cynthia was jumping up and down. 'Photo finish,' called the announcer. Everyone in the box was holding their breath. They replayed the finish frame by frame, which seemed to take an eternity. Miss Swede had held on. The crowd groaned, as they had all backed Slipstream, even though she had a late change of jockey. The numbers stood 4, 2, and 6. Under the circumstances, Daryl had done well, but the mood was sombre.

Cynthia had managed to get the VRC stewards to reissue the charge against Logan again with another downgrade, so he could be an assistant trainer, citing he needed to keep earning a liveli-hood. After the antics on YouTube of Masters in the tailor shop, the stewards knew it would be better for business for the future of racing if Logan was to be able to attend the race's meeting as an assistant trainer. He was also supposed to attend anger management classes, which Cynthia agreed to but never mentioned to Logan.

Logan and Tom had spoken to the stewards. They had been informed and were very sympathetic, but the rules stipulated that he had to be on the track by 2.15 p.m. if he was to ride the final three runners for Baker Racing. It was now 12.25 p.m. Logan walked back to the stalls, and the filly had just returned from the swabbing box, as the placegetters needed to be swabbed. The strappers were shell-shocked as well after hearing about James's disappearance. They knew if he had been riding, she would have won. Victoria texted: 'You alright darlin'?'

Logan replied: 'I'm going to stay down here at the stalls.'

'Okay. Love you xxx.'

Logan couldn't stand still and decided he would go for a quick walk. Logan walked up past the racehorses all waiting for their turn to run. He walked into the men's toilet to take a leak and saw Angus Masters, standing right there in front of him, drying his hands. Logan stopped dead in his tracks, as Master looked up. Logan didn't say a word. As far as Masters knew, Logan may have just had his first positive swab taken from the filly, as all three placegetters are swabbed after the race. He didn't know that Bill had not applied the tainted hoof oil to the other three. Sandra had texted Bill asking if he had done his job, and he replied yes. He also replied the dropped-off address for his cash, as he had been advised by the detective.

'Shame your gay little jockey didn't turn up. I reckon he would have won on her today.'

Logan decided he was done. He turned, and Masters thought he was leaving, but he locked the door. It made a click.

Masters looked a little worried, and quickly rushed forward to push Logan aside, so he could run out. But Logan lunged at him. They wrestled, and finally Logan had Masters' arm pinned behind his back. 'Where is he?' Logan barked.

'Fuck you!' Masters spat back.

'Bill told us everything. Your little plan didn't go through,' Logan told him, cranking his arm up higher until it felt like it was going to break.

Instead of screaming, Masters just started to laugh. 'You make sure your horses don't win or my guys will kill him.' He had Logan over a barrel—or so he thought.

Logan released his arm and stepped back. Masters whipped around, rubbing his sore arm. 'What's it going to be, asshole? Would you rather lose, or win and let the little fag die?'

Logan took a deep breath. 'Do you remember a Michelle Thompson?'

'What? What are you on about?'

'Michelle Thompson, Angus. Pretty English girl. Don't tell me you can't remember sowing your seed.'

Masters looked puzzled. 'What the fuck has that got to do with anything?'

'So, you remember her?'

'Yeah, I remember her. We only dated for a few months. What's that got to do with anything?'

Cynthia had told Logan the whole story that night and made him promise never to speak of it, ever. He was about to break that promise. 'Well, you got her pregnant. She told your mother, who demanded she get an abortion. But she was a good Catholic girl.' Masters still looked confused. 'Your father wrote her a cheque for $25,000, twenty-two years ago. The pregnancy triggered extremely bad depression and six months after her twins were born, she took her life. Custody of the twin boys went to her sister, Cynthia, my boss.' Masters was still silent as he was trying to take in everything. Logan took a deep breath, as this was going to feel like he was about to lose two boys he now felt were his flesh and blood. 'Tom and James are your twin boys.' The look on Masters' face showed the penny had finally dropped. He looked at Logan but didn't say a word. Logan spoke calmly 'Can you kill your own son? Are you that heartless?' Logan turned, unlocked the door, and left.

Masters stood there, stunned, trying not to believe it. Michelle's face flashed in his mind, then he thought about James and Tom. He quickly looked up photos of the twin boys on his phone and studied them more carefully. It was true. They had his chin, and they were both short like him. He looked in the bathroom mirror and Logan's words repeated through his mind: 'Can you kill your own son?'

Logan went back to the stalls and Victoria was there. She was worried and had walked down to watch the race with him. She took his hands and felt them shaking. 'What's happened?' she asked. He took her aside and told her everything that had happened in the bathroom with Masters. They sat and talked for at least 25 minutes, while he explained the whole story.

Suddenly, Logan's phone rang. It was Tom. 'They found him! They found James! He's alive! They found him, Logan!'

Masters had immediately called Joseph and told him to drop James within a kilometre of the track, and get the hell out of the farm and disappear. Sandra was told to go, and she headed for France. Masters knew that there was no proof it was him, but sooner or later he knew he would be held accountable. He was in a spin as he couldn't believe the way he had treated his own son. He finally stopped focusing on the winning and reflected on his affair, his obsession with Logan, and everything else that had led to this moment in his life. He realised he had reached the all-time lowest of lows. It was finally like someone had let the air out of him.

James arrived in the jockeys' room escorted by a steward and two security guards at 2.05 p.m. Miles burst into the jockey room with two security guards on his heels. The steward put his hand up and they let Miles go. He threw his arms around James and burst into tears. The whole jockey room stood still. Finally, James wiped his eyes and told Miles that he had to get ready. Anyone else on any other day would have been taken to the police station for questioning and further protection, but the prime minister intervened and said he didn't want to spoil the day for Her Majesty. Cynthia understood that James had to focus. If he withdrew or rode badly, they didn't care. But they weren't going to quit now. On the outside she was tough as nails and standing strong today. It was their day to shine, but the thought that her son may have been dead was like no feeling she had ever experienced.

Race four was the sprint, and Shark Tank won by half a length. Masters did his best to play it up for the media and press, but Logan knew he wasn't himself.

As Logan stood in the saddling enclosure, it finally hit him— *James is about to ride in the Derby, and he could win.*

CHAPTER 40

Trumped was backed into £2.20, favourite. The punters rallied and hit the bookies hard. Any horse that had been valued at over twelve million should be favourite. Cynthia decided to stay out of the pre-parade ring, as she didn't want to add to James's emotional state. She didn't trust herself to hold back when she saw him.

Logan looked over at James. 'You seem pretty calm under the circumstances.'

'It's my day. I'm here, and I have a job to do. And I am going to stick it to that fucking prick Angus Masters.'

Logan nodded. 'Don't worry. His time will come.'

Tom legged his brother on, and it seemed like the world stopped for a few seconds as they exchanged looks. James put his feet in the irons, and it was like a switch had just turned on. Logan hugged Tom. 'He's in the zone,' Logan whispered, looking up at the steely determination in James's eyes.

Logan and Tom joined everyone in the box. Pete had a few beers under his belt and roared, 'Let's do this!' Not really Royal Ascot behaviour, but no one seemed to care.

Trumped jumped midfield and James had him three back and on the fence. He was travelling like he was asleep, and the pace was a good solid tempo. At the five-furlong mark, James could see the other jockeys quickening the pace and looking for the right run. He had a lap full of horse under him. Rounding the final turn, the first and second horse laid out slightly under pressure. Within two strides, James made the decision to drive through the narrow gap. He pushed along hands and heels. By the two-furlong mark, he was two in front; by the one-furlong mark, he was six; and over the line with James standing in the irons. He had finished eight lengths in front and was the new English Derby winner.

They went crazy in the box, and Pete shouted the true blue Aussie celebration, 'You fucking beauty!'

Everyone laughed and Cynthia hugged him. 'Say that again!' she said.

Pete shouted, and they all chimed in with him, 'You fucking beauty!'

Logan skipped down the stairs like he was walking on air. He got to the bottom and turned back in embarrassment to see Victoria at the top. She smiled and gestured for him to go ahead. Don took her arm to help her down the stairs, since she had trouble with stairs ever since her toe was amputated.

Within seconds, Mick had grabbed Logan's arm. Mick tipped a hand to his head as if tipping a hat. 'Convict,' he said in a respectful tone. Logan didn't even think and kissed him hard on his closed mouth. For once, he was quiet. The crowd roared with laughter, and Mick raised his hand and they roared one more time.

By now, Tom and Cynthia had joined Logan. They heard a faint voice, 'Wait for me, you guys.' Miles was pushing his way through the crowd. James went an extra hundred metres up the straight and came back down past the crowd. This was his moment. He was the champion today; toughest on the course. Victoria joined Logan, and all five went out to lead the winner back in. Mick and Mr Tanaka joined in for the final few metres. He was now as valuable for the next two hours as the King. This was the moment James would remember for the rest of his life. He had just won the Derby.

He finally got down, and the live interviewer said, 'You look very emotional.'

'I've had a tough day,' James replied.

'Yes, we have heard you had car troubles this morning and missed the ride in the Oaks.'

He just laughed and shook his head. 'How about we talk after I win the Shergar and Queen Anne Stakes?'

'That's a confident statement in today's present company.'

James just looked at the camera and said, 'I just wish my father was here to witness what I'm about to do today.' He looked to the sky and pointed his whip, and the crowd roared.

At the winner's presentation, Logan let Tom do his thing, as he was back getting Everest ready for the next race and checking on Trumped, who had pulled up super. Masters walked past with Maximus's saddle, and he nodded to Logan as a way of silently congratulating him on the win. Logan returned a half nod to show he appreciated that Masters had done the right thing for once in his life.

James went back in and changed into the Baker Racing silks. Don headed up to the box with Cynthia, and the party was just getting started. Cynthia needed a drink and something to eat. Victoria had organised more food to be brought in, as Pete, Neale, Marc, and Shaun had made themselves right at home and were all now well on their way. Aunty Joy was over the moon, as she had won over £5,000, as she backed Trumped, but also got the trifecta.

Masters walked back past Logan and Everest. He was following behind Maximus en route to the wash bay to rinse his mouth out before the race. Logan didn't pay any attention this time to Masters, but realised in a split second that Everest was about to dive forward and try to bite him. Masters turned to see Logan and the strapper restraining the colt.

The clerk of the course rode past and said, 'Three minutes.' Logan stood in front of Everest. He placed his hands either side of his head, wiggled the bridle side to side, and checked it was the same length each side. He grabbed a brush, hoping for once he would let them brush him before the race. Everest stretched his head up as if to say, *No chance*. Logan shook his head and double-checked the saddle and girth. He let out a deep breath and said, 'Let's do it.'

It was hard to say who the pick of the yard was. Maximus looked every bit as good as Everest. Tom Rolfe had entered Mayday after being approached by Masters for the use of a pacemaker to tire out Everest. He had handed over a cheque for £30,000 after race one. Rolfe had no idea Masters was now going to cancel the cheque first thing Monday morning. Blake Boyle had the mount on Mayday, and had heard of James's kidnapping earlier on. Such an incident couldn't be kept completely quiet. 'James, can I have a moment?' asked Blake. He looked around and there was enough distance between themselves and the other jockeys. 'I hope you know Tom Rolfe has been paid for his horse Mayday to sit right on your tail and tire you out. He has already told the stewards he will be racing in the first two. I just want you to know; maybe you can take a sit today. You're a good young lad who has been through hell today, and I can't lose my licence over this.'

'Blake, I appreciate your honesty.' He had thought it would happen in the back of his mind already. Laying with a black hood over his head in the back of the van, he had plenty of time to run the race over and over.

James met Tom, Logan, and Miles in the parade mounting enclosure. 'Blake Boyle just told me that Masters has paid for Mayday to sit right on my arse all the way.'

Before Tom or Logan could speak, Miles said, 'You're jumping from barrier eight of twelve. Snag him back and cross over and bury him on the fence last. You know Everest can sustain a long run. Before the final turn, pull out and make your move, but go very wide and they will think you have run off. You will have used no petrol in your tank. Mayday has never run past ten furlongs before, and this race was an afterthought. Going forward will be suicide.'

They all stood there in silence contemplating Miles's suggestion. James teased, 'If you're wrong, no sex for a month.'

Miles poked out his tongue at James. 'And if I'm right, blowjobs for everyone!' he said, clapping his hands.

Logan put his arm over Miles's shoulder. 'Filter, Miles. Filter.'

Angela walked past Logan on her way to the members' area. 'Good luck,' she said. He was lost for words, so he just nodded. For so many years, he did everything for her, and now they were rivals. He walked into the box; everyone else was a blur to him, and only one figure stood out—Victoria. She walked over and showed her betting ticket. She had placed a bet of £10 on Everest.

He kissed her on the cheek and said, 'If he loses, you'll need to look for a job next week.'

James took a big breath in and gripped the mane on Everest's neck. The starter hit the button and James let Everest go for three strides, then pulled him back and veered right and positioned himself right next to the running rail. The commentator immediately said, 'Very different tactics today from Everest. He is settled last and twelve lengths from the front runner, Mayday.' Maximus was sixth; three back and one off the fence. He had the perfect trail.

James was talking to Everest: 'Steady, boy. Steady. Whoa, boy. Nice and steady.' Everest had heard this many times when he was allowed to run his own speed. Today he had a wall of horses in front, but he had a settled rhythm. After two furlongs, he settled more and more.

They rounded the first turn. Mayday had a lead of four lengths, and the pace was solid. Maximus was travelling beautifully for LJ. Tom called out from behind his binoculars, 'Everest is settled. Traveling super.'

Miles, always without a filter, said, 'Maximus is travelling better.' Everyone dropped their binoculars at the same time and looked at him.

They were now one furlong from the home turn and James could see Maximus was full of running. Miles had said to wait until the turn and go wide, but he wasn't the pilot. Close to 150 metres from the home turn, James peeled to the outside and let Everest have his full head. The broadcaster was glad some excitement was finally happening. 'Everest has made his move and caught them all napping. He is now two in front. Three in front now. Here they come around the turn into the straight. And here comes Maximus!' The crowd started to get up out of their seats. The media hype had worked, and they all wanted to see a thrilling finish.

With one furlong to go, Everest was ahead by one length. James glanced back to see Maximus was very close to his hindquarters. Everyone, including Tom and Logan, thought this was it. Maximus was wearing him down. James switched the whip from his left hand to his right, as he could hear the cracks of LJ getting into Maximus. In that split second, he knew Everest was giving his all. 'C'mon, c'mon! Pss, pss!' James decided he didn't need to hit his horse. He knew he was tough. Everest had looked for that split second and seen Maximus coming. In one stride, he saw Everest's left ear tilt back and he changed legs.

Tom grabbed Logan. 'He's pulling away. He's going to win!' Everest dug as deep as he could. When he changed strides, he got back on his preferred leg and this was when he broke Maximus's heart. The final margin was 1.5 lengths. Pete cried, 'You bloody beauty!' Everyone turned, as before he had said it with the F word. Pete turned up his nose. 'We are at Royal Ascot, you know.'

This time, Logan walked down with his wife. He started to shed a tear thinking how his mother and father would have both loved to be there. Frank had always talked about Royal Ascot, and he had woken Logan up to watch Shergar win the 202nd Epsom Derby. Trumped now looked every bit as good as Shergar.

Bill had been watching the races from his hospital bed with his leg elevated. He had been told to not say a word to Emma, but under the influence of morphine he let it all out. She closed the door to his room and sat quietly while he spilled the whole story. He didn't know the outcome, as all she had said before she left was, 'I'll bring the boys in tomorrow to visit you.'

It had spread through the jockeys' room—what had happened earlier on in the day to James. They couldn't believe he had still made the decision to ride. They all congratulated him with open arms. Finally, James felt he had been accepted by his peers. He sat down at one end of the room to focus on the next race—the Queen Anne. He knew he would just win on Trumped. He was confident on Everest. He knew the King was a superstar, but he had never really thought My Blue Boy was that good until two weekends ago. You could never take any Group 1 field lightly.

When he was a teenager, James had watched videos of champion racehorses face off. He must have watched the epic clash at the 1986 Cox Plate between the two champions from New Zealand, Bonecrusher and Our Waverley Star, at least a hundred times. They had gone head to head from the 700-metre mark in a head-bobbing duel right to the wire. Watching that race had changed James's life, and it had set his heart on racing. He told his twin brother that day, 'You train them, and I'll ride them.' They shook on it and told their mum of their dream. Eleven years later, they had delivered on their promise to each other.

Victoria told Logan she would meet him in the mounting yard, as he had her winning ticket to collect. She was very excited about winning £34. Logan had just won £68,000 in training percentages, plus Everest would now be worth in excess of eight million. Logan's deal stipulated that if any colts make stallions he was on a five per cent share of the sale price. Last week he had made £320,000, just for the fifty per cent sale of Trumped, and if a deal was done similarly on Everest it would be another nice payday.

Eighteen minutes until the start of the race. Logan's phone rang. It was Mick.

'Penguin.'

Logan just smiled and answered, 'I'm about to saddle up.'

'You want some more Japanese? Mr Tanaka wants to offer four million for fifty per cent, and he wants you to win the Japan Cup this year with Everest.'

Cynthia had just walked down with Tom, Mike, and the whole team to watch them saddle up. 'I'll put Cynthia on, and you can let her know the details.'

'Penguin, use less tongue when you kiss me next time.' Logan shook his head and handed the phone to Cynthia.

Masters walked by the Baker horses with the saddle for My Blue Boy. He tried to walk tall and keep his eyes ahead, but he couldn't help sneak a better look at Tom. The son he never knew he had was about to saddle up and run against his biological father, who had done everything in his power to ruin Logan and his racing career. Logan looked over and knew straight away what he was looking at. As much as he hated Masters for everything he had done in the last three years, for a fleeting moment he felt sorry for the man. That thought was broken when a punter yelled, 'You're a grub, Masters! Go home!'

Logan turned, as Tom arrived back with the saddle. 'How's James doing?' he asked.

Yet again, the man with no filter spoke up. 'If he wins this one, sex is definitely on the cards for me tonight!'

Aunty Joy grabbed him by the earlobe. 'You need to watch your mouth in public, young man. Man or woman, show some respect. Keep that kind of talk behind closed doors.'

She winked at Tom and Logan, but Miles took her seriously and nodded. 'Yes, ma'am. Sorry, ma'am.'

In perfect sequence, Tom and Logan worked together to saddle the King. After Tom had done the girth up, Logan moved out front and stretched the King's legs out to make sure the girth hadn't pinched him. Tom ran his hands down the near-side legs and picked up the feet to check the shoes. Logan did the same. The strapper had already done the checks, but it was a ritual that was always done. Logan went to his head and double-checked the length of the bridle straps and made sure they were perfectly aligned. They walked the King to the wash bay and hosed his mouth out. Logan then passed the second girth strap to Tom, and he tightened it. Again, Logan stretched his legs. He held the King while Amelia the strapper tightened Warrior King's race number vest that she was wearing.

'All good?' Logan asked.

Both Tom and Amelia said in unison, 'All good.'

'One minute,' called the clerk.

'Miles,' called Logan.

He came bounding over. 'Yes.'

Logan pointed to the King. 'Here, you walk on the off side and help Amelia.

'Really?'

'C'mon,' said Logan urgently, and Miles took his place. Some horses need two strappers to keep them settled in the parade ring, as the race anticipation is too much for them. The King was as casual as an old stayer, but it was a glorious moment, and Logan felt Miles deserved it. He was a huge part of the team success. Miles changed to game face. He could be a dill sometimes, but he was an incredibly loyal and focused employee. Everyone stayed back beside Tom and Logan. Even Darcy and MJ, as owners, left it to Logan, Tom and James. They had tactics to talk to James about.

Logan started by saying, 'This will be the toughest race you will ever have to ride in. It's not going to be handed to you on a plate.'

James smiled and said, 'The 1986 Cox Plate.' Logan knew exactly what he meant, as he was at the races strapping that day.

Tom said, 'You be Bonecrusher, brother.' Nothing else needed to be said.

The parade ring was extremely crowded. The live broadcast interviewer had made his way over and was asking for a few quick words. Logan had not said a word to the press or interviewers all day, as Tom was handling it expertly. 'Logan, how do you feel taking on your old horse My Blue Boy?'

'It's actually very hard to explain,' Logan replied. 'Perhaps I wouldn't be here today if the chain of events hadn't accrued like they did.'

'Have you gone to see your old horse since he arrived?'

Logan laughed. 'No. The invitation must have been lost in the mail.'

'Here he is now about to pass us. He looks tremendous.'

As Bluey approached, Logan's heart ached. They had shared an incredible bond for two years, and Logan wanted to reach out, hug him, and wish him luck. Logan let out a soft whistle and whispered, 'Bluey.' To his amazement Bluey stopped and turned. The strapper gave him a second, as any good horse had certain quirks, and he didn't want to start pulling at him before the race. Logan felt choked up, as he saw how much his boy had grown and improved. 'Bluey,' he said again softly. The interviewer signalled the cameraman to move back and get the shot. Bluey walked two steps toward Logan. The shot was being broadcasted live on the big screen. The crowd started to hush, as they recognised Logan and his old horse that had been stolen from him.

Bluey's strapper got nervous at the attention and gave the horse some slack. Bluey dropped his head and pushed against Logan like he had done hundreds of times. Logan habitually put his hands behind the horse's ears to scratch softly, and Bluey moved his head up and down. 'It looks like My Blue Boy remembers him after all,' the interviewer said quietly into his microphone. The camera swung around to get a shot of Angus Masters standing right alongside Angela. Masters looked like someone had just stolen his soul.

One punter yelled out, 'We love you, Logan!' and the same punter from before yelled out, 'You're a grub, Masters!'

'Move on,' called the clerk of the course, and Logan gave his ex-horse a pat on the neck and sent him on his way.

'I hope you were whispering in his ear to let us win,' Tom joked. Logan looked up, and Tom saw the tears in his eyes. Tom gave him a comforting pat. 'Harden up mate. Stop being a soft cock. We have to win this.'

They gave the honour of legging James onto the King to Miles. Tom and Logan saw them exchange some words. James was laughing, as he tried to put his toes in the stirrup irons. Tom shook his head. Miles couldn't resist cracking a joke, no matter the circumstance.

James flipped the switch and his expression turned to steel. It was up to him and the King now. LJ had the same expression as James. He didn't care about fairy tale endings. He didn't even care about James getting kidnapped. He cared about his five per cent in riding fees and his other promised five per cent if he won.

It was standing room only, and the private box was packed, as it seemed to have grown over the day. Tom had a young blonde following him everywhere. He said, 'An old friend.'

Victoria grabbed Logan's hand, as she could see it was shaking. She even tried to settle his nerves by showing him her new betting slip. 'I have £100 on the nose.' Logan thought it was cute that she thought that was a big bet. A person who worked with figures was not a risk taker at heart. Logan had gambled everything, every day of his life with horses.

Warrior King was moved in. He had barrier five—Logan's lucky number. My Blue Boy moved in to barrier six. They jumped and the King was slightly slower away than My Blue Boy. Armageddon took the lead and was setting a good solid pace. Triple Treat and Tongpo were in second and third. My Blue Boy and Sweepyouoffyourfeet were fourth and fifth. Miss Chang Chang was sixth, Romeo and Juliet was seventh, and the King was eighth, with two behind him.

Armageddon set a fast pace. James could see My Blue Boy was three back and one off the fence. He was having the run of the race. Five and a half furlongs to go. James was starting to think at the four-furlong mark, *I will start to make my run.* What he didn't know was that Masters had handed over £10,000 cash to Patrick Murdock to stalk James wherever he was from the five-furlong mark and put him in pocket. Masters' so-called backers were also money launderers for a prominent drug lord in Melbourne back home in Australia, so the cash was no issue.

James looked to his left and, within seconds, Patrick pulled up and had him pocketed with Miss Jamaica. James was at the five-furlong post. My Blue Boy was three from the lead and LJ was sitting so cool; the horse was travelling very well. James saw him look both sides and LJ couldn't see James coming on the King. James looked back once again and the remaining horse Smash and Grab had moved out three wide. Within two seconds, James pulled the handbrake on the King and, with all the cattle work, he responded instantly. Within seconds, he was last. The commentator called, 'Uh oh. Something might be amiss with Warrior King.' The crowd all held their breath.

Logan turned to Tom and said, 'It's going to be a long run home.' They knew what James had decided to do.

The commentator went on. 'Warrior King is now switched to the outside, and James Baker has let him loose. They know there's no horse in the world that could match his sprint, but the question is can he last four furlongs?'

LJ looked back and saw the King four wide and full of running. He pulled the left rein and angled My Blue Boy out and set him alight. He was two lengths in front of the King.

'It's on, ladies and gentlemen.' Everyone had hoped this would happen in the last two furlongs, not the last four. 'My Blue Boy has rounded the turn, Warrior King is coming fast. The Australian champion is not going to give in. Warrior King is starting to rally.'

They went past the two-furlong post. James was worried, as he hadn't been able to get any closer than one length. LJ was hard hands and heels. James knew the King had more to give, as he still hadn't lowered that extra bit as he always did.

On the final furlong, the race caller changed to his battle voice and this lifted the whole crowd to its feet. 'And it's My Blue Boy by one length, but Warrior King won't give in!' The crowd seemed to lift with the excitement even more. 'Can he dig? 150 to go! He is digging. Warrior King is digging!'

James felt him lower. Whether it was the roar of the crowd or, like many champions, he knew where the line was. 'It's going to be close. It's neck and neck.' LJ had gone for the whip. 'He is lifting. Is he going to get there?'

Right on the line, Warrior King stuck his head out and won by a half a head. 'THE WARRIOR BECOMES A KING!' Those words rang out all over Royal Ascot. The crowd erupted.

'You fucking beauty!' Everyone knew it was Pete.

James punched the air. He looked skywards and saluted the man who had raised him. 'Go,' Victoria said to Logan, and he ran down the stairs. You would swear his feet didn't touch a step.

When Logan was grabbed for an interview, they asked him how he felt. 'I just floated down the stairs.' As he approached the winner's enclosure, Logan simply couldn't help himself. He walked over and was first to pat My Blue Boy and kiss him on the head.

The big screen cameras focused on Logan. 'Ladies and gentlemen, that is what you call a true horseman.'

The Australian connections had just landed the biggest coup in Australian racing history: Aussie bred, U.S. sold, and the winner of the most prestigious and highest rated race in the world. Darcy, Jo, and MJ didn't try to take centre stage, as they were just along for the ride.

The Queen was so moved by the news that had now been shared with her about the drama that had unfolded for Logan and the Baker family, she decided that she would present the trophy to them. The presentation brought the crowd to a standstill. Her Majesty told of the drama today; the heart of such a young man to overcome incredible adversity; and the determination of Logan and the Baker family for holding it together and making the show go on.

Logan stood side by side with Tom, James, Miles, Mike and Victoria. Cynthia was giving the last speech in the presentation and was waffling on as usual after drinking too much champagne. Logan nodded in a direction and whispered, 'Ten o'clock.'

They all slowly looked over to see Don standing right behind Angus Masters. 'What's he doin'?' Victoria whispered.

'I don't know.'

Cynthia finished by saying, 'Once again, thank you, Your Majesty, and thank you to the public for making today even more enjoyable for our family.'

The presentation was over, and Tom, James, Miles, Mike, Victoria, Logan, and now Cynthia were all looking at Don. Angus Masters thought they were all looking at him. He bowed his head like a mongrel dog and turned to walk away. Don stepped towards him and bumped him. Masters looked up just as Don dropped his walking stick, pulled his right arm back, and said, 'You need redemption, son!' and landed a solid right hook on Masters' chin. Masters went down and looked up at Don in shock. Very quickly two security guards had grabbed Don by the jacket. He looked straight over at the team and saluted like a general.

It was just Logan and Victoria on the drive home. Don was released straight away by security (they hated Masters) and was driving back with James and Miles. As Logan and Victoria passed through Newmarket and started to head out of town back home, Logan suddenly pulled over on the side of the road. Victoria looked at him and asked, 'What's wrong?' He checked both ways and did a quick U-turn, accelerating back towards town. 'Logan, what's goin' on?' Victoria asked, more firmly.

'What's the time?' Logan asked.

'It's 5.50 p.m. Why? What's wrong?'

He accelerated quicker. 'Do you have cash?'

She fumbled to open her purse. 'Yes, yes. Why? What's wrong?' Logan reached over and grabbed £20 out. Victoria was starting to get very concerned. 'Logan, tell me what's going on *right now.*'

He looked over at her and winked. 'Chicken shop closes at 6 p.m. Hank pre-ordered this morning.'

NOTE FROM THE AUTHOR

Firstly, I would like to thank you for purchasing my book and I really hope you enjoyed reading the story as much as I enjoyed writing it.

I also recommend you head to YouTube and search 'Bonecrusher vs Our Waverly Star', as this is how I pictured the final race in this book between the two champions.

This book contains so many personal memories of my life throughout the story. All my life I have been around thoroughbred horses, lived in the country, and gone to the races. I've grown up with my share of heartbreak—divorce; myself, family, and friends suffering anxiety and depression; even suicide. Life is tough; it's not fair, it's hard, it's nasty, but it's also simply fantastic.

This book let me bring to life each and every character, from Logan through to my own little dog named Hank, who is exactly how he is described in this book. So many characters are based on my friends and people in the industry. 'Don' is exactly how he is portrayed in this book in real life. When I was down and out, 'Don' gave me the helping hand I needed, along with many others. 'Mick' is a bloodstock agent from Ireland who gives me stick exactly the same way, every time we talk. 'Victoria' is one of the most special people in my life. 'Aunty Joy' is my real Aunty Joy and very close to how I described her. 'James' is a young man who, like so many in this world, struggled to finally become who he actually is—that takes guts. The equine industry is filled with guys like Miles, and I based him off a mix of three of my very funny friends. I've also grown up around a few women like Cynthia, so that character was quite easy to write.

One character I closely based on my personal experience is Frank. So many parts of Frank are based on my own father, and Logan's relationship with him is inspired by the relationship I had with my own father; particularly the way my dad raised me and taught me everything he knew about horses. He could get the racehorses to settle on a piece of cotton, could feed them by hand, and made mates of the problem horses by treating them with forgiveness and kindness. I remember nights we would walk the racehorse barn at 8.30 p.m. to check how they had eaten, and how we did cattle work with the racehorses all the time to teach the shy horses to ride in groups, just like in the book. When my dad won his first Group 1 race, the 1977 Toorak Handicap, with a mare called Nunkalowe, he described it exactly like the book: 'I didn't touch one step on the way down the grandstand steps. I just floated down.' He never felt that he belonged in the elite group of trainers and owners, but that day he proved you can come from nowhere and win.

I hope this book showed you what thoroughbred horse racing is all about and the enjoyment and value that can be found in the sport.

I would like to personally thank the team at InHouse Publishing and my friend Daniel Morgan for their patience, understanding, and encouragement. Finally, I would like to thank Shannon, my wife, and William, Sebastian, and Edwina, my three children, for allowing me the freedom to write this book and for listening non-stop to my ideas and dreams. Writing is a selfish pursuit and their support and understanding while I focused entirely on my writing until all hours of the night has been invaluable. I never knew I wanted to be a writer, but now that I have written my first-ever book and have seen it come to life, it feels like winning my own Cox Plate.

Yours faithfully,
Stephen Irwin

www.ingramcontent.com/pod-product-compliance
Lightning Source LLC
Chambersburg PA
CBHW030349030726
47497CB00002B/253